# SECOND NATURE

## He Could Not Tell Whether He Saw the Past or the Present . . .

He took a step and found himself on the curled edge of a high cliff. Dawn was breaking over the Western Sea; there was no limit to the scene; he beheld sea and sky and there was a thunderous sound in the air, a kind of natural play on words, as if the dawn actually broke or was shattered. Far below him the water heaved and parted in three places and he saw the three protoheads come up. He saw the vast, rippling field of the seines and the dim bulk of the floating body. The sound was repeated: a sundering of the air that hurt his ears.

The Vail was rising . . .

Books by Cherry Wilder

The Luck of Brin's Five
Second Nature

Published by TIMESCAPE/POCKET BOOKS

# SECOND NATURE

## Cherry Wilder

A TIMESCAPE BOOK
PUBLISHED BY POCKET BOOKS NEW YORK

Another *Original* publication of TIMESCAPE BOOKS

A Timescape Book published by
POCKET BOOKS, a Simon & Schuster division of
GULF & WESTERN CORPORATION
1230 Avenue of the Americas, New York, N.Y. 10020

ISBN: 0-671-83482-7

First Timescape Books printing March, 1982

10 9 8 7 6 5 4 3 2 1

POCKET and colophon are trademarks of Simon & Schuster.

Use of the TIMESCAPE trademark is by exclusive license
from Gregory Benford, the trademark owner.

Printed in the U.S.A.

# Contents

# SECOND NATURE

# Prologue

## "A Long, Bright Day by the Sea of Utner"

*Before dawn the young girl, Maire, climbed up to the masthead and looked out through the narrows into the Western Sea. The caravel rode at anchor and the masthead wheeled in a lazy figure eight: Maire sat braced against the mast, astride the crosstree, and saw the water turn from blue-black, to green, to yellow-green as the sun rose. She looked back toward home waters, where the sea was blue and commonplace as the bustle on the deck below, the voices of the gulls and sailors. The Western Sea was shadowed, even under a cloudless sky; it was landlocked and old; its shores were hollowed out into caves and fragmented into islands. Maire was watching for the boat, coming back; in the hot light of morning she could not help looking for a movement under the waves. She dozed off for a moment and heard a voice in her dream, resonant, yet conversational. Then the ship woke her up and she heard her brother calling from the deck below. Maire would not answer; she was trying to recreate the voice in her dream.*

When I went on retreat to the Sea of Utner I lived in a cave with a good clearance above and below the waterline. There was a spring of fresh water just beyond the cave mouth on a sandy cape. One morning I found a legendary creature drinking at the spring . . . a minmer or nipper. It was long as my middle-foot nail and had black skin. I watched it for nearly the whole of the day; it drank several times and slept curled up in the lee of a stone. Toward evening it began hunting for food and speared a winkworm which it cut in pieces . . . with its nippers, I presumed . . . and stored what it did not eat beside its sleeping stone. When the light had gone I channeled quickly through the

11

sandbar and this was enough . . . the minmer was there next morning on an island.

To my surprise it had sloughed the black skin and laid it aside. The underskin was a smooth brownish-red and in places downy, like a sand flower. Unfortunately it had become dimly aware of my presence. The odor of its fear was sharp and distinct; it had no directional sense but seemed rather to guess the cave as a possible source of danger. It crawled behind its stone and as the sun rose higher a blue-green aura shone out from the minmer's body. There were jerks and breaks in the aura which made me investigate farther, and sure enough the minmer was making sounds, attempting some kind of sonic contact over land with the interior of the cave. I allowed the gentlest altered echo, a soothing whisper, and it registered, to me at least, as *ah-lo*.

The effect on the minmer was so great that I knew my reduplication had been very imperfect. The creature became erect, like a snapping shell; it advanced boldly to the very limits of its island and peered into the darkness of the cave. I magnified more than I had dared and saw two distinct eyes under a tuft of down on the nub of the animal. More arresting still was the single "nipper" . . . a metal spike, firmly grasped, giving off its own spectrum.

What is the measure of a true sentient intelligence? What are the lower size limits? The verts and dagomils, infinitesimal creatures, accrete vast habitations under the sea and tunnel busily on the land. But they operate under the rule of a blind patterning, without range, without color, without sonic impulse or spectral vision. I specialized one sensor and allowed it to come closer to the island. The minmer had a listening attitude. I listened, generally, and heard the sea, the sky, the local pulse of the land through the walls of that excellent cave. I listened with more particularity, through my sensor, and heard some approximation of what the minmer might hear. A grating of the waves on the island shore, a sucking as the waves washed into the cave mouth nearby, the cries of sea birds, a distinct susurration from within the cave, which I identified at once and took measures to correct. This sound came from my own body.

I drifted my sensor closer still and climbed it upon the beach. The minmer attacked at once in an access of terror; the sparkle of its nipper mingled with its bodily aura. I closed out sensation, but not before one or two sharp blows had penetrated. I prostrated the sensor and perfected its single eye and a coating of down. I writhed it in the sand and gave a little supplicating noise, half whistle, half groan, like a piron shell when it is forced open at a feast.

The minmer, which I now saw more clearly, drew back and did not attack again. It remained planted in the sand on a divided limb; after some moments it approached the wounded sensor. It made sounds that I judged were soothing ones; indeed I found them so. I whispered through the sensor a pleading "ah-lo." The minmer came very close, laid aside the metal nipper, then held out its upper branches, empty. I made a gesture of submission, flattening, crouching; it was not misinterpreted. The minmer cast off almost completely its aura of fear and anger; it became tinged with a pearly light about the upper half of its body. I soon learned that this denoted curiosity.

The minmer made sounds and I responded, mostly imitating. Then I slid the sensor back into the sea and returned quickly, from my own feeding seines, with winkworms and shells, appropriately small. I laid them before the minmer and it thanked me, bending its body and repeating several sounds. It insisted that the food be shared and opened the shells with its nipper. I feigned eating, when I observed how the minmer ate, and looked my fill, for my single eye was now functioning at a better level to observe my mythical beast.

Now at this first meeting it had become apparent that the minmer had a distinct patterning of sounds . . . a speech, a language. Leaving aside for the moment the question of any distinction between these two modes, speech and language, I decided to learn the pattern as quickly as I could. The minmer was only too ready to comply; it had nothing but friendly curiosity for the one-eyed amphibian, tall as itself. We accomplished the feat together in half the time it took to shed my skin. I feel a prickling sadness, now, at the memory of those summer days. . . . I have been influenced by the minmer's preoccupation with the passing of time, the actual passage of single days and nights in the continuum.

There was a harsh materialism about this minmer that grated at first, like sand in a duct. If I probed for sensibility, for breadth of feeling, I received "hard facts." . . . The minmer had been forced into the Sea of Utner by a storm . . . or figures spewed forth from the microcosm: the distances, in minmer terms, between the stars.

13

I was troubled by the deception I was practicing, even if the investigation were proving so successful.

"We don't come to the Western Sea," the minmer explained, "because there are tales of great sea monsters."

"What form might such a monster take?"

As the minmer replied it gave my sensor a strange look and a tinge of the old fear crept into the air around it.

"Who knows the shape of a sea monster?"

"Have you no legendary beasts?"

"Of course," said the minmer sitting up on its lump of sand. "The dragon—there is a great deal of material about dragons, not to mention the Leviathan, the Kraken, the Behemoth . . ."

It described all these creatures, then cocked an eye at my sensor.

"Have you seen anything of this sort in this Western Sea?"

"Of course," I whispered, "but you have not described them exactly."

"These are legends," said the minmer, "and off-world yarns at that. Perhaps the shape is nearer that of the plesiosaur, the ichthyosaur, the giant squid, the blue whale. . . ." And it was off again, speaking more wildly than before.

"Minmer," I said impatiently, "your brain is like a boru shell, full of little numbered grains of sand."

"Forgive me," said the minmer, "but I am nervous. I can't get off this island, my boat is gone, I am lost. Yet it is worth all my pain to talk this way with another life form."

"Agreed," I said. "We must speak further."

My retreat was nearly done; that night I made shift to provide the minmer with a new boat. It understood at once, for with daylight my sensor found it bailing water from the sloughed skin of my middle foot, washed up on the island beach. The minmer was active but not untinged with fear.

"What is that?" I asked. "The skin of a dragon's foot?"

"Something like that," growled the minmer. "Do you know how it came here?"

"Perhaps."

"Well, I am thankful. It will make me a boat."

"Come back," I said. "Come back if you have the spirit for it. I will be here again when the stars are overhead . . . including the one with the blazing tail . . . in exactly the same position."

"Whew!" said the minmer, looking up into the daylight sky, where I doubted that it could see more than the morning sun.

"That will take some doing. But truly I will come. Are you sure to be here?"

"I am sure."

The Sea of Utner was calm. The minmer had patched up a device to catch the wind from the black skin it had worn at first. It climbed into the boat and sailed off to the east, with an assisting breeze from the mouth of the cave.

*The boy, Paddy, kept watch from the lookout in the afternoon. He ate a red "rogue apple" to keep himself awake; down below, the captain was snoring in his cabin, the crew were drowsing in heaps upon the deck. Suddenly he saw something to the northwest; he knew it could not be his father's boat. A broad furrow curved about in the purple water of the Western Sea and then was gone. Paddy shivered, but it was only the breeze that had come off the black slip of water in the narrows. He had been bred not to fear anything the Western Sea might bring. He remembered his grandmother, pacing the bridge of her ship, intent upon the patterns of the stars.*

So the pattern was set and the minmer kept its word with fussy exactitude; I was forced, several times, to rebuild the island and reintroduce the spring of water. The minmer came in a new craft, towing the tattered relic of the "dragon's foot" as some sort of safe conduct. We talked.

"Minmer, what is the measure of intelligence?"

"Using tools? Building?"

The minmer had erected a wooden shelter on the island, neat as a soft crab's nest, and was mending it with a set of metal nippers.

"The larger sea creatures do not 'build' precisely, though they may reform their environment."

"Friend Ash, the monsters may be quite stupid," said the minmer. "There must be some upper size limit for an intelligent life form, even in the sea. They are simply too large."

"Or you are too small."

"What?" the minmer stared into the round eye of my sensor.

I was tired of this equivocation.

15

"Do you not know, minmer, that a sea creature lives in the cave?"

"It was thought so, once."

"Perhaps you mistake the part for the whole."

"Yes," said the minmer and it looked at my sensor very closely. The stink, the blue-green aura of its fear, washed over it.

"Tell me," asked the minmer, "what is the meaning of that name . . . Ash?"

"It means a tentacle." I slid my sensor back into the water, across the warm sand. The minmer ran to the water's edge, mastering its fear.

"Come back!" it shouted. "I will not be afraid."

I fixed it with my sensor's eye from the shallow.

"Then see . . . minmer!"

I reared up the full extent of my sensor to form a bridge leading into the cave and the minmer endured the test. It clambered onto the bridge, marched into the cave. It looked down into the swirling tangle of my seines, up into the darkness, where my eyes and scanners glowed of their own light, out to the forest of my sensors, coiled against the cave walls. But the sight was too much; the poor minmer reeled and could not take it in.

"Ash?"

"Minmer. . . ." I replied as softly as I could but the sound bore down on the minmer like a blow. It fell senseless against the nearest of my three land feet, planted against the cave wall.

I thought it was dead; I felt a grinding sadness, as if one of my own limbs had been lopped off. I bore the minmer back to the island with my adapted sensor, its own friendly one-eyed sea beast, and laid it on the sand. Presently the creature revived and seemed to have learned something . . . though not much . . . from its experience, We resumed our relationship through Ash, the adapted sensor; the word "monster" disappeared from the minmer's speech. At our next meeting the minmer put its senses to the test again and visited the cave; it became part of the pattern. The minmer confessed to an extreme difficulty in making the connection between my sensor and my whole body, yet at the same time insisted that it had "known all along," "suspected from the first" or "solved the mystery."

"Minmer, how is your city building?"

"Very well. We number a thousand."

"A thousand minmers!"

16

"Don't sneer. We are an ancient people. Our ancestors came from the stars. We are alone on your world. We have lost our technology."

"Is self-pity the mark of an intelligent life form?"

"Why not?"

And so we would speak and part until the tailed star rode in the sky again, over the Sea of Utner. But the cycles have passed until this time when I speak; I must divide and forget and be forgotten. When I told the minmer, it was sad and showed more pity for me than ever for itself.

"Ash, you cannot die. You are my heritage. . . . Your words are repeated in the city. We are comforted by this communication . . ."

For the first time since the dialogues began I experienced a twinge of emotion that I could share with the minmer. There had been comforting communication in times past with those lost ones, a race far from legendary. I understood the minmer but there was nothing to be done.

"Go well, minmer. The retreats are over."

"But need that be? The dialogue could continue . . ."

"How is that?"

"Send another in your place. There must be other beings like you . . . hundreds. . . ."

"Minmer, I cannot live as you do, numbering my companions, my days, like grains of sand."

Indeed my retreats, my dialogues with the minmer seem to me like one bright day by the Sea of Utner, a project half begun, a dream, a challenge. The minmer has set sail again in its red wooden boat, heading east toward the narrows. We cannot allow this creature to return to the world of legend; it has without doubt the beginnings of intelligence. There is more to it than fear and vanity. I have the feeling that there is some part of the pattern missing, some linkage that I have failed to connect. So I have entrusted my records and this preamble to the residual portion of my brain, to go to the repository for the earnest consideration of the Council. It might be enlightening to allow these dialogues to continue under exactly the same conditions.

*The long day was almost over; the light of the setting sun reached through the narrows into the Western Sea. Maire and Paddy still sat in the crosstrees, watching keenly. Suddenly Maire swung upright and gave a long, loud hail. Far to the west a sail grew in the half light; the caravel slewed about in the water as the crew shouted a welcome*

17

*and crowded to the rail. Brian Manin O'Moore, fifth hereditary envoy, stood at the helm of his red boat* Dragon-foot III. *He came in closer and was taken aboard.*

Landfall +10 to landfall +180 (1017 New Style)
When the population of the city of Rhomary reached 1000, in the year Landfall +163, this was declared to be the year 1000.

# Chapter I

## *The Dator of Rhomary*

A hot wind blew all day long and dust storms whirled their gray funnels up to the walls of the city of Rhomary. Time of the furn: a rustling in the streets, the fountains playing after hours in the gardens of the New Town. Maxim Bro stood on the city wall not far from the massive towers of the Sulvan Gate and stared into the moving grayness; he held a fold of his summer cloak over his mouth. He had spent the summer afternoon arguing successfully in committee with men and women twice his age. The dust of the encounter was in his eyes, in his mouth, he was choked with formality, with points of order and procedural madness. Yet he had won his concessions for the wrong reason: the thorn of progress was in their flesh.

The dust cloud suddenly cleared and he could look down over the irrigated land toward the Billsee, eighty kilometers to the south. The land sloped away from the city; the eastern sky was blood red where the unknown sun sank into dark banners of cloud. The tower of the gatehouse obscured his view to the west but he thought of the Western Sea. He had no special powers, he knew that, but a confounded uneasiness grew in him. He was trained to hold past and present firmly in focus; the flat incredibility of his world and its people troubled him. Maxim had no gods to address but sometimes he spoke in his mind to the Vail, the monsters of the Western Sea. "Look at the city of the minmers! You helped build it in the end. You helped quarry the stone for the Envoys' palace in a between-season . . ."

But the city was doomed. Twenty meters away the wall had been breeched and torn down, a broad straight road

19

ran out of the square behind him with its solid council buildings to the settlement of Dipper. It was the site of the new reed paper mills: the streets in Dipper were wide enough for pedal carts and twist-bikes. Dipper would mean the end of Carcut, the slum that had flourished for a hundred years beyond the wall. The unlicensed cribs and she-beens would be swept away, the dirt poor would be re-housed and lose their humpies. In the end the city of Rhomary itself would be an old dark slum in the midst of a new city of broad streets. Even Doctors' College would relocate. The city of the minmers would pass as the Vail themselves had passed.

The Envoys spoke bravely of the Leavetaking and the Outwandering: the plain facts of the matter seemed to be that the huge creatures were killed by the ten-year drought and the last of their numbers had died on the long portage overland to the Red Ocean. Yet there were no plain facts on Rhomary. "Where have you gone?" asked Maxim. "Are we more tenacious of life than the great Vail themselves? I must doubt everything. . . . Did we come from the stars? What of those others you mentioned? Those are the real fairy-folk, creatures of legend. I cannot stomach all the signs and wonders of this damned dusty place. I have no use for miracles. . . ."

Yet he knew they could all use a miracle. Time of the furn: the whirling dust ground into the minds of the people, tempers were short, there was fighting down in the Warren. A woman gave birth to a mutant lacking most of the brain, a blind mouth, and it died swiftly in the white recesses of Doctors' College. Maxim came down from the wall and walked up toward the Dator's house on the lowest level of the New Town. He heard a burst of music from one lighted window overhead, a shriek and a crash of pottery from another. He turned into the lonely tip of an alley and two shadowy figures laughed and ran off. Lovers? Something rolled into the gutter; he stooped and dipped a finger in whitewash from a broken crock.

It was dark as dust in the alley. Maxim scanned the mudbrick walls with professional enthusiasm . . . ah, there it was. The painters had completed a lengthy inscription before he surprised them. He took an erasing tablet from his britches pocket ready to note down the reference.

I saw a star begin to fall. I stood alone in the desert at night and the star shed its light all around me. A music of voices came from the star saying: "Heal the hearts and minds of all the people. The love of the gods does not hide in a white coat or in the roarings of the sea monster."

Jenz Kindl 3/7

Very neat. Maxim already knew the quotation. It had been executed with a stencil; one Jenzite kept watch while the other juggled roller and strip. The stencils were made of kelp; the Council used them for wall bulletins in the Warren and at the gates of the city. He had a grudging admiration of the Jenzites, no more; it was an area where faith mattered and he had none. He saw a carrying chair pass the alley and hurried on. The darkness of the dust was lifting, the sky in the east had faded to blue-green at the horizon. By the time Maxim turned two corners and came to the Dator's house the small moon of Rhomary was visible in the northern sky together with the evening star, the planet Topaz.

He walked all around the square bulk of the place in the twilight noting the crusted lizard nests under the eaves, the sag of the flat roof, the crack in the western wall which suggested that the place was literally bursting at the seams with the stored records of Rhomary. He was hailed as he came up to the front door again:

"Young man!"

A tall old woman with a rainbow cloak over black trews and tunic . . . housekeeper of a New Town family he guessed.

"Can I help you, Mam?"

"I need to place a letter. The lamps are not lit."

"I'm sorry . . ."

Maxim stepped into the spacious porch, took out his tinder box and lit the two oil lamps. The information slots were wide and inviting; an application of ferret-musk kept the flying gheckos from using them for nesting boxes.

"What, do you work here then?" said the old woman. "I will give the letter into your hand. Bring it at once to the Dator!"

"Madam," said Maxim Bro sadly, "I am the Dator."

He drew back his gray cloak and the bronze medallion shone on his breast.

"What? What?" the old woman drew back her hand with the letter. "The Dator is an old man, his beard is white. It is old Urbain Bro, I have seen him many times."

21

"My uncle," said Maxim, "the former Dator. I have taken over the office."

"O Vail send us wisdom," she whispered, "is the poor old man. . . ?"

"No Mam," said Maxim, grinning. "By no means. He has simply retired. Is the letter for the Dator? Then it is for me."

She came up to him, peered into his face and laid hands on the medallion. He saw with surprise that she wore a real rainbow cloak of old fine jocca cloth which drew out the shellfish dye into seven colors; today the cloaks were painted imitations. Her black clothes were finely made and she wore silver jewelry, ring and bracelet. An unusual servant. At last she put the letter into his hands. He looked down into her long brown face and her old blue-tinged brown eyes.

"Do not fail my poor lady," she said. "I will tell her the Dator is a young man now."

She walked off briskly, pattens echoing on the baked surface of the road, and he saw the carrying chair waiting at the corner. Maxim turned the letter in his hand and saw the crest: a tailed star, a comet, the same one that rode in the heavens this very night and for weeks to come. The letter was from the Palace of the Envoys, a place that even as Dator he had never visited. He stood in the porch stricken with the same hope that had plagued the city for so long and had finally died. Yet if the Vail had come again the brazen gongs would sound from the Palace roof, the fires would be lit from the Western Sea to the walls of the city. Or would it be so? A reliable sighting, maybe, and a quiet note to the Dator.

He had never visited the Palace because it was a sad forgotten place; the Envoys lived out their lives in a dream of annotation and unpaid back taxes. There were rumors of mutants born, of inbreeding and outwandering among the families themselves. He shook off the rainbow threads of this dead part of the city's past and went into the lighted hall.

The clerks and copyists had left the building. Ranuf, the senior archivist, was descending the stairs in cap and cloak ready to go home. He was a middle-aged, middle-sized man, round-faced and energetic. He had a tendency to fuss.

"Very late back!" he said. "Was it bad luck? Did you

strike a snag? Did you tangle with Macken? Or that old hag Bodril?"

"It went very well," said Maxim. "Where's my uncle?"

Ranuf pointed to a door on his left and Maxim moved away from it toward the foot of the stairs. He said to Ranuf in a low voice:

"We've been allotted the new premises!"

"What? That place? Oh sky, that's a victory. And the old man will bless you."

"It's a large house in excellent repair."

"I'm off!" said Ranuf. "Mind if I tell Bee and the girls? We'll celebrate up yonder, give a little festival in the garden!"

He bent close to Maxim.

"Maybe your uncle's old friends would . . . er . . . put in an appearance."

Maxim could not help smiling.

"The youngsters are on the bulk," continued Ranuf. "Good night then, time of the furn . . . will I get mugged on the homeward way, who knows, who knows . . ."

Maxim relaxed and went into the sorting room. Two young assistant archivists were drinking green-flower tea and playing Go. They had sorted the bulk into several piles: Requests, Answers, Justice, Other Departments and Mixed. In this basket besides the pile of reed papers lay three large stones, some melon rinds, a broken sandal and a wooden spinning top. The wide slots of the Dator's house were too inviting for the neighborhood children. Rab and Ginny watched as he cast an eye over this little heap of rubbish; Maxim made a face and they went off into laughter.

He skimmed the top off every pile: *"First request for a copying of my land deed laid in the Dator's house for fifteen years . . ." "Received with thanks payment for one hundred hardwood pens."* The pile for the Department of Justice was the one which depressed Maxim the most; as many as twenty citizens of Rhomary went to the trouble of accusing their neighbors every day. There was an anonymity about the slots of the Dator's house . . . it wasn't as bad as going to the Watch. *"Nehim Luck of Pechid Street, Third Level, keeps two dry-hogs in his house against city ordinance." "Ambel of Noag's Inn is a unregistered Hor" "Tadd Vitty and Fam are all Jenzite."* Most of the accusations were kept on file, could be examined by high-

23

ranking officers of the Watch; information about major crime was supposed to be passed on at once.

The pile for other departments was slimmer: Water Board, Weights and Measures, it was dry as dust. Literacy was increasing every day, thought Maxim, and the town was riding the crest of the reed paper boom. The bureacracy grew unchecked; the lure of free breakfast was bringing the beggars' children into the schools; advocates and ombudsmen were taking the place of public letter-writers. The city was overcrowded; Doctors' College was not wavering in the fight . . . infant mortality had been cut by half again in the past twenty years.

"Maxim. . . ?"

He realized that Ginny had been calling him several times.

"Sorry!"

"The Mixed is amusing," she said.

"Time of the furn," said Rab. "Signs and wonders are our daily bread."

"The old man has been asking for you," said Ginny.

Maxim scooped up the small pile of papers classified as Mixed and crossed the hall to the old reception room: an historical display for schoolchildren was mounted, some of it under glass. Books, printouts, viewers, a tape recorder, camera, binoculars, with lenses gone long ago to light fires . . . old engines that the kids couldn't work, couldn't believe in and couldn't touch. A scatter of old clothes: helmet, gloves, boots, suitliner but no suit; Doctors' College had six suits, would not release them for outside display. Photographs: involuntarily, he became interested. You could see on one a corner of something that might have been the ship. Mainly groups of unidentified castaways grinning in the mad light of a new world: sand, rock, half-made well, jocca palms, reeds. One photo out of sixteen had an inscription on the back, transcribed beneath it on a card: *"Olivia, Hank, John Higgins (supply) and self."* Taken from the effects of Commissariat Officer Leroy Lamartine, deceased Landfall +15. In the corner of the room there was a tableau . . . an old man with white hair seemed to be fighting with a huge full-color poster of a spaceship.

"Help me, you fool!" said Urbain Bro. "Get the top corners . . ."

Maxim reached over his uncle's head and tacked the poster. They put in more tacks, broke a few . . . the clay

24

heads came off the tack thorns . . . but finally the poster was secure. Reed paper of course; so much good jocca paper would have made the thing an art treasure. The colors were unbearably bright. Maxim knew the picture well. It came from the opening frame of a famous cassette book *Star Adventure 249*. The copying studio had signed in place of the publisher's name.

"That will give them some idea," panted the old man.

Maxim sat beside his uncle on a padded bench under the window. The old man stilled the trembling of his hands; after years of studied ill-health he was still going strong. Maxim covertly studied their two reflections in a glass case and saw no likeness. He took after his father Gregor, old Urbain's younger brother, who was a fruit farmer in Edenvale. Maxim was tall, could have slipped into the suitliner on display with only a few folds at wrists and ankles. His hair and beard were thick and half-brown, streaked by the sun, his eyes were gray. The former Dator was brown-eyed, compact, his olive skin unweathered. He said testily: "You're late back!"

"I was standing on the city wall."

"Time of the furn," grumbled the old man. "Dusty evenings, a madness everywhere."

"Come upstairs, Uncle. I have a few pieces of bulk to go through."

"I will sit here. I like this room. It was my interview room."

Maxim sighed but the old man did not continue with his train of thought. He collected his pile of paper from the corner of a desk where he had set it down and handed the sheets or scraps to his uncle one by one as he read them. Urbain took out a pocket glass and began to chuckle as he read. Maxim was making a separate pile.

"Six," he said at last, "six out of fifteen. What does that leave us with? Another outburst of ball lightning?"

"Madness," said Urbain, "the silly season. What is that longer one? Read it!"

Maxim sorted out the report which was well penned and neatly folded. It read:

Jules twelve before sunrise I saw three bright lights descending to the west. I was on the desert highway from Silver City, approaching Rhomary at the head of my parmel caravan. I looked back and saw the light and called my servant Lige to witness. We watched the

25

lights falling. They were round, colored from orange to red. The dawn was clear but as we came up to the outer wards after daybreak a thunderstorm began. I believe three meteors fell down somewhere in the west, may be worth looking up for the iron. I can be reached at Noag's Inn, the Warren.

Milt Donal, Merchant
Silver City

Maxim registered the name of the inn and recalled where he had just seen it.

"Is Noag's Inn a rough shop?" he asked.

"Never heard of it," said Urbain. "You want this checked?"

"I may check it myself."

"You go about too much on piddling errands!" snapped Urbain. "The office should retain some dignity . . ."

"I don't pull in ordinary citizens on a Dator's warrant, if that's what you mean," said Maxim. "Times have changed."

"Times changed," said Urbain bitterly, "before you were born. I used the warrant only in emergency . . . you will need it one day. I had a staff of four, you have a staff of fourteen."

Maxim had one thing left in his hands, the letter from the Palace of the Envoys. He showed his uncle the crest.

"What does she want?" asked Urbain. "How did you come by the letter?"

"Hand delivered by an old servant in a rainbow robe."

"Open it then. It is for the Dator."

Maxim broke the seal and unfolded an unnecessarily large sheet of jocca paper; the handwriting was old-fashioned and of great beauty.

"Well?" growled Urbain.

"Nothing. An invitation for the Dator or 'an experienced archivist' to wait upon the present Envoy."

Maxim examined the looping signature "Ishbel O'Moore Manin" and inhaled a faint sweet perfume from the letter. With his luck, he decided, she would be old, a very old shrunken white-haired creature who had spent a lifetime hoping for the Vail to return. But surely that was the Envoy before last? He did not dare ask his uncle the age of the present incumbent.

"The names," said his uncle suddenly. "I would not have believed the names could become so scrambled. Of course the bluggy fools scrambled the dates themselves, by decree, so that our years have four figures. But the names. All these damned Celtic Revival names. Another ship might have had a *Sociedad España* and we would be named in the Spanish fashion."

"We do not know if our name was Brown or Baronovski," said Maxim. "We don't even know that."

"*His* name was related to the Envoy's name," said Urbain reverently as any Jenzite. "Coll Dun Mor. What an archivist he would have made. A vesp who could lay his hands on a scrap of paper and see into its origins . . . I begged him to stay . . ."

Maxim was training himself to deal patiently with his uncle's loving obsession.

"Coll Dun Mor's destiny was elsewhere," he pointed out. "He went to search for the Vail when Jenz Kindl healed his blindness."

"I interviewed him . . . twice, three times in this very room," said Urbain. "A blind boy, who sat at the gate of the city . . . then he was healed . . . I must admit, I gave him a little money for the journey out of house funds."

"Uncle," said Maxim suddenly, finding an interesting question that he had never asked before. "Why did you not send him to the Palace of the Envoys?"

"Policy," said the old man. "I believed all of his story. I believed that the travelers who employed him were very queer customers indeed. The shape-changers. It might have excited the poor old Envoys too much to have a new gloss on the Vail's hints and scraps about a second extraterrestrial race on Rhomary."

A gong rang upstairs and Maxim felt that he was saved.

"Come to supper, Uncle. I have some good news."

Urbain gave his nephew a sad look and rose up without a word. He could be heard heavily ascending the stairs to the dining room. Maxim took the pile of Mixed information into the sorting room and shucked it back in the basket. Rab and Ginny were putting on their cloaks; they did not lodge in the house.

"Rab," said Maxim, "check on Milt Donal for me, the merchant from Silver City, lodging at Noag's Inn, down in the Warren."

"Sure," said Rab. "Where have we heard that name, I wonder?"

"He can't wait . . ." said Ginny. "He will check on Ambel, the unregistered whore."

27

"You know the procedure," said Maxim. "With the merchant, I mean. Take a statement on the prepared form, get him to sign it. Say we're grateful, we're looking into the matter. Refund his sheet of paper . . . he seems too well off to need a tip."

"Fine," said Rab.

Like nearly all trainee archivists he was a dropout from Doctors' College; Ginny was more rare, a lover of words. They shared two attic rooms in the Warren and went at nights to drink with the medical students in Carcut, beyond the wall. Maxim turned about when they had gone, thinking of his own boon companions, the high-bred girl intern he was slowly disappointing. He had been privileged to attend Doctors' High School because he was the Dator's heir; his friends had gone on to pre-med with its fifty percent failure rate and its fifty suicides a year. They had emerged as sleepless, dirty, hard-drinking interns. He might rather have boozed with them at the Glayster Bell but instead he trudged upstairs after a crotchety old man who still behaved at times like the head of the thought police. Even the supper would be cooked to Urbain's bland taste by the old houseman, Jon Witt.

The surprise that Maxim had been saving until supper time still had to do with the old man's narrowest obsession.

"Jon," said Maxim as he walked into the dining room, "bring a bottle of wine. We have something to celebrate."

Urbain, who had begun on his bean soup without waiting, choked down a mouthful.

"What's this, then?"

"We will move in four months," said Maxim. "It was approved by the Ex-Officio Committee. This house can be retained for storage of records."

"Good—good. . . . A notable victory!"

He could not tell if the old man was still sneering at him. Jon, a dour, gray man with a limp, brought in the palm wine and began to serve it.

"The new premises. . . ?" asked Urbain.

"Three and Twenty Spring Street."

The old man rose from his chair, trembling.

"But that . . . that property . . ."

"It is a villa called the Pleasance. Part of a deceased estate. The Council acquired it cheaply."

Urbain sat down in a heap, his eyes full of tears.

"Ah, this is the working of destiny," he said. "We have

the house where Coll Dun Mor was educated, where he read his precious books. Where he communed with *them* . . . all three . . ."

"You communed with them yourself," said Maxim, as gently as he could. "They invited you to dinner."

"I've explained," said Urbain. "You've seen the reports. This was part of a plan."

Maxim finished his cup of wine and poured another.

"Uncle," he said, "I find it difficult to believe. I have a respect for the Vail, I can take a certain amount of sooth-saying and true-dreaming, I believe in Vesps, oh yes, Vesps, and I appreciate the many remarkable qualities of Coll Dun Mor . . . but at these visitors I think I stick. I cannot swallow them. They were not the race of strange beings mentioned by the Vail. They were not off-world beings at all. These were human beings who lived at the Pleasance . . . what was it . . . twenty years ago . . . and if I obtained the villa for our use it was partly to lay their ghosts. It was my doing, it was not the workings of destiny. . . ."

"Finish your supper!" said Urbain.

"I will not be put off . . ."

"By no means," said Urbain ominously. "Finish your supper and we will go over a little of the evidence. And thank you, my boy, for getting us the Pleasance. We will lay the ghosts even if they are the ghosts of your doubts."

Maxim ate his bean soup. The dry wind rattled the shutters; he was stifling. He wanted to rush out into the streets of Rhomary, to the Warren, to Carcut or beyond to the farmed lands or the desert. The impulse was so strong he saw himself carry it out, fling down his spoon, clatter back his chair and run down the stairs, snatching his cloak from the wall. But still he remained. Time of the furn. A silly season where the mind played tricks. The hot wind circled all around the house like a live creature.

2

After supper they settled in the room that old Urbain kept as a study. It was a brownish place which contained, for Maxim, one interesting phenomenon: a wooden table. It was a heavy oval table of black kerry, a rare wood. Over the years books, paper, tablets, scrolls had been piled upon it until the sturdy wood bent under the strain; the table was shaped like a boat. To mark his retirement Urbain had removed most of the debris but it was creeping back again.

"What do we have then?" asked the old man. "This planet we are on holds many natural wonders. We are castaways with, I insist, a precarious hold upon the place, upon that small area we call the Rhomary land. We have never circumnavigated our globe. Howd and Ahern have been given up for lost. In the Red Ocean, going west, Gline was wrecked, Destris simply vanished. These are but four of the brave men and women who tried to move out from our shaky center here in the mud-built hive, the city of Rhomary . . ."

"Don't forget the outlying settlements!" said Maxim. "The Rhomary land extends for more than a hundred kilometers to the north . . . there was a tendency to move out and settle from the very first. A journey to Lemn Oasis in the early years must have been a great undertaking. Silver City is no longer a ridiculous boom town, it *is* a city. . . ."

"You sound like a Councillor at a banquet. We have an enormous capacity for self-congratulation. Yet what do we know? We gaze and gaze at the stars and name them and record their movements but we lost the ability to relate them to other systems of astronomy ten days after landfall. The ship burned, its wretched computers burned, more to the point Alois Kirchner, the senior navigator, was burned almost to death trying to save the maps, records. He named the planets, he insisted that our Sun is Delta Pavonis, but he died; our astronomy is based on his few surviving notes and the memories of assistant navigators and other officers in the first years. Now our astronomers grope about for the old systems or simply observe. We have never doubted that we came from the stars, to be specific from the planet Earth, third planet of a G0 star in a spiral arm of the Milky Way . . . how this empty rigamarole trips off the tongue. . . ."

"But there are doubts!" interjected Maxim. "What about the Marchers?"

"A bunch of cranks!" snapped Urbain. "But we must consider them, I suppose. A quasi-religious society has been growing in Silver City which holds that the inhabitants of Rhomary did *not* come from the stars. They hold that our ancestors migrated from another part of this planet . . . that we are the remains of a large overland migration and that, furthermore, the whole paraphernalia of the starfall theory is wicked invention, mainly on the part of Doctors'

College. These people call themselves the Society of Immigrants; they are called, popularly, the Marchers. They give no trouble . . . no hint of militancy, so far . . ."

"Of course," said Maxim, "both theories might be true. It is amply proven that a spaceship did come with a great many humans . . . but why must we be the only ones to find landfall on this hospitable . . . well, reasonably hospitable . . . world? Perhaps there *are* other humans on the other side of the planet. You've mentioned the difficulty of getting there or getting back."

"A very good point," said Urbain. "You have raised it . . . not I. Why should we be the only ones? Why should we be the only humans arrived here from the stars, and more particularly, why should we be the only *beings*? Other forms of intelligent life already exist here: the Vail and the Delfin folk of the Red Ocean. Still other forms could have arrived as we have done. . . ."

"I walked into that one," said Maxim. "But there is still no evidence . . ."

"Let us glance at what I call the evidence," said the old man. "Let us go back twenty years."

"Straight back to Coll Dun Mor . . ."

"Not quite. The matter of the three travelers, the merchants from Silver City, was first brought to my notice when I received a city official from that town in the year 1067. The man was a judge-advocate and he brought with him a long statement from a poor woman . . . a washerwoman . . . who had been accused of selling her twelve-year-old son into bondage. The charge had been laid by the boy's grandparents, the washerwoman's in-laws, who thought their son had married beneath him. The husband was a day-laborer, an easygoing fellow; there were five children."

"The husband was still living?"

"Of course he was still living . . . I expect he is alive and hearty to this day and the five children and the woman herself . . . they were a healthy, happy-go-lucky family. But to continue: the charge concerned the woman's second eldest son and it certainly looked as if he had been sold. He had been taken to work at a large villa in the town by three well-to-do merchants . . . yes, the story already follows a pattern. The mother seemed to have received presents or payments from these people; the boy didn't visit his home or his grandparents. Afterward the woman insisted there had been no sale: the merchants had been taken by the boy and offered to educate him and employ him as a servant.

31

"The grandparents laid the charge and talked their son, the boy's father, into going along with it . . . but he told his wife. She went at once to reclaim her child and she had a strange experience. The merchants, two men and a woman, received her kindly as they had always done. They confided to her that the boy was not quite what they had supposed; their plans to educate him were not working out. What they were trying to say was that the boy was too stupid. Yes, I had him tested, he had a low average IQ . . . no one had been literate in the mother's family for some years . . . but his manual dexterity was quite good. I remember wondering what on earth these people wanted in a house servant.

"The mother brought out the business with the child-selling warrant and the merchants became jumpy. They had all been sitting over a drink of small beer. The boy and his mother were left alone while the merchants retired into another part of the house. Suddenly they heard strange noises . . . musical sounds . . . they saw glowing lights. The woman thought the place was on fire. She went to a doorway, saw more lights, but then sank down fainting. The mother and child came to themselves in an empty house with signs of a hurried departure and the local watch beating on the door to serve the child-selling warrant. This was a strange story and the judge-advocate would have thought it only the woman's fantasy, something she made up to protect herself. The charge was dropped for lack of evidence. But the watch found something that was passed on: a single piece of paper, not jocca paper, covered with writing in a strange tongue. So this remnant came into my hands as Dator and I heard the story. . . ."

"I have read a version of the report," said Maxim, "but you kept back the mysterious scrap of paper . . ."

"It is a page . . ." said Urbain.

"Can you read it?"

"I can't," said Urbain. "It is Greek to me. In fact it is Greek to everyone. And in the length and breadth of the Rhomary land, then as now, there is no living soul who can read Greek, either modern or classical. I know the Greek alphabet . . . the Greek letters that were plastered over the spaceships of Earth, including our own . . . but in Rhomary it is one of the lost languages."

"But the provenance of the page . . ." said Maxim, "no need to make a mystery. There were several Russians among the first settlers . . . this was a page from some

Orthodox Christian prayerbook or testament tucked away as a talisman."

"Possibly," said Urbain. "I was interested, of course. In fact, as you must know, I was a great deal more interested than I let on to this good judge-advocate from Silver City. He thought of these mysterious travelers as child-dealers, possible troublemakers. But I was puzzled because I knew the three persons described in the washerwoman's report quite well; I might even have called them friends. They had sought out my acquaintance two years before by offering some books for the collection. They had even used the same names; they were three merchants who had rented the villa called the Pleasance. They were a married pair; Lural and Clay Ensor . . . he seldom used his first name . . . and a younger man Theo, Lural's brother or cousin. And I vaguely recalled a boy servant, somewhat older than the boy in Silver City."

"They existed, Uncle," said Maxim. "I know they existed well enough, but they were clever swindlers, hypnotists, charlatans. You saw them close up: they were human beings."

"I wonder?" said Urbain. "I had the villa searched at once, as soon as I got rid of the judge-advocate. It had been tidied and re-let twice to bonafide families of cotton-rich from the Billsee. There was no trace of anything suspicious; the landlady presented me with an object left behind. The bell."

Maxim rose up and reached it down from the shelf above the old man's head: a small bronze bell in a circle of fine turquoise ceramic, the whole resting on a wooden stand.

"They always left something behind . . ." he said. "Was it to lure you on? Are they careless?"

"Well," said Urbain, "they do not care. I had the feeling, always, that their relationship to things held in the hand, to objects, was slightly other than my own. I thought it was some affectation. Maxim, they were damnably strange. They were beautiful to look at; they were worldly; they were friendly and warm but I never once touched any of them. Think how strange that is, in Rhomary? Never to shake hands, to clap a shoulder, to brush against a person's hand, foot, cheek by accident . . ."

"Your recollection must be at fault!" said Maxim.

"Maybe, maybe. At any rate I searched for these travelers. The world was more thinly populated then than it is now and I was, as you say, more high-handed. I found no trace of the family but I did discover the name of their servant: Coll Dun Mor. This bell is the work of his mother Morag Dun Mor, a potter from Pebble on the Billsee. At first there was no trace of him either; I thought he had disappeared along with the Ensor family."

"Was there ever an Ensor family?" asked Maxim. "I mean in the Primary Records, from the ship . . ."

"Questions of names are the devil, as I said before. But there was an ensign aboard the ship with the second name of Ensor. There was no suggestion that this person was other than human. There was also no information on whether or not she survived the landing . . ."

"Ah, but the name was there . . . in the records . . ." said Maxim. "How careful they must have been . . ."

"Take care! You are beginning to be convinced," said Urbain. "Time passed . . . a year, two years, nearly three. Then I learned that Coll Dun Mor had returned to Rhomary city. He was a blind beggar who sat at the Sulvan Gate. He had a friend, a little waif from the Warren . . . Gurl Hign, the beggar's daughter."

"Now there is a real wonder," said Maxim, "and a warning not to make literacy the measure of all things."

"You go too fast. Gurl Hign's history, her success story comes later. I left Coll Dun Mor alone, I merely kept an eye on him, poor young devil. I worked on his dossier; it was simple enough. But finally a report came back from the farthest limits of the Rhomary land. A caravan fuhrer, Art Barn . . . whose name really was Baronovsky . . . sent a report of the Ensor family, large as life, cool and handsome as ever, traveling with his train. He took the usual circular route, hauling all manner of supplies from Rhomary to Stay A Bit, then hauling fruit from Stay to Lemn Oasis . . . changing his parmels there . . . going on to Bork with salt, raw jocca and any supplies that were left, and so from Bork to Silver City. The Ensors traveled from Lemn and struck out on their own to a tiny unnamed oasis near Bork. I waited still and I was rewarded by a burst of activity from the Lemn Oasis. Jenz Kindl began his ministry. He healed the sick, sweetened the wells, preached brotherly love, mystical communion with other starfolk and a hatred of Doctors' College. This last, I might add, was rather forced on him . . . you know how they resist any kind of faith healing. So finally after all this long time I took out a Dator's warrant and hauled in Coll Dun Mor, the blind boy at the Sulvan Gate. I felt sure that all the cases were linked;

34

the travelers had something to do with the washerwoman's son and with the blind beggar and with the preacher. I wondered, of course, if Coll might be a fake . . . a well-known blind man set in place for Jenz to heal . . ."

"Uncle," said Maxim, "we're back where we started with your feelings of certainty. I've read Coll Dun Mor's evidence and it tallies with your own and with the experience of the washerwoman from Silver City. Lights . . . strange noises. Three persons who are tall, good-looking, kind, rather untouchable. . . . But is this evidence that they were *not human?*"

"He brought out their intention!"

"Far-fetched. A Messiah for the Rhomary land. Careful grooming of the candidates who each had a 'miraculous birth.'"

"A miraculous birth *with reliable witnesses,*" said Urbain. "I was in fact their witness; as Coll put it they had been keeping track of me. I had been present at his birth years before during the floods on the Billsee. Coll Dun Mor was born soon after a tidal wave; his mother was rescued by some officials sheltering on the lighthouse platform."

"And the washerwoman's son . . . don't tell me . . . I remember. He was the survivor of quintuplets."

"The doctor who attended the mother in Silver City hospital was regularly wined and dined by the travelers just as I had been. Jenz Kindl who did become the Messiah was born on the second night of a great meteor shower: the whole oasis of Lemn were able to witness his birth. Oh yes, I'm sure this was the plan. There is something inhuman . . . non-human . . . about it. Were these folk kind or merely whimsical and cold-blooded?"

"You traced no connection between Jenz Kindl and the travelers?"

"He denied having seen anyone of this kind and so did his family back in Lemn. But he was absent in the desert for long periods. I think his preparation took place at some desert oasis on the way to Bork. Then he was made to forget the whole experience and substitute his own mystical revelations. Poor fellow . . . he believed in his mission. He was a remarkable man and he performed many cures."

"These travelers abandoned him to his fate," said Maxim.

"I'm not surprised, are you? Jenz embraced his martyrdom. Doctors' College were afraid; they brought him out on the twentieth day of his hunger strike. He had his followers carry him into the desert and he died there, by the tower rock. Of course he has reappeared to many of his followers."

"What did he look like, Uncle?"

"Medium height, longish, sun-bleached hair, bright blue eyes, thin beard trimmed back. He had a pleasant ordinary face, heavily suntanned . . . he always looked worried."

"Do you think the travelers produce these visions?"

"Not necessary. The Jenzites are persons of faith. Of course they will see visions?"

"Perhaps Coll Dun Mor saw visions?"

"He was a Vesp," said Urbain. "You have worked with a Vesp as preparation for this office. The power is well attested and I have used it many times. When Coll took my hand and in his own hand held this bell from the Pleasance, he could show them to me again. Lural, in a white gown, her marvelous ashen hair falling over her shoulders; the two men playing Go on a faience board with red and white pieces. I can still see Theo, the younger man, handling the pieces in that queer way they had.

"Coll Dun Mor upset their calculations. He was simply too clever and, in fact, too wise. He saw their intention and refused to become a Messiah. He had a certain spiritual power; he convinced me, in the end, that he was much more remarkable even than the travelers. No, I suppose that is exaggerating. He suggested the true nature of the travelers . . . pointed out the passage in the Book of the Envoys. Look . . . there *is* evidence: read it again."

Maxim took the clumsy folio book from the table and unfolded it to the woven marker. He read the rubric:

The Vail Arut speaking with the Sixth Envoy, Maire Manin O'Moore . . . a preamble on the senses of the Vail.

"There is no order of importance and no clear division in these senses; this passion for enumeration belongs to minmer thinking. Yet there are words, besides those of the minmer tongues, for those senses on which you rely. They may correspond to *Ul*, *Thet* and *Esoon*, seeing, touching and hearing, registering the presence of sounds. Is it common, minmer, to hear a sound and to be unaware of its origin, not to know what causes the sound?"

"I believe it is common."

"Remarkable . . . to isolate 'a sound' in the color and pattern of the sense fields."

36

"It is a matter of language. We might say 'a sound' when we mean a series of sounds."

"Language is always imprecise."

"Yes. A question, Friend Arut: where do you have these expressions Ul, Thet and Esoon?"

"I can hardly answer you, minmer, without touching on areas that are unretrieved. We do not swim into these waters of memory as willingly and hopefully as minmers do. We hold more of the universe, of all that exists, about us presently . . . in the present . . . simultaneously, perhaps. To answer your question is to disturb hidden currents of time and of feeling. There is regret here and innerlichkeit, even tristesse . . ."

"You feel sadness?"

"Not precisely. It is a more shredded emotion. For these words are come from a race of strange capacity, less known yet once more real to the Vail than ten thousand minmers or men. They are hardly to be seen unless they put on a shape to be beheld but their minds are spacious."

The rubic noted: Sensor withdrawn. No questions answered for the rest of the afternoon.

The two Dators were silent; Maxim was trying to picture the incredible scene. The dialogues had been recorded over a period of sixty years in that area of the Western Sea known as the Sea of Utner. The Vail preferred to receive the Envoys in those summers, seventeen years apart, when the comet, their tailed star, passed overhead. Later they agreed to meet them in between-seasons, during the heyday of Vail-minmer relations that preceded the Great Drought. The Envoys had had a tall platform built on a small island and the enormous creature, floating half in, half out of the water, spoke through one of its sensors adapted for the task. The Vail claimed ten senses; to the simple sight, hearing, touch, taste and smell they added a specialized visual sense, an audiovisual sense associated with the recognition of distance, a necessarily acute kinaesthetic sense, organs concerned with the transmission and reception of electrical impulses . . . or an electrical sense . . . and a tenth sense, if any or all of these things could be understood plainly as senses, compounded of emotion, space-time and racial memory. It was difficult for the Vail to shake off their first impression of the race of men as minmers, fairy-folk, of

37

minuscule intelligence. The fact that they swiftly invented and used this name for human beings was, in itself, a sign of discrimination for they were canny with names, as they were with numbers. When they allowed themselves to be named, after more than a hundred years of intermittent contact with human beings, it was a sign of recognition, of loving indulgence. The word "Vail," gleaned from the thundering "Ahvaal" of the beast's diapason, was probably nothing more than a version of the word "Whale," given by an early Envoy, for the Vail never forgot. The "personal" names, *Ash, Arut, Hema,* by which the Vail were distinguished in the reports and dialogues, were pet names given to a single adapted sensor, through which they spoke. The Vail became quickly proficient in English, French and German; they claimed to know one other speech besides their own modes of communication. The length of the Vail's life span and its method of reproduction were still unknown.

"I think Coll Dun Mor was right!" said Maxim suddenly.

"What, are you convinced about the shape-changers?"

"He was right to search for the Vail when he had regained his sight from Jenz Kindl. The Vail are a wonder; I am sorry they are lost. Do you think they will come again?"

"Who knows? After fifty years I am doubtful. Ask your Envoy tomorrow, she will let you know."

"Finish your story, Uncle."

"You are indulging an old man. Coll returned to me after he received his sight and spoke of preparations for his journey. We talked well. I still wanted to train him as an archivist. Perhaps he knew that he would never come again. He set off with his friend Gurl Hign . . . a cheeky, determined little thing . . . and it was a hazardous trip to the Red Ocean in those days. Word came back after more than a year that they were living with Frenck, the old trader at the Gann River. They lived there for five years working like slaves. Frenck became ill, sent me his written testament: he left the Station House and land to the pair of them. Coll Dun Mor was the Rancher. I often thought in those years of making the journey to see them, Coll and Gurl and their children on their kingdom. The Gann Station grew enormously. It has the biggest Jenzite settlement in the Rhomary lands. Coll was grateful to Jenz Kindl, even if he thought he knew the source of his inspiration.

Then there came this messenger with a cry for help . . . I sent a doctor to tend Coll Dun Mor in his fever but it was hopeless. He died far away and I never saw him again."

"Ten years ago and the Station still prospers," said Maxim. "Gurl Hign is the Rancher and a powerful one by all accounts. Uncle, why don't you make the journey . . . see the children, see Gurl Hign. The way is long but much easier now . . ."

"I am too old," said Urbain. "If they built Frenck's Canal over the long portage I might try it, but now? . . . No, I am too old. I have spent my life searching for lost things: lost languages, lost skills . . . the Vail, the shape-changers . . ."

"Uncle, remember the scrolls and tablets covered with so-called sightings, from the very early days of settlement?"

"Gathering dust!"

"We have changed so much," said Maxim.

He went to the window and peered into the night; the wind had dropped; there was a sprinkling of stars visible, he thought one might be the small yellow eye of the planet Topaz.

"What did they see, those poor castaways?" he asked.

"Why, spaceships, of course," laughed Urbain. "The skies were full of ships coming to take them home again. Spaceships of every known class, exactly described, and a whole slew of fantasy ships that were not known."

"And now?"

"I see your point. Now we see lights in the sky or meteors. It is years since the last UFO was reported. We have changed. But I still have the belief, the hope that these travelers were the shape-changers. They move in a mysterious way and they have traveled in space. I hope they turn up again."

"What would you do, Uncle?"

"Ah, I would tackle them boldly! They would have to change their shapes indeed to escape my questioning this time. Think, boy, they might know the old astronomy, they might help us circumnavigate or even communicate with our lost ancestors."

Maxim smiled at the unquenchable spirit of the old man.

"I will keep my eyes open," he said.

"And your mind," said Urbain.

He gave a sigh and rang the brass bell for their nightcap.

# Chapter II

## *Signs and Wonders*

---

The city was built of mudbrick and Doctors' College was faced with white tile but the Palace of the Envoys was built of gray stone, quarried on the shores of the Western Sea, with the help of the Vail themselves. The architect was Flor Manin, a scion of the Envoy's house, who had designed a good many of the villas on the upper tiers of the New Town. The palace was his act of faith: an unequalled piece of Rhomary baroque, a one-shot, a monstrosity, the expression of a dream. The building curled out from the city wall in two interlocking circles, twin-pillared porticos. The pillars were straight and smooth, of fair proportions, but their capitals branched into fantastic clawed projections supporting the roof domes of wood and gray tile.

Maxim walked to the left, through the pillars, and continued on a long, shadowy curved walk; the place was deserted. He passed through an open archway and found himself in a large hall. The light was greenish; he was walking on rushes; in the center of the hall was a tall monolith of black rock in a fenced enclosure of white sand. As he stood before this monument a servant boy in a rainbow cloak came toward him at last. The boy knew his name and office; he was led through the round hall in the opposite porch. It was more brightly lit, through untinted glass panels, and filled with columns of dusty sunlight. There was an air of sadness and dilapidation wherever he looked in this brighter hall. The plaster was peeling; the murals of the Vail and their meetings with Envoys were unfinished, their colors already fading. The stone basin for a fountain in the center of the hall was bone dry and stained with green mold.

They passed into a corridor and came to a long living

room, still furnished in a rather monumental style but not without life and comfort.

"Dator. . . ?"

Ishbel O'Moore Manin, about forty years old, swam up to him through the dark spaces of the room and kissed him lightly on both cheeks. The accolade as a customary greeting was falling into disuse, and for the first time Maxim thought this might be a pity. A scent of flowers lingered in his nostrils. The Envoy, who was slight and fine-boned, wore a straight silk robe and a massive silver necklace interwoven with the scented white blossoms.

"Madam Envoy," he said, clearing his throat. "How may I serve you?"

"I'm not sure." Her voice was warm and matter of fact.

She moved to a window and drew back a curtain so that more dusty sunlight streamed in from a courtyard. Leaf shadows danced on a corner of the long table; they sat down before silver cups of palm wine.

"I'm glad you were able to come at once," continued the Lady Ishbel. "The old man's memory is short. Of course we record . . . it is one of the few things we still record . . . but I wanted you to hear what he had to say."

"Is this to do with the Vail?"

"No," she said. "No . . . I don't believe so. We take notice of dreams and prophecies; we have grown old on them."

He nearly came back with some silly gallantry . . . "you are not old" . . . but instead he asked:

"This is a matter of prophecy?"

"I think so."

She refilled his cup and pulled a rope of plaited kelp that hung against the gray wall of the chamber. Far away he heard a clapper sound harshly.

"Vern Munn is our handyman," she said. "He is about seventy years old, comes from the shores of the Billsee. He was present when the last rock for this building was quarried."

"Then he has seen the Vail . . ."

"He has indeed, in a between season. Vern has had leave to record dreams and visions all through his life in our service. He has had several that remain unexplained but he has foretold many things."

"What kinds of things?"

"The Outwandering. He foretold disaster for the Vail, our friends and teachers. His vision showed the drought,

41

some two years before it began and was reinforced by a series of other dreams."

"The Great Drought lasted ten years," said Maxim. "I suppose the dates tally. Anything else?"

He realized as a slight shadow crossed her face that he had sounded exactly like his uncle.

"A fire in the year 1064; the outcome of certain city elections; the sex and birth-dates of a number of children; the mining cave-in of the year before last in Silver City. There is always a connection with Vern's family or with this foundation."

"In the case of the mine accident?"

"His grandson was trapped in the mine and released with others after ten days underground. Vern gave a warning to his grandson and I wrote urgently to the management of the mine."

"They took notice of these warnings?"

"Of course not," she said. "Prophetic dreams are not popular when they come from this Foundation. Vern was able to direct the rescue workers."

There was a tap at one of the doors and an old man came in. He was short, not much over one meter fifty, and heavily built with knotted brown muscles in his arms. He wore an old-fashioned overall of gray kribble and leather sandals that showed his big brown shapely feet. Maxim was plagued by one of his uncle's literary references when he saw the old man's feet; he hastily looked him in the eye. Old Man Munn had eyes that could be described as black rather than brown, the iris indistinguishable from the pupil; his thick gray hair had once been black.

"Good day, Lady," he said softly, with a sketched bow to Ishbel and another to Maxim. "Good day, Mister."

"Vern," said the Envoy, "I would like you to tell Dator Bro your dream."

"Gladly."

He looked toward Maxim as if expecting some preliminary questions.

"A dream, was it?" asked Maxim. "Were you asleep?"

"Yes, at first. The most of it was dream, a clear dream. Shall I tell you?"

"Surely," said Maxim.

The old man, who had remained standing, now sat down opposite Maxim and stared into his face.

"I saw the sea and the islands in the sea and in the distance a coastline black with forest trees. There was a flash

42

of light and a fireball overhead that divided into three; one fell in the sea, one over the trees, the third farther off. I came closer in the dream and saw where the fireball struck the water; there was a kind of explosion, the water bubbled and boiled, then wreckage floated on the red surface of the sea. I knew this was the Red Ocean. Next I seemed to be on a boat, standing in a crowd of sailors. There was someone I knew, young Jaygo, Lady Ishbel's child. Everyone looked at a figure on the deck. I saw him clearly: a young man, very tall, with yellow-brown hair and a pale face. He lay there unconscious and he had some hurt to his left arm. He wore a suit of silver cloth. I heard a voice say in the crowd: 'It is an old web . . .' "

"What? A web, w-e-b?"

For the first time Maxim felt an eerie excitement.

"That's right," said the old man. "I made no sense of it then or afterward but that was the word. I woke up at this point. I knew it was an important dream so I pushed back into it . . . it is a trick I can do sometimes. I shut my eyes at once and the dream landscape came back. Just a picture: this same ship was coming to anchor and an angry crowd of people were waiting on the wharf. Stones were flying. It was the Gann Station. That was all I got. I was wide awake then and I went at once to tell the dream and write it down."

"Mister Munn . . . Vern . . ." said Maxim earnestly, "have you even been at the Red Ocean and the Gann?"

"Yes, Dator, I have. I went with Lady Ishbel's father, the Envoy Shawn Manin, on an expedition to search for our friends the Vail in the year 1060. There was a party of ten persons from this foundation. We sailed on the Red Ocean as far as the Six Seven Isles. There was nothing at the Gann Station in those days except a mooring place and the Station House, Frenck's house. In this dream the place was much changed . . . houses . . . people . . . but I knew it for the Gann."

"What do *you* think this dream means?"

"As close as I can get to it . . . a starship has fallen from heaven within the last few days. There is this young man come down with it . . . he is not dead . . . I do not know it they have found him yet. The people at the Gann Station will take fright."

"Thank you," said Maxim. "I will take copies of this dream and all your former important dreams. Please do me the favor of sending me a copy of any further important dreams, Master Munn. You will be serving the city of Rhomary."

"Pleased to be of service . . ." said the old man.

He rose up quietly and when Lady Ishbel had nodded to him he went away.

"You are far from convinced," she said.

"On the contrary, I am much impressed," said Maxim. "I understand why you sent for me."

"Do you?" she asked, smiling.

She swung around in her chair and looked at a corner of the long room.

"We need more light . . ."

Maxim hurried to the second long shuttered window and wrestled with the fastenings. The sunlight came in and illuminated the dark corner opposite: Lady Ishbel was already standing there by a group of portraits. He went to her side.

Between the portrait of a young man posed in the open air on a sandy beach and the portrait of the Lady Ishbel, much younger, clad in a white dress, her hand resting upon a large scroll, there was a portrait of a child about thirteen years old. The artists, he guessed, had all been different, and the painter of this last work by far the most talented. The young girl . . . or was it a very handsome boy? . . . stared out of the frame with bare-faced pride, an extreme precocity that was unnerving. Maxim took in the thick dark hair, the delicate curve of cheek and brow, the set of the slim body and the white hands curled on the arms of a chair. He realized he was looking for signs of infirmity; did the look of defiance come from a twisted leg or shoulder?

"My father Shawn Manin," Lady Ishbel was saying, "My husband Jay Adam . . . and my child Jaygo. . . ."

Maxim looked now at the portrait he had missed, that of the husband, Jay Adam. He remembered the man's family, rich in Councillors and in cotton, and the accident that had killed him: a wall in a Council building had collapsed killing several office-bearers. Jay Adam was well set up and smiling, easily posed under a tree; his eyes were as green as those of his child; his portrait had been painted by the same gifted artist.

"I am widowed," said Lady Ishbel, "and Jaygo is called Manin."

"Vern Munn mentioned the name Jaygo . . ."

"He saw Jaygo in the dream. He dreams true when his

love and loyalty are involved. Jaygo is, at this moment, on the Gann Station."

"Why?" Maxim burst out clumsily. "What is this . . . a search for the Vail? A holiday? What age is your . . . er . . . your daughter? Who is with her?"

A look of fierce amusement grew on her face; for a moment she resembled her own child.

"Jaygo is now seventeen and generally passes for a young man," said Lady Ishbel. "I am still worried by the dream. Riots at the Gann . . . a panic arising from a fallen spaceship . . . I have made no report out of this foundation in all my time in office. Now I would like to convince Doctors' College of the reality of a dream."

She was trembling and there was a faint flush in her cheeks. As Maxim helped her to sit down again she leaned against him; a white blossom was crushed against his chest.

"You must explain," he said. "What has this to do with Doctors' College?"

"Jaygo has trained as an intern."

She held his gaze and gave one sigh. The heir of this dilapidated palace had taken, at last, another vocation. Maxim realized that he was talking not only to the Envoy but to the last Envoy: the search had diminished into a mere hope, some kind of formality. Or perhaps this Jaygo would keep Envoy as an old title, as the early Rhomarians had trailed the forgotten skills of their parents . . . "Navigator," "Computek." The Vail were passing into legend along with the Manins and O'Moores, their absurd edifice of power and influence. He looked back, wondering, to that other creature of legend John Maning or Sean Manin, the young Education and Media Officer, Second Grade, Secretary of something called the Celtic Society, who became a fisherman on the Billsee and was washed far into the Western Sea during a storm.

"You are shocked," said Lady Ishbel.

"Tell me about your son," said Maxim.

He knew there was more to tell, more from her manner than from certain puzzling references.

"Jaygo was educated privately," she said. "There was no question, at first, of the Doctors' High School. I wonder what you have heard about the dark secrets we nourish here in the palace . . . of monsters right here in our midst? My father was the only surviving child of four; his siblings were all mutants, severely deformed, one surviving to its tenth year. My own child is a mutant; Jaygo is an her-

45

maphrodite. At first we thought I had borne a girl child but the duality became clearer year by year. Jaygo has been in the care of certain doctors and they have used a fine discretion. He is extremely gifted and completed the pre-med entrance at the age of thirteen. I believe I think of him, now, as a young man. . . ."

"What is Jaygo doing at the Gann? Surely this is not a study tour or a posting?"

"He is attending his former tutor, the Third Consultant of the College, Dr. Los Smitwode, on an expedition to collect fever trees."

"Smitwode? The TC? He is at the Gann?"

The Third Consultant's reputation among the students was formidable; his gentlest nickname was Old Mel, short for Melanoma. Yet Urbain accepted his dinner invitations eagerly; he was one of the few members of the college that the old man held in high esteem.

"Lady Ishbel," said Maxim, "if Dr. Smitwode is there surely your child will come to no harm."

"And that is all the comfort you can offer me?"

"Yes!" he said, more fiercely than he intended, "What else could you. . . ?"

"Oh I expected Master Urbain!" she cried. "He might have helped me, spoken for me . . . used his warrant. They must send a party!"

"Lady, all you have is a dream!"

"Tell me the truth, have there been any sightings that support this dream?"

"Yes . . . fireballs, meteors. This is the time of the furn when people are shaken with all sorts of madness."

She stood by the window now, washed by the dusty sunlight; the droop of her head was exactly timed, he knew, but she had gauged *his* madness well enough and he could not help himself. He drew her into his arms and the scent of the white flowers engulfed them for a few seconds. He could not remember what he said to comfort her. Far away in the palace a silvery peal of bells sounded and softly, regretfully, again with perfect timing, she drew away from his embrace.

"Come," she said, "come with me. I have a duty to perform."

He followed her out of the room; the old waitingwoman who had delivered her letter stood at the door. They walked along dark passageways and came to a little curtained stair. They climbed steadily in bright light up the inside wall of the right portico and came to a small door in the gallery below the domes.

Lady Ishbel stepped out into the pale dust-colored sunlight and the furn, whipping over the rooftops of the city; Maxim followed, blinking in the light. They walked steadily along a figure of eight catwalk; the shabby humps of the domes were patched with a few of the black sun-trap frames that grew on other public buildings. They passed a heavily braced wooden stand like a yoke.

"The gong!" shouted Maxim, his voice blown away by the wind.

She drew back close to him, holding the fold of her silken cloak over her head.

"Sold long ago," she said, "mostly to keep up our charities. So much metal."

They walked on around the southern dome and there was the Rhomary land spread out below them. On a clear day, he guessed, one might see almost to the shores of the Western Sea. The observation platform was cluttered with broken pieces of equipment: the remains of at least two heliographs and a broken anemometer still twirling gamely. Lady Ishbel had the cover off the brass telescope before he could help her. She set her feet on certain markings, swung the instrument into position and looked out for about a minute. The bell in the tower of Doctors' College directly across the city began to strike twelve o'clock, two hours before midday, when Rhomarians took a snack before their lunch. Lady Ishbel paused, then looked again for a few strokes of the bell.

"That is all," she said. "That is the duty."

"What did you see?"

"The same as we have seen for fifty years. No signal fire. I looked toward one of our farms, one of our remaining farms, on the shores of the Western Ocean where it joins the Billsee. An old man and his wife keep a fire ready in a high place; they would light it if the Vail came. I look out in the late morning and in the evening; sometimes last thing at night."

"Lady," he asked sadly, "what would you do if the fire was lit?"

"I have no gong to strike," she said, "and no wish to cause alarm. Perhaps I would send word to the Dator."

"What is the Dator?" he said. "He holds another old hereditary office that some would wish away. In fact the office will pass, I know it; there will be nothing but a heap of dusty private archives consulted by scholars. The collecting of information will be in the hands of the Council; there will be more compulsion than ever there was in all of the Dators' warrants. Pardon me, Lady, if I see this as a loss almost as great as your own . . ."

"Oh, I will pardon you anything . . ."

She lifted a hand and laid it on his lips. He caught her wrist, playing their scene to the end, and kissed the palm of her hand. She went past him and they walked back the way they had come and descended the narrow white stairway in the portico, between faded portraits of the Vail. The old servant was waiting at the foot of the stairs.

"I must take my leave," he said.

The old woman stepped forward politely and handed him a scroll: the report of Vern Munn's dream.

"Believe me, Lady . . ."

"What shall I believe?"

"I swear that I will do my best to help you!"

"Why," she said, surprised, "I believe you will!"

She went into the corridor followed by the old woman and Maxim picked his way past the empty fountain.

"Sss . . . Dator!"

Maxim stepped out through a glass door with several broken panes and found Vern Munn lurking about among the columns.

"Is the Lady gone in? And the old woman?"

"Yes."

The old man stared up at him with steady, glittering black eyes.

"There was one more thing to tell," he said. "I did not dare say it before my Lady."

"In your dream?"

"When I saw that last picture. The crowd was angry and stones were flying," said the old man. "I saw Jaygo struck down by a stone. I saw it. The stone struck him about here and there was blood."

He touched his left cheek high up on the cheekbone below the eye. Maxim felt sick and giddy. He gripped the old man's shoulder.

"I'll take note of it," he said, "and something will be done. And you're sure of the word they used on the ship, an old web?"

"That was it."

He strode off along the broad street that led across town toward Doctors' College. Once he looked back and saw

Vern Munn, a dark hobbit creature, watching him still from the gray pillars. When he raised his head again he was passing the Guard House and the Watch barracks, strategically placed where steps ran down into the Warren. There was a steady press of people in the mean streets down below; peddlers and stall-keepers called their wares. A guard outside the barracks saluted Maxim and he turned to descend the steps.

He edged along in the crowd past some of the stalls. He saw a sign "Noag's Inn" and realized that he knew the place, it had been called The Seven Stars. He crossed the street, on impulse, and pushed between the kelp strips that hung before the inn door. The big room was dark and there was a comfortable reek of palm wine and cooking oil. He slipped into a booth and a boy with a laden tray served him a long-pot of wine and water. The Inn catered to farmers and merchants from out of town; he had come there with his father and mother as a child when they came up to market. Roast dry-hog was the specialty of the place and at this time of day most of the booths were full of families making an early lunch of delicious roast meat, garnished with salad grass and pickled fruit.

He cast an eye over the two serving girls and decided that neither of them was Ambel. They were sisters, fresh-faced, about sixteen years old, with braided hair and snapping brown eyes. Their sweet voices rang out as they passed the orders through the servery hatch. Behind the bar there was a hefty, smiling woman and a lean man came and went, passing the time of day with his customers.

"Mr. Noag?" asked Maxim as he came by.

"That's me!"

Noag looked down, took in Maxim and his official medallion, then slid into the booth opposite him.

"Something I can do for City Hall?"

"Dator," said Maxim. "Dator Bro at your service. I'm looking for a merchant name of Milt Donal."

"Young fella from your place was here earlier."

"Oh yes," said Maxim, not making too much of it. "Did he see Donal?"

"That's about all he did," said Noag warily. "Milt is feeling socked and sandy today."

"Was he celebrating then?"

"You know how things are when they come to town."

Noag was worried.

49

"Look here," he brought out. "Go upstairs . . . go up and see for yourself. His man's up there and my elder girl."

Maxim took out money for his drink but the landlord waved it away. He pointed to the broad staircase through an archway; Maxim went off in search of Milt and his hangover. He passed a man coming quickly down the stairs, took in the pale face, handsome, clean-shaven, about fifty years old, and the thick reddish hair, streaked with white. The man met his eye, gave a polite inclination of the head and a curious sideways step on the wide stair so that they passed within a meter of each other. He was carrying a satchel of some kind. Was it so bad, then, that Milt needed doctoring?

A shrill voice rang out from the top of the stairs.

"Stop him! Stop him, the bluggy mute . . ."

A girl came running down toward him.

"Stop him!" she cried. "Hey Dad! Dad! What are you waiting for, you great lunker . . ."

She pushed Maxim.

"The red-haired fella," she said. "He was getting at poor Milt again . . ."

Maxim ran around the corner of the stair and saw the flick of the man's green cloak. He ran and shouted. The courtyard at the end of the passage was full of dust; he plunged toward the roofed gateway and saw stars. A sheet of light flared up before his eyes, a glancing blow caught his head and shoulder. He turned as he went down and saw a second man, stocky, dark, holding a parmel whip with the thongs folded against the handle. Two figures whisked out of the covered gateway; he struggled up and Noag ran past him, looking into the crowded street outside. Hands reached out and were helping him to his feet; he felt himself brushed down.

"I'm fine," he said embarrassed.

"We lost him," said Noag. "Was it that prospector again?"

The girl had been brushing him down; now she stopped with her hands on Maxim's chest. She smiled at him. She was one of the prettiest girls he had ever seen in his life: white skin, masses of black hair escaping from its ribbons; a girl as lush as a black plum. Ambel of Noag's Inn. Oh yes.

"Sorry . . ." she said. "I took you for a farmer's boy. But you are something else."

"He's the bluggy Dator in person," said Noag. "Exceedingly sorry. What was it with that red-haired fella, Ambel?"

"He was hanging about in Milt's room," she said. "I swear he would have robbed him."

"Let us go up," said Maxim. "I wanted to see Merchant Donal."

Pot-boys and a few diners were coming to the stairs but Noag spread his arms and drew them away. Maxim followed the girl upstairs into a big, comfortable bedroom, one of the finest in the place. A muscular man in his thirties lay across the rumpled bed; his noisy breathing and the reek of palm wine should have told the whole story. Maxim stared into the merchant's flushed face and laid a hand on his forehead.

"What happened?" he demanded. "Ambel . . . Miz Noag . . . was this just a drinking bout?"

"Milt can take plenty," she said, "but he usually wakes fresh. I think that creature, the red-haired old prospector, slipped something in his wine."

"Another man hit me, in the courtyard."

"He had a servant."

"So did Donal, I thought."

"Old Lige? I finally got him to fetch a doctor or one of the duty interns."

She dipped a cloth in water and sponged the merchant's head tenderly. He noticed a silver ring with a large blue stone on her left hand. If he read the signs Ambel was moving up in the world, she would be the wife of a merchant.

"Tell me from the beginning," said Maxim. "Was this to do with anything Donal reported?"

"His meteors? For sure. I wish he had never seen them."

"I wanted to check his report."

"Every word is true!" she said indignantly. "He would have sworn to it. Milt travels often by night and he has spotted meteors . . . or he would say 'meteorites' . . . many times. He saw one fall by Bork two years back and pricked off where it fell and salvaged a hundredweight of iron. This fall was so big, two nights ago, that he decided to tell the city."

"He wasn't planning to go prospecting?"

"Oh yes," said Ambel.

She looked at him shrewdly.

"You have to keep secrets. . . ?"

"I am pledged to it," said Maxim.

51

"He wanted a city contract. He hoped to go into partnership with some prospector. Telling the city was the first step toward staking a claim."

"Was this red-haired man his partner then?"

"Not him. He turned up out of the blue, his servant rented a room yonder, he was rich enough, I can tell you. His name was Redrock. Milt got talking with him last night and I served their wine. Milt thought he might be the partner he needed but I was not keen on the fella."

Milt Donal let out a long groan and folded up on the bed. Ambel wiped his face again, talking urgently.

"Wake up, love. Here is the Dator to check your report. Milt . . . Milt . . . where did you put the map . . . ?"

The merchant opened his eyes, as if he were trying his best to wake; Maxim was embarrassed for the man. Ambel shook and prodded him but he slumped back into sleep.

"There was a map?" asked Maxim.

"A rough and ready one but Milt reads the stars. He could pick out landmarks, stars, line them up from his place on the road. Maybe that was what this Redrock wanted . . . to rob the map when he thought I was gone."

Quick steps sounded on the stairs and when Maxim turned to the door Ambel said:

"It is only Lige . . ."

He was a thin old man, very neatly dressed. He stared at them both with cold suspicion.

"I am the Dator," said Maxim. "I came to talk to your master about his report."

"You took long enough," said Ambel. "What about the Doctor?"

"A duty intern will call in two hours," said Lige stiffly. "I heard about Redrock. Did you see him then, sir?"

"He passed me on the stairs. Was he after your master's map?"

Lige went at once to a press by the window and felt in the merchant's saddlebags.

"Redrock didn't get the map," he said. "Here it is."

He tucked it into his belt, crossed to the bed and spoke in a low voice to Milt Donal. His voice penetrated as Ambel's had not done and the reaction was startling. Milt Donal began to whimper and groan; he uttered a few words, perhaps the name "Lige." Suddenly he swung bolt upright in bed, his blue eyes wide open and staring, his lips drawn back in a grimace of panic. A deep-toned cry leaped out of the merchant's rigid body. Maxim felt the hairs rise on the back of his neck. Lige, the old servant, stepped back, his hand going to his own forehead where he made a circle with his thumb.

"Sweet Gods, he is possessed!" said the old man.

"Jenzite mumbling!" said Ambel. "He has the shakes, or maybe he got a drug from that Redrock."

Again the terrible cry of fear was wrenched out of Milt Donal. Maxim knelt by the bed, grasped the merchant's hands firmly and stared into the mask-like face.

"Donal!" he cried out. "Milt Donal! Wake up, man! Come back to us!"

A tremor passed over the merchant's face and body; he relaxed, his eyes flicked shut, then after a few seconds opened normally. He smiled uncertainly at Maxim. Ambel flung herself down by the bed, reaching to take Donal's hands out of Maxim's grasp.

"Oh Milt, love . . . you scared us . . ."

"Praise the Word!" whispered Lige.

Milt Donal drew his hands up to his chest, like a child who didn't want to be fussed over by a nurse.

"Where?" he asked in a tremulous whisper.

"In your bed, of course," said Ambel. "At the Inn."

"Who. . . ?" said Milt Donal. "Am I sick? What's here? Who are you?"

Maxim said firmly:

"Can you tell me your name?"

Milt screwed up his face, childlike still, and came to the abyss and cried out again.

"I don't know!"

"Try to remember," instructed Maxim, "try to get the name!"

He stared into the merchant's earnest blue eyes and saw a slow struggle reflected there.

"I can't," said Milt Donal. "It has gone."

"Do you know this lady or this old man?"

Milt leaned back on his pillow and took a long look at Ambel, then at Lige.

"Should I know them?"

He smiled at Ambel with an admiring shy smile that was the reverse of a lover's greeting. Ambel did not cry or protest but her pretty face creased with worry and disappointment.

"Master Milt," said Lige steadily, "I am Lige, your servant, from your father's house in Silver City."

"Lige . . . I seem to have heard . . ."

"Wheeesht," said Ambel. "Lie still. It will all return to you."

She cast an imploring glance at Maxim.

"You will remember," he said. "Take it easy."

He was shaken and upset, anxious to be out of the merchant's sickroom. He could not forget the look of panic on Milt Donal's face; his memory was wiped clean, at least for the present. Was there some drug to do that? He remembered the strange sentimental errand that had brought him down into the Warren in the first place and decided to get on with it.

"When he is well enough I'll send for a report," he said abruptly. "Try not to worry, Miz Noag . . . go on with your good nursing. Good day to you."

He stepped out on the landing and Lige followed him.

"He cried out like one possessed," whispered the old man.

"It will pass off. May I see the map?"

"Surely."

It was not very clear to Maxim and he didn't believe it would have helped Redrock the prospector much. Had the man tried to question poor Donal with the aid of a drug, the so-called truthweed for example, in order to find out more than the map could offer?

"You remember the meteorites?" he said to Lige.

"I saw the lights," said Lige, "and I was filled with hope."

"Were they unusual?"

"Star-folk will come one day," said Lige doggedly. "It is written."

He pulled the bedroom door shut behind him.

"I have no love for doctors or those young devils the interns," he said, "but I could wish my master out of this place."

"You can't live his life for him."

"Little you know about it, sir," said the old man. "Noag would rob the shirt from a man's back. And the girl . . . *she* is . . ."

"I know what you think she is," said Maxim. "You carried Milt Donal's report to the Dator's house yesterday, didn't you? I read all the reports, remember!"

He went away down the stairs more anxious than ever to be away from Noag's Inn. He went out through the courtyard where he had chased the prospector; it was the time for siesta and the crowds had thinned out. He went on through dark fruit-smelling lanes and bought himself a straw basket of black plums at a stall. Only a few steps farther on he came to a well; no one was drawing water. Beside the well was a small square block of stone, weathered and dirty; Maxim sat down on the stone coping of the well and read the inscription.

**Philip Webb, Auxiliary Personnel, Landfall +75
'To Old Webb Who Carried Many Burdens'**

It was a little-known monument, but one which moved him more than the grander ones that reared up here and there in the city. He liked to think that Old Webb had been a beloved person. He had been in service for one hundred and ten years . . . some longer than others . . . when he laid his burden down in Rhomary. Philip Webb was an android, one of four who survived the landing. They had been of a standard height, one meter eighty; many of the human settlers had exceeded this height considerably. Now Maxim was very tall at one meter seventy-eight. There were giants in those days, fair-haired men and women in silver suits. He sighed and walked back through the drowsy streets and climbed out of the Warren, carrying his basket of plums. "What you need," he told himself, "is Jon Witt's food and a bit of siesta and a good long afternoon collating the new land register. The silly season has affected your brain."

When he saw Ranuf pacing in the front hall he knew that he was not to be permitted this kind of escape.

"The old man is asleep," said the archivist, "and I'm glad. He walked up to the Pleasance, had an early lunch and settled down for his nap. The post came and a letter by racing parmel."

"Someone has silver dollars!"

"It is the stargazing woman!" said Ranuf, excited but disapproving. "The hermit from Pinnacle . . ."

Maxim took the travel-stained fold of jocca paper slowly, with a kind of relief. Afterward he timed his decision from this moment; the bell at Doctors' College tolled one-third past thirteen hours; he knew what the letter would contain and what he must do.

"I'll read it while we eat," he said.

"I've eaten long ago," said Ranuf impatiently. "What did the Envoy have to say?"

"You wouldn't believe me if I told you!"

55

"Maxim . . . Dator . . . for heaven's sake."

"I'll read this letter!"

He started up the stairs and lightened his tread so as not to wake his uncle. Ranuf stayed below, fuming with impatience. Maxim nodded to Jon Witt who poked his head out of the kitchen and went to sit at the half-cleared table. He laid out the account of Vern Munn's dream and opened the report from Pinnacle. The stargazing woman, Faya Junik, was one of the links in the chain of his uncle's obsession; she was a trained doctor; she had attended Coll Dun Mor in his last illness. Some time after this she had given up her profession and retired into the desert. Most important from Maxim's point of view, she was a trained observer.

Exactly one hour by the glass before sunrise on Jules twelve 1102 a large radiant body entered the atmosphere on a low trajectory far to the northwest. I saw it explode, or more properly, divide, high over the reaches of the northwest continent. At least six smaller radiant bodies were momentarily visible; four were borne or propelled closer to Pinnacle. One must have fallen in the desert far to the north beyond Bork, three others fell in the area of the Red Ocean. I do not rule out the possibility that this was a large meteor exploding but I have seen many hundreds of meteors and this was quite atypical. I believe a space vehicle entered the atmosphere, seeking landfall, and divided itself into six landing capsules containing crew and equipment. I must leave the Red Ocean work to you, Master Urbain. I will take a driver and go at once to look for the impact zone in the distant north.

Maxim read the report a dozen times between untasted mouthfuls of salad and cold fish-cakes.

"Jon," he said, "Step down to Apprentice Rab in the sorting room and fetch me Milt Donal's report from yesterday."

"Milt Donal?" said Jon Witt, wondering.

"That's the name . . . and send Ranuf to me . . ."

Ranuf was already at the door of the dining room.

"Well, sir?" He was still put out.

"Read it. Read this, too . . . an account of a dream. Read the report of Milt Donal, the merchant . . ."

"The meteors? I've read it. . . ."

Ranuf's voice trailed away as he took in the words of the stargazing woman. Maxim pushed back his chair and they stared at each other wide-eyed, like two madmen. Maxim felt a fierce, joyful grin growing on his face and an answering one transfigured the round, cross face of Ranuf.

"Dry hell!" swore Ranuf softly. "Dear bleeding starfire. Is it? Is it?"

"Yes!" said Maxim. "Yes, it is, it must be . . ."

"From . . . the same place? From Earth?"

"It happened before!"

"Who will you see? Will they accept any of this? Junik is non grata at the College. Try the Council, the Ex-Officio that you saw yesterday. The Envoy's old dreamer is worth nothing . . . no one will accept it. Go to the Council . . ."

"You can work it out with the old man," said Maxim. "Have these copied instantly, I need to take all three. Use the apprentices Rab and Ginny, put two copyists on the bulk."

"Take the copies? Where will you take them?"

"I'm going to the Gann Station. I believe something important has come down in the area of the Red Ocean. I am Dator of Rhomary and I will see for myself."

"Right!" said Ranuf, distracted. "Yes, copies . . ."

He ran out of the room. Maxim went into his own room, still his student place, uncomfortably crowded, and began to put clothes into a leather saddlebag. He filled his wash-basin from the stone ewer and washed off the dust of the city and put on fine clothes. His holiday riding gear: leather britches, fine kribble shirt and an embroidered over-tunic of lightly padded jocca cloth. He was buckling his riding boots when his uncle erupted into the room with his hair standing up in peaks.

"You fool!" cried old Urbain. "What's this mad scheme? Did that pretty widow the Envoy talk you into it?"

Maxim went to his desk and took three stiff oblongs of jocca paper from a rack. He went on packing with both hands, seizing compass, gloves, writing-case, candles, sheath knife.

"I will send to the livery stable—Tam Hign's little place by Sulvan—I need a racer at once."

"And a driver?" said Urbain. "You think we're made of silver?"

"Uncle," said Maxim loudly, "this is myself you're talk-ing to. That is my saddle under the stairs that I won in the Stampede against all comers. I will ride to the Billsee, take ship over the Western Sea, ride again on the long portage. . . ."

Urbain capitulated at once and sat blinking on Maxim's bed.

"Oh, heaven," he said. "Oh, the wide world . . . my boy, how I wish . . ."

He took Maxim clumsily into his arms and held him tight.

"See them, greet them . . . Gurl Hign, the three children. I'll prepare a little packet. If this tale is true, then report, report, report . . . you've been trained . . ."

He went out of the room and began shouting for Maxim's saddle, for food, water bottles. Maxim unlocked his cash box and put twenty-five silver dollars into his money belt and fastened it around his waist. He sat at the desk and wrote on one of the oblong cards: his first Dator's warrants for immediate hire of one racing parmel, tanked up with its nails trimmed for a run to the Billsee.

When the sun set he was out of the market traffic and into lonely farmland, his young pied racer pacing sweetly, its flaps tightly rolled. The hot easterly wind that blew around the city on its plateau had dwindled into a warm breeze. The parmel answered to the reins, attached to the two soft growths of tissue beside its nostrils; he twitched lightly and it diverted to the Old South Road. There, after negotiating a few steep bends, he dug his heels into the bunched shoulder muscles and the parmel began to gallop.

Maxim bent close to the large smooth head and whispered encouragement. He adjusted to the sinuous triple beat, fore and mid and aft, as the three pairs of pads drummed at the sandy surface of the road. Presently the beast unrolled its flaps until they stood out around its body like a smooth, leathery cloak. The sensation of flying on a racing parmel was inescapable. Ahead of him he could see the stars and the comet, the tailed stars of the Vail, smeared above the Western Sea.

# Chapter III

## *The Rancher*

---

She woke in the darkness of early morning and heard voices on the ramp outside her door. What time? The thin darkness beyond the shutters showed that it was long before six bells. She turned aside into the warm emptiness of the big cane bed and relived the dream for a moment.

Her dreams these days were of haste, struggle, lists of figures, perhaps of the city streets, the alleys of Rhomary, far to the northeast. But this dream had been a wonder that left her shivering, washed clean, young again. They were in the Delfin, the old boat: herself and Coll and Alan, the first-born, sailing in the Red Ocean, far over the reaches of the world. The boat was seized in a rip that bore them along with magic speed. Coll stood at the prow staring ahead; his blue eyes looked the more keenly upon the world because he had once been blind.

Coll cried out and pointed. She settled the child on her back and came to stand beside him.

"The quest is over!" said Coll, in the dream.

She looked ahead over a vast plain of dark water and saw the Vail. The giant creatures had been drawn by human artists many times but one picture stayed in her mind. It was a woodcut made from sketches by Maria, the Third Envoy. Four serpentine protoheads came from the water and a fringe of long sensors, each thicker than a child's body; one land foot, the size of a small boat, gripped the rocky shore of an island. The swirl of threads upon the water were the Vail's feeding seines.

In her dream the Vail rose up out of the dark water in this form; its voice reached out to them over the sea. She could not recall the words. She stood beside Coll and they were borne swiftly along toward the great sea creature until the dream ended.

She was alone, Coll had been dead ten years; outside the door she heard Alan's voice, the voice of Bridey, the cook. A new voice now, Trim, the dock foreman. *"Wake the Rancher, for Old Earth's sake, wake the rancher. Cap LaMar . . ."*

Gurl Hign swore in the darkness, rolled from the bed and fumbled for her boots. Bridey was rapping on the door.

"Rancher? Rancher, my dear?"

"Coming!"

She opened her shutters and a thin, gray light came in. She looked up to the hills of the Divide and splashed water on her face from the washcrock. Some kind of accident? LaMar was her friend and the greatest trader on the Red Ocean. She shrugged into a work tunic, took her keys, strode out on to the ramp.

"What's the matter?"

Trim, the foreman, had a lantern, already paling as the daylight grew. Gurl saw that it was not bad news; Alan was puzzled, the old woman, Bridey, mildly excited, like Trim. The weather was fair, wind from the southwest; LaMar's vessel, the *Comet*, was berthed safely. The river Gann slept its late summer sleep between the flourishing silt plains and the irrigated fields.

"LaMar brought in something he wanted you to see," said Alan. "Part of a wreck."

"Dry hell!"

She looked crossly at the lot of them.

"Bridey . . . I'll have my tea. Alan, have you counted off the drivers and teams for LaMar?"

"Of course!"

He was a tall young man, blunt-faced and dark; she suspected that he looked like herself, a well-fed version of that black-eyed wretch, bred in the Warren: Gurl Hign, the beggar's child. She worked him hard, as she worked all her children, in fact all her kin. The remnants of the Hign clan who made it to the Gann Station in search of a successful relative either worked or went back. Trim was her cousin.

"What have they found?" she asked Alan in a low voice.

"Better look at it yourself, Ma."

They walked down the ramp to the kitchen with Trim at her elbow.

"It is a fragment," he panted. "Part of a boat? Part

60

of a building? Letters on it. I'm no good at letters but LaMar . . ."

"Oh hush up Trim, you old bell-ringer," she grinned. "Before I forget, how did LaMar go with the special order?"

"Badly, badly," said Trim. "Not much at all to give the bluggy Doctor's Eminence. Two solitary trees of one kind, maybe four of another . . . who knows how far away and the likeness not certain."

"Better than nothing," said Alan. "LaMar brought slips; we can try them in the plant shed."

The Station House was a tall, ramshackle building reared up around the solid cabin built by Frenck, the man who set up the trading post. It was set on a narrow shelf of rock, out of the way of the Gann flooding. Other cabins clung to the rocky shelves of the valley wall or rose on stilts on both sides of the broad river. There was a small hostel for guests just beyond the house; travelers from Rhomary and high officials sometimes came to marvel at the Ranch and find bargains coming from the Red Ocean.

The journey from the Rhomary land was no longer hazardous, merely frustrating. Gurl Hign turned back before she came to the kitchen and stared to the east, shading her eyes. The river Gann plunged down from the hills of the Divide, then curled round the valley on its way to the sea: it was no help with the journey east. The Long Portage: four hundred kilometers of scrubby tussock and salt ponds; three lonely corrals, then the town of Derry, on the shores of the Western Sea. Five days by galley to the Billsee and so to the roads of Rhomary. Old Frenck had been a visionary, already talking twenty years ago, when she first came there with Coll Dun Mor, of a canal in place of the portage.

Bridey had tea ready in the kitchen, the main room of the original cabin. Gurl drank standing often enough, but this morning she took a seat, ate some bread, glanced at bills of lading. Trim mastered his impatience.

"Alan," she said, "tell your sister to tend the meadow this morning."

The meadow, high up behind the house, was a graveyard.

"What is it, Ma?"

Alan put a hand on her shoulder.

"Nothing."

She stared at the familiar crevices of the stone room;

61

Coll's boot trees were still behind the cupboard, one of his leaf collages over the sink bench; she could not tell them that she had had a dream. Gurl Hign finished her tea and went out of the room with Trim at her heels, heading at last for the dock and whatever it was that LaMar had brought to light.

The unloading was at least up to schedule but a crowd stood around the old auction block. Children had come to look, and wharf laborers and Marko, the Jenzite preacher, who met every ship. On the block, pushing the spectators back, was Poll Grev, first officer of the *Comet*. She waved over the heads of the crowd and called:

"Step back! Let the Rancher get a look!"

Gurl went through briskly.

"This is a schoolday!" she announced. "I know it and so do your mothers. Get along, all of you!"

"Rancher," said a hoarse voice, "there is a revelation come . . ."

"So you say, Marko."

She had to be careful not to tease the preacher; he was an ugly, vulnerable young man, inept in the management of his own flock. Yet her loyalty to the Jenzites was and must remain unswerving; here they were firmly tolerated and their largest settlement stood across the river.

"There now," said Poll Grev, with a broad grin. "What d'ye think of that?"

Gurl turned her head this way and that and felt a permanent smile of wonder growing on her face. Vail knew what it was but it tugged at the imagination. A segment of tough molded stuff, maybe three meters by five at the widest part and shaped roughly like a leaf. At the wide edge a thick twisted overlay scarred by fire, some kind of metal. Between this metal, which might once have been silvered, and the other milky blue substance was a bunch of many-colored fronds, snapped off.

"Well?" cried Trim. "Well, Rancher? It's quite a find, eh? What d'ye say now?"

"Yes," said Gurl, "quite a find. Where did you catch this fish, Poll?"

"Way to hell and gone," said Poll. "LaMar has the place pricked off. Out by the Six Seven Islands."

"Can I see the other side?"

"*You* can . . ." said Poll significantly.

Gurl stepped on to the block and cried out:

"All right! To work, to school . . . this is no holiday.

Billy Dit, damn you, you're meant to be on tally at the gangplank. Get going all of you! Yes, Trim . . . you must go too!"

Everyone went away so quickly that she was displeased at the sound of her own harsh voice left in the air. Marko stayed, hands folded, light, astigmatic eyes fixed upon the mysterious pieces of flotsam. Gurl exchanged glances with Poll and received a firm negative; Marko should *not* see what was on the underside. Secrets! She could not imagine what it might be.

"Well, Marko, my dear," she said kindly, "what do you make of those letters?"

"It has come from the stars, Rancher, according to Jenz and his holy words," said the preacher.

He made no comment on the letters. There were two, two and a half; red letters painted on the metal. W.S. and part of a second S. And then again, if one looked closely, the blue substance, the inner layer with its strange moldings, was criss-crossed with small diagrams and lettered instructions.

"Go along now," said Gurl firmly. "If this is a revelation it doesn't need you to declare it. Please don't start any holy-shouts over at your chapel."

"Rancher . . . I must tell them . . ."

"Marko," said Gurl, "if there's anything here for you, I'll tell you. Keep the peace! Later today, end of the supper hours, bring me the scriptures and read to me about the stars."

His face lit up; he seized her hand and pressed it warmly.

"Bless you, Rancher!"

Poll watched him go; the two women were alone with the piece of wreckage. They took it firmly and turned it over. The moldings were shown as indentations, one deep as a cupboard, with no door but holes where a door had been. One cupboard was unopened, intact; the door, about forty centimeters square, was smeared with sand and mud.

"What's inside?" demanded Gurl.

"We didn't look," said Poll Grev.

She drew a bunch of flax-waste from her britches pocket and wiped away the sand and mud. The door was labeled with a single, square-armed red cross.

They stared at the symbol for a long time in silence.

"I don't think the Jenzites have had a revelation this time," said Gurl drily.

Poll laughed aloud and slapped her knee.

"You're a pearl!"

"Laugh away, Poll," she said, "but remember the Eminence up there in the hostel waiting for your fever trees. His timing is good."

"Show it to Doc Roak first," said Poll.

"I don't know . . . Gil Roak is only a field doctor."

They saw Cap LaMar hurrying toward them, his dark sea-cloak billowing. Gurl squinted at him in the sunlight; he was a muscular man in his fifties with a grizzled beard that half hid a scar on his cheek. He was truly dark skinned; the strain was thin but there were people in the Rhomary land whose ancestors had been black.

"LaMar!"

Gurl Hign stood up, smiling, and took his hand. He was an ugly old devil, she thought fondly. She saw in his eyes a version of herself that was suddenly not so ugly, not so workaday: strong, woman-shaped, high-colored.

"So you like this bit of a wreck?" he asked jovially.

"The Doctor's Eminence will like it!"

"I'm not so sure of that," said LaMar.

"Spell it out," she said. "Where did you find this and what do you think it is?"

"Found it floating beyond the Six Seven Isles," he said, "just within the compass of the second Gline map, in mid-ocean, about two hundred sea miles off the Northwest Continent. No other wreckage but as we came east . . . we were running home . . . we went through a lot of discolored water and fodder-fish debris."

"You found it clear of the islands?"

"Yes, well clear," nodded Poll Grev. "We altered course and sailed among them but found nothing."

"Well?" asked Gurl, facing up to LaMar. "Now your opinion . . ."

"Something came down. Something fell from the sky," said LaMar. "I don't want to make more of it than that. Perhaps there should be a search . . . this would mean more to us than the finding of those poor fabulous beasts, the Vail. The race of men have come from the stars a second time."

"Leave me my hopes of the Vail," said Gurl gently, "but tell me what you meant earlier. This little chest embedded in the wall of the thing has a medical symbol of great power, as great as the twined snakes. Why would the doctors, including the one we have up at the hostel, not be pleased?"

"If your power was based on spear and bow would you relish the discovery of gunpowder?" asked LaMar.

"No, you do our Eminence wrong," said Gurl. "He is cold and proud, but a doctor for all that. LaMar, you have done him a great service, finding the damned fever trees . . . now do me one!"

"Yours to command, Rancher, my dear," said LaMar lewdly.

"Go along!" she could not help smiling. "I want you to be with me when we have audience in a couple of hours. I will show him this wreckage."

"Please go to him alone, Gurl Hign," said LaMar. "Assure the Eminence that only my officers have seen the symbol on this chest."

"As you will. But LaMar, Poll . . . are there survivors, off-world folk out there?"

"Not close to the place where we found this wreckage," said LaMar. "Anything that came down with this is scattered far and wide over the ocean."

"No talk that I've heard of falling stars," said Gurl, "but we're badly placed here for stargazing. I hate to think of some poor devils . . ."

"Didn't we hear of falling nets?" asked Poll Grev. "Great balloons like Flip Kar Karn's Hot Air Balloon that helped travelers to earth?"

"We've been out of the air too long," said Gurl Hign. "The land and water are our two regions."

"That reminds me," said LaMar, "the Delfin know about this. I passed their chain and their flower formation on the way back. If there is a Delfin speaker about we could learn something."

"What do you think of those letters?"

"World," said LaMar, "World Star . . . I don't know."

"This is the world," said Poll Grev, shivering in sunlight. "I don't like to think of any other."

"I must get on," said Gurl. "Dine at the House, midday, will you? I'll keep this treasure apart until I can show it to the Eminence."

LaMar waved a hand in salute and went back to the ship. Poll had bound a strip of felt around the piece of wreckage; it was not heavy, but awkward to carry. Gurl looked about for a porter but would not call Trim from the unloading of candlewood and sea-moss and lime, the cargo of the *Comet*.

Suddenly she saw a boy of about fourteen leaping down

the paths and ramps that led to the dock. He was thin, with straight black hair; at this distance the likeness to Coll made her wince and when the boy came closer, in answer to her call, his pale eyes were the same as his father's. This was Ben, her youngest child.

"What are you doing out of school?" she asked gruffly.

"Old Denny gives me this hour free," he said. "I came to see this piece of a Mugoman ship!"

"Is that what it is? You can help me carry it to the house."

She was always surprised that the wild tales of the Rhomary children were so ordinary. They thrived on legends of Mugomen whose ships rose out of the sea to rob travelers; the Mugomen had long arms, sharp teeth, an eye in the middle of their foreheads. They robbed people and maybe ate them up. Gurl could not find them as frightening as the Vail or certain other beings who had once walked in Rhomary.

As they toiled up the paths with the slip of wreckage between them Ben said:

"I had a dream last night!"

She checked a little on the last ramp.

"Tell me about it."

"I was flying my new kite up at the lookout and this black bird came along and took away my slice of Feejo bread."

"Too bad!" laughed Gurl.

They came to the Ranch office, a new strongroom built of stone blocks, at the eastern corner of the rambling house. Gurl unlocked the doors and they laid the piece of wreckage down among her barrels of fertilizer and rolls of hide and kelp. She went to her desk, dragged Trim's bills of lading from her pocket and put them on an ironwood spike. A couple of faces appeared at the door:

"Rancher?"

"Wait in the hall!" she said. "I'll begin the session early, at eight bells."

She motioned to Ben to swing the door shut. Already they could hear through the wall a murmur of voices . . . men and women were arriving in the hall to consult the Rancher at her morning business session. She was collecting documents, an erasing tablet, various strange odds and ends: a new-blown hourglass, sixteen feet of priceless silk cord, a packet of nails. Ben was kneeling to examine the wreckage; his voice came to her like the voice in a dream.

"It fell down, Ma . . ."

She knew the tone of voice; it made her heart thump. The boy sat cross-legged on the dusty floor, his head upright, his eyes unseeing; he had laid both hands on the felt that covered the red-cross cupboard. Gurl went to him, took one of his hands, gripping it firmly. She had known for a short time that Ben had inherited his father's powers, he was a Vesp; in particular, like Coll Dun Mor, he could draw scenes and pictures from inanimate things, he could make the past live. Gurl had never experimented with the boy's power; she did not know if he could take others along with him to share the experience, as Coll had often done.

"Ben, tell me . . . show me . . ."

"Down . . ." whispered Ben. "They knew they were going down . . . oh Ma . . . can you see?"

She closed her eyes and for a moment it was clear, vivid as any of the wonders Coll had shown her and in some ways more terrible. There was a movement of men and women, suited figures; a long dark tube of a place lit by bands of light; the lights flickered, died, came alive again. A dense crowd of people moving steadily; she felt herself amongst them; strange clothes, bulging helmets. They were all afraid, yet mastering their fear. She saw, in that instant, a gloved hand reach out to the red-cross cupboard. The downward motion went on; a wave of nausea swept over her. Then Coll, then Coll's son Ben, released her hand.

"Ma . . . did you get it?"

"I got it, my dear."

"What does it mean?"

"Those were men and women," she said. "Are you sure of that?"

"I'm sure."

"It was a starship then."

"Are they all gone?" asked Ben.

"You could tell that better than I," said Gurl. "LaMar saw no more wreckage."

"Shouldn't we look for them? Ma, they might be out there. Remember the crew of the trader *Sweetwater?* Da found them after forty days, still living, in the bottom of a leaky boat, out by the Six Seven Isles. I remember when they were brought to the dock."

"You must have been four years old!"

"I remember," he said stubbornly. "They were skinny

67

and brown and you wrapped one, the Captain, in a pink shawl."

He finished on a note of triumph.

"I'll show this wreckage to the Doctor's Eminence," she said. "But don't get your hopes up, Ben, even if it comes to a search."

For a moment she considered questioning him about the contents of the red-cross cupboard, having him read it for her if he could. She decided against it. She brushed the damp hair back from his forehead and he shrank away from her caress.

"Get back to school," she said gently. "Not a word about this reading of the wreck. . . . I mean it, a true secret."

He nodded and went out, launching himself out of the door of the strongroom like a runner at the start of a race. Gurl sat for a few minutes at the desk; Coll had taken his last illness in the rescue of the *Sweetwater*'s crew but Ben could not know that. The fever had been in his body from that time and he died after the next harvest.

In desperation she had sent to Rhomary, to Urbain Bro the Dator, and the old pen-pusher had not failed them. The young doctor came and did what could be done but the fever was too strong. Gurl Hign sighed and shuddered; a bad time, even the doctor, young Junik, just out of internship, was depressed and star-crossed. What became of her? They had had other Doctors on the Gann Station from that time, doing their country service like Gil Roak, hoping for advancement.

Eight bells sounded from the watch tower. She gathered up her paraphernalia and went out and then in again to begin the session in the dining hall. It was a big room with a high-beamed roof and plenty of light from the wide tilted wooden shutters and small glass windows. As she walked through the cluster of sharefarmers, ranchhands, drivers, she felt again that whiff of desperate, enclosed fear. Down . . . the ship fell down . . .

"Morning, Rancher!"

"Morning, all!"

Gurl Hign settled at the high table; through the nearest shutter trap she could see a broad panorama of the Divide, a flash of green behind the house, the high meadow. She was down already, on the soil of the Gann Station, on the good earth of Rhomary. Never to sail again, to skim over the reaches of the ocean.

"Uschi Fott?" she looked wearily at the faces before her. "Mistress Fott? Here is your hourglass, my dear."

The schoolteacher from the Jenzite settlement, the only woman wearing a skirt, swished up to the high table and collected her precious piece of equipment.

"What do we owe you, Rancher?"

She was about thirty years old with a handsome, pinched face. Her expression was one of self-righteous hostility.

"Time is our great gift," quoted Gurl drily. "Take it in the name of Jenz Kindl."

"We must be thankful," snapped Uschi Fott, "even to those who live in darkness. Book of Jenz, four twenty-two."

"As you say," Gurl stared her down. "And in another place he says: 'Do not despise the beggar's gift.'"

There was an approving chuckle from those near the table and Gurl changed the subject abruptly.

"I have a question!" she called. "Can you all hear me?"

"Surely, Rancher!"

"In the past seven days has anyone seen a starfall? A meteor?"

There was a loud murmuring and she called again:

"Come on! You know the kind of sighting I mean!"

"Here, Rancher!" cried a woman. "Go ahead and speak up, you great fool!"

"It is Little Diggy Dit, Rancher," said an old share-farmer, Nat Dann, peering down the hall.

The crowd opened up and a young man was shoved forward. Little Diggy Dit, Billy's younger brother, was seventeen years old and out of school, more or less. He was a kind of giant, one meter eighty-five, the tallest person at the Gann.

"Well, Diggy," said Gurl Hign, "what was it you saw? Tell me from the beginning."

Diggy blinked and shuffled.

"It was early morning," he said in a hoarse sweet voice, "about six bells of last Sunday, five days ago. I was on the roof of this hall. . . ."

"What in dry hell were you doing *there*, Diggy?"

"Ain't you high enough already?" cracked one of the men near the table.

"I was fetching my boots down, Rancher, Mam. The boys put them up for a joke . . ."

"And what did you see?"

"I saw the lights falling. . . ."

69

"Lights?" she prompted quietly.

She thought of the time of day and the weather: with sunrise and the sea mist it was a wonder anything had been seen at all.

"Two lights, maybe three," said Little Diggy in a quiet singsong, screwing up his sandy eyebrows as if he would recapture the scene. "Two were clear. Round bright lights, like the meteors, year before last. They came down into the fog, out to the northwest, over the ocean. There might have been a third: I saw a kind of trail where it had fallen, far away beyond the hills."

Gurl relaxed, let out her caught breath.

"Thank you, Diggy," she said. "You tell it well. And no more roof-climbing, you hear!"

As Little Diggy tried to shrink back into the crowd she turned to Uschi Fott. The schoolteacher stood by the table clutching her hourglass; her face was creased with worry and uncertainty.

"I know the Jenzites watch the heavens," said Gurl Hign. "Are you sure you have nothing to tell me?"

Mistress Fott shook her head; Gurl knew that something had been seen. She did not press the point, but rapped on the table for silence.

"Back to business," she said firmly. "I have here a packet of nails for the Windmill Committee . . ."


2

Los Smitwode, M.D., Ch. M., Master Apothecary and Third Consultant, woke at eight bells after an unusually long sleep of six hours. The light through a small, badly glazed window hurt his eyes; he rose up promptly . . . the hard bed had done wonders for his spine . . . and took a cold shower in the small private bathhouse. He was fully dressed in fresh linen and a black silk robe when his assistant knocked at the door of his room.

"Come."

"Breakfast, Eminence."

Jaygo was in full uniform, even wearing cap and cuffs.

"I'll take it on the back verandah," said the Doctor. "And Jaygo. . . ?"

"Magister?"

"This is a holiday. Dress more simply."

"I will, then." Jaygo blinked insolently.

Green eyes, pure green, the doctor noted again. He took the tray himself and brushed past the young intern; his high pattens clopped on the wooden flooring of the guest hostel. He settled himself on the back verandah and gazed at the high hills, the walls of the valley, the pleasant checkered fields and sluices and the blue ponds of standing water. When he rang the bronze bell on his tray the housekeeper, a plump woman in brown britches, came at the double.

"Bring the red folder from the main room, please."

"Eminence . . . I have a piece of news!"

Clearly she was bubbling over with it. He inclined his head.

"The trader Captain LaMar of the *Comet* brought in a piece of an unknown ship!"

The doctor raised his fine eyebrows at her over the rim of his tea-mug.

"A strange ship," she continued, "not of this world . . ."

"A ship that fell from heaven!"

Jaygo's voice was husky, sometimes ill-modulated like the voice of an adolescent boy; the doctor noticed that the uniform had given way to a dark tunic, open-necked, over blue trunk hose.

"Ah!" said Los Smitwode. "And what has become of the wreckage, Mam?"

"The Rancher has it locked in the strongroom!"

The woman looked more cheery than ever; Smitwode remembered that his housekeeper was Netta Hign, wife of a foreman. Perhaps she relished the opportunity of "telling tales" on her in-law, the Rancher.

"Well, I am sure I will hear more about it," he responded. "The red folder, if you please . . ."

He turned to gesture the young intern to sit down but Jaygo was already sprawled in a seat beside him, running long fingers through a silky bob of jet black hair. The doctor stared, thin lips twisting with amusement: incredible quality of the skin, a pulse in the left temple. The line of the jaw was strong but still marvelously indeterminate; the forearms pivoted to reveal their soft underside when Jaygo pressed at the tabletop.

"You are 'double-jointed'," said the doctor.

"It is a secondary sexual characteristic," said Jaygo. "I also have a pronounced linea nigra and a rim of fine hair around the nipples of my breasts."

The doctor laughed sadly.

"I know all about you, Jaygo. Your case . . . or your predicament . . . must hang in the balance."

"For the present," said Jaygo, wolfing down the doctor's breakfast rolls. "When I am dead there can be work done on my pelvic bones."

"We will have achieved the X-ray long before that time!" smiled the doctor.

"At about the time we rediscover the Vail . . ." murmured Jaygo.

"Well, you would know more about that than I," said the doctor, unperturbed. "I know the X-ray must seem like a legend, however well-documented, but I have faith."

They fell silent as the housekeeper returned with the red folder; when she had gone the doctor asked:

"Did LaMar find the trees?"

"Three specimens at two different locations."

"What did he bring back?"

"A quantity of bark, leaves, branches and a number of growing slips," said Jaygo. "Alan Dun Mor, the elder son, sent word at first light."

"A well set-up young man," said the doctor.

"At least a young man," said Jaygo. "No doubts about *him*."

"Ah Jaygo, this bitterness suits neither of your personae," said Los Smitwode. "Was it this fellow who mentioned the wreckage?"

"No," Jaygo smiled at last.

"You have many sources of information."

Jaygo walked to the rail and swiveled the brass telescope on its stand. It was used for viewing the stars and perhaps the hills and the bird life of the station. Jaygo had it on a low trajectory: the green meadow perched above them. The doctor could see a figure moving about among the cairns and gravestones; he came to Jaygo's side.

"Your Eminence . . ."

The doctor found the lens focused upon a beautiful young girl. She was tall and slender; her hair was a rich auburn; she moved among the graves, her arms full of honey-pink and goldnoy.

"Ah," said Smitwode, "how have I missed her?"

"Not by design," said Jaygo. "I am sure no one thinks of you as a connoisseur. That is Shona Dun Mor, the Rancher's daughter."

"It has the ring of a ballad," sighed the doctor. "Does she speak to you, Jaygo? What does she think you are?"

"A human being," said Jaygo, with perfect good humor. "She is a very kind and sensitive girl."

"I wonder what will become of a beautiful girl in such an end-of-the-world place?"

"She has a suitor," said Jaygo, "and one you may approve. Doctor Gil Roak. I am sure he wants to go far . . . all the way to Rhomary."

"This place, the Gann Station, is unlucky for members of the profession," said Los Smitwode.

"You are thinking of Faya Junik," said Jaygo. "What became of her after the disqualification?"

"Junik was disturbed," said the Senior coldly. "She went into the desert beyond Silver City. For all we know she may be there still, living as a hermit."

He opened his folder and read with unbreakable concentration for an hour and a third until Jaygo, who had been prowling the verandah of the hostel, came to tell him that visitors were approaching.

"The Rancher and the local practitioner, Doctor Roak, carrying a piece of flotsam, or so I judge . . ."

Los Smitwode drifted into the main room of the house which was furnished with some sort of comfort, and settled himself into a long chair. Steps sounded on the front porch and to his surprise the Rancher led the way straight into the room. He knew her history but the solid presence of Gurl Hign always made him flinch.

The transformation of students into men and women of knowledge, presence and wisdom held less mystery than this transformation. She was well built, straight-backed; her dark eyes were fine and her skin not too much weathered; she wore a white leather tunic for the occasion over gray britches and heavy boots. The competence and authority were what baffled him. What divine spark lived in the beggar girls of Rhomary? Was she still inspired by her dead husband? Coll Dun Mor, that rare spirit, had been born with extraordinary powers, had communed with strange beings.

Los Smitwode flinched again; the Rancher and Doctor Roak carried in the piece of wreckage between them. It was still gritty with sand and had scraps of seaweed caught in its projections. The Rancher, reading the eminent guest's distaste, said at once:

"Your Eminence, I must bring this inside. You will see the reason."

"I hope so, Rancher."

Jaygo, behind the doctor's chair, watched and smiled. When the piece of wreckage was set down Gil Roak wiped his hands on his handkerchief and came forward for a full ceremonial greeting. He was a good-looking fair man of about thirty, not too old to get ahead, Smitwode reflected, but a sense of protocol would have told him when to dispense with it. Still the Rancher might have put him up to it or he might simply be trying to impress a prospective mother-in-law.

Los Smitwode carried out the responses and the touching of hands with an appropriate degree of reticence that worked against Roak's devotional vigor. When the ceremony was done Roak stood back but Jaygo, as intern, came forward too, ready to perform the Inferior Greeting. Los Smitwode watched with grim approval; he was conscious of using Jaygo's sexual neutrality as a test of other people. Gil Roak notably failed the test; he shrank back, swaggered, muffed the responses, then tried to make all well by a show of heartiness when he glimpsed the expression on the face of the Third Consultant. Smitwode saw that the Rancher missed none of this; she sat beside the piece of wreckage on a low stool, guarding it. His interest sharpened.

"Very well," he said. "This is a piece of wreckage brought in by Cap LaMar of the . . . er . . . good ship *Comet* from the area of the Six Seven Islands. Rumor says already that it 'fell from heaven.' "

"It did, Eminence," said Gurl Hign, bluntly. "I am convinced that it did."

"Jaygo," said Los Smitwode, "do some diagnosis of this remarkable find."

Jaygo stepped forward and examined the specimen. At a word from the Rancher Gil Roak opened two shutters so that sunlight streamed into the dark room and illuminated the object.

"A molded panel of heavy plastic," said Jaygo, "with a metal overlay torn away here. There are adhering scraps of insulation, a friable substance, synthetic. The metal probably a steel alloy, nothing in use on Rhomary. Between the two layers a bunch of . . . yes . . . fine wires wrapped in colored insulation. Inscription on the outer casing: W, arabic letter, point, S, arabic letter, point, and part of a second S. On the molded plastic: further fine instruction in English, German and two other languages, possibly Russian or Chinese."

"So far, so good," said Los Smitwode.

"If we turn the panel . . ." Jaygo did so and Gil Roak

74

stepped forward to assist, "and remove this felt wrapping . . ."

"Wait!" said Gurl Hign. "I want to assure you of something, Eminence . . ."

"Indeed. . . ?" the doctor raised his eyebrows impatiently.

"Only a few persons have seen the panel unwrapped," she said. "Cap LaMar and his officers and myself."

"Well, well," said Los Smitwode with lilting irony, marching right into the trap. "I will bear that in mind. Whatever can it be?"

Gurl Hign, with a gleam of anger in her dark eyes, reefed the covering of felt from the panel. The light blazed on the red cross that marked the cupboard. All three doctors gasped; Los Smitwode started up from his chair; Gil Roak cried out.

The Senior recovered his composure first.

"Rancher Hign," he said, "you have done right and I apologize for doubting your judgement. Are you sure no one has opened the medical chest?"

"I am sure," said Gurl Hign.

Jaygo and Gil Roak were overlapping eagerly.

"An off-world starship . . ."

"A first-aid box . . ."

Jaygo fell silent almost at once but Gil Roak babbled on with his indiscreet speculations.

"Sir . . . Eminence . . . a first-aid box of roughly the original dimensions of those in the Primary Records. Oh, this is a wonder! What they might have there now!"

He was silenced by Smitwode's gesture; the doctors looked nervously at Gurl Hign but she did not leave, and Los Smitwode suddenly did not want her to leave. He questioned her about the location of the find, forcing himself to keep calm, to drown out the promptings of all the doctors of Rhomary who had kept the faith for so long.

"We must search!" he said.

"What were you thinking of, Eminence?"

"This is your province, Rancher, more than mine. An immediate return to the area and a check of all distant outposts in the Red Ocean. We are searching for survivors and for more fragments. I know this will disrupt life on the Station but I authorize it in the name of my College and of the Council of the City of Rhomary. When does the next caravan leave for the Western Sea?"

"This evening, Eminence."

"We must send word to the College!" burst out Gil Roak. "We have made this marvelous find!"

"I will send word if I see fit," said Smitwode coldly. "It is a happy chance that I am here as Senior to examine this find and report on it. I will not alarm the College or raise false hopes. Have you racing parmels to take an emergency message, Rancher?"

"At your service, Eminence."

Gurl Hign turned aside as if about to leave, then turned back. Los Smitwode wanted nothing more at this moment than to commune absolutely alone with the red cross. He wished it were in his rooms at the College where the thick rugs, hangings, scrolls, charts and articulated bones told of civilization and luxury. But his diagnostic nerve was twitching and he knew the Rancher had something important to add.

"Gil . . ." she nodded at the young doctor, "Intern Jaygo . . . I will speak to the Eminence alone."

Gil Roak and Jaygo went out and their voices began at once out in the sunshine. Gurl Hign closed the shutters almost absentmindedly and the light on the red-cross cupboard was shut out.

"My youngest child is a Vesp," she said in a flat troubled voice. "He inherits this power from Coll Dun Mor, his father. He helped me carry this piece of wreckage from the dock."

"Tell me . . ." said Los Smitwode.

Her power of description was better than he might have expected. He put a few questions and she shut her eyes, trying to give back what she had experienced, but not, he believed, elaborating.

"With such powers," he said carefully, "the boy might see into any locked box."

Gurl Hign laughed.

"It crossed my mind, Eminence. But the answers might be uncertain and I don't care to trouble him with weighty questions."

"Mam Hign," said Smitwode, "I fully expect the box to disappoint us. It may well be empty; it may contain simple things we have on Rhomary. It may contain . . . worst of all . . . things we are unable to use or understand. In any case the contents may be spoiled. No, Mam, if I were a philosopher I would say that the box had been sent to remind us of our struggle and our failure here on Rhomary."

"We have not failed!"

"Of course we have," said the Doctor sadly. "It all got away from us in about the fourth year of settlement. You heard Doctor Roak speak of the Primary Records: these are the only records and I am proud to say they were kept by doctors and medical personnel. But the tale is confused; by the standards of those first castaways and the standards of Old Earth we have lapsed into barbarism."

"This is a good place," insisted Gurl Hign, "a world that we have just begun to explore . . . and in that time we have seen wonders."

"Too many wonders! What have they really taught us? Yes, I mean the Vail. How can we weigh up a series of dialogues against the lives of women dead in childbed, or polluted waterholes and fever epidemics? Mam, we have had more benefit from the jocca palm which gives us paper, alcohol, cloth and a half-poisonous distillation that produces abortion."

"You are too harsh!" cried the Rancher. "The towns and the city flourish! The land has blossomed. We had to adapt to a harsh life; the Vail gave us spirit for the task."

"Adapt is the word. What a sorry figure we will cut before any survivors of this ship . . . not that I expect survivors. Shall I cite facts and measurements from those holiest of records? Shall I reveal that we are a stunted, dark, flat-headed, splay-footed race of Rhomarians with a high incidence of six- and seven-fingered mutants? The race of homo sapiens, the human beings flung on this planet so many years ago, were by comparison a race of gods."

"Sir . . . how long have we been on this world?"

"What year is it? 1102? It is a good number. Have you heard of the band of people in Silver City who call themselves the Marchers? They claim that the starfall theory is a myth. They say that humans were always here; we migrated from the other side of the planet."

Gurl Hign laughed aloud.

"I've never heard of them, poor souls."

"I understand the comfort they take from this silly tale. Even in the early years of settlement, when the city was growing, we hungered for permanence, we wanted to dig into the sand like fish-toads. When the population of the city itself, not including the outlying towns, reached the figure of one thousand, that was declared to be the year one thousand. A good round figure. A dreadful twisting of the records. This occurred one hundred and sixty-three years after landfall. We have been on Rhomary two hundred and sixty-five years. But surely you were taught this at elementary school?"

Gurl Hign stared at him in the dark room and smiled.

"I didn't go to school, Eminence. Coll Dun Mor taught me to read when I was eighteen. I am the daughter of Bill Hign, a lame beggar."

"As I said—" the doctor could not help smiling back at her—"things got away from us . . ."

But he knew, obscurely, that her point was proved as well as his.

"One more thing." She sprang up. "The Delfin know something of this wreck. We need a Delfin speaker."

"Get one, then. The College will pay."

"There are several families of Delfin speakers on the fish farms on the south coast," she replied, "but there is only one here at the Station. Lem Fott . . . a Jenzite fisherman."

"Use him!" ordered Smitwode. "The College does not have dealings with Jenzites but this is an emergency. Lives may be saved, one way or another."

Gurl Hign went out and at last the Doctor was left alone with the medical chest. He stared at it in the gloom for some time then knelt beside the panel with some protest from his knee joints and ran his fingertips over the whole surface of the cabinet. A thought struck him and he sat back on his heels, laughing softly. Jaygo came back into the room.

"Eminence?"

"I was thinking of the Primary Records," said Smitwode. "Quasi-Medical Nine, perhaps you have read it too, Jaygo."

He extended a hand and the intern helped him to his feet.

"Not yet, sir," said Jaygo. "You mean the Diary of Paramedic Olivia Williams?"

"Exactly. In a red-cross box—as our garrulous colleague points out, a first-aid box, for lay persons—in one of these boxes which survived landfall and fire in a storage area of the ship the contents were distinctly odd."

"Wait . . ." said Jaygo, grinning. "I've heard of this too. The box had been looted, cleaned out, probably long before the emergency, and filled with personal items from the crew members working in that area."

"I quote," said Smitwode. "Ten tubes OSV, a stimulant;

quantity of candy bars and wrappers; pair of soiled socks, one E-gauge magnetic screwdriver and two thumb flicks."

"Thumb flicks?"

"Toys. Strips of color film, each in a miniature viewer. One showed two men and a woman engaged in sex play. The other a cook preparing a dish of meat and wine, with instructions."

Smitwode was hardly able to get to the end of this list straight-faced; Jaygo's expression of dismay was comical. At last they both stared at the red-cross cupboard and laughed aloud. The doctor felt in the pocket of his robe and brought out a small silver knife in a leather case; Jaygo stood very still. The doctor sighed and put away the knife; he drew out instead his stethoscope. It was made of silver and of wooden tubes jointed with leather. He listened to every surface of the box, then shook his head.

Jaygo burst out suddenly:

"Please, Eminence . . . Magister . . . please open it! It is in your interest. Open it now and I will witness or fetch the housekeeper if you need another. Gil Roak is not to be trusted; he will report to Rhomary."

Los Smitwode shook his head again; he saw that Jaygo was utterly serious. He remembered his own words: the Gann Station unlucky for members of the profession. Why had he been singled out to be present at this discovery?

"I will open it presently," he said. "I *am* to be trusted, Jaygo, and the College knows it."

He placed the tips of his fingers together, allowing a pulse beat after he had joined the little fingers of his two hands. The scars of his mother's scalpel had vanished but he often thought of the two shameful nubs of flesh that she had removed not long after his birth. Would they have grown and become useful? A twelve-fingered surgeon: an inhabitant of Rhomary.

"We are all mutants, Jaygo," he said softly. "We were mutants after the first year or the tenth or at the Centenary. I will eat lunch on the verandah if it is ready. Afterward we will open the box."

Jaygo was still not satisfied.

"Gil Roak has some link of patronage with the Eminence Alla Jons."

"The Second Consultant is equally trustworthy," said Smitwode. "She will understand our situation."

As he turned to go on to the back verandah the "bells" in the watchtower above the hostel began a brazen clangor. It separated into a melody; Smitwode and the young intern hurried out and were able to see the strikers, including Alan Dun Mor, standing in the open wooden structure that housed the bells. They wielded their hammers upon the open cylinders of bronze that had cost the Station five harvests. Netta Hign, the housekeeper, came running.

"Heaven," she panted, "they are playing 'Dodlo,' the music for a search!"

"Look!" cried Jaygo, pointing out into the farmland.

Men and women were coming from their houses and from the fields and canals. An echoing series of calls from horn, conch shell and drum rang out, "Dodlo" and again "Dodlo," with a *do do re mi, do mi re,* while the children sang and whooped the tune, until the whole valley rang with the sound.

"Sir . . ." said Jaygo.

The intern had a curious expression, absolutely devoid of languor.

"You want to go on the search?" said Los Smitwode, surprised. "Would they take you? What clothes would you wear?"

"I can get the young man some overalls and heavy boots," said Netta Hign. "Please, Eminence, let him go!"

He met Jaygo's clear green eyes and knew that he was pleased to accept the housekeeper's personal pronoun, a status less equivocal.

"Go along then," said the Doctor. "Take my smaller kit —the first-aid kit. And Jaygo . . ."

"Eminence?"

"Take care. And bring me back something worth preserving."

The Doctor stood on the verandah alone, caught up in the unending noise of the bells.

# Chapter IV

## Cold-Water Planet

---

He had been dying now for a long time and scenes from
all his death agonies flashed before his eyes. He fell down
or whirled end over end; variations in pressure made his
nose bleed and his eyes strain at their sockets; his skull
imploded like a monitor and his internal organs ruptured;
he burned, very often, or tried to beat out fire on another
human being's skin with his bare hands; he drowned in
nauseous gasses, in his own body fluids, in water many
fathoms deep. He was still drowning but the expected release never came, there was no respite from his anguish.
Then he was back in the capsule:

"Relax. All suited. Capem tree laden launched."

He was blind, deaf, swaddled, gloved, but he knew that
he was standing between two persons taller than himself. A
frightful buffeting descent; nosebleed; sphincters still holding. *O Mami, Pappi, Liesl.* . . . The godlike beings talked
over his head.

"Oxper. You?"

"Vippwatch."

"Yet even."

"Better capem. Howzit?"

They were talking softly into their helmets as the capsule plummeted down; his line was open; he screamed or
squeaked. The end over end began again; they squeaked
too. He gave himself over to fear and clutched the tall
man on his left.

"Relax, Meister."

The movement altered and momentarily his vision
cleared. He saw through four thicknesses of plex a sea of
pink cloud.

"Drogues out!" said the tall man.

81

"Yay! Getting down!" said the female voice in a dull, breathless tone.

He relaxed his hold a fraction.

"John Miller," said the tall man, introducing himself. "Hang in, Meister. How you called?"

"Valente . . ." he gasped. "Thank you. Not accustomed."

"Doing smooth, Doc," murmured the female voice. "Miller, read-off."

Miller read off a long jumble of letters and figures.

"Shee-it!" said the female voice. "Shangri-la."

"Capem Tree nearing landfall. Come in, fleet. Fiver, Sexer, Bulk One."

Miller was speaking to the empty air. He repeated the call, with variations, but there was no reply.

"Visual?" growled the tall woman.

"Nix," said Miller.

They rushed downward all alone; he saw a bright spot expand and sizzle on the wall of the capsule. The woman attacked the burning spot with a foam-pack; they were straining away from the heat and shouting. He dragged the woman's hand toward him and smothered the flames around her cuff. There was a hissing, rending sound and the capsule bounced on a hard surface; his skull rebounded from his helm as it struck the wall; his brain rebounded from his skull. He was unconscious.

But that was some time ago. Now he was in another place full of watery darkness; he struggled, hand and feet going in unison, swimming motions like an infant or a kitten. His head came out into sweet remembered air; still almost pitchblack . . . was he blind? His hand struck a floating object; he climbed back into the inflatable boat and felt about for the woman. Yes, she was there, and he remembered her nameplate. Chan T.N.R. She lay like the dead; he fumbled and felt her jugular vein. Still alive. He began to vomit water, then to shiver; the boat was moving slowly. He closed his eyes and saw another flashback.

The wall of the capsule was flung open by Miller, who dived out first; he and Chan, both conscious again, struggled after him. He heaved Chan through the opening, then fell exhausted; water was churning around his legs. Chan came back, gripped him around the waist, cursing, and dragged him out. There was light, bright daylight and thick watery spray, clouds with rainbow edges. Miller had already inflated the boat; now he wrenched the door unit from the sinking capsule and used it for his personal raft. He realized that Miller was auxiliary personnel, an android. He saw that his helmet was of a different design. He asked through the speaker, clearing his throat.

"Do you use any oxygen?"

"Some," said Miller. "Burn a little of it, for the tissues, y'know."

Miller urged the boat through the turbid green water from his own floating door; Chan had her helmet off. He saw dimly that she was brown-skinned with a broad slab of a face and thick shining black hair, beautiful hair that curled all around her head. Couldn't be Chinese hair, he thought. Chan shouted, tried to stand, and the boat went over a waterfall. He fell out into the odd-tasting water and drowned for the first time and was shoved back into the boat by Miller. The mists had not cleared; he took off his own helmet and breathed the air in sweet gulps. Shee-it! Shangri-la! He had spoken aloud . . . Chan was laughing.

"Where are we?"

"Some loozy cold-water planet . . ." smiled Chan.

"Instead of landfall I guess we made waterfall."

This was a huge joke. Miller and Chan roared with laughter. Miller was tireless, pushing the boat ahead of him through the mist. They went over another waterfall, unexpected, or maybe their reactions were slow, and everything broke up again. Miller was going and Chan was floating unconscious, buoyed up by the silversuit. He was terrified of losing Miller, tried to hold the boat and the door unit, but Miller was carried off, shouting. Hang in, Doc. Somehow he got Chan, every inch of her, back into the boat. They would die now, all alone, without Miller, who was exceptionally strong. The mist had cleared and he felt sunlight; he saw the sun, a hot white radiance in cloud. It stunned him; made him sleep.

He had a continuous stream of memories after this but he thought some of them must be nightmares. He woke at night and saw the moon overhead, a tiny disc of a moon, large as his thumbnail. He checked Chan T.N.R. The mist had gone and he could see a wide expanse of water. Inland sea? Lake? Tree shapes in the distance, then another clump of them, moving without wind. A swirling of the dark water. The forest walked a little and he was shaken with terror and disbelief.

\*     \*     \*

There is a disturbance of the air, a small sonic boom, globes of light dance before his eyes. He hears a range of impossible sounds woofing and tweeting over and under the water. The boat is propelled along through the waves of sound, very fast; he can do nothing but try to remain conscious. The sound becomes unbearable yet with a modulation like a huge voice that sighs above him.

"Minmer . . ."

He sees a moving frond in the water, poised like a periscope, bearing a single globe that could be an eye. Still the voice brays out above him; he is grasping the sense of the words but the blackness closes over him.

He woke again in some kind of backwater where the boughs overhead darkened the night; the lake had become a river. He had fallen overboard but he fought his way back and checked Chan. He felt for the words in his monster dream.

"Go down to the red sea. Keep the sun at your back."

Madness! Would a monster or a series of monsters talk like that? He found the right locker as the boat drifted back into the mainstream out of the backwater. The small moon had set but the night was less dark; he managed to get out a soup beaker and shake to heat. The warm drink put him to sleep all over again.

It was broad daylight when the lifeboat eased out into a red sea at the mouth of a great river. He saw islands on the horizon; there was no sign of John Miller, nothing that told of the other emergency capsules. His mouth was dry; he could have gulped the whole pack of distilled water. The water over the boat's side was greenish, not red; he put down a timid hand. The water was fresh and drinkable . . . it was river water, pouring out for several kilometers into the red ocean. He filled the storage tank and all the containers he could find with river water.

There were instruments strapped to Chan's wrist but he could make no use of them; he turned his back on the risen sun and urged the boat along the swampy tree-fringed coast. He took one of the paddles and began threading through the channels between the stumpy black trees. The work made him sweat. He took off the silversuit which he had begun to regard as a second skin. His own traveling overall looked foreign; he tenderly undid the zipper and took from their places against his chest his two leather-bound cases of medical instruments. He took out his passport, stared at the photograph and the irretrievable data on the punched card and sadly pressed the spool release for his voice print.

"Karl-Heinz-Jurgen Valente," quacked his voice, the voice of an eminent unfrightened man in excellent physical shape. "Karl-Heinz-Jurgen Valente, Physician and Surgeon."

"Ohayo, Doc!" said Chan.

She lay still with one brown eye open. He grinned and made as if to throw his passport into the channel.

"No!" she said. "Don't throw anything away. Matter of Ma Dana's law: you never know when something will come in handy."

"I had an aunt with the same law," he joked feebly. "Chan, how do you feel?"

"Bad. Is there water?"

He gave her water and paddled on through the series of channels among the swamp trees. They found one tree laden with long, black, good-smelling pods; some creatures were eating this fruit . . . not birds or insects but crustacea that scuttled crab-like back into the water as the boat came by.

"No!" he said as she held up a sample. "It might be poisonous or it might just give you diarrhea and dehydrate you. Anyway, do you have a directive on alien fruit?"

"Sure," she tossed the fruit into the channel. "I forget the signs to look for. Maybe with those bugs noshing."

She goofed off outrageously in the bow of the boat while he told everything that he could remember.

"Shee-it, that manual," she sighed. "Measure the loozy pressure, test water, test urine. Test my ass. Faggiddy moon-bus profees wrote that manual. Here . . . I'll take a day reading at sundown, okay, Doc?"

She remembered Miller going away.

"Don't worry. Oxper are forever. We don't do a perish here inna swamp and twenty years later Miller comes by. I'm old, you're old . . . all beard and wrinkled titties . . . but there is loozy Miller, lookin' the way he went down the waterfall."

She enjoyed the story of his nightmare.

"Tell over, Doc. That about the big bem and the vocal."

He told it over and the strangeness took hold of him again.

"How could it speak to me . . . it called me some name."

85

"No," said Chan. "Maybe there was a bem, a sea serpent. But I think the words were in your deep-mind, Doc."

"Chan, where are we and how did we get here?"

She screwed up her eyes.

"Second question first. About twenty-four hours ago, ship time, there was a violent perturbation of the IC . . . the internal navigation systems. There followed 'normal deviation' . . . the bridge tried to correct, they went hunting . . ."

"You mean they overcorrected?"

"Several times, I'd say, but the deviation went on and the perturbation took over. We went over or through or beside a black hole."

"I knew nothing."

"You were in the Vipp area, why would they tell you? They were tight with data to the lower ranks too. As a result of, or maybe just following, the big buzz-up the stabilizers failed, the correction still didn't work, the life-support systems began to turn brown at the edges. Zikko! Alles Raus! Abandon ship."

"But how did we get *here* . . . how did they find this planet?"

"Ho!" scoffed Chan. "This proves the point. Bridge used the emergency scanner, didn't they, the pratchiks!"

"Otherwise?"

"Kaput. Paradise button. Bite on that special molar."

"You think any other capsules made it?"

"Why not?" she said fiercely. "Just because we haven't heard . . ."

"What do you mean?"

She sighed and held up her right wrist, indicating a flat black instrument.

"All of the brass and most of the noncoms have one of these hide-and-seek bleepers. It is timed to send out identification every four hours and it has an open channel all the time to receive in-coming signals."

"Are you sure it's still functioning?"

"Yes!" she snapped. "And I'm not going to monkey with the setting."

"But no one has checked in . . ."

Her eyes had become hard and black; she turned aside and did not speak again for hours. He wondered about the stories of conditioning, the jokes that held space personnel for heartless robots. He knew that he felt very little, so far, for the crew of the *Serendip Dana*. He had not known them, he reasoned. He and Chan would go mad with excitement if there was a call from one of the other capsules, he knew that. But he feared they were alone; he could not imagine anyone else "out there." On earth, surely, he would have felt more pity for men and women lost, for a tourist jet crashing on takeoff, for a submarine trapped beneath the polar ice. The people he could pity were the citizens of the planet Arkady; he had been going to deal with an epidemic and to found an eye hospital.

He rowed on, fascinated by the maze of channels, each with a new vista of black glistening trunks, blue-green and blue-black fronds. Chan roused herself and began to take readings, squinting through a filter at the hard, hot, whitish sun overhead. They ate sticks of hardtack and enriched chocolate. He fed Chan one of his own routine stabilizers and she lay in the bow again, zonked out, as the sun sank lower and was lost to them before it dipped below the horizon.

"In the *east*, Doc," she said dreamily. "Those guys presented a schema and found us this entry corridor. The northern hemisphere of the second planet of a G star . . . one small satellite. . . . If my instruments aren't hopelessly perturbed the motion is widdershins. We're going east . . . with the sun at our back."

"But where . . . which star?"

"Hell, we can call it what we like. It is Delta Pavonis, old style. Should have a companion, class M4. Apart from that, Doc, the system is a lot like our own, they have a gas giant, further out, we can look for it. . . ."

They were wary of the darkness. The boat hung in a channel like the small moon hanging briefly overhead; they heard no sounds, nothing disturbed them. The stars came out; they stared at them greedily and found one, yellow, unblinking, that was not a star.

"Yeah . . . must be in the system," said Chan. "And hey . . . see the comet? Big smeary-tailed kahooter at fourteen hours."

"Yes . . . yes, I see it."

"Well, it's your comet, Doc. I give it to you. Valente's comet."

"Chan, would you call a comet a tailed star?"

"I wouldn't, but . . ."

He was sitting up in the boat trembling with excitement. He put his hands over his ears in an effort to bring back the echoing modes of the voice.

"The monster . . . the bem . . . it said, 'The tailed star rides . . .'"

Chan was excited too, but he could remember no more.

"Probably some back-formation, Doc," she said sadly. "You saw the comet and didn't know it."

They split a tube of lemon lift; the taste of artificial lemon made him faint with nostalgia for Earth, even for the horrible longeurs of the ship. He set the boat moving again through the channels, guided by the faint, white phosphorescence of the tree trunks.

"Otherwhere, otherwhen," said Chan, still lying on her back looking at the stars. "We've done it, Doc. We have joined the ghostly company. It don't happen so often but often enough so that the service is afraid of it. Ships that have 'gone darkside,' they've been digested or dissolved, they're listed GOK or NSA, they're in the no-more sector. . . ."

"NSA?" he queried.

"Never Seen Again."

"Never?"

"A few are crossed off the list. Wreckage found. They did a simple burn maybe. But the list itself is still there. At cadet school we memorized a lot of those old barges, just in case. You make landfall on some loozy asteroid and there is the carcase of the *Caroline Herschel* or the *Ark Terreste,* the *Kappa Kansas,* the *Rho Maryland,* the *Canberra EP19.* In a year or so they'll be listing the *Serendip Dana.*"

"We've been digested by this swamp," he said.

He was becoming restless and miserable because their landscape did not change. They rowed on eastward for five days and five nights; the hours of darkness and daylight averaged out, so Chan told him, into days and nights of fourteen hours and forty-eight minutes.

"That is a very long day!" he said sharply.

Chan fell about laughing.

"We'll kink that hour a little," she said, playing with her chronometers, "and have a straight twenty-eight hour day, give or take a minute."

"And that hour you kinked?"

"An hour, amigo, is now sixty-three minutes long."

"That will wreck the world!"

"Not this world."

They were both tired and sunburned, their faces turning red-brown, the color of the water in the channels. He saw that Chan was tired, she fought against a heavy lassitude; he thought of giving her a physical and the idea settled in his head and in his solar plexus. He wondered if she would call him a loozy stud or a faggidy breeder. The swamp went on; they saw a bird, an ugly gray lizardlike creature that flapped away and left them talking and speculating for hours.

"I'll bet it had teeth!" said Chan.

He did not dare take the stabilizers, they made him heavier than lead. Once at high noon he flew into a rage and shrieked and swore in German, English and Italian for a third of an hour.

"C'mon, pard," soothed Chan, lying back in the bow. "You're doing right. We're following the coastline of a landmass. Don't you know why we're feeling so bad?"

"No . . ."

He wondered vaguely if it had something to do with sex, with wanting to give Chan a physical.

"The gravity is a shade heavier."

"Shee-it!" he said.

He laughed hysterically, he felt as if he could laugh for another third of an hour. He rolled about in the bottom of the boat and Chan came and held his arms and smiled at him. He unzipped her silversuit and found she wore nothing underneath.

"We'll get ultra-violated . . ." she said.

It was hard work making love but he overcame all the problems; he lay beside her and streamed with sweat and she splashed him with water from the channel.

"We are lost," he said.

"We are a little high all the time," said Chan. She covered her big, pale-brown, woman-shaped body and laid his suit across his compact white nakedness, his black-furred chest and shoulders.

"Why do you say that?"

"It's true. I would guess the air has a shade more oxygen. We think and think but don't like to move."

They rowed for another day and another; they did not talk much but their silences were companionable. He asked.

"What are your given names . . . T.N.R.?"

"Tui Nirvana Rose Chan," she said dreamily.

"Those are beautiful names."

He saw for the first time that Chan was beautiful; he was lost on an alien planet with a beautiful woman. Things could have been worse.

In the late afternoon of that same interminable day she stood up and said:

"I see something . . . range of hills . . ."

"Mountains?" he said eagerly.

"No," said Chan in a strange choked voice. "And they ain't volcanoes either. Those are hills."

He stood beside, her, balancing the boat easily, and saw the hills, frowning, brown and sheer, near the sea's edge, where the swamp ended, then rolling off at erratic angles into the arid reaches of the inland.

"Yes," he said, "a range of loozy hills. Where are you from in the U.S.N.A., Chan?"

"Hawaii," she said. "And you, Doc? What part of Eucom?"

"Von der Schweitz. Switzerland."

He saw that a tear had traced its way down her broad, brown cheek; he brushed it away, fighting his own tears. Aloha, Mauna Loa. Leb' wohl, Matterhorn. The boat nosed its way through a last channel, eastward to the shore.

# Chapter V

## *Encounter on the Western Sea*

Maxim came into the town of Go Down before dawn, his beast in good condition, rolling its flaps and pacing serenely as they headed for its home stable at this end of the run. The little town, barely waking at this hour, was enclosed by groves of palm. For more than an hour he had been riding through the stately pillars of the Jocca, encouraged by years of irrigation. Suddenly, passing through a dusty plaza he saw the Billsee, still and grayish, spreading out beyond a thin bulwark of sheds. The parmel led him swiftly and sedately to the livery stable behind a rambling warehouse. The place was busy: a large caravan was mounting for the city. The young girl who dismounted him could not tell much about a place on a galley so he came to the boss, a fat man fretting in his little hutch of an office.

"Take your sleep, Mister," said the boss. "What is this sweat to cross the water? The first and only galley on this day, Freeday, sails at fifteen hours of the afternoon."

"I must go sooner," said Maxim. "Official business."

"What . . ."

"I am Dator of Rhomary. I can use a warrant for the hire of a boat or the requisition of the last place on a galley, if I need to."

The boss picked his teeth and fingered the silver dollar that Maxim had given him.

"Hire would cost you dear, warrant or no warrant," he said. "But if you're quick and ready to share a place . . ."

"Surely!"

"Then come, Dator, I'll show the way!"

He rolled off his stool and led Maxim through the muck and chatter of the stable yard to a side gate.

"Cut between the two silos, yonder, and you'll find a marina. A yacht, the *Arrow*, is sailing at first light under private hire."

"Who is the Captain?"

"Name of Ramm, Old Dag Ramm . . . say I sent you."

"Many thanks."

Maxim went off as fast as he could with his gear draped about him and the heavy saddle on his arm. He arrived at the marina short of breath and feeling the pull of tired muscles in his legs. He set down the saddle on the boarded wharf and gaped, in silence.

The gray water of the Billsee, with ranked gray-green jocca palms upon its further shore, ran up to the soaring headlands about the Narrows. Maxim peered into these hills, thinking of the old couple faithfully tending an unlit bonfire against the Vail's return. The Western Sea, a thunderous purple-green in the dawn, spread out to the horizon, trapping the furtive light in its wrinkled surface. The ragged shoreline was hollowed out into caverns and cavernous bays; the dark water heaved and puckered as if its depths were haunted still.

In these last instants before sunrise the elements of the scene . . . the headlands, the two bodies of water, the low clumps of buildings, the white, sturdy shape of the steam-yacht *Arrow* . . . stood out in relief. The sky in the west

91

was fiery orange; the sun's orb was obscured behind the headland but now the waters of the Western Sea took on color, shaded from purple to crimson, marked with shadows that glittered like onyx. A voice, high and sweet, was part of the scene: a woman in a rainbow cloak stood at the very edge of the dock, looked to the sunrise and sang a dawn hymn:

> *"The sun returns,*
> *The world awakens ...*
> *O Vail, return to us again!"*

The short stanza was repeated and Maxim saw the woman, quite unself-conscious in the renewed bustle and chatter of the marina, cast a few white blossoms into the water at her feet. Maxim looked harder for a moment but the woman was gray-haired, a stranger. His thoughts of Lady Ishbel left him empty and sad. What was the use of his adventure with no one, friend or lover, to share it with him? He looked around at the people on the wharf, half-afraid that they could read his thoughts, as if loneliness, a young man's loneliness, always tinged with sexual longing, were a shameful thing.

The hiring party, richly dressed, with servants, were trailing up the gangplank. The gray-haired woman guided a party of children aboard: few boats sailed over the Western Sea without selling every place. Maxim heaved up his saddle and hurried to the gangplank ready to tackle a crew member. He saw an old man, brown as kerry-wood, come purposefully through the clutter of loading nets and accept a salute from a sailor at the rail.

"Cap Ramm?"

"What is it?"

The old man was curt to the point of hostility.

"Dator of Rhomary," said Maxim. "I will hire a place."

"Nothing left. This is a private charter."

"I know it. The stable boss sent me. Must I use a warrant?"

"Be damned to you. Serve it in six days."

"Cap Ramm," said Maxim, "I need to travel at once. I can pay well. Ask your charter."

"It is my ship. I carry whoever I want."

Cap Ramm looked Maxim slowly up and down and gave a sigh.

"Is that your saddle, then?"

Maxim gathered it up again and followed the captain up the gangplank. The captain tipped the wink to a tall sailor woman, whispered and jerked a thumb. She led Maxim forward and down to a place beside the crew's mess room; she presented him with a cupboard and a key for the cupboard. He locked his saddle up and kept the key.

"Five dollars," she said, wiping a hand on her britches. "That gets you a place in the common room, food and small beer. Wine is extra."

"I'll need to sleep, later."

"Try the boat deck," she said. "Five dollars . . ."

"Have a heart," said Maxim. "Is there nowhere to sleep?"

"The ship is full . . . we sail only twenty and we're carrying five and twenty. I mean it about the boat deck. You can bunk in a lifeboat, no questions asked."

"Well, here is the fare and a dollar for yourself."

"Ah, good lad," she said, smiling at last. "Talk to Farb, the second steward. Tell him the bosun sent you. He will see to your food and drink and a mattress for that lifeboat."

He paid over the money and she dashed away. He followed, but she was gone; the engine thrummed through the paneling and a piercing steam whistle blew overhead. He passed a man in the corridor and climbed the stairs to the deck. On the top step he remembered. A dark man, stocky; without his parmel whip this time, but he had flinched, Maxim could swear it, when their eyes met. The servant from the inn yard who had knocked him down.

His anger and anxiety flared like the pain of the blow. He found his way to the bow, past clumps of children bent over the rail to see the ship move out from the wharf. He stood by the long bowsprit with its sails set and was carried away himself by the simple excitement of putting to sea. The *Arrow* curved out swiftly into the Billsee and headed for the Narrows in a bright haze of light dancing on the gray water. There was nothing much he could do, he reasoned, if Redrock and his servant had made fair time to Go Down and joined the ship. Or was the prospector aboard at all?

"Look there!" said a sweet voice at his elbow. "Was that a flying fish so soon?"

The gray-haired woman, the teacher, stood with two older children pointing eagerly at the sea. Maxim bowed to her and she returned the greeting. He saw that the children wore padded cotton jackets of uniform cut; the boy's leather boots were patched but well polished. He looked at the sea again as they came to the Narrows and the woman spoke to him directly.

"Sir? Will you pardon us? I must call the children together as we go through the Narrows. We will sing."

"It won't disturb me, Mam."

The girl ran off to fetch the other children. The woman continued to peer at Maxim. Her eyes were very light blue, she had a curious tilt to her head and her sweet voice was too piercing. There was something at once humble and demanding in her manner.

"I am called Cridge," she said. "This is a great time for us, a trip over the Western Sea. We don't live too far away but the road is long without shoes, as the saying goes. But we are helped, wonderfully helped, every year, for our holiday. We went to Rhomary city last year. I think you must come from Rhomary . . . you are an official person . . ."

The children had come up and arranged themselves on the bow quietly. Their hair was cut short; their cheekbones stood out; they were all so clean he could feel the scrubbing brush on his own fingernails.

"Maxim Bro, Dator of Rhomary," he admitted. "I'm pleased to meet you and your pupils, Mam Cridge."

"Sister Cridge," she corrected. "Why, we are honored. Do you hear, children? It is the Dator of the city. What does he do then, Peter?"

"Collects information, Sister," said the eldest boy patiently.

The shadow of the headland reached out for the yacht *Arrow*.

"What is your school, Sister?" asked Maxim.

"Why, it is the Chippan Foundlings School," she answered in a low voice.

They exchanged a look of pity and terror; she turned away abruptly and raised her hand to the children. As the ship entered the Narrows they began to sing. Nothing in his life had prepared Maxim for a choir of children singing expertly in three-part harmony. It was as if he heard a range of new instruments for the first time; their sounds flew up and were amplified by the rocky surfaces of the Narrows. They sang new words to an old melody, a kind of traveler's anthem, praising the beauty of the world and of the Western Sea in particular:

94

*"At last between the headlands*
*Behold the Western Sea . . ."*

He listened in a dream ravished by the music and by the children's dark history. The village of Chippan or its empty shell lay on the farther shore of the Billsee some way to the east. Seven years ago—he looked at the children—when the eldest boy Peter, for instance, had been about seven years old and some of the others no more than two or three, they had been orphaned in a night. Doctors' College, whose teams had come in the end to the dreadful stinking ruin of a harvest festival, thought they knew what had happened but no one else did. The neighboring villages and the town of Pebble, all across the water, experienced gruesome scraps of information, rumors that were never dispersed.

An old woman was found rowing a boat with three live children and their mother, horribly dead. A Jenzite couple collected another clutch of young survivors, rowed them to safety, then were almost stoned to death by the good folk of Pebble. Children and adults were never found, dead or alive; they might have drowned, starved, wandered away. There were tales of looting, blood, violence that could never be disproved. There was the awful particularity of poor Chippan, a place inhabited by a few locals and a large party of "Second Settlers," drop-outs from Rhomary come to look for an idyll.

These young couples lacked grandparents, servants; they put their children to bed at a reasonable hour. They engendered mistrust with their city ways and sunbathing; signal rockets fired that night were ignored over the water. At twelve o'clock, or thirteen, they drank a toast to the future, all from the same keg of spaggin-beer, newly opened. And so died, swiftly and inevitably. The spaggin-moss was a fungus; there had been other bad mistakes.

The imagination of the people of Rhomary, hovering between the everyday and the unbelievable, reeled off into nightmare. Maxim wondered if any of the children had been adopted, if any had surviving relatives. As the lovely song drew to a close he felt cold and sick, plagued by the workings of fate and the irrationality of human beings. The yacht *Arrow* chugged into the Western Sea and a breeze filled its sails; the stoker, aft, laid back on his faggots and shut the damper.

Maxim was applauding the song vigorously for the breeze flung the sound away; then his clapping was reinforced.

The party of finely dressed persons, the hiring party, looked down from the rail of the upper deck. He saw a man and a woman, a young couple; she wore an enveloping cloak of jade-green jocca, lined and embroidered, and the man was splendid in crimson leather. They were handsome and they smiled with a genuine sweetness; Maxim's first thought was of a wedding party.

There were two servants . . . a young girl and boy . . . who came right to the rail and flung down, showered down, sweetmeats, nuts, small coins, even small toys, favors done up with fringes and ribbon. The children dived for these rewards and Sister Cridge smiled and bowed to these bene-factors. She gave a single nod to the children and presently the eldest girl came forward with all the coins. Maxim caught the eye of the young couple and bowed; they re-turned the salutation with easy smiles. They were still ap-plauding the children's singing or rather they were playing a clapping game of their own, the girl allowing the young man to clap one of her hands. The young man cried out:

"Sister, may we hear another song?"

"Surely, Mr. Heath . . ."

The children had already closed ranks, eager to begin, and as Maxim stared out over the sunny waves they sang a round about a little boat. He felt a surge of well-being as unbidden as his former worry and discomfort. It was as if the singing bound them all together, the singers and the listeners. The *Arrow* struck out to the northeast across the bright water.

He saw that this water was still a curious color, a trans-lucent dark green; trails of red-brown plankton lived in the hollows of the shallow waves and colored the foam where the *Arrow*'s keel made a path. The northern shore was lit with a rim of sunlight; caverns and curled cliff-tops and sea-pines, picturesquely gnarled, crowded one upon the other until the traveler fell into a trance at the sight of so many "vistas." It was impossible to think that the Western Sea had any face but this: the storms of Sept and Oct seemed as mythical as the historic drought that his uncle had been summoned to witness.

Maxim thought of the Vail and tried to superimpose their picture upon the romantic scenery. A heaving of the water, a thickening of the wave that did not settle, the dripping rise of the three giant protoheads to tower above the yacht. He thought suddenly: "They will never believe us . . . never believe the wonders of this world." And the thought was more terrifying than thoughts of the Vail. *Those others . . .* human beings, tall men and women in silver suits, a race of godlike beings ready to judge the inhabitants of Rhomary.

"Dator!"

The song had ended and Sister Cridge touched his shoulder. The young man from the upper deck was trying to attract his attention; he held between his hands a brass telescope. His voice was clear and slightly nasal; he looked down at Maxim with a half smile.

"We may observe the Sea of Utner."

"Thank you."

Maxim reached up and the young man retreated his boots of crimson leather a step from the rail. The servant boy took the telescope about its shaft and passed it down. Sister Cridge had marshaled her choir and now proceeded to march them off to breakfast.

"Please join us, Dator," she said in a low voice, "if you are free."

"I will indeed. Sister . . ." he was half whispering himself, "the young lady and gentleman. . . ?"

"Ah," she said, "they have done so much. If it were not for them . . ."

"Mr. Heath, you said?"

"And his wife, her given name is Ulla, they do not stand on ceremony. Heath and Ulla Redrock. Their holdings are mainly on the southern shore of the Billsee. Not far from the site of Chippan."

"Thank you."

It was a puzzle; he found it difficult to associate these prepossessing people with the set-to at Noag's Inn. Yet when he looked there was definitely some kind of likeness: the young man's hair was the same reddish brown. In any case the prospector Redrock had been handsome, respectable; Maxim recalled that he had taken him for a doctor. He raised the telescope and adjusted the focus.

The Sea of Utner was the name given to a wide bay marked off by headlands; it was a point of debate whether the Vail called only this region by the name or whether it was used for the whole of the Western Sea. Maxim searched and found his objective. The great Vail had passed and gone and all that remained of their presence was this: on a tiny island close to the shore there was a weathered wooden platform about twice the height of a man. The old speaking platform built by the Envoys so that the race of minmers could converse with the Vail. Maxim felt a melancholy surge of pride. "Vail," he said in mind, "we are tenacious. We are not easily discouraged."

He felt his eyes sting and blur with tears which he blinked away. He laughed and handed the telescope up through the railings.

"The minmers built well!" he called cheerfully. "Many thanks, Mr. Redrock."

"Oh yes," it was the young wife, whose voice chimed like a bell. "They are excellent carpenters . . ."

Both young people laughed so hard at this that Maxim wondered if he had missed something. He stood, reaching up awkwardly, and had to wait until the pretty servant girl bent down and took the telescope from his hand. The lordliness of the Redrocks verged on rudeness. Very rich, he supposed, one had to make allowances. He decided to meet them face to face and introduce himself; he went briskly round to the broad steps that led upward.

When he came to the upper deck they had all gone. They had left behind a scatter of the ment leaves that were used to wrap sweets and a ripe rogue-apple in a basket. He took this up and ate it as he promenaded all round the upper deck. The captain's bridge rose up centrally, before it the yacht's mainmast with sails set, and aft the long wooden funnel strapped with metal. He got in the way of the crew, peered into one of the lifeboats, then into another. The one on the port side had a mattress under its enveloping cover of brown bark cloth and did not look a bad place to sleep.

Maxim had just begun to learn a basic fact of life as a ship's passenger: there was nothing much to do. He went below and joined in the children's breakfast. For the whole of the long, bright day he gave himself up to the experience of sailing upon the Western Sea. He began a report in shorthand for his uncle; he played Go with the two older children Peter and Gem. At siesta time he dozed in the day cabin which served as the children's common room.

He heard the Redrock family, their clear, loud voices and very often the music they had accompany their strolling. Once he saw Redrock senior pass by a port, in profile; he was stricken with relief, it was not the same man. Then the prospector turned his head and Maxim recognized him at once. The handsome set face, smiling now, the white streak in reddish hair.

At last, after supper with the children, he called Farb the second steward, a smooth-faced man in a buttoned jacket, and ordered a nightcap of wine and water.

"The elder Redrock has a servant, hasn't he?" asked Maxim.

"His driver, name of Bevin," said Farb. "A city man. Not one from their usual stable."

"What d'you mean?"

"The Chippan Foundlings. Most find employment on the Redrock estates," said Farb. "You might say they had solved the servant problem."

This information did not surprise him. He wondered if he had some innate prejudice against the very rich.

"Farb," he said, "why do you think they hired this boat?"

The steward glanced about the boat deck as they came round to the port side and said in a low voice.

"The word is out, Dator, that it's iron they're rushing to meet."

"An ironrush then," said Maxim. "And the route?"

"Overland from Derry, where the long portage begins."

"Keep an eye on that Bevin for me," said Maxim. "Talk to him about his recent doings in the city . . ."

He drained his mug of wine and gave Farb some loose change. The steward nimbly pocketed it, set down the wine cup and spread the blanket he was carrying inside Maxim's lifeboat.

"There you are, Mr. Bro, snug as a gecko's house."

Maxim climbed in and settled. He lay awake for a few minutes watching the red unwinking eye that was the planet Ruby, shining through a small rent in the bark cloth covering. Then he fell asleep quickly, rocked in the cradle of the deep.


"Dator Bro?"

A light shadow fell across his face. His dream of sea and sunlight dissolved; he sat up awkwardly in the deck chair. It was midday of the second day out. Heath Redrock in a white ruffled shirt, stood above him holding a book, balanced upon his palms.

"I was dreaming," said Maxim. "Good day, Mr. Redrock. Is that a book you have there?"

The young man bent somewhat awkwardly from the waist and set the book in Maxim's lap. He had to straighten his knees and grasp the warm leather-bound book so that it did not fall on the deck.

"We wondered what you would make of it," said Heath, still standing, "since you are an expert on books."

"You're joking, I think," said Maxim. "There are no experts on books in the Rhomary land. Even my Uncle Urbain would not qualify himself as one."

Heath cocked his head, smiling, and Maxim examined the book. The cover fooled him for a few seconds . . . its working was particularly fine and traditional . . . but he knew the jocca paper at once. It was a book printed and bound in Rhomary: *Songs and Ballads.* There were a few authors listed but more often the origins of the work: *Traditional, An Irish Air, As passed down in the Green family, Based on an Earth text.*

"Why, this is fine work!" Maxim turned the pages eagerly.

"The text?"

"Everything. I think I have read a number of these songs before or heard them sung. The book is most finely made . . . one of the hobby printers. The plates are excellently done."

"We made it," said Heath. "We have this small press. As you say, we are hobby printers. The plates were drawn by one of our young men."

"May I read it then?"

"Oh, it is yours," said Heath smiling. "Please place it in your archives when you return to Rhomary."

"Why, I am deeply grateful!"

"How long before you return?"

"I am traveling to the Gann Station. I think that will take some time."

Heath sat down before him on the deck, ignoring the other deck chairs; he looked very young, the texture of his pale skin was girlish. He grasped one knee and rocked to and fro, staring out to sea.

"Late summer in the Rhomary land," he said. "I like to travel at this time of year. Do you know that the most meteorites fall to earth at this time? It is eighteen years since the fall of the Big Boy meteorite. Do you have a listing for that, Dator?"

"Third largest," said Maxim. "It fell on the southern shore of the Billsee."

"It fell on our estate," said Heath.

"You were in luck, then."

"Oh, we are a lucky family. We attract iron like a magnet . . . or perhaps it attracts us."

"Then you need little help to find it," said Maxim. "Where do you think it lies this time?"

"Surely you could tell us that, Dator?"

The book had suddenly become rather heavy in Maxim's hands. He saw himself handing it back to Heath, passing a lofty remark about bribes and the pledges of his office. But instead he looked at the Western Sea . . . which he was crossing at a great rate . . . and wondered again about the behavior of the rich.

"Truly," he said, trying to look Heath Redrock in the eye, "I am not interested in meteorites. If I did have certain knowledge of a fall of any reasonable size I would have reported it to the city."

Heath now stared at him with an expression of calm unbelief. Between one pulse beat and the next Maxim was seized by a sensation so strange that he could explain it only in terms of physical sickness. Time spun out, a slow lightning shock struck some part of his brain; it was as if he had awoken from sleep to hear the tail end of a mighty shout. Then he was himself again, rubbing his eyes and shaking his head.

"Are you all right?"

"Thank you, Sister." Maxim shied away from Sister Cridge who was bending close. "I felt dizzy for a moment. Perhaps it is the motion of the ship."

The Sister had come on to the deck as part of a larger party: there was Ulla Redrock in a painted gown and spreading straw hat, the servant girl laden with sunshades, the musician, two stewards with baskets of food and drink. Heath did not stir from the deck, but he cried out:

"Have you brought us a picnic then?"

"A festival!" chimed Ulla.

She sank into a chair under the first sunshade to be erected and smiled at Maxim.

"The Dator must have a shade," said Sister Cridge, "or he will be sun-smitten."

"Too late," said Maxim gallantly. "I am smitten already with this beauty and good company."

The young servant girl, whose name was Dorit, snapped up a lilac shade over his head and caught his eye, blushing. Heath had given a command to the musician who began to play a gentle thrumming accompaniment. Heath and Ulla began to sing in clear fluting voices:

*"We have stayed too long*
*By the sweet wells of Rhomary,*
*We hear the watchman's song*
*And the sound of the wind in the jocca palms.*

*"We have traveled far*
*On the brown roads of Rhomary,*
*We see a distant star*
*Giving light to the days of forgotten worlds."*

Before the song was over Redrock senior had joined the "festival"; Maxim stared as keenly as he dared. The man glowed with health and wealth in this setting; in Rhomary he had been paler, more contained.

"The days are too long," he announced. "The days and nights of this world are a challenge to our ingenuity. Dator, are you rested after your ride from the city?"

"Well rested, sir!"

Maxim took a draft of the excellent fortified palm wine and gazed at Ulla Redrock on his left some distance away. She really was an exquisite creature, narrow featured and fine, her hair red-gold, tarnished in places to a coppery green by some of the colors of her sunshade. Her gown of painted jocca cloth was a puffed and slashed creation that spoke to Maxim of ancient earth; a single blue stone on a silver chain flashed fire when she turned her head. Her ambience was not warm or sensuous; Maxim found that he admired her as he would admire a work of art. Her conversation was controlled; when he looked away from her the bell-like voice might have come from someone older, more worldly.

"Oh I have good grounds," he said, in anwser to one of her questions, "I have the best grounds in the world for traveling to the Gann Station, Mam Redrock."

"Then you must travel for love," put in Heath ironically.

"Surely," said Sister Cridge, "the Dator travels on a matter of life and death."

"Perhaps he follows a dream," said Redrock, smiling.

"Too close," said Maxim. "If you know that, sir, I must suppose you have been prospecting for information."

Redrock laughed boldly and Ulla took up the thread.

"Information is your special province, Dator. *We* must suppose there is little you do not know."

"Well, you must enlighten me, in the interests of the

city," he said promptly. "Where are you going? Why are you traveling across the Western Sea?"

"The where is easy," she said. "We go to Derry, then we trek to the northwest, to our summer lodge in the Obelisk Hills."

"And we travel for pleasure," said Heath. "That is the reason for everything we do."

"Not true," said Sister Cridge. "I have much evidence of your kindness. A life of pleasure is surely a selfish one."

"Dear Sister," said Redrock kindly, "do you take no pleasure in what you do?"

"Oh I do . . . especially when the results of my labors are to be seen . . ."

She held a hand out to Dorit, the young girl, and to the young musician who began to play again on his ribboned guitar: Maxim saw that they were her former pupils.

The yacht sailed on in clear summer weather, set on its course for Cape Loron, the first port of call, and the festival continued. The food and drink was delicate, varied and delicious, very different from the plain fare Maxim had shared so far with the foundlings. In fact he worried, as he picked at the shellfish salad mixed in a plate-sized piron shell, that the children would still be on plain bread and fish-cake.

"It is not food for children," said Sister Cridge, "your conscience is too tender."

"Sister, I wish you would do something for me when this holiday is over."

"What then?"

"Please write a report of your school. Its origins and history."

"Ah, you know that."

"I have read the reports of the tragedy but nothing that happened later. Were none of the Foundlings adopted?"

"Some are left in the school although they have close relatives," said Sister Cridge. "Prejudice and fear. Look here, Dator . . ."

She turned back her rainbow robe where it covered her right arm and pointed to an old scar on her forearm.

"A stone," she said, "thrown by a passerby in the very first months, as I took two of the elder children shopping in Pebble."

"You have been with them so long?"

"I was the district nurse," she said. "Chippan was within my district. I was on leave in Rhomary, the first leave in five years, and I came back on the morning after. I was called to the wharf at Pebble when the very first survivors came in. I came with four children and an old woman to the hospital in Pebble and they made over a large recreation room to house them. I went straight away to Chippan and saw what had to be done and came back with a boatload of children. By the time I returned the hospital authorities had been prevailed upon: we were housed in an old long-house used for quarantining dry-hogs . . ."

"You saw the truth at Chippan?"

"It was very bad but I had helped in a flood and an epidemic of fever. I had read and heard tales. We are lucky in this land, Dator; we have had no battlefields."

"What happened in Chippan?"

"It was plain to see. They were poisoned with false-spaggin in a new keg of beer. There was no mystery at all. There were no mysterious disappearances and no looting . . . unless you count the few poor coins I took from the parents' bodies to buy food and fuel for their children. I saw all this and I spoke the truth in Pebble, to the doctors even, until my voice gave out. I made ten, fifteen trips to the village in a leaky boat, rowing with the help of a young boy, just orphaned. No other boatman would make the journey."

"'There was a Jenzite couple . . .'"

"Good people whatever their creed. They were injured."

"But what in the Vail's name were the people afraid of? What caused this evil reaction?"

"They were afraid of a new disease, an unknown infection," said Sister Cridge. "Dator, they were afraid of the unknown. It was as if the Rhomary land had struck back at them."

"Ah, but the land is kind," said Maxim, "or it would have killed us all long ago."

He shuddered in sunlight. Sister Cridge had fallen silent, staring out over the Western Sea which was suddenly crossed by purple cloud-shapes, as if huge creatures moved under the waves.

"The Redrocks are good people," she said awkwardly. "We owe them much. They are the only real benefactors of the school."

Before Maxim could reply she went on:

"Please trust them. Tell the reason for your journey. I think they are anxious to know it."

He turned to her in surprise but she hurried away. Maxim

was hailed at once by Redrock senior to referee a game of quoits; if he expected some straight questions he did not get them, only an invitation to drink more wine.

The festival was at its height. Cap Ramm came down from the bridge, downed a liter and called two sailor girls to do their rope-gathering dance. It involved mock-fighting, cuffing the air and striking the coiled rope on the deck to make the sound of a slap. The crew and passengers either had no siesta at all that day or a longer one than they had planned. The children gathered on the lower deck, sang songs and were rewarded again with fruit and sweets. Suddenly the long hours of daylight had passed and colored lanterns flowered in the dusk. The lookout had called "Cape Loron" and the ship was approaching the distant lights of the settlement. Maxim sat under his absurd lilac sunshade squinting a little at Heath and Ulla who seemed to be sharing a chair.

"The day is simply too long," said Heath. "Mind and body cannot stand it."

"I can't imagine any other day," said Maxim, "and I can't remember any day that I have enjoyed as much as this one. The great Vail are gone and we are still here, making merry on the Western Sea."

"Human beings are remarkably durable creatures!" put in Redrock from his place at the rail.

"You sound like the Vail," said Maxim. " 'The race of minmers or men, though puny and purblind, has certain durable qualities . . .' "

"Very good," said Redrock, "but you must remember that the Vail so-called never sounded like the books of the Envoys."

"How did they sound?"

For a moment Redrock puffed up his handsome face as if he were preparing to utter some extraordinary sounds but he thought better of it. Ulla and Heath joined in his laughter. Maxim took up the book Heath had given him, bade the family good evening or good night and turned to go below.

"A meteorite?" asked Redrock suddenly.

Maxim laughed and shook his head, negotiating carefully between two fallen chairs. Below deck in the paneled washroom he dowsed his head in cold seawater; the steward Farb hove into view.

"You have a cabin now," he grinned. "Courtesy of the Captain."

It was a narrow sliver of a cabin, aft, with a bed made up on a large coffin-shaped box beneath the port. Farb had brought Maxim's cloak and saddlebag with his writing things from the corner of the day cabin where they had been hanging. He was suddenly conscious of the few poor documents he carried in an inside pocket of his tunic: a dream, a report of meteors, a tale from a hermit stargazer.

"Sail-locker," said Farb. "Used as a sick-bay sometimes."

"I'm glad of a bed," said Maxim.

He fumbled in his pockets and gave the steward half a credit and a sweet wrapped in a ment leaf. At that moment there was a grinding and shuddering as the *Arrow* edged up to Cape Loron wharf. He knelt on his makeshift bunk and saw a parmel with a páck harness, a gnarled sea-pine and a jocca palm, a single mudbrick building. He saw the civilization of the Rhomary land.

"Not much in Loron," said Farb cheerfully.

When the steward had gone Maxim found himself slightly more sober than he had been but hardly less sleepy. He heard a heavy tread in the passage and looked from his door just as the driver Bevin came past, carrying a pack. Maxim breathed deeply and slipped out, blocking the man's way. Bevin cringed; he was thickset but much shorter than Maxim who saw himself filling the narrow corridor, hulking and not quite sober.

"Bevin?" he said. "We met at Noag's Inn."

Bevin licked dry lips.

"Never knew it was yourself, Dator," he said. "You were chasing my boss."

He hefted his pack and said anxiously:

"Please let me through . . . I'm leaving the ship."

"What did you two do to Milt Donal, the merchant?"

"Nothing!" said Bevin in panic. "Nothing! I did nothing! Is he . . . ? How is he?"

"Tell me, damn you!"

Maxim seized the man by the slack of his tunic and pulled him close.

"Let go, dry hell . . ." whispered Bevin staring into Maxim's face. *"He'll* come down. I beg you! I have to start the trek!"

"The ironrush?"

"Maybe. I take a parmel train from here to the Summer Lodge and get it ready. The family comes on from Derry."

"What was with Donal?"

"Truthweed," said Bevin. "Let me go. It was truthweed

106

he used and some kind of thought reading, some Vesp thing. To *see* . . ."

"To see what?"

"Dator, protect me, don't split on me. To see what Donal saw, the meteors."

Maxim released the man and stood aside.

"Get along," he said. "I won't make trouble."

Bevin raced off; there was shouting and the sounds of the gangplank going down. Maxim sat on his bunk in the little box of a cabin thinking of Milt Donal with his mind washed clean by the truthweed. He was not sure that he believed the story about mind reading; Redrock simply had his servant bluffed and frightened.

There was a light tap on his cabin door; he sprang up and bumped his head on the ceiling. In came the young servant girl Dorit carrying a large pottery goblet of wine, the sort called a loving cup. She wore a loose robe instead of her tunic and britches and her light brown hair was unplaited. She stared at Maxim, shy and bold.

"I was sent with your nightcap."

"Who sent you, sweetheart?"

It sounded harsh; he stood beside her, slipped an arm around her waist. She drew breath but did not flinch.

"Mam Redrock and the others sent me. I was supposed to ask . . ."

"What?"

"If you had everything your heart desired."

"Well, that is kind."

He took the goblet then drew Dorit close and kissed her. But it was too much, he couldn't play the game; he was conscious of her reaction, blushing, uncertain how to yield or to turn the kiss into an embrace. He was conscious of his own reaction, knew that he would not have hesitated if he had been close to Ambel of Noag's Inn. How long was it, three weeks since he had lain with a girl, since he had shared the bed of his tired, comradely intern, Nell Jons. Now that he had been sent this virginal creature who could pass for sixteen with her hair braided he felt angry and nauseated. He moved away and now he raised the cup to his lips and thought of Milt Donal. He sipped and passed the cup to Dorit.

"Have some yourself!"

She took a gulp still staring at him. He had no idea how to let her down lightly; he shook his head, ran a hand over his hair.

"Good night, Dorit," he said.

She gasped, set the cup down on the only shelf in the narrow cabin, and ran from the room. He sat down on his bunk again feeling cruel and foolish, probing the rest of the wine with his fingers in search of a slow-dissolving seaweed pod. He found nothing but he poured the wine into Loron harbor through the porthole. He lay down trying to recapture the pleasant tipsiness from the long, happy festival on shipboard. He stripped off his clothes and lay down under the quilts. He had spoiled the day with his suspicions or the Redrock family had spoiled it with their gentle, cynical pressure.

He fell into a heavy sleep and half woke when the yacht was under way again on the last lap of its journey to Derry. Then he slept again and dreamed he was walking through the orchards, home in Edenvale. He saw a girl in a most beautiful flowered green cloak but when he ran through the trees and stretched out a hand to her she changed, shimmering, into a tree, and walked disdainfully away. Maxim was afraid in his dream; his father came up, looking like his Uncle Urbain, and said, "Use your senses, boy!" Maxim looked down at the ground and saw that a torn book lay open at his feet, the fine pages ripped out, screwed up and flung about in the orchard grass. With painful anxiety he began collecting each one, smoothing it out; but the tiny letters crawled on the page and he could not read a word.

He was wide awake, back in the sail locker of the yacht *Arrow*, sailing on the Western Sea; he gave a sigh of relief for his escape from the anxiety of the dream. The small oil lamp on the cabin wall had burned down and for a while the cabin was black. When his eyes became accustomed to the darkness he scrambled into some clothes and took his cloak. The corridors were empty; a lamp or two burned low in the wall brackets. The galley was empty, with hot tea in a straw and clay warming pot; he helped himself to tea and bread and prowled up on deck, amidships. Here he found signs of life; the watch were at their posts; a light burned on the masthead and the bridge was warmly lit.

He walked around the lower deck and came to the bow. The silence was broken only by the music of the ship as it rode swiftly over the Western Sea. Maxim looked at the dark, glittering plain of the sea, the line of the distant shore, the parting bow wave where it turned to flakes of reddish fire. He looked up at the sky and saw the great comet blazing down from the place it had seized among the familiar planets. Ruby, the gas giant, had set but small Topaz shone in the east and the planet Connor overhead; human beings perceived and named the system and used the names they liked best.

The jewel names had been chosen by Kirchner, the senior navigator, whose name was not known any more except by archivists. He named the planets *Topaz, Smaragd, Saphir, Rubin,* but *Saphir* became *Connor* for the commander who had done the impossible, and *Smaragd* was *Rhomary,* not so emerald green in the place where landfall was made. *The Rhomary Land* . . . it was a nickname, a play on words, as if its people did not dare speak the name of that vanished shape that had sunk into their deep minds: Rhomary was named for the ship itself.

Maxim searched the western horizon and found the strangest light of all, the smudged golden eye of Brother, the dark companion of their sun. In the north the small moon had set, the little Pearl. A soft whistle sounded from above; he saw the wave of a hand on the bridge.

"Come up!"

Cap Ramm's voice, perfectly pitched to carry through the still night. Maxim waved back and climbed. The Old Man stood at the wheel in his warm kelp-smelling cubby with a thin young sailor dozing at the chart platten.

They stood in silence for some time, watching the sea, then Ramm remarked:

"We'll see the eastbound galley if they're making time."

Maxim looked ahead keenly but he saw nothing until the lookout gave the call, "Galley to starboard." It was a splendid sight, a long low ship with a single bank of oars.

"How many rowers to an oar?" he asked.

"That is the *Derry Queen,*" said Ramm. "She is lightly built and packs but six to an oar."

"In off-world times, on Earth," said Maxim, "galleys were rowed by slaves."

"Is that a fact?" Ramm cocked a bristling eyebrow. "Times have changed, or so the owners and galley-masters will tell you. They think they are the slaves of the Rowers' Union."

After the galley passed and the sleepy sailor had made a note in the log they went on in comfortable silence. Then Ramm said again:

"We are over the Nirut deep, what they call the Black Hole."

"The Envoys sent divers down here, looking for the Vail during the drought," said Maxim.

"No use," said Ramm. "It is some kind of canyon undersea but too narrow to hide them big fellas. It is part of the net of rivers that feed this sea."

"How many underground rivers?"

"Hard to tell. A whole lizard nest of rivers and springs, some giving up and others beginning."

"Have you traveled much beyond the southern shore?"

"Not far," said Ramm. "If no one has settled there it is because the climate is harder and hotter than any other in these lands. Even the sea can't make it bearable."

"It is on the equator then."

"As we commonly reckon it."

"What are our chances of getting around this world, Captain?"

Ramm chuckled drily and scratched his ear.

"Did you ever hear of a sailor called Hilo Hill?" he asked. "I thought not. He said he had been around the world."

"Sailors tell tales," said Maxim.

"He told a good 'un. He sailed with Gline."

"Some of Gline's crew were brought back from the Red Ocean."

"Hilo Hill took the long way around, so he said."

"How long did it take him?"

"Fifteen years," said Ramm. "He was mad, of course, and past sixty years old."

"Where did he turn up again?"

"Where would you suppose? In the far east. He was at a fish-drying plant at the eastern tip of the Billsee, working as a useful."

"No reports? No ballads or rumors?"

"I don't know. His daughter found him there and took him home to Derry, where we're heading now. His family took him with a grain of salt."

"And what did he find? Golden City? The Land of the Marchers?"

"Nothing half so fine," said Cap Ramm. "In fact the other side of the globe was so bluggy dull by his telling that I was inclined to believe him. The best he could do was a tribe of lizard men."

"A wonder they didn't eat him up!"

"Oh, but they did," said Ramm, straight-faced. "The old man lacked a middle finger on his left hand . . . said the lizards took and ate it so he could join their tribe."

The sky at the horizon beyond the western shore had just begun to lighten. The sea was still black as night but criss-crossed with white wavelets and phosphorescent trails. There was movement below on the boat deck; two of the Redrock servants, arranging chairs; was that Dorit standing by with her arms full of colored quilts? Three chairs were set out and on each a quilt, one was caught by a beam of light and it gleamed silken green, a color that made Maxim faint and squeamish.

"Dawn coming," said Cap Ramm, "the star passengers will watch the sun rise."

The Redrock family assembled by the light of a lantern, all in long bedgowns, golden brown, amethyst, coral; Ulla's veil and a few strands of her bright hair were lifted by the morning breeze. Maxim remembered his dream; he saw the green-robed figure in his dream, the girl who changed into a tree. He narrowed his eyes until the figures of the three travelers became soft blurs of color. *Shape-changers?* He went on talking to the captain as if two portions of his brain were rushing to some conclusion.

"Look here," he said, "how could you be sure the old sailor *was* Hilo Hill? After fifteen years and with parts of him nibbled away and his wits gone?"

"It was him all right, I knew him."

"I'm interested in identity," said Maxim. "You didn't take his fingerprints or his palm prints."

"No," said Cap Ramm, "I recognized him in the ordinary way. He had a look of Hilo grown old."

Now the family were settled; as Maxim watched their slow perfect gestures, the way they bent toward each other or waved the servants away, he thought of actors in a play. He remembered the very first time he had seen Redrock, on the stairs at Noag's Inn. The odd sidestep the prospector had made upon the stairs to avoid contact. He steadied himself.

"Then there was no proof," he said.

"Yes," said Cap Ramm, "there was proof. Some things cannot be changed."

He lifted his gnarled left hand from the wheel and held it before Maxim's face. There was a tailed star tattooed in red and blue upon his broad brown forearm.

"Hilo and I had this same star, done on the same day

by Fan Kells, the skin artist at Pebble, when he was Bosun of my first ship and I a ship's boy. Such a mark will last through wind and weather."

"That is proof, I think." said Maxim.

But what proof was there for the wonder before his eyes, the three travelers sailing on the Western Sea? He cast about for some question the captain might answer.

"How long have you known the Redrock family?"

"A few years," said Cap Ramm. "They float up to the top, these rich folk, but not all of them stay rich."

The western horizon had changed from purple to rose; the travelers would not have a long vigil.

"When do we reach Derry, Captain?"

"Give it four hours," said Cap Ramm. "Time for another sleep if you need it."

As he went down the ladder from the bridge Maxim found that he was trembling. For a moment he was filled with an urge for violent action: he wanted to run to the boat deck, seize Redrock by the hand, shout aloud, question fiercely. But all he did was what befitted the Dator of Rhomary. He rushed to his cabin and began to write in that shortened language that was almost a code, a report for his uncle.

Little enough to go on . . . or was it so little. The alleged "untouchability" of the shape-changers that Urbain had noticed twenty years ago was still apparent in the Redrock family. Yet when he thought about it Maxim saw it more as a quirk, an idiosyncrasy. They were solid enough, their pale skin, the flesh that held out their elaborate clothes, these things appeared as touchable and durable as human flesh. Their way of handling common objects was certainly strange. The young servants they had always employed might be a necessity; Maxim wondered if there were certain finer physical actions—threading needles, writing, using a tinder box—that they could not perform.

He noted down solemnly every scrap of conversation he could remember and it was tendentious nonsense that added up to nothing. These were rich, feckless people, used to getting their own way, eager to find out the whereabouts of another iron strike, nothing more. But the hypothesis that they were the shape-changers altered the very shape of their words. Had Redrock really conversed with the Vail in ages past? Did Ulla really distance herself from the race of minmers or men?

He groped for the words of that artless song: *"We have*

112

*stayed too long by the sweet wells of Rhomary . . . distant star . . . forgotten worlds. . . ."* But were these clichés of former Earth-dwellers? Maxim stopped short, pen poised, and realized for the first time how deeply he was gripped by the old fantasy "Earth." He was not and had never been an Earth-dweller: he was a creature born and bred on another world, a creature every bit as strange in his own way as a shape-changer. He was an inhabitant of the Rhomary land.

The smart knock on his door was a summons, he knew it. Sister Cridge peered in when he answered.

"Breakfast," she said. "Breakfast with the family. It is two hours until we dock. They are waiting in the saloon."

"Thank you, Sister."

"Don't be late now!"

She gave him a quick smile and popped her head out of his cabin again. He wanted to question her, to warn her; he was tempted to tell tales on the Redrocks . . . about Dorit, for instance . . . but he could not, he did not dare. He was by no means sure that the Sister was ignorant of the truth; the Redrocks commanded her loyalty for the sake of the children. She had experienced too much irrational cruelty to be bothered by peculiarities of behavior in a family of rich benefactors.

Maxim broke off his report, ignored the twanging of his nerves, and spent ten or twelve minutes putting his possessions in order. He cleared out the cabin, stuffed clothes and papers into the saddlebags and transferred them to the saddle itself in its cupboard. He managed to change his linen, to wash and brush up, to comb his beard and to tie the tapes of his shirt with trembling fingers. He stood outside the door of the saloon, the splendid forward cabin where the Redrocks usually dined, and heard their voices beyond the door. He caught a glimpse of himself, wide-eyed, in the brightly polished wood; he knocked and went in.

The handsome paneled room was full of watery sunlight; reflections from the water moved on the ceiling. The Redrock family, dressed for traveling, had never looked more healthy, normal and human. Ulla was sipping green tea from a painted bowl; Heath played some game with fork and knife; Redrock was eating pancakes.

"Bravo!" said Heath. "We thought you might miss breakfast."

"It is our last chance to talk to you," said Ulla, smiling at him over the rim of the bowl.

Last chance . . . the words rattled in his head like two stones. He was alone with the family; Sister Cridge had not shared their meal.

"Sit down, Dator," said Redrock. "What is it, man? No ceremony . . ."

"No," said Maxim. "It is just that I have something most particular to say to you all."

Their faces turned toward him, mildly interested but, he could swear, absolutely secure.

"I would like you to know my reasons for traveling to the Gann Station," he said. "If you would care to read these three copies of reports . . ."

Maxim drew out the documents that he had been guarding so carefully and laid them on the breakfast table. They seemed to him faintly absurd: Milt Donal's workmanlike script on reed paper; the long jocca scroll with the carefully penned account of Vern Munn's dream and the seal of the Envoys hanging from a ribbon; the doctor's firm handwriting of Faya Junik, the stargazer from Pinnacle.

The Redrock family all gave exclamations of delight.

"Oh, this is fine!" said Redrock. "But what's the mystery? Tell us yourself."

Maxim shook his head and sat down. He had not intended the documents themselves as any kind of a test but he watched now and he was afraid and wished his uncle could be by his side sharing the moment. Ulla did nothing. Heath, who was within easy reach of the documents, hauled the bunch of papers down the polished table with his fork, lips drawn back with the effort of such a maneuver. Then with painful slowness Redrock unfolded the papers, weighted the corners with pieces of pottery and began to read at what appeared to be a normal speed.

Ulla cried out: "Ah, but the dream . . ."

Their faces turned to him again and they saw that he was watching. Redrock sat across the table from Ulla; she had not moved; there was no way in which she could have read the documents. Slowly, playing the game without fuss, Redrock turned the papers so that Heath and Ulla could see them; yet Maxim was sure that all three knew the contents. The information had passed from mind to mind.

Heath let his fork clatter onto the table and made a face. "No iron then!"

"Who knows?" said Ulla. "Perhaps some samples of new alloys, but probably unworkable."

114

"I still think it is a very long shot," said Redrock, "but I can understand the Dator's interest."

"I have a human interest!" said Maxim fiercely. "Survivors! Men and women from Earth!"

They stared at him politely; Maxim shivered. Their coldness reached into the very marrow of his bones; he thought of a plunge, deep down, into the waters of the Western Sea.

"You had an interest in my mission," he said. "I'm sure you understand the need for discretion. I don't want to cause panic or raise false hopes in the people of Rhomary."

"Secrets?" said Heath. "Oh yes, we are good at secrets."

"Please repay my confidence," said Maxim. "Please answer a few questions."

He thought it was a bad beginning. He was never sure how much they knew. There was no glance exchanged, no closing of the ranks, not a sign of the least concern. Redrock ate a last mouthful. Maxim cast about for a thoroughly improper question, bristling with traps; a double and triple-stringed "Have-you-stopped-beating-your-wife-yet" that would trip anyone. He asked, rather lamely:

"Have you always used the name Redrock?"

"It *is* our name," said Ulla.

"Have you not used another name? Shall I suggest another name you have used?"

There was a little tension among them now but they still did not look at each other, only fixed their eyes on Maxim.

"Changing names . . ." said Heath in a wavering voice.

"Do you think my Uncle Urbain would recognize you, the three of you, if he met you again?"

"The Dator . . ." said Redrock, softly.

"I am the Dator now," said Maxim. "I am pledged to keep personal information secret."

"Secrets . . ." echoed Ulla.

The timbre of her voice had altered, become even more bell-like.

"We haven't any idea what you are talking about," said Redrock smoothly. "What . . . Dator, please forget these strange thoughts."

"I *must* question. I believe you can help us all!"

"Help you!" said Heath, his voice wavering. "It is no more than your damnable curiosity."

"My human curiosity!"

"No proof!" said Redrock.

The words re-echoed from the three of them all together.

"No proof!"

"I have some evidence," said Maxim. "The reports of Coll Dun Mor. Is that name strange to you? The reports of a certain washerwoman in Silver City. Yes, all these things happened long ago. But what were your dealings with Milt Donal, the merchant?"

"No proof!" said Redrock again.

"I wonder if any one of you would care to take my hand and swear this is all my imagining?" said Maxim.

He walked toward Redrock down the side of the long table with his right hand outstretched.

Everything changed with stupefying suddenness. There was a burst of muted sound racing through the cabin, bell-sound was the nearest to it. Maxim had time to turn his head, to realize that the sounds came from Ulla and Heath. He saw them imperfectly in a haze of light as if sunlight had flooded the cabin; he felt that slow lightning strike at his brain as it had done once before on the deck. He blinked his eyes shut and heard Redrock say, very close, at his ear, inside his head:

"... but not here. When we are disembarked."

He heard himself utter one cry. He opened his eyes and it was his last conscious act. He saw nothing but a moving spiral of light. Then he had a sickening sensation of falling; he fell away, he fell or floated upward, he was loosed from his body. He looked down from a corner of the cabin ceiling and saw himself pause and shudder and clutch the table for support. Surrounding him were three bright, wavering figures. Then he dived back into some recess of his own brain and was forced to sleep.

# Chapter VI

## *Night on the Red Ocean*

Gurl Hign sat in her chair at the fireside and watched Shona lacing up the sea boots. It was the time when the family sat together at the end of the day, but this day was just beginning.

"Can you manage?" she asked Alan. "Can you get off that damn caravan?"

"Of course. Go along and have your sea voyage."

Gurl reached out guiltily and touched Shona's coppery hair.

"Take care of Ben," she said.

Shona looked up at her mother and Gurl was glad to see a spark of resentment in her eyes. At nineteen the girl was beautiful and uncomplaining; Gurl knew this was too good to be true. Somewhere there was a touch of Coll's spirit or her own.

"Where's your doctor?" she asked.

"Working!"

Shona knotted her mother's bootlace savagely.

There was noise and bustle in the hall tonight; a flimsy screen painted with desert scenes separated the family place from the rest. Alan fetched his mother a plate of bread and meat from the supper table before the unlit fireplace.

"LaMar will send for me to go aboard," she said. "First I must meet with Lem Fott, the Delfin speaker. Marko is bringing him."

"He'll know by now that he is wanted for the search."

"Lem Fott is a mild enough little man," said Gurl, "his sister is the prickly one."

"Watch out!" said Alan. "Lem is every bit as fanatical as Uschi Fott."

Ben came in through the kitchen and cried accusingly:
"You're sailing on the *Comet!* Oh, Ma. . . ."

He was furious, his fists clenched, his face red and frowning. Gurl laughed helplessly and stretched out a hand to him, but he stamped childishly and turned away.

"Behave yourself, you devil!"

Alan grasped Ben by the shoulder and shook him.

"Ben," said Gurl, "get your plate, then sit by me."

Alan saw that he obeyed and settled him on a stool beside his mother.

"One day you can sail with LaMar," she said. "I promise."

"I hate him!" said Ben. "I hate the *Comet*. You should stay home, Ma."

"Oh stop it, you sulky baby," she said. "When all this dies down I'll come up to the lookout and fly that kite with you."

He still glowered a little but she could see that this offer pleased him. Was the boy jealous . . . jealous of LaMar? Trim, the dock foreman, poked his head around the screen.

"Marko the preacher is here, cousin."

"Come along, Trim," she said. "Take my chair and have a bite of supper. I'll speak to the Jenzites."

She gathered up her oilskin and kitty . . . a leather satchel like the ones the sailors carried. She embraced Shona.

"Good-bye, my dear . . ."

"Ma!"

"What is it, child?"

"Gil is going to lose his head with this red-cross box that was found!" said Shona.

"Well, he can't hold his tongue, that's certain!" said Gurl.

"He'll send his own word to Rhomary!" said Shona. "He's sure it will mean promotion. He had this good grading long ago from the Second Consultant!"

"Tell him not to be a fool!"

She ruffled Ben's hair, clapped Alan on the shoulder and left Trim in her place, gobbling his supper. She met Marko on the hall verandah, with Lem Fott and his sister Uschi, the schoolmistress. After Marko had prayed and made a blessing Gurl said:

"Lem Fott, we must have your services as a Delfin speaker. You will be paid by the City of Rhomary but I will make a donation out of station funds to your sister's school and to your church."

"Fine, Rancher," said Lem uncomfortably. "Suits me. I never look to be paid for speaking to these folk."

"He should not work for the doctor!" burst out Uschi Fott. "That High Eminence Doctor is one of the same breed that sent our blessed Friend into the desert."

"The search is to save lives," said Gurl. "Wouldn't Jenz Kindl have approved this work?"

"I think so," nodded Marko. "Mistress Fott, dear Sister, remember your hourglass, another gift from the Rancher. Do not be so harsh."

"Lem . . . don't speak to your Delfin folk!" said Uschi.

"I will, but!" said Lem with unexpected firmness. "It might save a life. What's more, I can maybe calm their fears. If anything fell down, Rancher, it fell on their domain."

"Thank you, Lem," said Gurl Hign. "I sail on the *Comet* to catch the evening tide. Is your boat ready to go along?"

"All shipshape!"

"I'll brief you before we set sail."

Uschi Fott sat stiffly on a bench, leaning against the wall of the veranda; Marko the preacher fumbled for his gospel.

"A few lines," he said. "Remember, Rancher . . . you promised to have me read the Book to you after supper."

"Go ahead!" smiled Gurl.

She was not uninterested. This was another time of miracles and all things strange. The life of Rhomary was rough and primitive, as the Eminence had said, but this was part of its texture as well. She leaned against the wall herself and heard the preacher read in a strong voice:

"I was born in the oasis of Lemn in the distant north of the Rhomary land on a night when the heavens were filled with falling stars. My mother, Dita Kindl, told me that the people believed starships were coming, but I came instead to bear witness to the love of the gods. I would wish that if the gods would show their bounty yet again they should send that sign. I would wish the skies to be filled with ships as the sea is filled with the Delfin folk and the earth of Rhomary is peopled with loving human beings."

Gurl Hign sighed. It had the authentic ring of the Jenzite scriptures. She could almost hear Jenz Kindl's voice and see his worried sunburned face. She saw Uschi Fott and her brother making the circle of blessing on their foreheads

119

and she felt a sad emptiness in herself, complicated by guilty knowledge. She knew too much about Jenz Kindl and the sources of his inspiration ever to be a believer. She trusted the loving kindness of human beings rather less than he had done, but his words were comforting.

"May his wishes come true!" she said. "Come, Fisher Fott. It's time we went to sea."

When the *Comet* came to the mouth of the Gann, at twilight, and nosed out, through a low tidal bore, into the Red Ocean, there were searchers in smaller boats already returning. Other boats had been sent to the distant fish farms and pearl havens and these small craft that were now returning had patroled the river banks to the sea and the near reaches of the north and south coasts. To the north there was the broad expanse of the Blackpod Swamp; it reached for hundreds of kilometers, past the point where the Divide met the sea, and on almost to the shores of the Sooree River.

Lights flashed from a small boat and LaMar, with Gurl upon the bridge, had the *Comet* heave to. Other search boats came to them like fireflies over the red-brown waters. Ahead of the *Comet* Gurl saw the black sail of Lem Fott's little boat take the evening wind and scoot off to the northwest.

"Ahoy!" came the cry from below. "Is the Rancher there?"

"Ahoy yourself!" called LaMar. "What do you have?"

"I'm here!" Gurl spoke into a wooden cone that sent her voice echoing over the sea. "Is that you, Billy Dit?"

"Me and Little Diggy, Rancher. We got a couple small pieces. Sending them up."

The small pieces came up in a net and Poll Grev carried the dripping bundle to the bridge. LaMar held up a lantern. They saw a small container, blue plastic, and some absolutely unidentifiable piece of soggy, colored pulp.

"Yes!" said Gurl Hign. "A hit, I think . . . especially the bottle. But what in Vail's name is that mess?"

LaMar prodded it gently, first with his boot, then with a forefinger. He laughed.

"Rancher, my dear, I swear it is a great find. It is paper!"

Gurl bent down and peeled away a flake, saw a blurred patch of lettering.

"You're right!"

She took the cone and called:

"Hey Billy . . . that was a good haul. Troll along the

120

edge of the swamp for more of the same. Do you have spoon nets?"

"We do, Rancher. Shall we try entering the old devil . . . the Blackpod?"

"Have you had fever, Billy?"

"I have, Mam, but Little Diggy ain't."

"Don't go in among the trees, Billy. It is a pesthole. Troll a little, then turn in. You've done fine."

"We must dry out this paper," said Poll Grev. "I'll have it to the galley and see what Sim can do with it."

"Every precious flake goes to the Dator at Rhomary," said Gurl. "Tell Sim to go very easy."

LaMar went to the port side and addressed the search boats beneath.

"Send up any finds in the nets!"

The haul from these boats was disappointing: wood, crab shells, a promising piece of shaped stuff that they identified as a root of seaweed, three fishing floats, a wooden bucket that had sailed away from the Gann Station.

As Gurl leaned over the rail to thank the searchers she saw a larger boat rowing in awkwardly with its dark sail furled. There was some jostling and laughter as the other boats let it have a wide berth.

"That's bluggy Finn Connl," she said to LaMar. "What's come to the poor pizz this time?"

"You mean Mudflat Connl?" grinned LaMar. "He's enough to set the search back by half a season!"

He leaned down as the craft swung in toward the thick leatherweed fenders of the *Comet*.

"Mudflat, you great fool, hang away from my ship!"

"Please Rancher," came a piteous voice. "Me old man has an arm broken . . . and the young doctor . . ."

"Milly Connl?" said Gurl. "Has Finn hurt himself? What's this for a doctor? Is Gil Roak sailing with you?"

She saw a handsome boy at an oar in the Connls' unlucky boat and could not place him for a moment.

"Intern Jaygo, Rancher. I set Connl's arm. We found something that may change his luck."

"Come aboard and bring your find, intern," said Gurl.

"You boys and maids please help my wife bring in the boat!" called Mudflat Connl. "I tell you plainly, our luck has changed and we will be called Full-Catch from now on!"

There was a chorus of hoots and jeers but two young men hopped nimbly through the bobbing small craft and took the oars. Jaygo climbed up the ladder on to the *Comet*'s deck.

"Is that boat, the *Pearl*, so unlucky?" he asked.

"Finn Connl and his Milly are bad sailors, more likely," said Gurl. "How did you get a place on her?"

"Gil Roak set me aboard," said Jaygo, smiling. "See here, Rancher Hign. I think this is of some interest."

The find was wrapped in Jaygo's own silken scarf: a tube of thick silver fabric, ridged in places, torn at each end. Gurl and LaMar stared at it in the lantern light and the crew of the *Comet* tried to peer over their heads.

"All right," said Gurl. "It is a great find, I give you that, intern. But you must diagnose it for me."

"Mam Hign," said Jaygo solemnly, "it has certain curious features, I admit, but the object is undoubtedly a sleeve!"

Gurl turned aside and went immediately back to the rail.

"Finn Connl," she cried. "Mudflat . . . where was this found? Did you get a reading?"

"There, I told you!" shouted Mudflat.

He waved his good arm and sat down without warning in the watery bottom of his boat.

"I got no reading, Rancher, but I put out five markers. Due northwest, no more than five sea miles. The Delfin are there."

The crew had returned to work but LaMar and Jaygo still stared at the silver tube in the patch of lantern light. The wind was tugging gently at the shrouds.

"Any traces of blood?" asked Gurl.

"Not a drop," said Jaygo. "Oil, signs of charring."

He pointed to a blackened, melted area.

"Some fragments of . . . er . . . skin," he went on. "I have them in a specimen case."

"Take it all below," said LaMar. "When the boats have moved off we will sail further and meet with Lem Fott. Did you see the Delfin, Master Intern?"

"They saw us and gave the *Pearl* a wide berth."

"They're not stupid," laughed Gurl Hign.

She climbed up to the bridge again with LaMar. The lights and voices of the searchboats dwindled as they crossed the mouth of the Gann; the *Comet* slowly came about. Gurl Hign remembered her dream: this seemed enough to explain it . . . she was sailing again at last and in the Red Ocean. LaMar put his arm around her shoulders and as she looked into his weatherbeaten face she saw more love, more warmth than she had seen for a long time. This was his homecoming after a long trading voyage and he would have come to her room back at the station. She smiled back at him and slipped a hand around his waist, under his sea-cloak.

The ship sailed on to the northwest. An unmistakable sound between a whistle and a bell note came toward them over the sea, then a humming chorus that lasted only a few seconds. They heard the voices of the Delfin.

They sailed on, beyond the point where the lookout had spotted Finn Connl's five markers, until the faint riding light of Lem Fott's boat bobbed ahead of them. The night was undark and the small moon of Rhomary . . . the Little Pearl or "Baby . . . added its grain of light in the northern sky above the planet Topaz. There was a light swell; LaMar looked at the unfurling clouds overhead and put out a sea anchor. They could hear the Delfin all around them but see nothing. Gurl Hign took the flaplight on the bridge and made contact with Lem Fott. He signaled at once:

"Come, Rancher. Quiet."

She gave him back the OK and consulted with Poll.

"Take the longboat," said Poll. "I'll get Tug Trant, our strongman, and another rower."

"No need," said Gurl. "I'll take the cocker and young Jaygo can come along."

"What, that soft-handed little twix?"

"He has plenty of spirit," said Gurl, "and it's a flat calm out there."

"Don't stay out too long. There's a squall coming."

The cocker was a tiny boat; as she rowed steadily and silently Gurl was aware of the shapes in the water.

"All around us," murmured Jaygo. "Are they so intelligent then, Rancher?"

"Very much so but in their own way. They have no wish to be anything but Delfin."

"Are they as intelligent as the Vail?" he teased.

"How shall we measure it? The Vail claimed ten senses. We have five or six. I don't know the senses of the Delfin."

They drew alongside Lem Fott's boat and saw him as a dark figure in the bows. He opened his flaplight and they saw his odd reclining attitude, surrounded by his gear. Two long jointed tubes of wood and leather descended into the water; a drum, a small reed pipe, lay by his hand. He waved to them and began hooting into his tubes. They did not hear the reply.

"Here comes your greeting, Rancher!" he said.

There was a quick spattering of underwater sound, then four Delfin broke the surface some way off and set up the humming chorus.

"Steady," said Gurl Hign to Jaygo. "We are going to see the Leader, the One-In-The-Middle."

The water was parted in a golden cloud and the Leader danced upright, underbelly phosphorescent green, brow ridges stern, eyes moist and glittering. The great Delfin let out a loud screaming cry. Gurl Hign cupped her hands to her mouth and roared in the hollow tone they heard best:

"Ahoy! Ahoy Leader!"

The Leader dipped its beak, sent a welcoming jet of water into the cocker boat and uttered two words in reply.

"It spoke!" whispered Jaygo in astonishment. "It said 'Ahoy Gurl'!"

"That's my name, after all," she grinned. "It's easier for them to say than Rancher."

The Leader swam very close to the cocker boat and Gurl went on with the greeting. She extended a hand and lightly touched the highest brow ridge; it felt hard as bone and cold as the depths of the sea.

"This is Doc Jaygo," she articulated into her cupped hands.

"Doc Jay-go!" The Leader quacked and sent a jet of water into Jaygo's lap.

The intern cupped his hands and with a wild look at Gurl Hign he replied:

"Ahoy Leader!"

"What news?" asked Gurl.

"Show! Show!" replied the Leader.

It retreated, sent out a lofty column of water through its blowhole and was gone. The audience was over.

"Rancher," said Lem Fott, coming aft, "it is all true. They saw lights falling."

"The place?"

"Away to the west, above the Six Seven Isles."

"How long ago?"

"At least eight days."

"Where was the *Comet* at this time? How come LaMar and his crew saw nothing?"

"The *Comet* was even farther west, making landfall."

"Searching for the damned fever trees," said Gurl. "Pardon me, intern, but I would have had a human witness

124

as well as the Delfin. Lem, what else? What will they show?"

"Wreckage fell and sank; they have the place pricked off. Other lights went to ground by the Sooree River but this is a place where the Delfin will not go."

"I know it," said Gurl Hign. "It used to be thought they were put off by the fresh water."

"It is some old taboo for them," said Lem Fott, scratching his head. "I can't learn the cause."

"There were no survivors?" put in Gurl Hign.

"No, Rancher. I asked most particular," said Lem. "They say that three pieces of wreckage have been sent in the chain. One has arrived. . . ."

"Would that be the sleeve?" asked Jaygo.

"I expect it is," said Lem Fott when he had heard of the silver sleeve. "The next pieces will be here within the hour, so they say."

"Did you ask them for dead persons, Lem?" asked Gurl Hign.

"I did, Rancher. They made a strange answer."

"Tell me . . ."

"The sounds for floating-on-the-surface, which usually means a dead body. But they added a strong question . . ."

Lem Fott produced three hollow sounds.

"It is like they are asking what? what? what?"

"Perhaps it is a body in strange clothes," suggested Gurl.

"They don't take too much notice of that."

Jaygo and the Rancher sat as comfortably as they could in the cocker boat and watched the moonpearl dipping down and the stars overhead.

"The comet is there," said Jaygo. "It is the time of the Vail."

"The tailed star rides," said Gurl, remembering her dream.

"I suppose the Delfin have been questioned about our vanished sea monsters?" asked Jaygo.

"They deny all knowledge of the Vail," said Gurl Hign. "In fact they give back that strong question: what-what-what?"

"Master Fott," said Jaygo, "where did you learn this strange art of Delfin speaking?"

"From Old Robs, at his pearl farm, out there to the southwest," replied Lem Fott. "Are you a doctor, young fellow?"

"Not yet. I will be a doctor in one year."

Lem Fott scrawled the Jenzite sign on his forehead with a wet thumb and would not speak to Jaygo again.

After some time a ripple of activity spread on the sea around them; Lem Fott began speaking and listening with his long tubes.

"The second piece of wreckage . . ." he announced.

There was a flurry of motion, then a large Delfin flipped a ribbon of scarlet weed into Lem Fott's boat. He began to haul on the line steadily, then a bunch of weed appeared with a white object enclosed in its branches. He swung it into the air and shone the lantern. Gurl made some exclamation and Lem Fott uttered a cry of horror and disgust. Jaygo climbed surely across from the cocker and sat in the thwarts of the large boat, disentangling seaweed from the fingers of the white water-logged hand that was the second piece of wreckage.

"It is nothing to be afraid of," said the intern.

Then Jaygo gave a sharp intake of breath and Gurl Hign, watching the finely chiselled young face in the lantern light, swore that he was suddenly afraid, too.

"Rancher, could you take hold of this thing we have here?" Jaygo whispered.

"I can take a human hand, a dead hand," said Gurl Hign, "though I don't care for such a pitiful thing."

"You must be my witness."

"What is it?" she asked. "Lem Fott, please bear witness, too."

The fisherman peered, lips drawn back, then he gave a chuckle and reached forward.

"Ha!" he said. "It is not flesh and blood, Rancher. It is some poor devil's fake hand that he wore, like a peg leg. Very fine work, one would swear the skin was human skin."

"Let me see . . ."

Gurl Hign accepted the poor thing in its carrying package of seaweed branches.

"It was cut loose when the arm became entangled with saber nettles," she said. "There are deep cuts and nettle-marks at the wrist."

She looked at Jaygo and saw that his anxiety had not grown less. The workmanship of the hand was unbelievable; in the Rhomary land artificial legs were made of wood, hands were sometimes replaced by a metal hook. She had heard of a fine pair of metal tongs that Doctors' College had made to replace a hand but had never seen such a thing.

"Intern Jaygo," she said, "this is finely made. Doctors' College might learn much from it. Why does it bother you?"

"Perhaps I have a mad fear of such things," said Jaygo sharply. "It is nothing . . ."

Lem Fott, she noticed, was gloating a little over the intern's discomfort. He spat over the side of his boat and made the sign again on his forehead. Jaygo was already climbing back into the cocker boat. He gently touched the hand again, flexing the fingers; he stared at the Rancher with wide, girlish green eyes.

"The third piece of wreckage . . . much larger . . . is coming in the chain," said Lem Fott.

"It is hard to know when to speak and when to remain silent," said Jaygo. "I am afraid . . ."

Lem Fott chuckled again as if to say "we can see that" and Jaygo said nothing more.

"Tell us," said Gurl Hign. "Jaygo, what are you afraid of?"

"I won't violate the Primary Records in this company!" said Jaygo harshly.

Gurl Hign sighed. She wondered if the Rhomarians had become small-minded in their mutant years upon the planet, as well as stunted and splay-footed. Here in the night, on the wide expanse of the Red Ocean, with only the dim bulk of the trader *Comet* to remind them there were other humans in the world, the Jenzite and the young intern were sparring about their factions. She would not have believed it of Lem Fott; she had underrated the fisher as a simple soul whose only accomplishment was this Delfin speaking. It was equally mad to have Jaygo, quick and sensitive, hiding behind the Primary Records, that old buttress of the medical mystery.

"Coming now, far off," said Lem.

He replied to the underwater speakers who were keeping him informed and laid aside his equipment. He looked to the west; the humming chorus of the Delfin grew in that direction and Gurl saw that many Delfin were gently breaking the surface all around them.

The chorus swelled and at last they all beheld the formation of the chain itself, racing toward them across the blood-colored water. A ring of Delfin leaped with great swiftness and precision, their re-entry scarcely raising a flake of foam. Behind this swift-moving ring were other Delfin of all ages and sizes, some very young and tawny,

127

others deepest bronze with age. They moved in double lines but irregularly and with many pauses to frolic and to form their own moving circles.

She could see that within the ring of the escort there were two or three large Delfin supporting and bearing along with equal swiftness a piece of blue and silver wreckage that served as a raft. On the raft lay a human figure and as the chain reached them Gurl Hign saw that it was a youngish man in a suit of thick silver fabric. One sleeve had been torn away and the exposed left arm, pale and muscular, lacked a hand.

The raft was urged between the two boats; Gurl drew in an oar and came as close as possible to the piece of wreckage, supporting it. She shouted her thanks to the Delfin; there was thick spray everywhere and the air rang with their curious speech.

"What? What?" cried Lem Fott, giving the grand question himself. "Is he dead then?"

Gurl balanced the boat and Jaygo, without a trace of his earlier fear, swarmed half onto the raft and laid hands upon the man's body.

"Still functioning!" he said. "But he's unconscious—if that is the right word."

"Alive? Why didn't the Delfin say they had found a live man?" grumbled Lem.

Gurl found that she already knew the answer to his question. Jaygo drew back and handed her a small metal nameplate.

"Rancher," said Lem, "what is the matter?"

"Nothing," said Gurl Hign. "This is a strange find, Lem Fott. We have here a copy of a man. There is a word for it . . ."

"It is called an android," said Jaygo. "I will say . . . there were three in the Primary Records, who came to Rhomary with the Ship. Perhaps they were not so advanced."

"I was thinking of another word . . . roobo . . . robot . . ." said Gurl Hign.

She stared at the firm pale face and shone her flaplight directly upon it. The eyes were not fully closed; the face was relaxed, soft, the face of a child. She felt for the undamaged right hand and it was cold but a little circle of warmth lived in the palm of the hand. Gurl Hign made her decision but at a level so deep that it seemed to have been

128

made for her; there was nothing one could offer such a being but acceptance, even love.

"His name is John Miller," she said. "We must return him to the *Comet* and take him to the Doctor's Eminence. He must be mended."

As she spoke John Miller's hand closed gently upon her own for a few seconds.

Lem Fott scrambled to the bow of his boat and began to stow his gear noisily.

"Thank them . . . thank the Delfin," said Gurl Hign. "Say that they have done us great service and we will divide a catch with them seven times, as we have done in the past."

"If you say so, Rancher."

There was a round of ceremonial thanks; Gurl Hign stood up and addressed herself to the circling tribes of Delfin. Then, with the suddenness that is bound to exist between friends in two elements, the Delfin dived off and went away.

"Lem Fott," said Gurl, "come and look at this man's face. I don't want us to be afraid of him."

"I'm not afraid," said the fisherman doggedly.

He shone his light on John Miller and Gurl was puzzled by his expression. He did not show fear or disgust but prim disapproval . . . the look of Jenzites at a boozy harvest festival. For the first time she realized that she was cold and wet. The wind was rising and there was a difficult task ahead.

"What is the matter?" she repeated Lem Fott's words to herself.

"This is not a man, Rancher," he said. "I think it is a slave. I think it has no heart. It offends against the Book of Jenz."

"I don't remember the passage," said Gurl Hign flatly. "You must help us bring John Miller and this piece of flotsam he is resting on back to the *Comet*."

Lem Fott shook his head.

"I'll see to my gear," he said. "If I did right I would sink this evil thing forever in the sea . . . but I will not spoil the territory of the Delfin."

"Lem Fott, you bluggy fool!" she felt her anger surge up but she could see that he was determined.

"I will bring John Miller into this cocker boat," said Jaygo.

"It is too small for the three of us," said Gurl. "We must try and tow in his platform."

"Yes," said Jaygo, "but I will give up my place to him in the boat. I am a strong swimmer . . . I will go on or beside this raft."

As they worked to get Miller into the cocker and make the raft fast to its stern Lem Fott deliberately edged his boat away with a single oar. The wind had swung around; the squall was coming. Gurl saw the fisherman put up his sail and beat down into the darkness, heading for the river mouth.

When John Miller was curled awkwardly in the cocker boat . . . he was twice the size of Jaygo . . . the young intern lay upon the raft. Already the sea was choppy. Gurl Hign began to row, feeling a deep anxiety and a selfish one. What if she lost Jaygo, the Eminence's servant, even his favorite, in this recovery of one android, "still functioning?" They came slowly toward the *Comet,* hidden now in the spray and the darkness. Gurl used her lantern and hailed and the long boat was with them at once. She realized that it must have been standing by to help them. She was weary and trembling, hardly able to hold the ladder, to help lay out John Miller upon the deck.

She stumbled against LaMar who held her fast and offered a tot of grog. Gurl Hign drained it, cursing feebly.

"Where's Fott?" he demanded. "Why did he leave you to carry this fellow back?"

"Fott is a hard-headed Jenzite, but the intern is a pearl."

"Now what's with this water-logged specimen, Rancher, dear? Is he dead?"

"John Miller is not dead," she said. "Call for more light . . . take him below to the mess room. I want to speak to the whole crew, LaMar, if you will let me."

LaMar was watching the progress of the squall; no sooner was the longboat safely stowed than the wind hit the *Comet* broadside. Her sea anchor was in and she wallowed westward in the Red Ocean.

"We will lie out till morning," he said.

There were five lanterns shining onto the mess table where John Miller was lying; if he looked inhuman it was because, in all this light, he was one of the tallest and most handsome persons anyone had seen.

"By Jenz . . ." said a sailor, "it is an angel."

Gurl Hign wished that Lem Fott had taken this line.

"This is John Miller," she announced to the clustering

faces in the light. "He has come in an off-world ship as our people came to the Rhomary land years ago. He is a kind of helper: a robot, an android. There were some of these fellows in the Primary Records and I will ask the intern here to say their names."

Jaygo, who at one stage had looked angelic, was thin, ruddy-faced from Poll Grev's toweling, a cabin-boy wrapped in a blanket.

"Two androids were Jerry Turner and Philip Webb," he said. "Have you heard these names?"

"Phil Webb . . ." said an old sailor woman. "Strong as Old Webb, is what they used to say."

"He survived seventy-five years from the Landing," said Jaygo, "and died—wore out—at a human age of about one hundred and ten."

"Has no one heard of him besides Lilla?" asked Gurl Hign.

"Eh, Rancher," said the old woman again, "I know about him particular because he has a memorial in the Warren at Rhomary, outside my mother's house. The stone says: 'Old Webb who carried many burdens.' "

"This then is such another," said Gurl, "and we must welcome him and not fear him."

"Rancher, my dear," put in Cap LaMar, "perhaps the intern can tell us how this fellow came to be called *Old* Webb. Did he indeed grow old?"

"That is a mystery," said Jaygo. "Maybe his face did become weatherbeaten and his hair lost its color, bleached white."

"Another question," put in Poll Grev. "Is this a true man?"

No one was in any doubt as to what she meant and she received some teasing hoots for the question.

"He is made to look like a man," said Jaygo, unblushing, "but I do not think he can act like one. And certainly he cannot reproduce."

"Fair enough," said LaMar. "I think we have heard all we need to know. We should all do our best by this poor John Miller. What's more, I think he can hear what we are saying . . ."

There was a murmur of astonishment; everyone crowded forward. Then a long gasp echoed through the room; Gurl Hign felt the motion of the ship. John Miller's sound right hand slowly clenched and unclenched before their eyes; the corners of his mouth turned up minutely in the beginnings

131

of a smile. She looked at the crew, going back to work, and knew that John Miller had worked his magic a second time. There would be no talk of monsters or slaves. She called to them on impulse:

"Has anyone on this ship a copy of the Book of Jenz, the Jenzite scriptures?"

No one had such a thing.

"Were you planning on some gospel reading?" asked LaMar.

"Well, I had not set my heart on it," said Gurl Hign.

"Turn in, my dear. I'll be down presently."

Only a single lantern remained in the mess room. Jaygo dozed in a big chair, bolted to the deck; John Miller, lashed to the table, slid a little with the movement of the ship. Someone had placed a pillow under his head. Gurl Hign stumbled off to LaMar's cabin thinking of her long day, of the long years that had been lived on Rhomary till this moment, of the Delfin, bound by the time cycles of the sea, of the sweeping time waves where the Vail lived, each long, bright day encompassing many human lives.

## Chapter VII

### *Country Service*

Los Smitwode lay in darkness and listened to the intruder. A reasonably quiet and skillful intruder, but the timbers of the guest hostel were too sensitive. A step on the back veranda, two boards that creaked beyond the door to the doctor's own bedroom . . . not an assassin at any rate. There was a long silence; he sat up in bed and saw a faint glow of lamplight beneath the door.

He could move very silently himself, given the time; there was even a certain exhilaration in moving so stealthily. He remembered the cold passageways of Doctors' College in the dawn; as students they climbed back into the building after a night in the Warren or in Carcut, beyond the city walls.

It had not occurred to him to come armed; he went along the short hallway in four slow muffled steps. Was it Jaygo returned from the sea? Was it bad news that they were afraid to bring? There was nothing to steal in the main room of the house. Then the doctor remembered that something *was* there. He gave a sharp exclamation and strode into the dim light, preceded now by his own tall shadow. Doctor Gil Roak was crouched over the slip of wreckage examining the red-cross cupboard with the aid of a small, shaded lamp.

"How dare you!"

He heard his own voice, harsh and shocked. The young man did not speak; his expression was determined. The Third Consultant suddenly did not know what to do; he wished he had someone to consult. This was more than a breach of discipline in college and in any case breaches of discipline were handled with a moralistic ritual that he did not find relevant. Men and women had lost their scholars' places and been disqualified for less than this. He wondered if Gil Roak were mad. Had the thought of the box so worked upon him?

"Doctor Roak?"

"Eminence," whispered Roak through dry lips.

"What did you have in mind, man?" exclaimed Smitwode wearily. "Why are you doing such a stupid thing?"

He went to the supper table where a pitcher of cold herb tea was covered with a bead-fringed square of fine linen. He poured two beakers and motioned Gil Roak away from the wreckage impatiently.

"Sit here . . ."

Gil Roak obeyed, not taking his eyes from the face of the Senior. His words came with a rush:

"It must go to Rhomary. There's a racing parmel ready to take it on the portage. Have you opened it yet? Is there a report on the contents?"

"I've made a report," said Los Smitwode. "Were you intending to take it yourself, Doctor?"

"Yes," breathed the young man. "Yes, Eminence, let me take it. I've been favored by the Second Consultant, Mam Jons; she will remember. I've been five years in this place . . . really a time of testing, wouldn't you say, Eminence? My leave is due, but now I'm certain to be transferred."

133

"But your practice. . . ?" inquired the Third Consultant silkily. "Would you leave your practice, Doctor Roak?"

"Nothing pressing," said Gil Roak. "The accident rate is very low. All pregnancies midterm."

He took a gulp of herb tea; Smitwode reflected that his ambition had an effect like drunkenness.

"Technically," said Gil Roak, "there would be two practitioners left here: yourself, Eminence, and the intern. And when I came to the College bearing this . . . this unique discovery my promotion would follow speedily."

"Doctor Roak, you have close ties with persons on this station. I'm sure you would be missed."

"Yes," said Roak, "but there's nothing to keep me here."

"Not planning to marry?"

"What? No, not me. Difference of background."

Los Smitwode sighed; his patience with the young fool had almost run out. He believed that Roak's lack of style might not have mattered if he had made his appeal more directly, including the girl, Shona Dun Mor . . . if he had wished to advance himself and his beautiful young wife.

"Perhaps you are hasty," he said. "The city of Rhomary is comparatively old and plain. Everyone responds to a beautiful young woman."

Gil Roak moistened his lips; he gave a knowing smile.

"Of course I've heard stories. A beauty, as you say, may gain powerful protectors. But, of course, she would have to be schooled in all the civilized arts. Would you know any . . . eminent person who could arrange such an apprenticeship?"

"No!" said the Third Consultant sharply. "Doctor Roak, what has brought you to such a pitch of desperation? You are the son of a family of market gardeners. Your specialty was to be midwifery. Your grades have been fair to good. You are rated as hard working, of good address, even charismatic. I would be hard put to affirm any of these qualities!"

At last Gil Roak understood his own plight.

"You have deceived me!" he said in a loud, trembling voice. "I shall make my own report to the Second Consultant. Your judgment is clouded by evil influences . . ."

"Go away, you young fool, before you say another word!"

"The intern—Jaygo . . . living here with you . . ." panted Gil Roak.

"Jaygo is a brilliant student with connections of which you are unaware," said Smitwode coldly. "Quite immune from anything you might say, even if I were not."

"And the box . . . you were going to let me take it to Rhomary. We were here when it came," cried Gil Roak. "It fell from the stars into our laps. It is the chance of my lifetime. You have forgotten what it is like to lack advancement, if you ever knew it. Five years in this vile place among bluggy peasants and Jenzites!"

"The box was empty!" said Smitwode.

"Empty!"

Gil Roak sprang back to the piece of wreckage and tore open the door of the red-cross cupboard. The interior was of a sharp clinical whiteness and brilliantly lit. A complicated network of straps showed where the contents had been secured.

"You emptied it!" shouted Gil Roak. "You cleaned it out, you old idiot. This is one of your decadent games!"

"It was empty," reiterated Los Smitwode, as if he hardly took note of the abuse, "empty except for a large tube of antibiotic regenerative ointment."

"What? What was that? A new ointment?"

"For minor cuts, scratches and abrasions. Also good for sunburn. But the idea is not new . . ."

"Was there some mentioned in the Primary Records?"

"The formula was different and it was called Neo-Derm. This present cream is called New Skin," said Smitwode. "I am not sure if this indicates an anticlassical spirit or simply better taste in the choice of names."

He had already decided what to do in the case of Gil Roak. He reached for his red-leather folder which lay on the table and unlocked it with a silver key which he wore around his neck on a fine chain.

"Is your racing parmel ready to start?" he inquired.

"Yes," said Gil Roak.

"Then you will take the piece of wreckage and a small sample of the ointment, plus my written report that I have here."

"You are sending me to Rhomary?"

"For the present."

"Eminence, forget what I said. I was mad. This deep kindness . . . I'll be worthy of your trust . . . I was driven mad by five years of country service . . ."

Los Smitwode was engaged in melting a stick of wax in the flame of the lamp; he let the heavy drops fall on the folded jocca paper and sealed the package with his black ring engraved with the caduceus.

"When I was a young man," he said, "I did my country service in the settlement called Bork . . . two hundred kilometers north of Silver City. Population at that time about three hundred permanent, plus the daily parmel caravans."

"Very small," said Gil Roak.

"Very small and remote," said Smitwode. "I was there seven years. I really can appreciate the effects of country service on an ambitious doctor."

Already Gil Roak had recovered his composure.

"Is the report addressed to Mam Jons?" he asked.

"No. It must go to the First Consultant, the Chancellor himself," said Smitwode. "But it will be handled by his secretaries since Dom Artur is very frail."

"I understand, Eminence."

Los Smitwode shook his silver fountain pen until a shower of dark red drops fell on the table cloth. He began to scribble on a fresh sheet of jocca paper.

"This is my authorization for your transfer and for a Locum to be sent at once to the Gann Station," he said, without looking up.

He wrote three, four lines in a busy, minuscule script and sealed the paper into a tight three-cornered fold. Gil Roak kept his head elaborately turned aside.

"I will try to be worthy of your trust," he said again.

"Good!" said the Third Consultant briskly. "Now these will go in a mail pouch . . . I have one here. Wrap up that specimen . . . the first-aid box and its parts adhering . . . in that piece of felt the Rancher brought along. It can travel very well in an ordinary pack sling."

Before he attended to these preparations Gil Roak rose to his feet and went solemnly into the ritual of dismissal and departure. The Third Consultant made the responses with less restraint than usual. Two bells sounded from the tower behind the hostel and Los Smitwode checked his antique solar wristwatch. He lit a second lamp. When Gil Roak was ready to leave he looked up from his reading and said:

"Send the housekeeper, Mam Netta Hign, to make some fresh tea and to bring me news of the search."

After the young man had gone he sat for a long time in the lamplight thinking of the oasis called Bork: the vile heat, the lizard plagues, the dank cold of the nights. The population had more than doubled by this time; Gil Roak would be kept busy in his new practice.

The present incumbent . . . a woman, as far as he remembered, they stood up to the heat better . . . she would undoubtedly find the Gann Station a paradise, even as a Locum. He remembered that he had dreamed for years of his relief coming in just such a way . . . a sudden call, a letter of immediate transfer. It had never happened. He had served out every minute of his seven years in Bork at a time when his mother was Superintendent of Surgery at the College.

He heard a rattle of stove lids in the kitchen; then a shy voice said:

"Psst . . . Eminence?"

It was a thin, bright-eyed man in a gray cloak.

"Trim Hign, your Eminence, Dock Foreman. You asked for news. Alan Dun Mor said I should come tell you . . ."

"Of course!"

"The boats are long back and the boat of Lem Fott, the Delfin speaker, came back three hours later as a squall was coming up."

"A storm? Where is Intern Jaygo?"

"A squall, Eminence. Bit of a blow, that's all," said Trim, as the doctor strode anxiously to the hostel's front door and flung it open to look at the weather.

"It don't reach this far," Trim went on. "See? The Gann is no more than a bit ruffled. The young intern is on the trader *Comet* with the Rancher and Cap LaMar. They will ride out the squall and come in at first light, I'd say."

Los Smitwode looked down to the docks which were still busy and brightly lit with torches. Across the river he could see more lights, a string of pearls winding among the dark huts of the Jenzite village.

"What are they doing over there?" he asked.

"A holy-shout, Eminence. Middle of the bluggy night and all but sometimes they do that," said Trim. "When the wind is right you can hear their bell and their singing."

The night was cool; a breeze tugged at Smitwode's dressing gown of padded silk; he let Trim bolt the door.

"Mind you," Trim was saying, "this is a queer thought that Lem Fott has gotten hold of . . ."

"The Delfin speaker? What does he say?"

Trim hesitated and at that moment Netta Hign came in with the tea tray. She gathered Trim to her side with a fierce look and Smitwode recalled that they must be husband and wife. They stood together, small, dark strange-looking folk, Rhomarians; he did not look much different, he supposed, but he did not care for his part in the tableau . . . a senior doctor in a rich robe questioning the bluggy peasants. Suddenly he noticed that Trim had a filthy rag of a bandage on his right hand.

"Let me have a look at that hand, Foreman Trim," he said.

"It's nothing," said Trim. "I grazed it with a stone rasp, cleaning the bottom of my rowboat."

"Bring some warm water, Mam Hign," said Smitwode. "I'll see to it . . ."

"Eminence . . ." she protested.

"Come along," said the Third Consultant, smiling. "I am a doctor. In fact I am your doctor now, for some days. Did Doctor Roak get himself off?"

"Surely," said Trim, mystified. "Alan Dun Mor saw to his racing parmel and a driver and loaded that piece of a wreck into a sling."

Netta gave him a push and he settled into a chair and held out his injured hand. Los Smitwode went off to wash and to bring his own splendid leather-bound box of equipment. The graze was a bad one; Smitwode cleaned it and smoothed on New Skin. It had a thick silky texture; he did not mention where it had come from.

As he was cleaning the wound he asked:

"What was this the Delfin speaker had to say?"

"Ah, that was strange," said Trim. "You heard it, Netta: 'the body of a slave . . . a thing to be cast out . . .' "

"A thing to be cast aside," corrected Netta. "Yes, that was something from their scriptures."

"Did he mean that a body had been found?" asked Smitwode. "The remains of some poor off-world man from this sky ship?"

"Yes," said Trim, "a body and part of a body. He came in shouting and crying out to his own people."

"The way he put it sounded very bad," said Netta. "Something strange, monstrous, 'a thing with no heart.' And this is the thing they have aboard the *Comet*."

"I shall be interested to see it," said Smitwode.

He was puzzled; was it simply an unsightly corpse that had upset the Jenzite?

"Alan is hoping for no trouble when the *Comet* docks," said Trim.

"There has been coming and going across the river,"

said Netta. "The station people are upset. We don't get much excitement and now with this so-called wreck and the search."

"There was drinking . . ." said Trim.

"If you would hold the bandage so, Mam Hign," said Smitwode.

He fastened the knot with a little flourish and neatened the ends with his scissors.

"I hope things become quieter," he said. "Will the bells be rung when the *Comet* returns to harbor?"

"No!" said Trim. "No, by no means . . . that might set them all off, ringing the bells. We will send to you, Eminence, when the ship appears."

He surveyed his bandaged hand.

"I swear it is better already," he said. "How honored we are to have such doctoring!"

Smitwode, to his own surprise, felt pleased by the little man's gratitude. He had not busied himself with any procedure so simple for ten, twenty years. He went back to his room and, thinking of a sudden awakening, he dressed and lay down in his day clothes, an old student's trick.

Yet, as he lay on his bed waiting for dawn he began to feel angry and disappointed. He had been mixing in local affairs, punishing Gil Roak, punishing himself and Jaygo, for they must remain until another doctor was sent from Rhomary. Now there was riot and commotion threatened. And the starship that might have renewed their knowledge had sent, so far, a tube of New Skin. Formula far too complex to be produced in their laboratory. He shut his eyes, pierced by the moment of disappoinment: the damnable emptiness of the box.

He woke to the angry clangor of the station bells; it was broad daylight. The first confused sounds became regular, not a melody like Dodlo, the music for a search, but a strident three-note call. Hadn't Trim been afraid of an alarm?

The sound *was* alarming and to anyone in the hostel it was deafening. He looked from the back door and saw a fight develop in the bell tower; half-a-dozen men and women began shouting, inaudibly, and trading punches. One bell was silent, then another; the third went on ringing. Los Smitwode ran to the front of his wooden cabin and peered through the shutters: yes, the *Comet* had docked. He could see its masthead and banner above the crowds on the wharf; he could hear shouting and the chant of the Jenzites. The third bell had fallen silent.

There were quick steps on the back verandah and Shona Dun Mor ran into the hostel.

"Eminence . . . you must come with me. There's trouble!"

She was disheveled, there was a bruise on her upper arm.

"Were you fighting in the bell tower?" he asked.

"Jenzites," she said. "They rang the alarm. Please, Eminence, you can't stay here. Alan is waiting."

He took up the leather-bound kit, crammed in the red folder, took his cloak.

"Where am I to go?"

"We'll take you to the house first of all. We can get across behind the hedges."

"Is Intern Jaygo still aboard the *Comet?*"

"No. My mother, the Rancher, sent him off as soon as the ship docked. He's at the house. Please come . . ."

They ran out of the back door; Alan Dun Mor, some way off, screened by thin bushes, raised his hand. They ran to him stooping low. The hillside below them was dotted with figures; there was aimless shouting.

"Come, sir," said Alan Dun Mor. "We must get you off the station."

Before the Third Consultant could say a word Shona tugged his hand again and they ran past Alan down a long irregular slope into the back regions of the house, where Trim was waiting to pass them into the hall. Los Smitwode was blinded by his transition from daylight into semidarkness; then he made out a number of people keeping watch through the shutters.

A cluster of dark figures stood around the long hall table and drew back at his approach. He had some foreknowledge of what he would see, a fear being realized. Jaygo lay on the table unconscious; blood oozed, yes, thank heaven, still oozed from a ragged gash on one cheek.

He was already checking pulse, respiration.

"What happened?" he demanded.

"The Jenzite stoned the intern," said Shona Dun Mor. "Trim, you saw it?"

"The Rancher sent him off, double quick," said Trim, "before the trouble was half started. Then the damned preacher and Lem Fott started shouting . . . someone threw a stone. Alan and I and the teacher, Mr. Denny, we went in and got him out. But the poor lad fainted as we brought him here."

"Bring some light!" he ordered. "Is there a nurse aid?"

"I am one," said Shona Dun Mor.

The light, when it came, was barely adequate; it was, he told himself, more an exercise in self-control and concentration than anything else. He dismissed the anxious faces around the table.

"The intern is not badly hurt," he said. "Stand aside if you please."

As he prepared to stitch the wound Jaygo sighed and opened one eye; the other was puffed and darkening.

"Lie still," said Los Smitwode. "This will hurt. Three, four stitches."

Jaygo's pale lips moved; he bent down to hear the words. *"Save ... John Miller!"*

"John Miller?" he found himself whispering, too. "Who is that?

*"Must be saved ... report ..."*

The notebook was firmly clutched in Jaygo's hand.

"I'll see to it," said Los Smitwode. "Lie still. I've put on a local."

He laid a hand across Jaygo's eyes, closed them, then he turned for the needles that Shona Dun Mor held ready in their dish. He played over in his mind a difficult Caesarean he had performed five weeks previously. Jaygo's lips were compressed; no sound, then a faint groaning. *This is not to be borne, this helpless distillation of love and pity. A scar on the cheek, almost inevitable, but fine, the finest, this is fine work ...*

The last silver needle rattled back into the dish. Jaygo had fainted again. Los Smitwode, trembling, dabbed on New Skin and laid a dressing on the wound.

"Treatment for shock," he said to Shona Dun Mor. "Get him another pillow. Try the smelling bottle ... there, the blue flask."

He prised the notebook from Jaygo's fingers and walked into a thin shaft of daylight to read the report. Presently Alan Dun Mor came to his side.

"The dock is a little quieter, Eminence," he said. "You must leave. The intern can be carried. You can cross the Gann above this house at the falls ... we'll have a litter, parmels waiting. We can't risk ..."

"Do you know what they have aboard that ship?" asked Los Smitwode.

"I don't know what to call it," said the young man frowning. "A doppler . . . a copy of a man."

"An android," said Smitwode. "John Miller . . . still functioning. How can I tell you how important that is!"

"Eminence, we are responsible for your safety . . ."

"Alan Dun Mor," he said, "I cannot leave the Gann Station, for one thing, and for another we must have John Miller off that ship. You have some cool heads among the station people?"

"Yes," said Alan Dun Mor, "there's Mister Denny . . . Mam Dit and her sons. Besides my mother and the crew of the *Comet.*"

"Call them to me . . . I'll speak to all the people who are hereabouts . . ."

The Rancher's son looked at him in alarm, then he smiled, looking more than ever like his mother, and began calling to the folk in the hall. Los Smitwode went forward boldly and flung open the double doors onto the porch of the great hall. Daylight streamed in and the sound of raised voices from the dock.

"Trim . . ." he called loudly, "bring my cloak from the table!"

"Yes, Doctor!"

Los Smitwode stepped deliberately onto a bench and pitched his voice to penetrate a packed lecture hall.

"You know me!" he said. "Call your names . . . What's that? Billy . . . yes . . . and Mam Cross. I know Mam Netta Hign . . . Mam Dit . . . Is that tall boy called Little Diggy? Mister Denny . . . thank you for bringing the intern to safety. Who knows what they have in the ship *Comet*? Yes, indeed, it is a 'rooboter.' It is an android called John Miller. This poor fellow brings us the wisdom of Old Earth."

"The Jenzites have something in their book against these beings!" called Denny, the teacher.

"I can't believe it!" said Smitwode. "Jenz Kindl never saw an android. If he holds forth against, what was it, 'slaves,' or heartless monsters he probably meant doctors. Now I am a doctor . . . I am the Third Consultant of Rhomary, a high office . . . but right now I am *your* doctor. I have taken the place of Doctor Gil Roak while he travels to the city. And I tell you we must have John Miller off that ship! Therefore, all of you, stand with me, for I am going down to the dock!"

He paused and spun about his shoulders his long cloak of black silk emblazoned with a red cross.

## 2

Gurl Hign was below decks, choking down a bite of breakfast, still full of rage and fear. Poll Grev came and said:

"Something doing . . ."

"Are those bluggy fools attacking the ship?"

"More like a counterattack!"

She climbed up, right up to the bridge where LaMar strode, looking like a storm.

"There's a go!" he said, pointing.

She saw a little knot of people, no more than fifteen souls, moving slowly down from the Station House. She saw Alan, Diggy Dit, Trim and Netta; they came on slowly, in silence, descending the rough steps and ramps as if they were taking part in a procession. Alan was carrying a staff, so were some of the others. At the head there walked a slim black-clad figure that she could not place, and then suddenly she could.

"Great Vail! Look there LaMar, my dear . . . see who is coming to get us out of this hole!"

LaMar looked and began to laugh.

"The little beggar has some nerve!" he said. "The Doctor's Eminence in person!"

There was a reaction all through the *Comet;* sailors lounging all just out of sight or out of range of the dock stirred and peered out. Between the ship and the rescue party there stood about a hundred persons, some chanting or shouting, some standing about. The station farmers seemed no drunker than the Jenzites who never touched wine or beer. From the bridge of the *Comet* Gurl could look down on a sea of faces that looked all angry and half crazed. But if she looked more closely she could pick out here and there the face of a child or the troubled face of Marko, the preacher, or Mudflat Connl, boozed to the gills, and supported by his wife Milly, pale and sober. Gurl looked with something like hatred at the Jenzite elders, men and women in dark "seemly" clothes, the families of Dekk, Nujons, Fott, Peel, all chanting.

The party from the house took their stand on a last ramp almost as high as the ship's bridge. For a moment the noise of the crowd rose up; she seized the speaking cone and ran to the bridge rail. Then as the noise died down a little an extraordinary voice rang out, clear and sharp and penetrating as the wind in winter:

*"I have come to speak to the Rancher!"* announced Los Smitwode.

The voice struck at the crowd like a whip and in the few seconds' breathing space Gurl called into the speaking cone:

"I am here, Eminence. We're all unharmed in this ship, waiting for these folk to go to their homes."

"There is your Rancher speaking!" cried out Smitwode. "Go home, all of you. Let the crew and passengers come ashore!"

There was a roar from the crowd and a drunk shouted "And who the hell are you?" Then there was a hush, for the answer, because most of those watching had placed the stranger.

"I am your own doctor in this place," said Smitwode, "since Doctor Roak has gone to the city. I am more than that, for I am a member of the highest Councils of the Rhomary land and I order you to return home. There will be no listing and no trouble if you all disperse at once. What d'ye say, Rancher Hign?"

"Well said, Eminence!" shouted Gurl, thinking of two cross-talk comics in Flip Kar Karn's Tent Show. "Go home, you silly folk! Let us come ashore. There will be no taking of names. . . . How can you shame us with a riot at the Gann Station, the place of peace, before the Eminence here?"

Then Marko uttered the question they were all waiting for:

"What of this cursed slave, this thing with no heart?"

His question was echoed among the crowd: "rooboter . . . what of the bluggy rooboter. . . ?"

"I will tell you!" said Smitwode in his harsh schoolmaster's voice. "This is John Miller and he is called an android, which means a being made like a human. He is a helper. He is not a slave. Four of his kind came with our people long ago when our ship first fell down and landed in this world . . . they helped to carry our burdens long ago. Why should we fear John Miller? He brings us new wisdom. He comes from our ancient home . . . the planet Earth!"

And he lifted his white hands toward the blue sky with all the fervor of a Jenzite preacher. The crowd murmured, wavered. Then a Jenzite woman . . . Gurl thought it was Uschi Fott . . . screamed:

"*Doctors . . . murderers . . .*"

Gurl Hign looked into the cleared space that had opened up below the ramp where Smitwode stood and saw Lem Fott scooping up a stone. She called with all her might:

"Lem Fott . . . stay his hand. . . ."

Then of all people Mudflat Connl, reeling, casually raised up his good left hand and brought his fist down on Lem Fott's head. The tide turned at that moment; there was a spreading wave of laughter, directed at the Jenzites. Marko called some word of power and his people began threading themselves out of the crowd and heading for their boats which were moored behind the *Comet*. In some places they were hustled and Smitwode called again:

"Let those folk go to their village in peace. And stand from the *Comet!*"

"Now or never!" said LaMar.

He went tumbling down the steps from the bridge calling the names of sailors and Gurl saw the waiting stretcher with the form of John Miller brought up from below. The gangplank rattled down a second time.

"Coming ashore, Eminence!" called Gurl Hign.

"Thank you, Rancher!"

The crowd drew back to a respectful distance and John Miller was brought off the *Comet,* ringed around with sailors. They carried him over the dock and handed the stretcher up to the outstretched hands of the party from the Station House. Alan Dun Mor, Trim, Denny and the Dit brothers took the precious burden. Already the crowd was half gone; Gurl took her kitbag and gave LaMar a kiss.

"The old Eminence has pulled off something," she said. "Come to the house and eat."

"At midday," he said. "I'll see what can be done around the docks. Some cargo has taken a pasting."

"Fool, fools . . ." she said. "Have I made such a bad job of running the station to be put down with a show like this?"

"This is a once-in-a-lifetime show," said LaMar. "Not every day a rooboter falls from heaven."

She went down the gangplank and stumped across the dock not looking to right or left though voices hailed her, shyly and ruefully. She climbed the ramps and followed the procession ahead, the banner of the Doctor's cloak. Half-way to the house she looked back and saw the fleet of little boats taking the Jenzites across the Gann to their village.

# Chapter VIII

## *Finding Bulk One*

---

They slept in the boat hauled up onto the sand beside a tiny brackish stream that came from the jungle. Chan walked about, insisting that the air was fine and that she had the hang of the loozy gravity. She stared into what they called the jungle, a thick expanse of "trees," "vines" and fungoid growths without analogy. They were at some kind of watershed on this strip of beach below the hills: The jungle, ranging in color from pale moon-green to black, rolled off thickly toward the sunrise. There was a line of demarcation, a rift in the crust of the planet that began as a shallow ditch on the sunset side of the little stream. Beyond this deepening valley the vegetation developed fantastic desert shapes; a wide belt of stunted and twisted trees reached as far as they could see, merging into the brown desert sand.

On the second day as he walked on the strip of beach he found the pug mark of a large animal. He shouted for Chan and they bent over the footprint, measured it, sketched it, speculated, peered into the swamp, cracked as Crusoes.

"At least *he* knew what to expect!" said Chan.

Before their eyes in the moist gray-brown sand a second footprint appeared; the hair rose on the back of his neck: the invisible creature had hopped half a meter. Then the pair of them gave a bellow of relief and disappointment and began to dig in the sand. The culprits were bronze, clover-shaped creatures resembling sea urchins, about half the size of the pug mark they produced. Chan boiled them up for supper out of sheer revenge.

She spoke up after they had eaten, in the blue evening, when the comet rode in the sky.

"Doc, I'm oriented. We have to go look for Bulk One."

"Which part . . . ?"

"The left radial arm."

She drew a diagram in the sand and he peered at it in the twilight. The shape of the *Serendip Dana* was something he could not associate with its cool interior, the endless corridors and the womblike luxury compartment he had inhabited.

"It was set to come down about two degrees northeast . . . call it that . . . of where we went into the big lake," said Chan, "and that would put it right in there. . . ."

She turned and stood pointing into the jungle over the stream. He thought: I don't want to go in there. Then he looked at the twisted trees and the desert . . . that might be worse. He looked at the hills and felt vaguely tempted. What was beyond the hills? A particular dip in the brown contours pleased him, he thought of it already as a pass, a pass in the hills. But the lure of Bulk One . . . other humans . . . bulked large in their thoughts.

Chan filled him up with information as they lay naked in the boat:

"There was a low complement on Bulk One. Twenty-one, twenty-five, I don't know."

"But our capsule had only three . . ."

"It was a mutch-up. We coulda taken four more, but it went too fast. I put in the call, last thing I did. Shee-it, Doc, we were scared. I was set to go back down the gang, grab couple mensh from the Fiver . . . they were crowded . . . but the panels were alight, the walls were screaming for let-go. Miller came, said he was assigned so I didn't haul nobody. Then we were let go."

He remembered her vaguely: a tall, competent figure mothering him into his suit and into the capsule that had made up a corner of his suite. Now he felt her trembling in his arms.

"You did fine. Tell me about Bulk One."

"Shee-it, it is the biggest. They had the best chance. They had growing plants, livestock. Doc . . . imagine that."

"What did they have?"

"Faggidy guinea pigs, rats, coupla *dogs,* coupla goats, a whole raft of canary birds and budgies. Oh Doc, to see those types flying around *here. . . .*"

"What about Fiver?"

"Biggest complement. Fifty-five souls. They were strung out to the northwest, then came Four, Two and Tree, that's us, all over the landmass. Who knows. Sexer was a smaller capem, only a little larger than ours. It would have come down in that red sea, I reckon. Sexer had the brass, the log-banks. Faggidy sharp-heads . . . I can see them floating around out there shouting to the sea serpents: 'Take me to your Lead-ah!' Only maybe they died, drowned. We nearly drowned, up the creek . . ."

They slept fitfully and rose up in the dawn. They checked their suits, took water, filled their rucksacks from the boat carefully. Chan packed a hand weapon that she called a blaster. He cast about for ways to blaze a trail; they must be able to find the boat again. The boat yielded a spraycan of virulent yellow marker dye to be used in an emergency splashdown. They set off, Chan leading, and once they were out of the roots and suckers of the swampy foreshore made fair time. He could look back and see the screaming yellow trail he was making from tree to tree, from growth to growth.

The gravity tugged at them. He told himself resolutely that this was nowhere near as difficult as a trek through old-time jungle, the Amazon basin, back home. But the strangeness of the terrain made him shudder. The soil between the sticky tree-stems was porous and damp, sometimes chocolate-colored, sometimes almost white. The stream climbed laboriously away from them up the edge of the rift formation. Chan deliberately struck further east.

On earth such a jungle would have teemed with life but the count of living creatures increased slowly. Chan drew back, stepped on his foot, breathing hard. A gray shape twisted away into the fleshy fronds of the undergrowth: lizard or snake. Then came the bract insects, leaf-shaped, leaf-colored, hanging in clumps or flexing gently on the sinuous branches of the trees. When they sank down exhausted after five long hours they had to sweep away a whole colony of these creatures, some dead and transparent, some still living.

There was a horrid pulpy softness about the place which made him long for rocks and logs. He walked on, trudging in Chan's soggy footprints; she tried to climb a huge black umbrella of a tree and it bent down under her weight. She went on pushing angrily at the soft tree growths, trying to find one that could be climbed. She wanted to look about and he found himself just as anxious for an überblick.

He dreaded the coming of night; it was the swamp all over again, the awful stillness had swallowed them up, digested them. The ground seemed to ooze and heave under the ground sheet as if they were on the back of a leviathan. There was no wind, but a light mist exhaled from the moist landscape. They sat in a damp, black cave with a bright sky overhead.

"*That* is in the system," said Chan. "Little yellow planet overhead and maybe that red one just there, through the trees, you see?"

"Psst . . ." he had imagined another sound.

They listened. Nothing disturbed the enormous damp, black stillness of the night. No predators howled, no bright eyes peered through the trees, no noxious insects came to suck their blood. He deliberately doled out sleeping capsules and they slept, pole-axed, until the slow dawn crept through the blue-black trunks. They found on this second day out a tangle of tougher vines that allowed Chan to climb up a few feet. He climbed up beside her, rested a foot on her shoulder and looked over the low roof of the jungle.

"Look for breaks!" called Chan hoarsely. "Wreckage, anything solid—"

He saw hectares of unbroken, leathery foliage. It was unnerving, but for the first time almost beautiful. There were no breaks but the ground to their right began to slope upward, the colors of the vegetation altered a little. He came down and they wound to the direction Chan called north. He was seeing a new, strange beauty everywhere. He drew back his hand with the trusty spraycan of yellow paint and marked a tree trunk rather than a bunch of "leaves" with turquoise lights in their ruched edges.

They slept another night and next morning the landscape changed under their feet with every step. It became drier; the soil was less unearthly. The undergrowth, then the trees themselves, were interspersed with tougher, more woody species. At midday they encountered their first hard wood or hardwood tree.

They stood slapping at the smooth, hard trunk and staring up into the branches fifteen meters overhead.

"It still ain't right," said Chan, "but it sure is hard."

Nothing was right about the forest even yet. The trunk of this tree was hard as metal, dense, shiny; it had a thin rime of red-black bark and beneath this the substance of the tree was black and hard as basalt. He snapped off a piece from one of the new woody bushes: the interior of the brittle stem was divided into tough longitudinal segments full of dusty, crystalline pith. It looked weird enough

149

to him, he couldn't imagine what a botanist would have made of it.

"Okay," said Chan wearily, "but how we gonna climb this big stack and get a look around?"

"No problem . . . if we can get a rope over that branch . . ."

He was already paying out the nylon rope from his pack.

"Easy said," grumbled Chan.

She fiddled with setting of her blaster and fastened the rope to a metal spike.

"What makes you so sure you can race up this monster, Doc, even if the loozy rope goes the right place?"

He grinned and shook his head. How could he explain that ten years ago . . . was it so long? . . . he had gone up the north face of the Eiger. Chan motioned him aside and took careful aim; the blaster gave an unsatisfying soggy plop and the rope sailed obediently over the branch after the metal spike. The thin bark gave a better foothold than he had hoped and he had the satisfaction of looking down at Chan's face, astonished. The remark that floated up had something to do with a mountain goat.

He climbed higher and looked out. He saw that they had climbed the side of a deep valley. This long curving ridge, which rose a good deal higher than the point they had reached, was covered with the lighter, brownish-green foliage of the hardwood forest. He could see where they had come, the dark, moist expanse of the "soft" jungle, and it stretched almost to the horizon in the east. To the west the ground fell away in that rift which had begun at the shore; he guessed that beyond the rift again the landscape shaded into that forbidding place of twisted trees on the edge of a desert.

He looked down more keenly into the valley below him; he saw the line of demarcation between moist and dry. He saw, not far away, a deep scar, black on black, in the soft jungle. He blinked, screwed up his eyes, felt his heart thumping painfully. He saw a thin strip of blue, hard and bright, just above this scar on the far side of the valley. He began shouting and Chan understood him.

"The drogue!"

She jumped about and slapped the tree trunk.

"Doc! Doc! We found them . . . take a line on the drogue. Come down . . ."

He came down so quickly that he burned a hand on the rope.

"Chan . . ."

"Come on Doc . . . oh heaven, to see Bulk One . . ."

"Chan, the scar was black . . . the break in the jungle was black."

He gripped her fiercely around the chest.

"Chan, the section burned."

"How can you tell?"

She broke away from him, staggered and sat down awkwardly among their scrambled gear at the foot of the big tree.

"Doc, please . . ."

"Don't . . . don't *hope*, Chan."

"We have to go there!"

"I know it. I know it better than you do!" he panted. "But it is a crash site."

He led the way down the ridge; he had "taken a line" as best he could. The landmarks he had chosen, two more hardwood trees, a paler clump of vines, were easy to find. They came into the soft jungle again and both floundered, panting and cursing, driven by a painful anxiety. He believed the line was lost, he was leading them away from the site. Then Chan cried out.

She had seen an alteration in the forest roof, ahead and to the left. They were on a sharp downward slope, tobogganing down through the dark softness; the smell of burned vegetation enveloped them suddenly like a patch of fog. The jungle had melted stickily at the bottom of the valley, the smell was like overcooked fruit, burned jam. They came to a place where a huge shape blotted out the light.

They clung to a fused mass of vines; all they could see was a long wall of blackness towering above them and breaking into ragged crenelations against the sky. He stared for a long time and made out little more than a hint of metallic structure. The wall branched away from the point where they stood in two directions. Large grayish flakes of ash broke off and fell into the sumpy trench that surrounded the wreck. Bulk One. He guessed that the bottom of the valley had been unusually soft, even for the soft jungle; Bulk One had landed in a swamp.

Chan squelched out from behind him and went right up to the wall of blackness, sinking in past her boot-tops. With a rasping sob, loud as a scream, she struck out, not with a stick for there were none in the soft jungle, but with a rubbery plant, uprooted. The ball of mud and root fibers struck the blackened skin of Bulk One with a muffled resonance, an oxidized clang that vibrated through the whole structure.

He was suddenly anxious to get her away. The blackened shell filled him with dread: the loss of hope, the certainty of death and destruction would destroy Chan's reason.

"Come this way . . ."

He struck off to the left, around the wreck, trying to stay clear of the syrupy water that spread out from the crumpled metal. Chan followed without a word. They saw portions of the surface less charred, ghostly projections and illegible lettering under the coating of ash and mire. More light shone before them; the thickets of the soft jungle had been destroyed by the wreck. The light had changed, inexplicably, to a haze of pure green. They waded and trudged around a hideously bent and misshapen dome of metal and came into another world.

They came back for an instant to their own world. The sky overhead was blue and the leaves were green, an unforgettable sweet, bright, succulent green. Chan reached out and plucked a spray of the rioting green. The vines were earth plants, quick-growing, some common as weeds: morning glory, busy lizzie, philodendron.

Bulk One had fallen, burning, into the valley and had curled and bent on impact. The tail section, the last thirty meters, lay higher, on a hump of ground; the blue drogue that had broken its fall was twisted in the trees. He guessed it was the only drogue that had opened. The tail section was scorched silver and brown; it had not burned. They could see the green vines spilling out from the open cargo doors; in ten days of the new world they had half covered the tail section and the hillock on which it stood and were working along the shore of the dark pond on the inner side of the wreck.

Chan caught his arm; her lips were drawn back against her teeth.

"Doc . . . there's one . . ."

The first. He sniffed the air and put on his gloves before pulling back handfuls of green. A dead man, no, a dead woman in a silversuit. The face calm, only a little bloated although the suit was ballooning with decay. Cause of death: head injury; a wonder she had come so far. The woman had staggered out to die in the air. He collected the name tag and motioned Chan away. He thought of the products of decay loosed upon the soft jungle, saw Bulk One for the first time as a source of pollution, an alien pustule suppurating in the quiet valley.

"Gloves . . ." he said to Chan.

"Must have come from the tail section," said Chan.

They went forward again; he passed the name tag into Chan's gloved hand.

"Girl with red hair," she said, "worked with the animals."

She slipped the tag into the kangaroo pocket of her suit. Without warning a cloud of small birds rose up churring and chattering.

"I told you!" shouted Chan, "Look Doc . . . the earth birds have landed!"

He recognized budgerigars and finches, saw them in an instant spread out over the whole of the new world. They began to climb up the small green-covered hillock on which the tail section rested. It was an unusual formation to be found in the soft jungle; he wondered if there was rock beneath the spongy covering of soil and plant growth that nourished the earth vines so well. Perhaps a meteorite had landed here. . . . They were on the slope near the cargo doors and a voice said quietly:

*"Chan . . ."*

The leaves made a curtain; Chan parted the leaves and stepped through. He peered around her.

*"Chan . . ."*

She went down on her knees.

"Hello, Ed."

The man lay propped against a gray molded chair ten meters from the open cargo doors. The leaves had grown loosely over and around his legs but his chest and arms were free. A big plastic jerrican of water and a Q-pack of emergency rations rested beside him. The man's beard, sprouting in black tufts, showed up the awful pallor of the skin. As he checked the man's pulse, laid a hand on the clammy skin of his forehead he read the name tag: Ryder E.D.D. The voice was weak and wheezing.

"Hey, what you pull, Capem Tree, Chan?"

"Ed, this is some break, some loozy break all along the ine."

"I have to examine him," he said.

"What the fag . . ." wheezed Ed.

"This is the doc, the V.I.P., the supercargo," said Chan.

153

"We hit a ways down southeast, came here by boat and walking. It is a medic, Ed."

The man stared at him with sunken, glittering eyes; they shared a guilty secret, a total lack of hope.

"You get any bleeping?" whispered Ed Ryder. "Anyone else meld themselves?"

"Not a flicker," said Chan. "Your pickup still working?"

"Not sure. Had a weak signal two, three days ago, maybe longer, I lose track; since then nothing."

"Shee-it," said Chan. "My loozy pickup is out for sure."

He cleared his throat gently to remind them of his presence. A piece of bedside manner that came as naturally as breathing.

"Go in the holds, Chan," said Ed Ryder. "It ain't bad. Go bring me some OSV from the green store locker."

Chan stood up and turned toward the open cargo doors.

"Anyone . . . ?"

"No," said Ryder. "There were only three of us. The other two, Voychek and Bateman are both . . . gone."

"We found Voychek," he said.

"Bateman is yonder, I guess."

Ryder pointed vaguely toward the far side of the hillock.

"Go in the ship, Chan," he said. "Let the doc look at me."

She put down her pack and went off, tearing aside the vines in great handfuls. He began to do the same with the green that surrounded Ryder.

"I don't . . . want . . . to . . ." said Ryder feebly.

"What?"

"Dead," said Ryder. "My legs are dead. Hole in my back."

It explained his attitude, the way he lay propped against the chair.

"Dead from the waist down," said Ryder. "Hate to look."

He screwed up his eyes.

"Been . . . planted here for a long time, it feels like."

He had already uncovered Ryder; the tough silversuit was pierced and torn, Ryder had worn it rolled down to the waist; he cut him out of it. What he saw *was* hateful. When he rolled him onto a ground sheet and began cleaning him up Ryder moaned at last.

"Your chest . . ." he said.

"One, two ribs," whispered Ryder. "Painful . . ."

He had come to the borderline. Ryder was more than

154

half dead, his tolerance must be minimal, yet he wanted Ryder to wake and talk again. He gave him a shot that would have been pre-op for a docile child and Ryder was out so completely that he wondered if he had lost him. The pulse still fluttered, the breath heaved and gurgled in the damaged chest. He went on cleaning the flaccid body, using too many of his precious cleaning packs. As he approached the frightful wound on Ryder's back he used the little japanese suction cleaner; it was meant for fine work but on a broad setting it vaporized dirt and scraps of proud flesh.

He cleaned on and on, changing his disposable gloves, until he was at the point where the patient should have been handed over to a team of nurses who would wheel him away and get him ready for a surgeon. But there was no team and, reason told him, there was no other surgeon ever anymore. He was on call forever; he was on call now, on the ground sheet in the clear light, among the waving, intrusive tendrils of the escaped earth plants and the rubbery excrescences of the soft jungle.

Chan came back, her arms full of food packages.

"How is he?"

"I need a board or a tabletop," he said, "and a clean ground sheet or something like it."

"I'll set it up near the ship," she said. "There's a table."

She went away and he heard a crashing and tearing. Chan swore, then he heard her voice become gentle, she whistled, pleaded, muttered. He could not leave Ryder. She came back again and said:

"Okay, Doc, shall we move him?"

"Who . . . what were you talking to?"

"Something ran off," she said. "Reckon it was one of the dogs. Small stuff, guinea pigs, gerbils, have been put down in their cages. Birds let loose . . . plants *got* loose . . ."

They carried Ryder a little way up the slope and laid him on Chan's table. She had put down a metal door, topped by a dural crate and topped again by a tabletop, metal, from a lab trestle. He doubted that he would have been able to move some of these things. There was a clean plastic cover on the table; he dressed Ryder in a new thermo-pack suitliner, cut a hole in it, cleaned his hands with the Yamamoto Little Giant, put on surgical gloves and went to work. Not to think, not to think too much about infection, risk, assistance, post-operative treatment . . . here and now he must do it.

Chan stood by Ryder's head, propped on a foam chair seat, and listened to his breathing. He worked alone except for the instruments; the magic of some of them was still impressive to him although he had been "welding" nerves and using the sonic scalpels for years. He knew this was probably their swan song; they were good for three earth months without a recharge, but he was just as confident with steel. And though he worked for two hours and was fed OSV by Chan and turned to the hopeless task again, he could do no more than patch the man up, for all his art.

Ryder was hovering in and out of consciousness. He applied tissue regenerator, analgesic dressings; he strapped Ryder's ribs.

"A silversuit would be best," he told Chan, "We could connect the waste system."

"He can have mine."

She stripped off her suit and went back to the hold wearing her boots and underpants. She came out again arrayed in green work trousers of slippery, shiny synthetic and a big red and white anorak over a T-shirt.

"Faggidy trade goods for the colonists. . . ."

He found her beautiful and strange, a colonist herself now. They put Ryder into the silversuit with its possibilities for dealing with double incontinence. Ryder had been made comfortable. He sat by him for hours, afraid of shock, wondering why shock had not killed Ryder long before this. After some time Ryder asked for water; he blinked at the light and said:

"Did you see her? She don't come much during the day, but evening she's always here . . ."

Chan shot a wild glance over Ryder's head, then asked cautiously:

"Who should we see, Ed?"

"She's a little shy," said Ryder, "but eating well and not only stuff from the ship, y'know. Getting acclimatized."

"What became of the dogs, Ed?" she asked.

"Their handlers took 'em back into quarters," said Ryder. "They . . . went . . . with the rest."

He sipped more water and went on in the same flat, determined voice.

"Pure chance, y'know, pure chance I came down, joined the zoo people, Voychek and Bateman, after split-off. Beattie, you recall Beattie, he was ranking in Bulk One . . . no sooner I'm here checking the seal on the cargo doors than Beattie slammed all bulkheads down. Shields and electrics

156

musta been on the way out before split. No chance . . . no chance *not* to burn. The freak accident was that we didn't. Insulation better . . . I don't know. I talked with Beattie . . . for quite some minutes. . . ."

His pale face twisted; Chan covered his mouth with her hand.

"Enough . . ." she said gently. "Eh, Doc."

"Enough," he agreed. "We're making camp, Ryder. Here beside you."

He heard a sound, a real sound in the tangle of greenery and saw that they had all heard it.

"She's coming . . ." whispered Ryder. "A dish . . . needs a water dish . . ."

The incredible sound was repeated and then, as they all stared, the leaves were parted, not even knee high, about two meters from where he was standing. A pretty white head appeared, drooping ears, *O Schwannli, O meine liebe Schwan* . . . Ryder made feeble clucking noises; Chan, moving very softly, poured water into a box that had held a dressing and passed it across to him. He knelt down in the morning glory and moved the offering toward the little black and white goat. She withdrew her head, he thought he had lost her and crooned and clucked like a mad mother. He set the dish down and she stepped daintily through the leaves and drank. Her human audience watched in breathless admiration; she began to nibble the empty container.

"Nein, nein . . ." he whispered.

He brought out a protein stick from his pocket and she ate it down, went off into the green. They were giddy with delight.

"A goat," said Chan, "a goat like Cook left behind."

"African dwarf goat," said Ryder faintly, "dunno her proper identification."

"Just one female?" he asked.

"Pregnant," said Ryder. "Voychek said so. And she'll have two, male and female. There was her mate too, only he didn't make it, I guess. She was the only thing ever came, her and a few bloody budgies. Now you're here."

Ryder's face glowed with a fearful joy, as if the skull were visible beneath the skin.

They made camp, mostly Chan made camp, he was jittering with post-operative nerves. They took turns sitting beside Ryder all through the long night, holding him when he coughed, giving him sips of water. They talked a good deal to keep the patient from talking too much. He found

157

himself telling Ryder about their own adventures, about Miller, swept away down river.

"You could have done with this Miller," said Ryder sententiously, "they're towers of strength, the old oxper."

But he was already full of doubts that he dared not express. Would he and Chan have become so close in the company of any third person, even or especially an android? Three's a crowd. Chan came to take over at first light and he fell into an exhausted sleep on their ground sheet. He forgot the jungle and the strange stars overhead and the dreadful black shape of Bulk One looming nearby. He slept deeply and naturally and returned in dreams to Earth. He woke with the sun high in the heavens; Chan was shaking him.

"Doc, come and look!"

"Ryder?"

He snapped wide awake.

"Ryder is holding," said Chan. "Come see around the back of the hill."

He got up, sucked guiltily on another tube of the spacer's favorite high, orange concentrate with supravite, then checked Ryder himself. The big man was dozing under the canopy of vines they had rigged to keep the sun off his face. He followed Chan around the back of the hill. The earth vines gave way to the soft jungle again; they stepped between two umbrella trees. He saw an exquisite round carpet of pale blue bracts and darker leaf growths. It was beautiful and unexpected, a jewel hidden in the bottom of the valley; he thought of a mountain meadow covered with gentian flowers.

"Watch this!" said Chan.

She jumped on the spot with all her might. A slow ripple edged through the blue carpet but did not reach the center. She fished from her pocket a dressing box and threw it like a frisbee into the middle of the circle. They watched the light object disappear, slowly, slowly sucked under. Chan ducked under the umbrella tree on her left and led him by the hand along the banks of the quagmire.

"Bateman found it!" she said, pointing.

There was a distinct trail of slithering boot marks down the steep bank; out among the blue bracts, delicate as butterflies, they could make out a scatter of foreign bodies. A glove, a Q-pack, some kind of folder or wallet. As they watched, the glove was sucked under again, then with a soft pop some other object rose, some distance away.

"What is it?" he asked.

"Helmet," she said. "He had it off, I guess. Came through here and slipped."

She stood up and the treacherous soft ground retreated beneath her boots; she was sliding just as Bateman had done. He flung himself flat, caught her arm, hauled back as hard as he could. There was no sound but their rasping breath. Chan reached for a handhold but the sticky growths came up in her fist. She swung her body sideways and they got clear, millimeterwise, like snails on a slope. They went on crawling, rolling until they could barely see the blue surface. Chan was sweating with fear; her new clothes were heavily streaked with mud. He held her in his arms and experienced the pain of love, the fear of loss.

"In a silversuit I might not have made it," she said. "You should get out of that loozy thing, Doc. We're all colonists now."

They staggered back to camp and he changed Ryder's dressings; the patient was perceptibly weaker; he had long periods of drowsiness.

"Keep me awake, Doc. I must tell . . ."

"Rest . . ." he said.

"I will," said Ryder. "Lemme talk now . . ."

He fed Ryder another of the fruity vitamin boosters . . . blackcurrant lift . . . and let him talk.

"It was bad when we made landfall," said Ryder. "Hotter than hell inside those holds; the company up front had stopped talking. We were set to break out in seconds when she touched, to escape frying. We had to wear our full tack, y'know, helmet and tank, we were afraid of the tanks blowing but we had no idea what the air would be like.

"At the end it went very fast, felt like we bounced, rolled; I heard Bateman cry out. Last thing I did was open the seals and spring the hatches, then a loozy crate crushed me against some broken metal. I couldn't move. There was a lot of noise from the front end . . . hissing, popping. I had fouled the tubes of my gear, nearly suffocated until I got the helmet off. Shee-it, was that some sweet air.

"I tried to call to them. I saw Voychek go past outside, staggering; I never saw Bateman, just heard him crying out, slipping and crunching in that jungle. Then there was no sound, no other human sound, Doc, and I was scared, especially in the night. The front end took days to cool; it made waves of heat, stinking heat. I had my Q-pack and Voychek had given us all these big jerricans of distilled

159

water. The crate came off me more easily than I had thought; I took a long time to drag myself out, just the arms and shoulders."

"Hush," he said, "take a break, Ryder."

Ryder paused and drifted off again into his half-sleep. He wandered away to the open hold; Chan was playing about outside with pieces of ply and duro from the broken crates. He climbed inside Bulk One; the plant-and-livestock section had been separated from the cargo hold proper and there were two sets of cargo doors side by side. Most of the supplies lay behind the bulkhead; the whole structure had taken a half turn. The confusion and destruction reminded him of a filmset, artistically crumpled. The crated supplies in the outer hold were mainly clothing, brightly colored and old-fashioned in cut: trade goods for the colonists. He searched until he found a small pair of the shiny pants, a yellow sweatshirt, a good anorak.

A crate spilled out some queer footwear: thick soles, nonmagnetic . . . he thought, laterally, of a wall built of shoe soles. He picked up a sample and found these were long loose boots, waders, of heavy-duty synthetic, yellow and black, something the colonists had need of in Arkady. The hold had a dry warehouse odor, but he smelled, underneath, a stink of burning. He had meant to change his clothes but instead he remained in his silversuit and found a pair of the waders to fit. He had somewhere to wade, he realized.

"What have you got there, Doc?" asked Chan.

"I have to check . . ."

He pointed.

"Leave it . . ." said Chan softly, "you got no reason."

"For the record."

He hitched the braces of the black waders into position, took the handlamp they had brought from the boat and began to wade through the black sumpy water surrounding the burned section of Bulk One. He was heading for a break, a gaping hole in the innerside of the long twisted cylinder. In some places he sank in nearly to his chest; he clung to the slippery trunks and fronds as if they were old friends. He came to the black hole which exhaled a smell of damp soot like a rain-wet chimney. He shone the torch into the hole and like every dreadful thing it was not, at first, half as bad as he had imagined. There were no bodies to be seen, simply a section of what might have been corridor. There was a totality of destruction, everything changed, fused, melted.

He climbed in with difficulty. The wall held his weight, the floor was canted above his head; struts and projections, whatever they had been, crumbled when he touched them. He edged to a position but it would not budge; he crawled through rags of wall-padding, turned to sludge and ash and a door, lying sideways, yielded to his double kick. The blast of foul gas was so strong that he choked and rolled away back to the air, stuck his head out and panted. He tanked up, filled his lungs, quickly slithered back and shone the light and looked. Then he came out, right out, and strode back through the black water. Destruction complete. A number of human beings in that compartment . . . *verkohlte Leicher.* . . . No pockets of unburned oddments this trip, not even the unburned feet in the sturdy boots.

Chan came and helped him out of the swamp.

"Satisfied?"

He could only shake his head, lips compressed. He clambered out of his waders, then out of his silversuit, and ran uphill, through the vines and the sunshine to the place where he had left his clean clothes. Behind him Chan laughed, then choked off her laugh as if she had remembered where she was.

He sat beside Ryder for nearly the whole of the long day, doing what he could, which wasn't very much. He played at being an intensive care unit and Chan played with her pieces of ply and duro. The little goat came to be fed and sniffed at the edges of the ground sheet which marked their camp. He sat idle, sniffing the air himself; he did not trust the place, even the green hillside felt unwholesome. When it was evening he went and asked Chan what she was making.

"A sled," she admitted. "We have to take Ed Ryder out of this loozy place."

"Come and eat something," he said.

When she hesitated, he said:

"The goat is back . . ."

She came then and they sat on the ground sheet until the night came down and they were in the familiar black cave with the strange system overhead and the small moon. When Ryder rallied again they turned on the handlamp and let him talk; they took turns sitting beside him. He had talked so much after days of silence that his throat became sore, he had to take medication for his throat. But Ryder still talked in a thin, clear voice.

"Don't worry, Doc. You don't have to worry about me. Look after Chan."

"I'll do that," he said.

"She was a real friend, Doc. You don't know what it means to see a real friend, an old friend, this way. Oh sure we made it for a while, couple years ago, but lately it was just friendship. I guess you heard the talk about spacers, how they fuck around, close quarters, orgies in the sky . . ."

"Oh sure . . ."

"It's like that and it isn't," said Ryder. "On a good ship like the *Serendip* the atmosphere is . . . friendly."

"I went to the South Pole once on one of the big Russian Lab Ships," he said. "I guess the atmosphere was something the same. Friendly . . ."

"Shee-it, Doc," said Ryder, "you get around. I always wanted to see the South Pole."

Then, changing the subject, he said:

"Chan said something about a plesiosaur-type creature making speech-sounds."

"I expect I was hallucinating," he said, "but we took its advice."

He told all that he could remember; it was a memory he often replayed, trying to recall more words.

"I swear it is all inside my head," he said.

"Doc," said Ryder, "this world is going to be full of surprises. I have something I haven't told Chan."

"Something you saw?"

"Something Beattie saw . . . almost the last thing. He was gasping and shouting but he knew what he was saying."

"What?"

He gave Ryder a sip of water.

"It is stuck in my mind," said Ryder, "the way it is with your lake monster. He said: 'Ryder, believe me, believe me. We all saw it. Northeast on the landmass. Lights on the ground. Lights on the ground. Looks like we are coming in to the Alice.' That was about it. There was more shouting . . . he switched off . . ."

"Alice? A girl's name, Alice?"

"I knew what he meant," said Ryder. "You think about it, Doc. Beattie was a training buddy of mine, we both trained at Woomera; he came from California, he knew I was a native son."

"Alice Springs is a town in Australia, is that what you mean?"

"Chan said there is desert, some kind of scrubby desert northeast of this place."

"Yes, that's true."

"Alice, the Alice, is a desert town," said Ryder. "A desert town."

The faint voice choked; he saw that Ryder was weeping, tears were running down his pale cheeks. He remembered how he and Chan had been moved to tears by memories of Earth.

"Promise me, Doc," said Ryder, "promise me one day you'll check it out. Lights on the ground like a desert town."

"I promise, Ryder."

"You can tell Chan," said Ryder. "Later, you can tell her."

He let the thought rattle around in his head while Ryder lay still. What else could look like a town but a town? Lights on the ground? A collection of luminous giant fungi, a scatter of oil ponds, the bed of a salt lake. What creatures could make a town or something that looked like one? Oh, it had been a trick of the light, a variant of an UFO sighting. Beattie was facing death in a burning comcen, seeing the lights of Earth in his last agony.

He lay on the ground sheet and tried to sleep while Chan and Ryder talked and Chan sang songs. He tried to stir up some hope for the three of them, especially for Ryder, but he had no real hope. He might have tried to pray to the gods of this new world, to the lake monster, if he had known what to ask for. He popped medication and slept and when he awoke one of the prayers he had not dared to utter had been answered. Chan was asleep at his side; she had doped herself heavily. Ryder was dead. She had covered his face.

They left the crash site as soon as they could. It was difficult to bury anything in the soft ground and burning was out of the question. They slid the bodies of Ryder and Voychek into the dark pool beside Bulk One. There was extra food, clothing and building material to take along, so Chan used a modified version of her sled. He caught and tethered the little goat and fed her by hand.

"What's her name, Doc?" asked Chan.

"I call her Alice."

"Poor old Alice in Wonderland," said Chan, petting the pretty white head.

Ryder really had not told her the story.

When they started back he carried the goat over his shoulders in a sling until they were away from the swampy crash area and the dark shadow of the wreck. Then he let her down and she led them through the soft jungle, jumping along at the end of her lead. The track they had made coming down to Bulk One was wide and clear and blazed with yellow; the pack sled moved smoothly. He kept looking back at Chan; he was still afraid that her grief would become unmanageable. They traveled a short distance uphill and came again to their hardwood tree. They didn't make camp but he climbed up again and looked at the site of the crash. He looked toward their beachhead and the tops of the brown hills. He stared through the harder upland vegetation toward the rift valley and the haze of the desert.

Chan led for the rest of the day and when the night enclosed them in their silent cave she was overtired, full of aches and pains. Their companion, sweet Alice, cuddled up to their warmth, tame as a pet dog. They made good time the next day, singing old songs along the yellow trail. Sometime after the eating break and before they made camp Chan stumbled and fell. She picked herself up, shying away from his touch.

"Loozy vine tangled m'feet!"

He knew she was sick. When they made camp he found that she had a high fever; she burned from head to foot. He dosed her tentatively; she had a fine pinkish rash under her chin and behind her ears; her eyelids were inflamed, her mouth was tender. In the night she was stricken with a rigor; long chills shook her body, then passed off. They were a day and a half away from the beach, in the heart of the soft jungle. Chan knew that she had to go on.

He hardly dared think what she might have because he doubted if it came from the area of the crash; he thought of a longer incubation period. They dragged through the dark vines, umbrella trees, blue-frills; he hitched Alice behind the sled and pulled it while Chan staggered on ahead, shivering again. They made an early camp and the fever had returned, worse than before. Chan's rashes had gone but the fever was eating into her; she was dry-skinned, bright-eyed. He looked at the selection of medication that remained in his drug kit with absolute terror. The disease was something like malaria, just as the growths around them were something like trees. An endemic disease: a gift from their new world.

He sat awake through the night while in succession Chan burned, then sweated, then was wracked with chills. In the morning he packed the sled, left Chan on the ground sheet with water, took Alice and the sled on as quickly as he could. He came to the beach again, the small brown corner of beach hemmed by the black, marine swamp, the bare brown hills, the jungle, the desert. He tried to make a camp, got up the small tent from the boat as best he could; it was either damaged or not foolproof. He fed Alice and tethered her; she bleated after him as he plunged back into the jungle and went back to Chan.

The D-Quin had worked, Chan was able to stand; he supported her and they began to walk. Her head was not clear; she laughed and swore and called him by the names of half-a-dozen people. Chan fell down, shivered, then burned; he heaved her up after a few of the long alien hours and they went on. When they came to the beach at last he was so exhausted that he wondered if his turn for the fever had come. When he had Chan safely in the tent and medicated he slept himself and felt better.

Chan's fever lasted for five days and he was afraid that she would die. He built a larger shelter incorporating the little wrinkled tunnel of the tent. It was a wretched, ramshackle thing, cobbled up out of plastic sheeting, the molded panels they had brought back on the sled. He became distrustful of the purification tablets and began boiling the water. The stove from the boat broke down and he made bad driftwood fires; the dried seaweeds and swamp trees burned, at least. The stuff from the soft jungle only melted with that awful burned fruit odor that recalled the crash site.

When Chan was convalescent they crouched over his miserable fires in the long purple evenings. He watched certain birds that he had christened hawks wheeling over the gap in the hills. Alice, the goat, was perfectly happy; she romped on the beach and nibbled the sparse brown grass that grew near the stream.

Once he was certain that Chan was out of danger he took the sled and made a trek along the base of the hills. He found the bones of one or maybe two animals, larger or at any rate longer than a draught horse. He loaded some of the long bones on to the sled, took them back to camp and added them to the shelter.

"There's a place in the hills about one kilometer inland," he said at night by the fire. "I think there is a pass through the hills."

"You still think we could get up there?" yawned Chan.

She was thin and weak from the fever; he had a vision of her long bones lying in the drifting sand. She reached out and touched his bearded cheek:

"Doc . . . don't *worry!*"

Part of their closeness was an unspoken agreement not to say too much, to let be, to bring out only what could be remembered without pain. Technical subjects were good; he spoke of operations he had performed; Chan told him about docking procedures. They watched Alice, her flanks rounding ever so slightly; they laughed and cried over the plots of old TD shows. He felt them both turning resolutely away from thoughts of the crash site but he still saw it in his dreams. The new world had narrowed to a warm, interminable day on the small strip of sand and brown grass.

"That mensh . . ." said Chan at night by the fire.

"Which mensh?"

"That mensh between the devil and the deep blue sea . . . he had it made!"

# Chapter IX

## *The Long Portage*

---

Maxim found himself sitting at the table; still here, still on the ship, was a half thought. He cleared, slowly, a patch of mental fog; he felt cold, his legs were cold. He groped for a discovery, just out of reach like a dream fading. *They . . . where were they. . . .* He was more deeply asleep, if that was the word, than he had realized. As he fought his way back to consciousness a sound penetrated: a parmel nickered close by. He felt himself falling forward, shoved

166

with his arms and was awake. He was seated at a rough wooden table in a bare mudbrick room; by the light it seemed to be late afternoon. The ship, the shape-changers, the bright morning had vanished; a cold wind whipped through the uncurtained doorway around his legs.

He was shocked and afraid but he tried to cope with these feelings quickly. He tightened his muscles, breathed deeply of the cool air and felt a momentary rocking, a memory of the ship in his body. *Where? And where were they?* He looked around cautiously and found himself alone, in a sort of rough anteroom; there was an inner doorway with a leather curtain, behind it a glow of light. In a corner of this anteroom was a heap which turned out to be his own saddle and saddlebags. Outside the parmel nickered again; from the inner room came a thrum that was almost the sound of voices. Maxim shuddered from head to foot.

He stood up and crept to the open doorway in three long, silent, crouching steps. Outside the wind whipped at sand and scrub; the land raced away to the horizon in undulating, gritty ridges. He saw smudged hints of water, shade, rough country: it was the long portage. To his left there was a belt of sea-pines and beyond that, at the foot of a hill, a town, the town of Derry; he could see the Western Sea gleaming in the distance. The building was at a crossroads outside the town; the road behind it led toward the Obelisk Hills, a last outcrop of the Dividing range which began at the shores of the Red Ocean. There were three parmels tethered in a pen. He had no idea how he had been brought off the ship but his way was clear. He had only to take his saddle and take his pick of the beasts.

He thought again. *They* had made him unconscious, apparently without laying a finger on him. Milt Donal had had no truthweed at all, Bevan was mistaken. It was all mind-power of a lazy strength that he hardly liked to consider. He wondered if they could play with humans like tethered birds, bring them back with a word, if they wanted them. Was he being given a choice? To stay or to go? But Urbain's words rang in his head: "They do not care . . ." He couldn't believe that they did. They had passed him out to avoid a momentary embarrassment, and if he ran away they would shrug and continue to do what pleased them. If he tried again perhaps he would be brushed aside again. But they *had* taken him along. "I would tackle them boldly!" said Urbain in his mind.

"Damn you, old man!" said Maxim aloud.

He ran a hand over his hair and his clothing, stepped up boldly to the lighted doorway, drew back the curtain and went in.

He was less afraid than he might have been because he simply did not understand what he saw. There was a pleasant light in the room and he saw clumps of bright fabric lying about. A man sat at a table hardly better than the one in the anteroom and passed his hands through and through a pool of colored lights. They danced like bubbles about his fingers and their light seemed to shine through the skin and bone of his hands as if they were transparent. In the corners of the room where the light was softer he had an impression of pillars, as if rolls of carpet or sections of jocca stem had been stored.

"What's this? What's this?" said the man.

He had Redrock's voice but not quite Redrock's face. He was darker skinned, his hair in long ringlets.

"Redrock?" Maxim felt his voice tremble.

"Of course," said the man. "You should have been 'absent' for hours longer. What do you say, *liebe Kinder*? Has the Dator some convolutions we know nothing about?"

The room was filled with the musical answer: incredible sounds, tinkling like laughter, whining like a sharp wind. And Maxim saw more clearly so that his knees were weak. An oily movement of light deep within the two dark columns. He saw what Coll Dun Mor had seen in the garden of the Pleasance at Rhomary, twenty years before. He realized that the clump of silk nearest him was Ulla's gown, vacant, as if the shape that filled it had flowed out of it like mist.

"Sit down, man," said Redrock. "This is what you were after, I don't doubt. Here, help me, I need your hands."

Then Maxim saw that under the dancing lights on the table and Redrock's shadowy hands there lay some object. Redrock lifted up his hands and they were gone, there was only a strong band of light flowing from one cuff to the other of his dark gown. Maxim slid across the table an ornate leather case; its silver buckles were unfastened and inside was a silver-backed mirror.

"But what . . ."

"If you would fasten it please."

Maxim did up the buckles. There was a tinkling and churring which he interpreted not so much as thanks but as an exasperated comment on the ease with which he performed this simple action. He cleared his throat and looked down at the table as he asked.

"How could you exist on any world without the ability to . . . ?"

"The conditions were very different," said Redrock, lightly, "and besides, there were what you might call handlers."

"When did you leave this other world?"

"Long ago. Even its light has faded now."

"You are three?"

"Oh, there is one other," said Redrock, "but it has chosen a different mode of existence."

"Have you been long on Rhomary? On this world?"

"Not by our reckoning. We come and go. Take no notice of us. We are . . .'"

He seemed to search for a word and a second voice that Maxim could just associate with Heath sighed through the room. Yet the figure before him was still speaking:

"We are lost. We are displaced. There *is* no place for us unless we make one."

The third voice chimed in, the voice related to Ulla; the figure before him had become a simulacrum, a mask.

"Think of us as what we appear, the Redrock family."

"You must be able to understand the human situation on this world," said Maxim eagerly. "We have made a place for ourselves, more or less, but we are displaced too. You can help us with your superior powers."

Redrock, more comfortable to watch speaking in his own person, laughed aloud.

"You are a self-pitying race. Even the Vail, so-called, remarked on this capacity. How do you imagine we can help you?"

"Well," said Maxim impertinently, "not by the creation of an ersatz Messiah such as Jenz Kindl!"

The reaction was violent and, he thought, angry. The room was filled with sound: tinkling, chiming, stridulating, and the light grew to a rainbow glare. Redrock spoke as if striving to keep his face from changing:

"You——assess——too soon!"

"How can we circumnavigate the globe?" asked Maxim, "Have you done it, over land and sea?"

"We have done it in our own way," said Redrock.

The room had become cold and still.

"Please," said Maxim, "you could have maps prepared.

What lies on the other side? Is there a promised land or . . . or a race of lizard men?"

"Oh, leave them alone!" said the voice of Heath. "He must mean the . . ."

The word or expression was soft and guttural; he did not dare ask to have it repeated. The distrust for the human race that he felt emanating from the shape-changers was beginning to oppress him. He felt that he had lost all chance of the other side of the world once he had let drop this scrap of legend that he had picked up from Cap Ramm.

"Do you recall your friend Coll Dun Mor?" he asked.

There was no reply, not a word or a ripple of sound.

"Will you speak into the record an independent account of the race called the Vail and their fate?"

Again his words fell without an echo and there was no sound in reply.

"Oh, trust us a little," he said softly. "Have you no human confidants? Your servants?"

"They are trained," said Ulla, the voice very cold. "They forget anything unusual that they have seen."

He knew this was meant literally.

"In the way Milt Donal forgot?" he asked.

"His brain is congested," said Redrock shortly. "He could not endure the least scanning."

It was persuasive. Maxim did see the merchant as a possible candiate for a stroke. Ambel, if time permitted, would not only be a rich wife, but a rich widow. The thought of this warm, greedy, ordinary world of the city filled him with despair. He was displaced indeed.

"Is there no way in which we can begin a dialogue?" he asked.

"What?" laughed Redrock. "'Do you want to become our Hereditary Envoy?"

"I want to learn your nature!"

"You are afraid!" said the voice of Ulla.

A long finger of light darted from the corner of the room and struck at Maxim's face so that he threw up his arms to shield it.

"Can't you understand my fear?" he said, controlling his voice as best he could. "You must know your own powers!"

"Yes," said Ulla. "You are vulnerable. You are afraid of the snake, the lion, the elephant. You are afraid of death, of ghosts and demons, of . . . what is it . . . bacterial infection. You are afraid of losing face."

170

"I know nothing about lions or elephants," said Maxim, "but ghosts or demons do not scare me. I don't care about losing face, if I understand the expression correctly. I will do my best to control my fear if it upsets you."

"Your feelings are of overwhelming interest only to yourself," said Heath. "We are easily bored. A stint as a hideous multilimbed marionette takes some getting over."

"It is boredom then that makes you so cruel and trivial!" said Maxim. "Or has a little of our humanity rubbed off on you after all?"

There was another cold, heavy silence. Maxim heard the parmels outside and longed for the desert, the sight of the natural world.

"This is all wrong!" he cried suddenly. "What good thing, what hope, what knowledge can I carry back to my Uncle Urbain? He at least is a good man worthy of your trust! He has worn out his life hoping to find this race of superior beings who would add to the sum of knowledge that we have scraped together. Must I tell him that your true interest is in iron meteorites? Must I tell him you use human beings as shamelessly as they use each other . . . their heads, their hands, the bluntness of their senses as compared to some of yours? Are you moved to hear that Coll Dun Mor loved his teachers, even though they blinded him? Would you have continued to live on this world if the ship had *not* cast away our ancestors in this place?"

There was a chiming response, soft, almost reluctant.

"Perhaps . . ." said Heath.

The sounds and the atmosphere of the encounter became gentle and conciliatory.

"It is time for us to move on," said Redrock. "Our servants are far ahead by now. We go to the Obelisk Hills."

"I must get on to the Gann," said Maxim. "My papers . . . ? The dream, the report from Faya Junik?"

"In your pocket," said Redrock.

"How was I brought off the ship?"

"You said good-bye to the Sister and the children and walked off in our company."

"Do you need all three parmels?" asked Maxim.

"Go out and see which one you like," said Redrock.

The silence was broken again by a lilting burst of their sounds.

"Thank you," said Maxim.

He stood up and bowed feeling like a hideous marionette.

"I hope I will be able to keep the record of this interview in my memory."

He walked out into the anteroom, collected his saddle and went out into the blue light of early evening. The eastern sky was fading to deep rose and gold; the desert was still painted with sunset colors. He gulped at the fresh air and forced himself to walk upright without staggering. He was struck with the notion that he should have offered to load the baggage for them but he could not go back. On the way to the parmel pen he stumbled and felt strange and the air thickened around him.

He did not have time to feel afraid; he was warm and light and weightless, moving through a hazy darkness. He felt that he was no more than a meter or two above the ground. He saw desert plants moving dimly ahead of him and felt the padding of his saddle against his arm but not its weight. It was a dream of flying; it was a dream of sweet sounds, half heard, falling through the air like leaves. He was relaxed, exhilarated, protected; time spun out again but the lightning did not strike at his brain. He saw, after some time, a light growing ahead in the darkness. He was borne closer to the light and felt his boots light softly upon sand. The warmth of the flight diminished and he was clear headed, more or less, standing in the desert at the edge of a patch of light. The stars were out, it was really night.

The circle of light came from a small camp fire; a man sat by the fire scribbling industriously in a rough bundle of jocca paper. Maxim could see him dip and dip with his wooden pen; his inkpot was hollowed out of stone. It was an extraordinary thing for the man to be doing at night in the desert all alone.

Maxim stared with quickening interest; he could not tell afterward if he always knew this was something to be looked at, a scene, a spectacle. He made no attempt to walk into the circle of firelight or address the man. He watched as the man laid aside his pen, stood up and held out his hands to the starry heaven. He knew the man from his uncle's description and from the awful embroidered pictures and colored prints put out by his followers. This was a middle-sized, long-faced man with sun-bleached reddish hair curling to his shoulders. He had a trace of beard and a complexion marked by the sun until it was a coppery mass of freckles and sunburn. His expression was one of intense concern; deep wrinkles were graven in his forehead and ran from nose to chin; his eyebrows were high-arched and shapely, lending his blue eyes a grave beauty. This was Jenz Kindl, the prophet and healer from the Lemn Oasis.

With the thrill of this recognition came another. The man relaxed after a few moments of prayer or meditation and as he turned back to his place by the fire he side-stepped awkwardly. Maxim saw the snake lying across his path, an unusually large rock adder, thick and red-brown, marked with blue diamonds. Like many of the snakes of the Rhomary land it had rudimentary legs, six stumpy appendages just above the crawling skin of its belly, and a trace of a row of dorsal spines ending abruptly at the place where its tail could be dropped. The bite of the rock adder was deadly; the rare antivenin did work but a rough amputation was the only recourse in an out of the way place.

There was a flicker of movement and Jenz fell to the ground. He cried out, but Maxim could not be sure if he heard the cry. He saw the bite on the man's ankle distinctly, blood ran down. Jenz reacted very swiftly and before the snake was through a cleft in the rocks he had crushed its back with a stone. The diamond painted tail writhed and thrashed and lay still. Jenz sat on the sand dabbing his ankle with the tail of his long burnous; he began to weep. He bound a strip of cloth torn from the hem of the burnous tightly above his ankle. He limped to the fire and drank from his water bottle. He crouched by the fire in an attitude of intense concentration and devotion. Then he came back to the rock pile and tenderly extracted the body of the dead rock adder from the cleft.

He sat cross-legged on the sand with the blood-stained length of the dead creature across his knees, raised his hands to the stars, laid them upon the snake. His strong sun-marked hands hovered above the body, tense and stiff, then descended gently to touch the snake's skin. His hands were stigmatized with the snake's blood. After a length of time that it was impossible for Maxim to measure he saw the Healer's face relax. He lifted his hands for the last time; the body of the snake was whole again, still blood-stained. The snake quivered, flexed awkwardly, flowed forward out of Jenz Kindl's lap and across the sand into the darkness. Jenz was exhausted; sweat stood out on his forehead. The scene was beginning to fade; the snake had lived and Jenz had lived too, had written up the incident.

Maxim was in a euphoric state, but he had no doubt that the shape-changers had done everything, had conjured up the scene and transported him to this place. He felt them close by and spoke a little; he was answered wordlessly. His critical faculty was not quite dulled for he remembered asking or thinking: "Did this happen?" "Where?" "I cannot find anything to stir *my* faith in the scene, it is all within, it is all Jenz Kindl's faith. A Jenzite would see it differently. It is a mystery." Yet he did not ask *"How* did it happen?" He knew that his companions could perform miracles.

Then he was taken up higher than before and carried through the air. He saw the stars with a marvelous clarity and the comet among them and the planets of the system, like jewels. He heard a series of strange names and he gave back the story of Kirchner, the astronomer, and the names he had given and how they had been changed. He saw a rain of fragments on to the earth below, tiny meteorites and larger ones and far to the east a great yellowing fireball. He could not tell whether he was in or out of time, whether he saw the past or the present, but at last he was softly set down and again the darkness wavered.

He took a step and found himself on the curled edge of a high cliff. Dawn was breaking over the Western Sea; there was no limit to the scene; he beheld sea and sky and there was a thunderous sound in the air, a kind of natural play on words as if the dawn actually broke or was shattered. Far below him the water heaved and parted in three places and he saw the three protoheads come up. He saw the vast, rippling field of the seines and the dim bulk of the floating body. The sound was repeated: a sundering of the air that hurt his ears.

Large globes of light, so defined that he had the impression of bubbles, bounced on the water or hovered about the heads of the Vail. The sounds that came from them he recognized: tinkling, chiming, vibrating; the shape-changers ringed the Vail with sound and bright outpourings of light. The Vail lifted two, three, five sensors into the air like fronds of a marine forest and its voice came from them. It repeated the sounds of the shape-changers and uttered its own sounds. The voice of the Vail was resonant, harsh, there was nothing he could compare it with.

Before his eyes now the globes of light elongated, "put on a shape to be beheld": the shape-changers rode upon the surface of the Western Sea as dark, semitransparent tubular shapes, more than man-sized. The Vail and its three companions continued to exchange sounds and moved slowly through patches of light and shade. Maxim felt a

174

hopeless longing, a sad envy for their communion. "O Vail, return to us again . . ." He saw now that the waters were parted in several places; other Vail were feeding and at times exchanging sounds. He knew that he beheld a golden age when the shape-changers wandered freely, when Rhomary was an unnamed, unspoiled planet. On his imaginary clifftop he experienced the nostalgia of the shape-changers, his companions in the present, for this vanished world. He expostulated gently with them: "Have we changed things so much?"

Then he lay at full length on the turf and watched his fill, like a boy staring into an aquarium; he watched the Vail, he strove to imprint them upon his senses. The purple-brown and blue-black of their bodies, the delicacy of the sensors, which changed color and shape as readily as the shape-changers themselves, the crisp wordlike utterance of certain sounds and the thrumming sweetness of others, hanging in the air like music.

As the scene faded eventually and he was carried away again he sighed and said aloud:

"But the Vail could *not* remember in this way. They have said as much. They cannot bear to remember, perhaps because they sense too much in every moment of their long lives. Is this something we share with your kind, this ability to remember?"

For answer he was teased with sound and warmth, rolled in the air. "Pish, tush," protested his invisible companions, "how absolute the knave is!"

Presently it was night in the desert again. He heard human voices and thought that the whole dream was at an end, he must endure an awakening. There was only a very little light, much feebler than Jenz Kindl's camp fire. Two voices, talking and laughing quite naturally; a young man and a girl. Now at last he saw them, sitting in a boat of all things, with a small rush-light on a thwart between them, the desert rushing away on all sides. They sat becalmed in the middle of nowhere and held hands on either side of the small flame.

"I can see," said the young man. "I can see in the dark like a cat."

"What is a cat?" asked the girl.

"Silly, it is an off-world animal, perhaps a bit like a ferret, with very soft fur. I have seen a picture of a cat."

"C-A-T," the girl sounded the word phonetically. "Is that right?"

"Right."

He was able to see their faces: the young man dark and striking, the girl pretty and lithe with a mane of dark curls and huge dark eyes. He had no idea who they were but the scene was as moving and important as any he had witnessed. Perhaps these feelings were subjective and came from the shape-changers. Perhaps from himself because he envied them both: together, loving, in the midst of the wilderness.

"I will write your name in the sand," said the girl.

"The wind will blow it away, no one will remember my name."

"They will, don't worry!"

She had climbed out of the boat and was writing in huge letters on the sand with a pointed stick. Now she began to unravel a double set of traces, made of rope and leather.

"Come along, see in the dark if you can!" she said. "We'll do another stretch before we camp . . ."

Then the young man sprang up, smiling, and looked at the starry sky with a sort of furious delight. At last Maxim knew who he was. The pair slipped into the traces and went off into the darkness, dragging their tiny boat on the long portage. All that was left was a name written on the sand but Maxim thought he could read COLL DUN MOR, before the wind blew the letters completely away.

Maxim experienced no doubts at all; he had witnessed a past time and it was a gift for him and for his Uncle Urbain. He was whirled up high again and carried along in a vortex of light and darkness. He was on the point of understanding the nature of his companions; he was assured at last of their good will. Even the periods of transition were gentle and pleasant: traveling down, returning to a zone of time and verbal contact. He knew his location; he knew finally that he was alone.

He was in the desert at night and there was a light up ahead. The First Corral, ten hours overland from Derry at a caravan pace, four or five hours by racer. He still had his saddle; he hauled his cloak from its place under a thong of a saddlebag and put it on against the cold of the night. He felt light-headed, a little hungover. He found the road, the beaten track toward the lighted homestead, and lay down beside it, looking at the stars.

He tried his best to bring the whole experience under control before it engulfed him altogether. He longed to sleep, to sleep for ages and to wake, pretending the wild trip had been a dream. Maxim breathed deeply, tried to relax and went over the events of the day as carefully as he could. He was often sidetracked into his own memories, plans and fantasies. He thought of festivals and discoveries: New Year in Edenvale, of learning to swim in the leaden waters of the Billsee, of learning to read under the kitchen table from a book prepared by his Uncle Urbain. He thought of the day he first lay down under the trees with a sweet, plump girl called Ann; he thought of that great day of sun and dust and shouting when he had won the Stampede and had asked himself "Is this all? Is this the finest thing that can happen to me?" His answer then had been a firm negative; there was more achievement in mastering his calligraphy, winning the medals for English composition and for verse. There was the moment when his uncle, Urbain, had at last admitted he was an Archivist. And now this bewildering adventure: Was this all? Was this the finest thing? Fine indeed but . . .

Maxim sat up and said aloud: "No! This is only a beginning!"

Up ahead lay the homestead of the First Corral; he could just see the outbuildings and the parmel pens. He began automatically adjusting the times and preparing a story. He supposed this was what the shape-changers must do very often to explain away things that were quite natural to them. He took the girth of his saddle and hacked with his knife at the thongs holding the hardwood buckle until the buckle slewed sideways. Then he trudged on toward the homestead and hailed when he came up to the lighted doorway. An old man came out wiping his hands on his apron.

"Where did you spring from?" he rumbled. "Did you dismount by yourself, eh?"

"No," said Maxim, "I was thrown a mile or so back when the beast's flap-nail caught in my girth."

"Ha! Not properly trimmed," said the old man. "Come in, then! Are you hurt? Couldn't catch your beast, I'll be bound."

"No harm done," said Maxim, "but the parmel's to hell and gone."

"I expect the beggar will show up here one day soon."

The old man gave his name, Tom Gard, manager of the corral, and shook Maxim by the hand. As they came into the big warm kitchen-common room of the homestead he whispered:

"There's company, Mister Bro, through in the good sitting room."

"From Derry?" asked Maxim.

"Coming from the Gann. His driver is still sleeping. They're going through with the best racers, bound for the city!"

"Let me sit with this man," said Maxim. "Here, I'll buy a feed for myself and a round for the company."

The old man took the silver dollar and hesitated.

"I dunno he will. It is a doctor, sir."

Maxim's first thought was of the TC, Los Smitwode, sitting fastidiously in his black silk robe in this scruffy waystation. Surely it could not be the young person Jaygo, the intern.

"Truly, Mister Gard," he said, "I must see this doctor. I'm going to the Gann on important business."

He had not given his title so he was announced simply as Bro, a traveler bound for the Gann, from Rhomary. Tom Gard came back and began serving wine.

"Go in," he said, "you're welcome. I'll bring the food and drink."

Maxim would have liked to wash at least, before fronting up to the Third Consultant, but he wiped his palms on his cloak and stepped into the room. A man not much older than himself sprawled in a cushioned chair; he was fair, ruddily handsome and clean shaven.

"Doctor . . . ?"

"Roak. Gil Roak, M.B."

"Maxim Bro."

Roak gestured with an open hand.

"Sit down, sit down!" he said. "No ceremony. Is the old fella bringing wine? Good!"

They grinned at each other warily; the initiative was all with the doctor.

"You look shaken up," he said. "The old man said you had been thrown."

"Yes," said Maxim humbly, conjuring up a picture of his imaginary parmel. "The beast was ill-trimmed."

"That's what they all say!" laughed Roak. "Own up! You should have hired a driver. Riding a parmel on the Portage is a very different thing from a little pleasure riding on the roads of Rhomary."

"I'm recovered," said Maxim.

"Warm up," said Roak. "Get that cloak off and come nearer this piddling fire . . ."

178

There was a brazier of thorn branches in the fireplace against the chill of the desert night. Tom Gard brought in an excellent hotpot and two tall jugs of wine. Maxim took off his cloak and checked his pockets: his letters were inside, safe, and his medallion of office.

"Why in the name of Luke and Esculap are you going to the Gann Station?" demanded Gil Roak.

"Is it such a bad place?" asked Maxim, stalling.

"Bad? It's the arse end of the world! No society, nothing but the farms, the wharf, the river and the sea beyond. The Jenzites glooming about with sour-pod faces . . . you're not a Jenzite, are you?"

"Not me!" said Maxim hastily.

Then feeling vaguely guilty he added:

"But I think they should be tolerated. Any I've met have been honest folk."

"Oh, surely," said Doctor Roak, "but it's another thing to have the wee buggers underfoot all the time or making difficulties about their doctoring. Anyway they weren't the only thing that bored me at the bluggy Gann. Not the Jenzites or the awful pretensions of the Dun Mor and the Hign clans—our Rancher, Mam Hign, tough as old boots, the sort who'll bury more than one husband. No, it was the feeling of wasting one's life. I need to be in the center of things, in Rhomary. What do you do? I can see you're not in medicine. Did you have a tutor or go to one of the merchant schools?"

"I went to Doctors' High School," said Maxim.

"Ha-ha, a dropout!" cried Gil Roak. "Didn't even make it into internship, eh? Well, it's better than the rope or the spaggin-cup, like some poor fools. A friend in my year . . ."

His good-looking face creased with sadness but he recovered himself, quickly.

"We won't dwell on that. Back to my original question. What brings you to the Gann?"

"I'll pass up that question for the moment," said Maxim seriously. "It has to do with my job, my calling, let us say. And I hope you'll forgive me, Roak, if I ask you the same question. Why are you rushing away from your practice? Has something happened at the Gann?"

Gil Roak did not like to be questioned or even addressed in this way, Maxim could see, but he was so full of excitement he could not keep it in.

"You take a lot on yourself, Mr. Traveler Broo or whatever you call yourself," he said, "but since you're going to the Gann I might as well tell you. Something amazing *has* happened. I've been rescued by a miracle, literally a fall from heaven!"

"Tell me . . ."

"Wreckage!" The doctor leaned forward, his blue eyes very bright. "Section of an off-world ship, found in the ocean."

Maxim heard it with a sort of relief.

"Where? Who found it?"

"Out by the Six Seven Isles," said Gil Roak. "Brought in by a certain LaMar, an old bully of a trader, reputed to be the Rancher's bedfellow. Makes you laugh at their age. . . . At any rate LaMar brought this thing in and there's a search in progress or was when I left. But the point is that there was something of medical interest in this wreckage . . . I'll not go into details before a lay person . . . and by good luck I was able to be in on the discovery. There was even a bit of college brass at the Gann to send me on this trip and entrust me with the bringing of the good news."

Maxim could not resist it.

"Let me guess," he said. "That would be the Third Consultant, his Eminence Los Smitwode."

Gil Roak gasped.

"Dry hell, you're well up in things. Have you met the TC?"

"Only once," said Maxim, "I doubt he'd remember me."

"Well, he's lording it at the Gann, all right," said Roak. "Acting as *my* locum now, if you please."

"You'll go back after you've brought this find to the city?"

"Not me!" cried Gil Roak cheerfully, sinking another beaker of the wine.

He leaned forward and tapped an inner pocket.

"In here I have my notice of transfer. Good-bye to the Gann. Country Service is over for me, thank the stars."

"May I ask about your new posting then?"

"A secret, even from yours truly," said Roak. "Oh I'm not expecting too much. A junior residence in obstetrics, maybe. Perhaps the old Magister gave me a posting to Silver City General . . . I wouldn't mind that."

"He has an intern at the Gann as his assistant," put in Maxim tentatively.

Gil Roak shrugged and grinned.

"Jaygo," he said flatly. "What can we say about the good

intern Jaygo? Bright, certainly, and very young and the TC mentioned something about family connections. Couldn't stand the lad myself but that was because I was so fed up with the Gann. The intern was getting special treatment and I was a bluggy field doctor. I say . . . do *you* know the family?"

Maxim was suddenly on the spot. He didn't want to deliver Jaygo's family history to this genial, destructive character. But under all the bluster and the crude ambition he sensed something that was almost likable. He could sympathize with a man of his own age whose life irked him to distraction. He decided not to lie or to pull any kind of secrecy.

"I've met Jaygo's mother," he said. "A beautiful lady with a strange destiny."

"Sounds intriguing," said Roak. "Who in the world. . . ?"

"Please," said Maxim. "Let this be between us two. You, as a medical man, must know about keeping confidence. Jaygo's mother is the Lady Ishbel Manin O'Moore, the Thirteenth Envoy."

Gil Roak whistled with astonishment.

"And Jaygo is an *intern!*"

"I thought it strange myself," said Maxim. "Have you given any thought to the problem of the Vail?"

"Pah! What problem?" growled Gil Roak. "I ask you? Why should I waste my time thinking about a vanished dinosaur? That's another thing I've had a bellyful of at the Gann: this damnable mysticism. If it wasn't the Jenzites chanting heavenly rubbish then it was Rancher and her push with pious hopes for the Vail's return and hints about the mysteries of Rhomary. I believe in what I see!"

"So do I, up to a point," said Maxim. "How about showing me this piece of wreckage that fell from the stars?"

"You'll have to do better than that," laughed Gil Roak. "You strike me as a pretty mysterious character yourself. You know a hell of a lot. You appear out of the night and ask questions, but you're very stingy with answers. Just why should I show you that find?"

"All right," said Maxim, laughing too. "I'll be more forthcoming. Here, will this satisfy you, Doctor?"

He laid his medallion on the table between them.

"Maxim Bro," he said, "Dator of Rhomary. Heir to Urbain Bro. Traveling to the Gann to investigate reports of a fallen spacecraft."

Gil Roak passed a hand over his face and looked rueful.

"You devil," he said, without rancor. "Letting me gab this way."

He sprang up, a shade unsteadily, and took the lamp from its shelf. "Come on then. It's in the pack shed."

Maxim followed him out, feeling the effects of the wine, and in some recess of his brain, of the experiences of that day. They went through the empty kitchen and walked slowly toward the pack shed, both reeling a little with the cool air. The comet blazed overhead; Ruby hung low in the southern sky; Connor and Topaz kept watch to the north. The endless scatter of the distant stars made Maxim lower his gaze.

"I'll miss the stargazing at the Gann," said Gil Roak unexpectedly. "There's a lookout in the hills of the Divide, just above the Station House. Good place for an observatory."

"Was anything seen . . . lights in the sky . . . six days ago?" asked Maxim.

"Mam Hign asked that question," said Roak, "and got an affirmative from one of my favorite patients, Dixon Dit."

"What, you had a favorite patient?" teased Maxim. "Is he reliable?"

"Blessed if I know," said the Doctor. "His condition might have affected his judgment, who knows. Poor young beggar is a pituitary giant. He'll make two meters, two and a half . . ."

They went into the shed and Gil Roak reefed away a pack sling and a piece of felt from a long ovel shape. Maxim stared; he felt the world turning under him. He bent down and laid his hands on the various surfaces, he fingered the insulation and the bunched cables.

"Oho, Dator," whispered Gil Roak, "that's not all!"

He bent down and flipped the piece of wreckage over so that Maxim saw it: a red-cross cupboard.

"What's in it?" Maxim found himself whispering too. "Can you tell me? Has it been opened?"

"Nothing," said Gil Roak. "There was a bit of—medicament. Nothing special. How's that for a bluggy disappointment! You should have seen the TC's long face."

He hurriedly wrapped the strange object again and lifted it back into the pack sling. Maxim waited with a feeling of anticlimax. Would that be all? No survivors, nothing, an empty medical chest. But the stargazing woman from Pinnacle had spoken of six "emergency capsules." Could they all have landed badly?

182

"Have you ever heard of a woman called Faya Junik?" he asked Gil Roak as they came out of the shed.

"Bird of ill omen!" said the Doctor. "One of the martyrs of the Hign push at the Gann. Attended the late lamented Rancher Dun Mor when he died o' fever. But she's poison to the medical profession."

"Because she left it and became a hermit?" asked Maxim.

"More to it than that," said Roak shortly. "She was a reformer. Before her time. Anyway, what's your thought? How do you come to the Junik?"

"She gave the best report of the fall of an off-world ship," said Maxim. "By her description we still have a few hopes left."

"Pah! I don't believe it!" said Gil Roak. "The folk in that ship burned or drowned."

"But if it divided into rescue capsules or something of the sort?"

"Divided into burning fragments, more likely. No, a meteorite doesn't fall in the same place twice. We are the miracle of Rhomary; that landing old Connor made years ago was miracle enough."

"I don't agree!" said Maxim. "Rhomary has a few miracles left."

He felt suddenly tired and his muscles ached. He really did feel as if he had ridden a parmel from Derry and been thrown. As they wandered back to the homestead Gil Roak said gruffly:

"I had a girl back there at the Gann. Perhaps I should have taken her along after all. Couldn't stand her family."

"You could send for her if you get a good post," said Maxim.

"Not me!" said the doctor. "My destiny is otherwise, little brother. But I'll bequeath her to you . . . you're much more her type anyway. She's gentle and thoughtful; frankly I don't know how her old battler of a mother ever bore such a child. Shona Dun Mor, the Rancher's daughter."

Maxim laughed uneasily as they came into the homestead; the roughness of Gil Roak was beginning to grate on his nerves. Suddenly he delivered tit for tat.

"I met a beautiful girl in Rhomary a few days ago," he said. "The handsomest girl in the city."

"Rich? Well-connected?" Gil Roak grinned, pouring the last of the wine into their beakers by the dying fire.

"Engaged to a merchant," said Maxim, "but the poor

fellow is sick and may not get well. His jewel is named Ambel Noag of Noag's Inn, the Warren."

"Ambel, the Innkeeper's daughter," murmured Gil Roak. "I'll take a glance at her. Why are you smiling, Bro, you old bookworm?"

"Ambel is very ambitious," said Maxim, "and so are you."

Gil Roak laughed aloud. They drained their beakers and stumbled off to the big empty dormitory where Roak's driver was snoring loudly. There was a bed made up for Maxim by the shuttered window; he lay with his hands under his head listening to Gil Roak still splashing about in the washroom. He began to sink into his strange dreams and visions . . . Redrock, Ulla . . . the movement through the air . . . the face of Jenz Kindl lifted to the stars. Ah, but it had happened, it had happened and there was no one he could share it with until he returned to the tumbledown Dator's House in the city. He was suddenly overpowered with sleep.

The morning was already blazing hot outside the homestead when he awoke; he had no hangover and an appetite for breakfast. The homestead smelled of tea and kippered round-fish. As Tom Gard dished up his food in the kitchen Maxim asked:

"Have the others gone on?"

"Loading up," said the old man. "Were you and the Doctor . . . late to bed?"

"Were we under the weather?" laughed Maxim. "No, not especially. Why, what's the matter, Mister Gard?"

"Something has cast him down."

Gil Roak came in at that moment, dressed for traveling. Maxim was shocked at his appearance; the man was gray-faced. His first thought was of illness.

"Dry hell, Doctor!" he said. "Are you sick?"

Gil Roak dismissed the landlord with a fierce look. He stood against the wall avoiding Maxim's gaze.

"Forget all our talk last night," he said. "All of it. Let me trust you to do that."

"Of course," said Maxim. "What has happened?"

"I can't talk about it. I've been a fool and I've been treated like a fool. If that tea was false spaggin, by Luke, I'd drink it."

"Tell me . . ."

184

"I can't," said Roak. "I'll abide by my own foolishness. There's nothing else I can do. Perhaps it is . . . destiny."

There was none of the old bravado left in the man, only a bitter lack of hope. He stood in silence for a few moments until the driver, a sturdy dark-browed young man stuck his head around the door.

"Set to mount up, Doc Roak!"

"Thank you, Sid."

Maxim stood up and offered his hand. Gil Roak clasped it strongly.

"I enjoyed meeting you," he said.

"Is there any way I can help you?" asked Maxim.

"I'm past help," said Roak. "Ask for news of my posting when you return to the city."

He strode out of the homestead. Maxim watched the racing parmel take off, flexing its flaps in the heat. The drivers white burnous and the white canopy of Gil Roak's howdah shone like stars in the hard morning light. He came back inside and called for Tom Gard.

"What was the doctor doing this morning?" he asked.

"He was reading," said the landlord, as if this activity might well produce violent symptoms. "I don't pry, Mister Bro, but I see what there is to see."

"What did he read?"

"Letters, I would say. And I saw one thing he did . . ."

"Speak up man, I won't tell!"

"He slipped the seal on one letter with a hot knife. Then I reckon he sealed it up again, after reading."

"He was upset by this letter?"

"He gave one cry, he cursed," said Tom Gard, "then when I went in he was as you saw him. Hard hit, with all the life gone out of him."

"Say nothing then," said Maxim. "I'll be on my way to the Gann as soon as I've mended my girth. Have you a good racer for me?"

"The best!" said Tom Gard. "I'll have her tanked and trimmed."

Maxim sat munching his breakfast and thinking of Gil Roak's bad news. He had looked at his letters of transfer and found that Smitwode, the TC, had given him a bad posting. Some little dry-well town on the Billsee, nothing half so fine as his imagined "junior resident" or even a stint at Silver City General. And there *was* nothing he could do. He was not even supposed to know about the transfer position until he reached Rhomary with the equivocal piece

185

of wreckage. Poor Gil Roak. He was hard to take sometimes and he might have overreached himself but Smitwode must be a cruel devil.

Maxim mended his girth and set off in midmorning. The parmel he hired was rangy and fierce but very fast and she flew along the road to the second corral, flaps out, pads striking sparks from the stony ground. He rode at top speed for two hours then slackened down until his mount altered her gait. He ate in the saddle and admired the small "morgana," the wayside mirages of shimmering water. Then off they charged again and reached the handsome homestead which marked the Second Corral in the early afternoon. A caravan was resting on its way from the Gann.

As soon as he had washed off the dust he went to speak to the Caravan Fuhrer, a gnarled and surly woman called Min Hunt. She had worked the long portage for years and bore out the story that after awhile drivers got to look like parmels. Her face was long and gray-brown, her nose flattened, her eyes hooded against a fierce light. As he expected, her train of pack animals, laden with early wild-kelp, rare woods, spices, pearl-shell and lime, had left the Gann almost ten hours before Gil Roak; he had passed them on the way.

She could add nothing to the story of the wreckage although Alan Dun Mor had spoken of it when he saw to the loading of the train. Maxim had shouted two liters of small beer for Mam Hunt and was almost content to leave it at that. He asked for a sighting, for lights in the sky, but so far as they could work out the time Min Hunt and her six helpers had been asleep at the First Corral when the lights fell.

"What do you think, Mam Hunt," he asked, "should I question your people?"

"No use," she growled, "we sleep sound."

"How long have you been traveling the portage?"

"Fifteen years or thereabouts. Times I go back to the city and take a few hauls on the round route."

"Which way did the Vail go? Can you tell me that?"

"You've got nothing but stories and tales in your head, young fella," she grinned, "but I'll tell you. They went this way until Palm Spring . . . which has dried up long since . . . then headed south. The road was changed, because the parmels would not walk in the way of the Vail."

"Have you talked with the Rancher about this?"

"She knows it better than I do."

186

"But they did not come to the ocean along the Gann River!"

"No, they took the southern bank, if any were able. Walked right through the place where the Jenzite town stands. The going was easier."

"But where does all this come from?"

"From old leather-arsed parmel drivers, men and women long dead. They knew. All the data is not stored in the city."

"And the bones of the Vail, any that died, why were they not found?"

"What are bones?" asked Min Hunt. "All bones ain't the same. Your bones and mine would be preserved by the sand but theirs would turn to yellow dust. Even parmel bones are other than ours . . . they dry out, turn soft, in twenty years they are gone."

Maxim gave her a silver dollar to buy a drink for her caravaneers. He did not care much for the Second Corral although its rooms and service were several cuts above those offered by Tom Gard. He set off before sunset on a quiet gray beast which went lame after forty kilometers. He trudged beside the limping creature while the stars came out then made a small camp and soaked its pad in a salt pond. Then he bound up the foot, heavily padded, and rode slowly through the night; he arrived at the third and last corral at midnight.

It was a cheerful place with the homestead and outbuildings of stone and wood; it had a bathhouse and a friendly reek of the fish-oil varnish used to preserve the wood. In fact it was an introduction to the Gann Station, its style and atmosphere, quite other than the city or the towns of the Billsee. He was the only traveler but there had been visitors and relatives coming and going from the Gann with supplies and gossip.

The Third Corral was ringing with news. The host and hostess, whose name was Cross, could talk of nothing but the trouble, the riot on the dock, the lights in the sky which one, two, four persons had seen. Instead of too little information now Maxim had too much, none of it solid. The Rancher had been hit by a stone, no, it was the doctor, the old one or the young one. Doc Roak had gone off carrying a case of magic medicine from the earthship, the head and hand of a dead earthman, the mechanical heart of the rooboter that the old doctor was mending.

A rooboter? Why surelee, breathed pretty, plump Mam

Cross in her country brogue, a young man, pale as a pearl, tall as Little Diggy Dit, why a good head taller than Mister Bro himself although he was an upstanding man. Mind you, Little Diggy would beat them all, poor pizz, because he was *still growing*. But the rooboter, yes that was a thing. He lay as if sleeping, yet smiled and heard what the Doctor's Eminence said to him and he had a human name: John Miller. What could be more friendly than that? Why she knew of women at the Gann who were already planning to call their children that when the time came. But perhaps the Dator could tell her, would John do for a girl child? So Maxim gave out with Joan and Jean and Johanna and Joanne and felt a twinge of responsibility for these future souls who might be so named.

It was all as comfortable as his mother's kitchen at Edenvale. With the host, Stan Cross, he talked about the sea, the red ocean that sent its skinny gray gulls inland to this corral in stormy weather. The skyship couldn't have picked a better time: the stormy season was past, would not come again until after the kelp harvest and the field harvest. This was the best time of year for a search but Vail knew if anything could be found. Mind you, there had been marvelous rescues in the past, trader crews had endured for many days, had been blown incredibly far from their course, had been brought in by the kindly Delfin. Destris, Mallin, Gline, sea captains of old time, had made many rescues although the ocean claimed their own vessels in the end. What lay westward? Why, more land and another ocean, the largest of all the seas, which stretched to the end of the world.

They talked late and Maxim had only a short sleep, but he awoke full of excitement for the end of the journey. His parmel was a young male, skittish, but strong, taking the last of the desert highway in its stride. For the hills of the Divide came nearer on his right hand and on his left in the far distance he saw a blurred plain with trees and a blueness that must be the swamp forest or jungle. Ahead the land soon grew green and he was able to pick out the course of the Gann River itself. He could not see the falls but the riverbank nearest him was settled, it would be a town itself soon. There were larger buildings on either side of the river, barns or warehouses, and further away to the left, the south, some hurrah's nest of timber.

The road skirted the settlement and he went on, nodding to a few people weeding their fields. He could look up and

188

admire the falls now and see the bridge over the river and beyond it something that might be the roof of the Station House. The hurrah's nest had sorted itself into a shipyard; two sizable vessels were being built and a third was in dry dock. There was a marina at the bend of the river with smaller boats, pleasure boats but he guessed the wharves were further on.

He came about eleven of the morning to the last corral and it was totally deserted; no one was expected in or out. He tied up his beast, sluiced it from a tank, stored his saddle in a big tack room where saddles just as fine were left unattended. Then he took his saddlebags and headed for the bridge.

There was a handsome noticeboard standing left of the bridge: BOATS FOR HIRE. DAN KELLY'S MARINA. THIS WAY, 200M. Maxim walked on to the bridge and looked upstream. He saw a mill, with a millrace and pond; the trees, probably hardwood, bent over the stream and the place was greener than the garden of the Pleasance, back in Rhomary.

"Where did you spring from?"

The voice was loud and clear but a shade hesitant. A girl came out from under the bridge by the far bank and walked up until she stood on the road.

"Good day," said Maxim, "does anyone live hereabouts?"

"Where are you from?" she asked again.

He saw that she was tall and shapely; her hair was a dark, rich red, an incredible color. Sky, she was more beautiful than Ambel, was this what they bred here at the Gann?

"I fell down with the earthship, of course," he said coolly. "Take me to your leader!"

The girl laughed.

"If you fell down why are you wearing Rhomary gear?"

"Well, I came upon some humanoid creatures riding a six-legged beast," he said. "They ran off so I borrowed some clothes from the saddlebag. My silver suit was hardly decent."

"You have all these strange words off pat," she said. "I would think you were a doctor if you had no beard."

"You have doctors to spare, here at the Gann!"

"Come along," she said. "Do you really want to see the Rancher? She is in a meeting but it will be done soon."

She came up to him and they stared frankly at one another. He could not look so directly into her light but

189

turned aside and leaned on the bridge rail again, looking down at the mill. What he wanted to do, suddenly, was stay with this girl.

"What trees are they, by the mill?" he asked.

"They are Earth trees," she said. "They grow nowhere else in Rhomary . . . except a few gardens in the city, I guess."

"But how did they come here?"

"Frenck brought them here, Albert Frenck who began the trading station in the year 1031. He had some seeds and slips from many trees but only these flourished, here by the water."

"What are they called?"

"Weeping willows," she said, "and the strange thing is there is a hardwood tree, a native, that looks like them. So it is called a native willow."

"I wonder if they have bred true, the Earth trees?" he said. "Or has the planet changed them the way it has changed us?"

"Are we so much changed? I mean in our human nature?"

"Have you seen the android, John Miller? Does he look like an inhabitant of the Rhomary land?"

"No," she said, "but then, does he look like the men and women on the spaceship? Perhaps these androids are made more perfect than creatures of flesh and blood."

He looked at her sidelong and thought she was perfect, but could hardly frame a compliment.

"Will you tell me your name?" he asked.

"Will you stop all this fooling and tell me yours? And why you came here?"

"I'm recruiting for Flip Kar Karn's circus," he said dramatically, flinging back his cloak. "I hear you have a promising young giant, name of Dit."

"Oh stop!" she could not help laughing. "He is a nice boy, you must not tease him. Besides he is not much taller than you . . ."

"Oh, well," said Maxim, "I will settle for some young women to wear transparent jocca robes and ride about on snow white parmels. Will you come along?"

"Oh stop talking all this quatsh!" she said. "You don't know much about the circus! Tell me who you are and I'll take you to . . . the Rancher."

Something in the way she said these words told him who she was. His heart lurched and sank.

"You are Shona Dun Mor!" he said.

"I make no secret of it."

As they walked over the bridge she gave him a slow smile that made his head reel.

They climbed a path that led to a ramp, built of wood and packed earth. The Gann Station began to show itself as they came higher. Maxim caught exciting glimpses of green and gold fields, houses on stilts, dams and ponds. He saw the river broad and blue-green, flowing on to the distant reddish line of the ocean. The Station House rose up ahead like a castle of Old Earth. He knew that this was the most beautiful and interesting place he had ever visited; Gil Roak must have been mad not to appreciate its wonders.

# Chapter X

## *Revelations*

---

Gurl Hign went in empty-handed to the business meeting; she had nothing to give out, the next caravan from the east was not expected for at least five days. She was careful to keep her expression cheerful and noncommittal, yet she looked at ranchhands and farmers with a sort of alarm. She saw faces, dark, quiet; she saw defects and differences; a twisted lip, patches of blanched hair on a youthful head, a squint, a game leg, a hand with six fingers, the roomy sandals that hid an extra toe on each foot. There was a large turnout this morning because a new ship was due in from the south coast with the first of the kelp harvest. The *Comet* had sailed to load up kelp and redweed two days ago; already another ship was in dock, the trader *Colleen Cross*, and they awaited the *Seahawk* within the hour. Tomorrow or the next day it might be the brig *Dancer* returning from further west.

"Extra hands to clear the third kelp barn," she said. "Thank you Dan, Shawn. Sure you have time?"

"Surely, Rancher," said Dan Kelly. "We're slack at the shipyard and the marina."

"Be ready for a wave of visitors in the next few months," said Gurl. "Any more? Thank you, Molly, Trim . . ."

No shortage of volunteers. The kelp harvest was the biggest ever; it was an omen for their own grain and fruit, now ripening well. She looked every morning at the big new plantation across the river, planted well above the flood-line on "enriched tussock land."

"No one from across the river?" she glanced through the hall again.

"Beggars still sulking, I reckon," murmured Sam Cross, a Committee Man who stood by her table.

"There are a few at the dock," called a woman. "Skeleton shift every day now since . . ."

"Do they still fish with the fleet, Mister Fell?" asked Gurl.

"One or two. Skeleton fleet, you might say," said the old fisherman.

"Is there anyone . . ."

She looked about and saw a young man, brick red.

"Ah yes, Herm Dann, you're keeping company with Hope Nujons. Will you go visit her?"

He came close to the table, a picture of anxiety, twisting his straw hat in his hands. It was difficult at any time to keep company with a Jenzite girl but Herm had persevered with his Hope. She felt sure it would make a marriage; perhaps young Herm would join the Friends and settle over the river.

"I been across once since, Rancher," said Herm Dann. "I . . . I was planning to go again today."

"What's the mood over there, Herm?" she asked.

He hung his head; it must be worse than she had thought. The church elders or Companions must have ruled against full contact with the Station. The Jenzites would not join in the life of the Station fully until John Miller was removed. She could not help calculating; five, ten, thirty days to the harvest, what arrangement could she make about the new plantation which was partly on Jenzite land? Then she felt the inevitable twinge of anger: Coll had persuaded Frenck to give them this land in the first place. Ingratitude. But she was making trouble before it came; the Jenzites were practical enough not to let their grain go to waste.

"I'll give you a letter to Marko and the Companions," she said. "Don't worry, Herm, nothing is your fault. This is a difficult time, but we'll all come through, Jenzites and Station people both. Come to me after the midday meal for the letter."

Poor Herm Dann could only nod his head. She felt a sudden anxiety: what was the matter with the boy? Had they forbidden him to see Hope, the daughter of Nujons, a Companion? She couldn't question him before the meeting. A young girl called from the back of the room:

"How is our John Miller, Rancher?"

"Here's the report . . ." said Gurl, bringing it from her pocket.

"Following the shutdown while his left hand was replaced, according to his own instructions, John Miller has reported as follows in writing, as he did on the first day he arrived at the Gann Station.

"'The space vehicle which divided over the landmass eight days ago was World Space Service Class AR for Argosy Transporter, Number 04, Name: *Serendip Dana*. Complement 139 souls, including 90 regular crew members, 36 members of the Silver Cross Air Space Maintenance Unit, 12 members of the Mixed Media Team KONO and one civilian passenger. Destination: Port Garrett, Arkady, Alpha Centauri System.'

"John Miller has limited information on the fate of those listed above. We are working to restore speech and movement; there will be other shutdown periods but regular reports will be given.

"Los Smitwode, Third Consultant."

This was damnably difficult to read and she stumbled over the hard words although she had practiced them and checked some of the meanings with the Doctor's Eminence. The Station people followed with breathless interest, and when Sam Cross tacked the report to the notice board they crowded around to read it again if they could.

Gurl Hign watched them eagerly taking in the Primary Records of the *Serendip Dana* and knew that something had been loosed upon the world. Generations had passed in the Rhomary land without a scrap of news to compare with this. So far as she knew old Smitwode was not exercising much censorship; Shona assisted the two doctors and helped prepare the reports.

"Rancher," called Sam Cross, "what in dry hell is a mixed media team KONO?"

Gurl Hign laughed sadly, for she had asked the same question.

"Team of singers, dancers, musicians and such," she said. "KONO was the name of the team."

At that moment a weird thuttering cry echoed as far as the Station House and the news readers turned away laughing. It was the conch sounding aboard the trader *Seahawk*, Cap Swift's call sign as she came sailing down the Gann. Every captain had a personal call: LaMar used a bell, Holly of the *Colleen Cross* a bell with a different note. The hall emptied quickly and Gurl Hign was left alone with the sunlight falling across the boards. She must get down to the dock. But she sat at the high table reliving that first encounter with John Miller in this place, soon after he had been brought in and set down.

She stood with Ben, who would not leave her side, and they saw John Miller waving the fingers of his right hand in a curious seeking gesture. Los Smitwode took out his silver fountain pen and a notebook. He placed the pen between John Miller's fingers and laid his hand upon the block of reed paper. The pale, well-shaped hand knew what to do: as they watched one word was printed followed by a question mark. "Human?" asked John Miller.

"Yes," said Los Smitwode drily and distinctly, leaning toward Miller's face.

There was a fumbling pause, then another question: "Who?"

A moment was at hand that Gurl had imagined quite differently. The Earth folk, the newcomers, were lifted from wreckage or from the sea. They were amazed or frightened to find human beings on this planet, but there *were* human beings. Flat-headed, splay-footed dark runty types they might be, but the people of the Rhomary land were fellow humans, brothers and sisters . . . tears of recognition and of joy were shed at this first meeting. . . . Now, in fact, the information was delivered in the doctors's crisp college speech.

"We are the descendants of Earth settlers cast away on

194

this planet some two hundred years ago. We call the part of the planet that we inhabit the Rhomary land."

John Miller's face moved slightly after this pronouncement. After some time he wrote "Spell it."

The watchers laughed uneasily and were silenced by a flashing glance from the Third Consultant. He spelled the word. Rhomary. Pronounced Romarry or something nearer to Rummarry in country districts. There was another pause and the fine hand made a single notation.

"Yes," said Smitwode, as if he approved a pupil's work, "the greek letter Rho."

The moving fingers wrote again, a longer expression that threatened to run off the page until Shona reached out and turned the notebook a little sideways.

"Yes," said Smitwode, "you have written the name of the ship. We are the descendants of the crew and passengers of the *Rho Maryland*."

His voice wavered very slightly. Gurl felt the tears spill over from her own eyes and course down her cheeks. Ben gripped her hand tightly and spoke everyone's thoughts.

"Oh, Ma," he said, "they still remember. . . ."

Another squawl from Cap Swift's conch shell brought her back. She went out and in again, into the office for her clipboard. Bluggy bills of lading. The tail end of a cry followed her; there were quick steps on the ramp and Shona came in. She was bright-eyed; the skeins of her hair matched the dark rust-red of her old jocca overall.

"What is it?" asked Gurl.

"A man! Someone has arrived from Rhomary city!"

"What? So soon? Oh, it is just a chance. . . . What sort of a man, anyway?"

"He knows about the earthship, Ma. He asks the strangest questions."

Shona stood at the door and opened it a crack.

"Look . . ." she said. "Take a look, Ma. What do you think of him?"

Not just a man then, but a man who interested her hard-to-please daughter. Gurl peered out obediently. A young man, tall and well built, was striding up and down impatiently on the ramp. His hair was thick and the sunlight brought out lights in his beard.

"He's lovely," said Gurl. "Better keep him off the wharf or those randy sailor gals will have the breeks off him."

"Ma, behave yourself!"

195

"I was thinking of a merchant . . . or maybe he is a merchant."

"No, he's acting too mysterious."

"Just wants to get you interested!"

They both peered through the crack of the door and fell back laughing when the young man turned toward them. Sky, thought Gurl, I like the cut of his jib better than poor Gil Roak.

"He has some letters to be delivered into your hand," said Shona.

"Come on, then," said Gurl, "stop looking at your reflection in the window and we'll solve the mystery."

She opened the office door; the young man squared his shoulders and flicked back his cloak as if he sensed an occasion. Who was he then?

"Rancher Hign?"

He smiled and the smile was, momentarily, for her alone. Then he looked at Shona and swung away and took in the whole of the Gann Station, from the hilltops to the docks. He held his arms wide and then let them fall as if he could hardly express his gladness.

"To be here . . . to be here at last!"

He whisked a small packet from under his cloak like a magician and pressed it into her hands.

"From Urbain Bro, in fond greeting!"

"Is that where you come from!" exclaimed Gurl Hign. "The Dator's House!"

"More than that!"

"An archivist?" said Shona. "Is that what you are?"

"Well, I am that!" said the young man, teasing.

Gurl Hign had read what was written on the packet and now she laughed. The nephew, of course, and old Urbain had retired at last.

"You're nothing like your uncle to look at," she said.

In answer to Shona's look of exasperation he announced formally:

"Maxim Bro, Dator of Rhomary!"

"I'm sorry I didn't push you off the bridge," said Shona.

"Mam Hign," said Maxim Bro, "I came here on some strange and unconfirmed reports of the earthship that has fallen. I met Dr. Gil Roak on the way and saw the piece of wreckage. Then I heard much more at the Third Corral. How fares John Miller?"

"The Doctor's Eminence is putting him in order. He has made a few written reports about the ship."

"Mam, how is the TC and how is his intern?"

"Both well," she said, "but Jaygo had a small . . . accident."

His questioning look made her go on.

"There was trouble when we brought John Miller in aboard the *Comet*. The Jenzites have something in their book that they read as forbidding these rooboters. They're still sulking about it."

They stood and stared at the neat white houses of the Jenzite settlement. Those near the levee bank rose on stilts; the Jenzite wives hung their washing under their houses on rainy days. Shona pointed out the new plantation and the chapel and at that moment the morning wind brought a couple of bell notes, abruptly silenced. Gurl Hign shivered; were they cleaning the bells?

"There is a ship just coming in," said the new Dator, "Might they have a further sighting?"

"They might," said Gurl Hign. "The *Colleen Cross* had talk of lights in the sky and the *Seahawk* went further southeast, to the Robs Station."

Maxim Bro set down his saddlebags at the office door and was ready to run off down to the docks in search of information.

"Come along!" said Shona. "Shall I take him down, Ma?"

"Oh, take him, take him," said Gurl Hign.

She put the letters and the baggage in the office and then went down to the docks at a fair clip. The world was full of wonders. The crowd on the dock were shouting and calling; the sound of raised voices in this place was shocking to her. She felt a rush of fear and anger again although she knew the trouble was over. The Station people were shouting for news: did the *Seahawk* crew see the earthship, had they found flotsam, were there lights in the sky?

Gurl Hign strode through the crowd and came to the young Dator standing with Shona at the edge of the dock. The tall stranger was attracting curious glances but he seemed unaware of it; he looked about him with a sort of joy.

"Listen to that, Mam Hign!" he said.

"They have become news-hungry," she said.

There was a final blast of the conch and Cap Swift appeared at the rail with her trumpeter, a barrel-chested young sailor. The Captain was a burly woman in her fifties; she leaned on her great sunburned forearms and called in a harsh wheezing voice:

"Where's the Rancher?"

"Ahoy, Captain!" Gurl lifted up her voice.

"Come aboard!" commanded Cap Swift.

"I'll bring the Dator!"

"The what? That young fella?"

"The Dator of Rhomary!"

Maxim Bro took his cue and bowed to the captain. Cap Swift turned to a pair of sailor women lounging at her side and made a remark that set them laughing.

"Come aboard!" she said again.

The gangplank was already rattling down.

"Whew!" said Maxim Bro. "Is she a friend of yours, Rancher?"

"We work well enough together," said Gurl Hign.

"She's an old devil!" said Shona.

"The *Seahawk* was the name of Gline's ship," said Maxim.

"Vera Swift sailed with Gline," said Gurl Hign. "Devil or not she's a good sailor."

"Won't you come aboard with us?" Maxim turned to Shona.

"Not invited," said Gurl, overlapping with Shona herself.

"I'd rather stay clear of the *Seahawk!*" she said.

They were at the gangplank and Gurl ushered the young man ahead of her. She turned back, halfway up, and called to the people on the wharf.

"Back to work!" she shouted. "If there's anything to be known I'll have it posted for all to read."

The crowd dispersed obediently and she felt the same thrill of fear from the time of the riot. That time they had not gone about their business; her nerve was badly shaken. She had done what had to be done for a long time: she had led and they had followed. But what if they refused to follow? She steered the Dator through a clutch of grinning sailor women and they went on into the Captain's cabin. Swift had power of life and death over the crew of the *Seahawk;* her strong hand never loosened its grip.

The cabin was lined with rare woods, polished to a high luster, and the Captain commonly drank from silver beakers.

"We have something you will want," said Cap Swift waving a hand at the upholstered benches.

Gurl Hign understood the look on her weatherbeaten face, but the Dator was more innocent.

198

"More wreckage? Where is it, Captain? It's important for me to see it exactly as found . . ."

"Not so fast," said Cap Swift showing her excellent white teeth. "The Rancher and I have some business to do. What's with those sorry wowsers, the Jenzites, by the way?"

"They have the Station under ban," said Gurl. "Did you hear of our visitor, John Miller?"

"We've heard nothing else."

"And you want to add to our store of knowledge?"

"Somewhat," said the Captain. "I think it's worth an overall increase in the price of the cargo."

"Not a chance," said Gurl. "Bonus or nothing. I don't care if you've twenty Earthmen in the hold."

She saw Maxim Bro's shocked face and hoped he would keep quiet.

"You can afford it!" said Cap Swift. "Squeeze the increase from the Rhomary subsidy!"

"Your cargo will spoil," said Gurl reasonably. "It must come to the drying racks. We have not much use for the kelp and weed here on the Station, we buy it for the city refinery and for Derry. You know I'm shorthanded without our holy friends from over the river. A bonus for yourself and all hands!"

"Twenty and two!" said Cap Swift.

"Five and one-half," said Gurl Hign. "I'm buying a dry-hog in a basket. If this is poor stuff I'll back out."

"The stuff is good. This fine Rhomary stud could write a book on it," said Cap Swift. "Eat your heart out that your old man LaMar never hit on it first. Ten and one."

"Done!" said Gurl Hign. "I trust you, Vera, my dear."

She shook hands with the captain.

"What is this rate?" asked Maxim Bro softly.

"Credits," said Cap Swift.

"Allow me, Mam Hign," said Maxim. "I'll pay the captain's bonus in silver. Nine for ten."

Cap Swift smiled.

"Ah, this is a good-hearted boy," she said.

Maxim counted out the silver dollars into her broad palm and she bawled:

"Duty officer!"

A bearded sailor stood in the cabin doorway, smiling.

"Unloading can begin. Send in the flotsam."

She threw one of the silver dollars and the man caught it nimbly.

"Relax," said Cap Swift, pouring drinks from a leather bottle. "Try this sugar-vine schnapps from Robs Station."

They sank the fiery spirit from their silver cups and waited.

"I understand you sailed with Gline, Captain," said the Dator.

"I was his second mate," said Cap Swift. "I brought home the *Rover* and sailed the first rescue expedition."

"Did you know a sailor called Hilo Hill?"

The captain's cheerful face had clouded. Whether it was a reaction to the sailor's name or a reluctance to talk about the whole expedition Gurl could not tell.

"I can't recall every hogger and swabber," growled Cap Swift.

Steps sounded outside the door and two women heaved in a bundle on a stretcher, shrouded in grass matting. They set it down in the middle of the cabin and ran off even before the Captain had time to wave her hand.

"Take a look," said Cap Swift to Maxim. "It won't bite."

Gurl Hign rose at once and twitched the covers from the stretcher. The piece of flotsam was a bulky package, striped black and yellow, about two meters by three, the outer casing of tough, smooth fabric. On the upper surface were two wrinkled, collapsed sections.

"Found floating?" asked Gurl Hign.

"Old Man Robs had a tip-off from some of the Delfin strays that hang around his station. He knew something had come down and that a piece of wreckage had been seen southeast of the Six Seven Isles. The main crash area was northwest of the islands . . . dunno how this piece come so far. Maybe it was caught in one of the eddies around the islands. Another few days and it might have beached. We kept watch on our homeward way and sure enough there were two swim-bladders, yellow, showing above the water like some giant woman lying there. Do you know what it is?"

"Not a glimmer," said Gurl Hign.

She followed Maxim Bro as the young man walked around and around the thing, prodding the sides occasionally with a finger. No labels or handgrips, a square red patch on one of the short ends.

"Did you try to open it, Captain?" asked Gurl.

"Thought about it," grinned Vera Swift. "Truth to tell the boys and gals were scared of the bluggy thing. Said

200

there was a dead body inside or a floating bomb. What do you think, Dator?"

"Neither of those things, Captain. And it's lost a label with instructions, very likely." The young man tweaked aside a small corner of the red patch, then replaced it. "Do *you* know what it is?"

"Vail bless the child," said Cap Swift, "of course I do!" She smiled so widely that her gray eyes disappeared into folds of flesh.

"And weren't you curious?" asked Maxim Bro.

"Surely, but I had my duty to all the data-lovers back in the city, didn't I? I decided it was worth more the way it is. I have to live, Dator, and keep the crew happy. When the harvest is unloaded the *Seahawk* goes into dry dock here on the Gann and we poor sailor folk head for Derry and for Rhomary to spend our few credits."

"Sing me a ballad," said Gurl Hign, laughing. "You're the richest trader hereabouts. And I'm not in the secret . . . I don't know what we have here."

"Take it away," said the captain. "Let this young fella play with it in the hall, that's my advice."

Maxim Bro nodded to Gurl Hign and she saw that he was anxious to unload the new object.

"Fine," she said. "We'll return your stretcher, Captain."

She heaved up the front end of the stretcher and the Dator took the other. The package was heavy; she was glad they had no ladder to climb. They came from the cabin to the deck and down the gangplank and on the wharf took a rest while curious dock workers downed tools and came to stare. Gurl told off two new porters, Little Diggy Dit and one of the Cross boys, to take the package into the hall. As they followed it Alan came up and she introduced him to the Dator.

"What's *that?*" said Alan. "It looks like a two-colored coffin!"

"Come to the hall," said Maxim. "We'll give a little show. Where is your daughter, Mam Hign? Will she watch too?"

"Shona has gone to the hostel," said Alan. "Helping the Doctor's Eminence."

They went on up to the hall; Gurl let the ordinary work of the day be pushed to the back of her mind. Bills of lading, the kelp barn . . . guests for midday food . . . she must speak to Bridey; and where would young Bro sleep, with the Third Consultant and his intern plus one rooboter cluttering up the guest hostel. The old watchroom upstairs, perhaps, the room where she and Coll had slept on summer nights, watching the stars above the hills.

In the hall they found Little Diggy and Tad Cross, bolder than the members of Cap Swift's crew, poking and prodding the yellow and black bundle.

"Go canny!" said Gurl. "Let the Dator look at it, you two great goobies!"

"Do you know what it is, Rancher?" asked Little Diggy.

"Not me," said Gurl Hign, "but I think the Dator knows . . ."

"Here now . . ." said Alan.

Shona had come in through the back door of the hall with Jaygo, trim and erect, in that uniform which made him look, Gurl thought, like a nurse aide. The young intern shook the Dator by the hand and Maxim Bro said:

"I have spoken with your mother."

Jaygo's green eyes were fiery for a moment.

"She worries unnecessarily. What signs, what lights in the heavens brought you here at such a great rate, Dator Bro?"

"I have discovered an old man who dreams true," said the Dator.

Jaygo laughed aloud.

"Vern Munn! Did he dream all this then?"

"Down to the presence of an android and the cut on your face!" said Maxim Bro.

Jaygo was angry; the color rose in the intern's pale cheeks. Gurl Hign wondered what his parentage was. Surely he came from some rich Rhomary family . . . merchants, doctors. The talk of dreams was mysterious.

"Is that what Cap Swift brought in?" Shona was trying to change the subject. "What in the world . . . ?"

"The Dator won't tell what it is," said Gurl, smiling. "We're waiting for enlightenment."

"It's a lifeboat," said Jaygo sharply. "The design hasn't changed much in two hundred years!"

The intern strode up to the striped package, ripped off its red patch.

"Still a ringpull!" he cried.

"No!" shouted Maxim Bro. "No. . . ."

But Jaygo had tugged firmly on the ring; a thick cord came away and a loud hissing sound filled the hall. Little Diggy and Tad instinctively cowered away. The striped package began to heave and swell and then it took off.

The swelling yellow-black mound charged at the Dator, Gurl, Shona and Alan, and they scattered. It changed course, bounced toward the beams of the hall overhead and fell down on Jaygo where he had fallen off the ringpull. It charged at Little Diggy who had come to help the intern, pursued him in a half circle, caught him in the back of the knees and threw him over its back. Gurl Hign began to laugh.

"Ma," gasped Alan, half helpless with laughter, "here it comes again . . ."

She ran, cannoned into a crowd of watchers at the outer door.

"Don't let it out!" she shouted.

They put up a forest of hands and the yellow and black monster bounced off this wall, rode right over Jaygo and the Dator who was dragging the intern to one side, headed for the side wall and stopped. A lifeboat. A sturdy fabric construction about six meters by three with a hooded cabin, a thick inflated rim, countless pockets and compartments. She went to stare at it again, warily, with the others, and saw that they were struck with the same thought. A marvelous contraption like this, but unused, unopened. No survivors had used the lifeboat.

"Poor devils!" said Jaygo. "What will you do, Bro, log it here on the spot?"

"Log every inch of it," said the Dator, looking at the lifeboat with consuming interest. "Cap Swift said I might write a book on it and by the Vail she was right."

"I'll take the liberty of extracting the first-aid case," said Jaygo.

"I'll turn it over unopened," said the Dator. "Where can I work on this treasure, Mam Hign?"

"Right here, if you will," said Gurl Hign. "You can have screens if you want them."

"No need," said Maxim Bro.

Gurl went off to the kitchen and found old Bridey watching and smiling through the door.

"I've made extra," she said. "For the officers of the *Seahawk* and the young man from the city."

They looked at the young people working on the boat. Little Diggy and Tad helped heave the thing away from the wall; Alan had brought out a measuring tape; Maxim Bro and the intern made notes. Then in an instant it turned to play: everyone climbed into the boat and sat down as if they were playing castaways. Maxim had produced a white paddle and was showing Shona how to use it, a thing she knew, probably, much better than he did. Jaygo sat alone in the boat and the others hauled it about on the floor. Alan called attention to something on the underside of the boat so Jaygo was unceremoniously tipped out while the underside was examined.

Gurl left them to it and sat at the kitchen table, seeing the old leaf collage over the sink that Coll had made, remembering the day when the first slip of wreckage had arrived with LaMar.

"Rancher," said Bridey softly, "I wonder if you thought to ask . . ."

"I forgot," said Gurl Hign. "Pardon me, Bridey. It was the excitement with the Dator coming and this lifeboat."

"Is that what it is?" said the old women, wondering.

"We can ask the captain at dinner for news of the *Dancer*."

Bridey's grandchild, Paddy Rork, was aboard the ship that had sailed to Gline's Cape at the edge of the map or beyond to hunt the giant black-rays, gather moss-fowl eggs and spice berries and continue the search for fever trees. A week or more overdue but that was nothing, they would start to worry after a month or two.

"Bridey," she said, "do you remember Gline and his crew?"

"Like it was yesterday," said Bridey, stirring a cauldron on its hook. "Hal Gline was a high roller, a true dream merchant. Vera Swift, second mate, was slim as a young palm. Rork was a strong man with both of his long legs."

"Was there a sailor called Hilo Hill?"

"Surely," said Bridey. "He was their cook. A brown man, middle-sized, about forty, with pleasing ways. But Rancher, this is in your time too. . . ."

"When we came," said Gurl, "everyone was waiting for Gline. He was six months overdue."

"Everyone . . ." laughed Bridey. "A few sailor wives and their children, besides Al Frenck. Three or four huts besides this stone house. Rork had begun me a stone house but when he was brought back peg-legged it would have gone to ruin if Coll and yourself hadn't helped us to haul stone."

The old woman drew breath and wiped her sleeve across her eyes.

"Hush up," said Gurl Hign gently. "Too much talk of the past. The *Dancer* will soon be home."

But she did think . . . what if the *Dancer* does not come? . . . And this worked like a premonition. For the days lengthened out into months and there were wonders to behold and work to be done but the brig *Dancer* never sailed home.

## 2

Los Smitwode sat on the back verandah of the guest hostel at the end of another long day; he felt the familiar pull of tired muscles in his neck and shoulders. He shuffled the new pile of papers that inhabited his red folder with an altogether unfamiliar feeling of incompetence. For all the diagrams, the slow explanations in neat script, the notes that he had made himself, he could reach no full understanding of the workings of John Miller. He could only follow instructions where possible. Two pages in Miller's handwriting, part of the material that the Third Consultant had designated General Recall, he read again with particular care. Then he tucked one away, brought it out again guiltily and let it lie in a clip with the rest.

"Eminence . . . ?"

The young man stood by the steps; he carried a large platten woven from kelp. Smitwode knew who it was and also recognized him, more clearly than he had expected to do from their brief meeting in the city.

"Dator Bro!"

"Please don't get up," said the Dator. "I know you must be tired."

"It is the natural condition of a doctor," said Smitwode. "How is your uncle? How goes the city?"

"My uncle is lively enough and the city was in the grip of the furn when I left it."

"What have you got there?"

The young man propped the kelp platten against the house wall and the doctor saw that it had a map pinned to it. The Rhomary land, from the deserts of sand east of the Billsee to the deserts of stone in the far north; the jungles of the south and the limits of the Gline voyages in the Red Ocean.

"I have this from Jame Denny, the schoolteacher," said Maxim Bro. "You will see that I have marked . . ."

"I do see. Please tell me what you think these markings indicate?"

"Why," said young Bro, bristling slightly though he lacked his uncle's temperament, "the breakup of the *Serendip Dana* into six rescue capsules over this northwestern area of the landmass."

"How do you arrive at these positions?"

"By comparing the sightings," said Maxim Bro. "And I postulate a seventh section, unmanned, which fell to earth in the innermost part of the unexplored jungle about a hundred kilometers northwest of the Sooree River. Then the capsules: one striking in the Red Ocean near the Six Seven Isles, another inland, near or on the Sooree, a third in the jungle directly north of this station, beyond the hills of the Divide, a fourth in the desert beyond the town of Bork. The two remaining ones, uncertain, but both farther north and northwest, in jungle or conceivably in the Red Ocean or the extension of the Red Ocean beyond Gline Cape, the area which Gline wished to call another sea."

"Remarkable. And what have the College and the Council to say to this? What action has been undertaken?"

"None that I know of," said Maxim. "This is all conjecture from unconfirmed observations. I left my uncle to bring what we had before the Council but there are reasons why they might take no action at all."

"What possible reasons. . . ?"

Maxim smiled and handed him a piece of jocca paper; he knew the handwriting at once although he had not seen it for ten years.

"Junik," said Los Smitwode, unable to keep the bitterness out of his voice. "Well, she has gathered her wits about her. She observes the stars."

"Can you confirm?" asked the Dator eagerly. "Has John Miller confirmed any of these placings?"

"Yes," said the Third Consultant reluctantly. "So far as we can work out your placings are correct. I can even give the numbers of the Capems or emergency capsules."

"And the wreckage, the lifeboat brought in by Cap Swift and John Miller himself all come from this one capsule which landed in the Red Ocean?"

"No," said Los Smitwode carefully, laying a hand on the papers before him. "No. He came on *his* piece of wreckage down the Sooree River into the ocean. From Capem Tree or Three. The one which yielded the lifeboat and the first piece of wreckage was Capem Sexer or Six. A most important one for the *Serendip Dana* for it contained their administrative officers and their records."

"I have been thinking about this capsule," said Maxim Bro, "the one that fell into the jungle beyond the Divide."

"That one?" echoed Los Smitwode. "Its name is Bulk One by the way. For a rescue mission?"

"No, sir. I would not pick this as most obvious for a rescue mission. But when they came down in the early morning, I expect they were clearly visible from Silver City. And the light of the town would be clearly visible to those aboard."

"Would there be lights at this time?"

"In Silver City, yes," said Maxim Bro. "The mine workings are brightly lit with palm oil lamps."

"It is all conjecture," said the Third Consultant sadly. "What were you thinking would follow from this? That the people aboard Bulk One . . . it also carried animals . . . would march out of the jungle, cross a hundred kilometers or so of desert heading for that cluster of lights? Why, they would scarcely associate them with a human habitation. . . ."

"No," said Maxim, "but perhaps the other way about. The people of Silver City might be eager to find a large meteorite. There are a number of . . . prospectors in the Rhomary land."

The young man's look was so strange that Smitwode put it down to a trick of the light. He got up wearily and gathered papers into his folder.

"Come inside. We can see John Miller. It is a so-called shutdown period for the regeneration of his synapses."

"Wait," said Maxim Bro, "wait, before we see him. Mr. Smitwode, can this be the sole survivor?"

"I can't believe this is the sole survivor," said Los Smitwode, "the jungle may be full of them."

"We must search for them at once!"

"Easily said. You see what we have here . . . a fleet of trading vessels!"

"You have made no plans?"

"I have something in mind . . ."

The Dator was frowning with impatience.

"Who was aboard the Capsule Three?" he demanded. "How many others? What became of them? John Miller must have told you!"

"Only two persons," said Los Smitwode. "It was the smallest capsule and it contained, besides Miller, one passenger and a noncommissioned officer. They may, with the greatest good luck, be in a lifeboat on the Sooree River."

"Then we must find them!" said Maxim Bro. "Eminence, how can you hold back?"

"I don't hold back," snapped Los Smitwode. "Stop this damned foolishness!"

"Great Vail, don't you want to find these people?"

"More than anything else," said the Third Consultant. "The passenger aboard the *Serendip Dana* was one Karl-Heinz-Jurgen Valente, a physician and surgeon!"

"Then we *must* . . ."

"I learned this today," said Los Smitwode, keeping his voice even. "John Miller's passages of General Recall have been short and disturbed. I have already made arrangements to speak to the Rancher tomorrow morning. You can be present, Dator. You will have your search, be sure of it, but it will go at the pace of the wind and the sea, like everything else on the Gann Station."

He swept the last of the papers into his folder and strode into the hostel. A lamp was already alight in the passageway; he turned it up and carried it into the sitting room. The bulk of John Miller, flat out upon a trestle table, filled the room. A padded quilt covered him to his chest; the skin of his face, of his massive shoulders and arms, was very pale; it seemed to give off its own light.

Smitwode set down the lamp, lit another and checked the android's responses in places that were not determined by his human anatomy. He peeled back the neck flap, studied the pectoral panel. He looked back at the Dator and saw his own queer image reflected in the young man's awe-stricken look. The mad doctor himself, inhuman as the creature upon which he worked.

"You may come closer," he said.

Maxim Bro stepped up and was reassured, as Smitwode knew he would be, by John Miller's face, gentle as the face of a sleeping child.

"How many of the ship's company were 'auxiliary personnel?' " asked the Dator softly.

"Twenty-five," said Smitwode. "And there were another ten in the maintenance engineering team they were bringing to the Arkady spaceport. I have kept these figures out of the reports."

He went to the table and poured two glasses of the fortified palm wine he had brought from the city . . . ages ago . . . for his nightcaps. He sat down with the Dator in two chairs against the wall of the small plain room and they still spoke in low voices. Now and then small threads of sound came from the body of John Miller.

"You made good time from Rhomary," remarked the Third Consultant.

"I traveled in a private vessel over the Western Sea."

"You had great faith in Junik's report!"

"It was confirmed when I met Doctor Gil Roak on his way to the city."

The Third Consultant wondered if there were no more comfortable subjects in the world. As he refilled their glasses a light step was heard and Jaygo came in through the front door. The intern looked tired and pale, like every other intern that Smitwode could remember, including himself. The epicene beauty, he realized, would gradually change and harden, as if it were no more than a lengthy adolescence. At thirty Jaygo would look like . . . a doctor, robed, beardless.

"Surgery was packed," said Jaygo, setting down the Third Consultant's massive leather case. "Luke knows how schoolchildren break their fingers."

"Playing swing-volley," said Maxim Bro promptly. "They have the leather ball filled with sand."

The two doctors laughed aloud.

"Make a note," said Los Smitwode. "The swing-volley syndrome, as described by the Dator."

Jaygo went to John Miller and examined the chest panel.

"When will the shutdown end?" he asked, and without waiting for an answer, "Well, Dator, have you received any know about the passenger?"

"I do, and there will be a search!" said Maxim Bro.

"They are searching for *you* in the hall," said Jaygo. "Shona Dun will show you to your quarters in the old watchroom."

To Smitwode's surprise the Dator sprang up and began to take his leave. A fine specimen. Something to show the earthlings. No giantism, like the unfortunate Dit boy. He tried to think of John Miller, who emitted a faint whirring noise at that moment, standing upright in the small room.

When Maxim Bro had gone, Jaygo said:

"I thought that would shift him. What do you think of our Dator then?"

"He is much more of a bully than you are," said Los Smitwode.

"He is not your intern," smiled Jaygo. "Are you on night duty or am I?"

"My turn," said the Third Consultant. "Fetch the supper tray that Mam Netta Hign left in the kitchen."

A small lamp was left burning on the front door of the hostel to show that a doctor was always on call. Los Smitwode read for two hours after Jaygo had gone to bed, then stretched out on the long settle in the main room. John Miller was never left alone. Los Smitwode slept at once and more deeply than usual.

He woke in a dark hour, early morning before any streaks of dawn were in the sky. Certainly no light penetrated into the small room; it was some time before he could distinguish the shadowy outline of the window, the profile of John Miller. He did not know what had woken him: then he heard a stealthy footstep and another. Los Smitwode was suddenly afraid. He thought of the unbolted doors, of the unprotectable bulk of the android in the midst of the small wooden house. He rose to his feet silently and stood by the trestle table.

More footsteps, then a gentle tapping on the front door. A voice, a whisper; he could not tell if it was a man or a woman. . . .

"Doctor?"

He was relieved. A timid patient, that was all. In fact most night callers were apologetic, here on the Gann Station. He went to the front door and opened it. There was no one at the door; the darkness lay heavily over the settlement, the river, the distant sea.

"Who is it?" he asked sharply. "Do you need a doctor?"

There was no reply. The night lamp on the door had not burned out; he unhooked it and shed a pale circle of yellow light beyond the doorstep. He looked down and saw, just before the step, two dim packages. Was it that then? Offerings of fruit or simple gifts were sometimes left at the door: this time a scroll and a round straw basket. He bent down to retrieve the scroll first of all and before his hand stretched out for it the Third Consultant's sharp ears caught a dry rustle inside the basket.

He leaped back with a cry, holding the lamp high, and kicked the basket sharply away. The lid flew off and the brown whip-snake came out savagely, hissing and striking at the ground. He saw that the creature was tethered by the tail to the basket itself. He turned quickly back into the hostel, took up a cloth from the instrument table and the

210

sturdy hardwood poker from the fireplace. He hung the light on the door again, turned high as possible, then stepped outside. He covered the writhing snake and beat it to death. He took the light and went back into the hostel with the scroll. The noise had not wakened Jaygo in his small room by the kitchen. Los Smitwode sat alone when he had bolted the doors and checked the functioning of John Miller. This was all, he felt sure: the snake in a basket and a page from the Book of Jenz.

He had read the passage ages ago but in that hour it seemed remarkably fresh.

> The children in the schoolhouse were shown the picture of a city on the planet Earth. I sat on the steps in the sunshine and fell into a dream of those stone towers.
>
> I saw a million men and women who walked in the roaring streets. Their faces were gray, their eyes were full of pain, they walked as though their feet hurt. The sight of them filled me with pity.
>
> I saw other creatures in that crowd. Their eyes were lifeless, their smiles were cold. It came to me that these were slaves; these were creatures with no heart. Some were machines, made like men, but some were of flesh and blood and these were the worst for they had lost their humanity.
>
> I saw watchmen, White Coats, leaders, masters, and they were the same. They were empty and cold. They had no pity and no understanding.
>
> Then I came out of my dream and saw the village street, the watchhouse and the clinic. Let there be no heartless creatures in the Rhomary land.

Los Smitwode could only shake his head. What was it then? A simple, even simple-minded plea for warmth and tolerance plus another jab at the medical profession? Perhaps the man was honest, he had never ruled out that possibility. It was easy to imagine young Kindl seated on the schoolhouse steps in the Lemn Oasis, dreaming of Old Earth. But why had he persistently, even before his "healing ministry" began, withheld his tolerance from doctors, the hated White Coats. What sort of doctors did they have in his village but young men and women, just out of the hard days of internship, brimming with ideals, bored to extinction with country service? Los Smitwode felt a pang of con-

211

science even for the egregious Gil Roak, sent back to the rigors of Bork. Were any of these doctors, even young Roak, "heartless creatures"?

And now, he thought grimly, the same not particularly cryptic words of the prophet had urged the Jenzites to reject androids and to send him a poisonous snake in a basket. I must seem to them the model of a cold, heartless creature. The detachment of the surgeon is another thing again; I have cultivated this detachment. Be damned to the Jenzites, they are fools!

It was daylight. He got up stiffly, took the hardwood poker again, and went out of the hostel. He cleared away the remains of the snake and left them under his step to show the Rancher. He walked slowly all around the hostel, brushing at the damp grass, shivering a little in his silk robe. There were no signs of an intruder. He came back to the warmth of the sitting room and shut the door again.

*"Meister?"*

The voice made him jump. Then he stood where he was, rigid, unable to move. With a light thrust of sound, a heavy body disturbing the air, John Miller sat smoothly upright on the trestle table, turned his head and stared at the Third Consultant. His speech was heavily accented.

"Are you the doctor?"

"Yes!" he said. "Yes . . . Smitwode . . ."

He laid aside the blood-stained staff and came forward with outstretched hand. John Miller's handshake was bone-crushing. They stared frankly at each other, each measuring the other's humanity.

"How's the hand then?" asked Los Smitwode. "Any movement?"

He took a padded jocca quilt from the settle and wrapped it around John Miller's shoulders.

"Not much movement," said John Miller, "but it will improve."

All his movements and the play of expression over his handsome features were smooth but slightly lagging. He swiveled his gaze around the hostel sitting room.

"This is the guest hostel," said Los Smitwode, "at the Gann Trading Station, remember?"

"Reminds me of a 1-log cabin," said John Miller. "Shee-it, this is some prime turnup. . . ."

"What will you do?" asked Smitwode. "Have you . . . are you . . . restored?"

"Almost." He opened his mouth and took in gulps of air. "I'll sleep," said John Miller.

"Sleep?" echoed the Third Consultant, stupidly.

For answer John Miller smiled very slowly, then curled himself around on the trestle table, laid his head on the pillow before the Third Consultant could reach out to plump it up and fell sound asleep.

## 3

Maxim listened to the sound of the Station waking and thought of his home at Edenvale. The clatter of wooden pails; heavy steps; work-voices in the cold air of morning. His muscles ached from travel and his mind raced like a treadmill; it was all too much, too fine, he would never get it all down for old Urbain. He breathed deeply to calm himself, stared at the stone walls of the watchroom and lost himself in a dream of red tresses. When a knock came on the door his prayers were not answered; it was not Shona in a loose robe but Alan, shivering, in two towels.

"Bathhouse!" he said, grinning.

"Fine!"

Maxim sprang up and followed the Rancher's son down a back stair to the steaming wooden tubs. They sat and scrubbed and heard some kind of slow alarm spreading through the tiers of the ranch house. Running footsteps, then a door slammed, then a rumble of voices, more slammings and a call, high and clear, about a boat.

"Now what?" said Alan.

The old creaking door opened and this time it *was* Shona Dun Mor, fully dressed.

"Something doing across the river," she said. "Ma is going."

"Good morning!" said Maxim, trying to catch her eye.

She gave him a fierce look that struck him in the solar plexus, at any rate below the level of the hot water, and went off.

The two young men struggled out, cooled themselves and sprinted back up to the dormitory level.

"What's with the bluggy Jenzites. . . ?" grumbled Alan. "Can you find the kitchen, Bro?"

"Surely."

When he came down, minutes later, Gurl Hign was drinking her tea standing. The table was spread with food: dry-hog shinken, fresh pechids, bread and brose.

213

"The Jenzites have lighted no fires and sent out no boats," she said.

"Do you all work here on a Freeday?" asked Maxim.

"No, not much," she said, "but we cook our breakfasts. The Jenzites worked rather more on Freeday than we do. Anyway, it was their morning to service the beacons down the river. I'll have to check."

"I'd like to come along, Mam."

"Come then . . ."

He took up meat wrapped in bread that the old cook Bridey had made for him, gulped a few mouthfuls of tea and went off after the Rancher who was striding as usual. She went burning off down to the quiet dock with himself, Alan and the foreman Trim as the tail of the comet. A small boat was prepared, behind the still bulk of the trader *Seahawk;* Ben Dun Mor attached himself to the group.

"Ma, can I come too?"

Gurl Hign looked at her son and then at Maxim with an expression he could not read.

"This once," she said.

A mist lay over the river; they could not see the far bank, except in patches. The Jenzite village shone out, still, white for some minutes, then a light swirl of mist hid it from sight. Gurl Hign rowed strongly and Ben held the tiller, peering ahead. The mist cleared again. Maxim could distinguish the wharf and landing stage, then the village itself, partly downriver.

"Are the docks never affected by the floods?" he asked.

"No, there's a highwater point," said Gurl Hign, "where the levees stand on both banks. The levees have not gone down in ten years."

The Jenzites' houses shone out again, some perched on their stilts like the baba-yaga, then the mist came down more heavily than before. Gray shapes passed them on the river.

"Dator," said Gurl Hign, "that is a foghorn by your hand."

It was a gourd with a wooden mouthpiece; it sent out a dismal hooting when Maxim blew with all his might. Two boats crossed their path.

"What do you think," said Maxim, "are the Jenzites on strike?"

"They call it 'in retreat,'" said Gurl Hign, "but I don't know. I have a strange feeling about this new carry-on."

They saw the wharf again and Ben said:

"Their boats are tied up, Ma. But a few have gone."

Maxim felt a chill in his bones that had nothing to do with the cold morning. There was absolutely no sign of life in the swept streets; no wisp of smoke. He found a thought, a word that made him shudder.

"What is the matter?" demanded Ben Dun Mor. "Mr. Dator . . . what did you think of?"

"I shouldn't say," said Maxim. "It is too alarmist. But rowing over the river . . . the village . . . Mam High, have you heard of a place called Chippan?"

"By the Vail, that is a cold word for this hour," said Gurl High. "But I don't think you're right."

"What happened in Chippan," whispered Ben, "was that the place where. . . ?"

"You should ask Marko," said Gurl High. "He was there. His Ma and Pa were near stoned to death over in Pebble. But it has nothing to do with this present trouble."

So they drew up to the silent wharf; Maxim came out last and Gurl tied up. Ben stood for a few seconds then he ran off the wharf and they saw him cut under one of the stilted houses and run up the village street. When his mother called after him he took no notice.

Maxim and the Rancher walked away from the landing stage and at the door of a warehouse Gurl High called for the first time. The shout echoed around; nothing stirred. Maxim followed her up the outside staircase of the first house; they both called and Gurl High hammered on the door. On the outer windowsill of this first house sat a saucer lamp with the wick just about to burn out. They came down the stairs and went on in silence up the village street. The confounded neatness of the place, the freshly whitened bricks, the weeded garden beds, made the emptiness more uncanny. There was a sound of running footsteps that made them both turn eagerly; Ben came down an alley and stood in the middle of the street.

"No use to call, Ma," he said. "They have gone."

They walked down the broad street to the edge of the village. Along the way Gurl High flung open a few house doors and Maxim did the same. There were signs of departure; a good deal of furniture had been left behind. They came to a sandy track leading to the orchard and saw the way that the Jenzites had taken. The sand was a mass of footprints and the rough grass was flattened by wheels and sled-runners. Maxim knelt down and examined the tracks. Children walked beside their parents; men stood and hauled when a wheel stuck. Ben Dun Mor crouched beside him and laid a hand in one of the footprints.

"I could show you them going," he said, "but it is plain enough."

"What time of day?" asked Maxim.

He saw the boy's light eyes, hawk-thin face and dark hair as the image of Coll Dun Mor himself. Ben had inherited his father's powers.

"Twilight," said Ben. "They were over the rise there before the light faded."

"Left the oil-wicks burning on their windowsills," said Gurl Hign, "so that there would be lights in the village."

The three of them stood and stared to the south. There was one low hill, covered with orchard trees, and beyond it they could see hardwood forest, thickening on the crest of a ridge.

"What is the country like?" asked Maxim. "Will they get into the swamp forest, the real jungle?"

"There's the hardwood," said Gurl Hign, "then a stretch of tussock, with low hills. Grass country that is not found anywhere else. Frenck thought of farming it. The Jenzites will have their Happy Valley."

She was stern and sad. He could barely understand what she was feeling; some of it was a practical anxiety. They went to look at the unharvested plantation of rye and rik; the mist had given way to bright sunshine. The Jenzites had emptied their granary, cleared the lazy beds and potato pits. They had taken the bell from the chapel; the schoolhouse was empty save for a large poster of Jenz Kindl standing under a palm tree and a handsome hourglass on the teacher's bench.

"They are unforgiving," said Gurl Hign. "I made them a gift of this glass on the day the first wreckage came. How did poor old Jenz spawn all these hard-necked sons and daughters?"

"Was this Outwandering foreseen?" asked Maxim, staring at the empty schoolroom.

"By Jenz Kindl, you mean?" asked Gurl Hign.

"By his creators!" said Maxim.

The Rancher looked at Ben who was drawing on a wallboard with a charcoal stick.

"Ben," she said, "there's that big plum tree by the hog pen. Go and see if the fruit is ripe."

The boy grinned and ran off. His mother sat down on a scholar's low bench and stared at the dusty floor.

"I think of them," she said. "I've thought of them every so often for twenty years. The shape-changers . . ."

"Have you heard anything that could suggest . . . ?" asked Maxim warily.

"I was going to ask you the same question," she replied. "Has Master Urbain kept his eyes and ears open? Has there been another sighting?"

So Maxim was hard up against her direct question and the sudden surprising knowledge that he probably knew more of the shape-changers than anyone else in the Rhomary land. More, perhaps, than Coll Dun Mor, whom they had taught. More than their servants who "forgot" their special knowledge. It did not make his experience any easier to carry around with him or any easier to tell.

"Yes," he said hoarsely, "yes . . . I . . . there has been a recent sighting."

"*You* saw them!" said Gurl Hign quietly.

"Yes."

He could not look at her.

"I saw them, I traveled with them," he said. It was like pulling teeth. "I can't . . . the whole thing was so strange, Mam Hign. I can't talk about it."

"They know about the starship, the *Serendip Dana?*" she asked.

"They have an interest in meteorites," he said flatly. "For the iron, you know. But not much interest in the coming of more human beings."

"That answers your first question," said Gurl Hign. "They set up the Jenzite thing but they did not foresee the end of the work. The Jenzites could certainly call *them* 'creatures with no heart.'"

"No!" he said. "I'm not sure."

He turned to her at last and found her staring at him with the look of concern he had found very often on his mother's face.

"I must write a report," he said, "for my Uncle Urbain. I felt they did it . . . revealed themselves . . . partly on his account. I will show you the report."

"Thank you," Gurl Hign smiled. "Try not to worry yourself, Maxim."

She took up the hourglass and he followed her into the sunshine. As they walked to the landing stage Ben came panting up with a wooden bucket filled with black plums.

"Looting!" said Gurl Hign cheerfully. "No sooner are these folk over the hill than we fall on their fruit."

217

"It shouldn't go to waste, Ma!"

"Wipe your face," said the Rancher.

As they rowed back across the broad, sparkling water Gurl Hign said:

"Herm Dann knew of this," she said. "He kept company with Hope Nujons, child of a village committee-man. I was going to send a letter to these Companions with him yesterday but he never turned up and I forgot the letter."

"This trek into the wilderness was planning for a long time," said Maxim. "The robot was no more than an excuse, I think."

"Perhaps Herm has gone with them," said Ben.

"Do you know that?" asked his mother, sharply.

"No," said the boy, "I'm guessing."

They rowed on in silence. Out of the blue Gurl Hign remarked:

"Hilo Hill was Gline's cook. What's the story about him?"

"Why," said Maxim, off the top of his head. "He went around the world!"

And for the rest of the journey across the river he told them the silly tale and watched Ben's delight. But as they came to the dock again Gurl Hign gave a muffled curse. He saw a group of four persons standing together, a woman heavily pregnant, two girl children half grown and an old man, the grandfather.

"The Dann family," said Gurl. "The mother, Caro Wills, is near term with her fourth. Herm has gone, the eldest son, seventeen. The father, Young Nat, sails with LaMar on the *Comet*."

She leaped ashore, leaving Ben to tie up, and went straight to the family with only curt facts to the few watchers on the dock. It was Freeday and there was not much going on; Maxim saw the word get around; men and women stared across the river. Gurl Hign came back, took her hourglass from Maxim, and led the way up to the Station House. A thin black-clad figure loomed on the verandah.

"The Doctor's Eminence is early for this bluggy meeting," said Gurl Hign. "What now? I hope Bridey gave him tea."

When they came up, the Third Consultant gave that wintry smile which forbade impatience and anxiety.

"Good morning, Rancher," he said. "Good morning, Bro. I hear that the Jenzites have gone."

"Gone," said the Rancher, "and taken one of our young men along with them."

"They left symbols," said the Third Consultant, somewhat reluctantly.

Maxim found the story Smitwode told of the scroll and the snake left at his door puzzling and unpleasant. He could not picture Jenzites doing such a thing, but the fact was that they *did* go in for tricks and happenings. He remembered the young men who had run off from the alley in Rhomary leaving their crock of whitewash in the gutter. He wondered if young Herm Dann had been forced to leave the symbols as some test of faith. And there was the time factor . . .

"But, Rancher," he said, with some excitement, "this trick was played in the early morning . . . and the Jenzites left hours before, at twilight. . . ."

"Well I can think of ways around that," said Gurl Hign. "There are one or two on this Station who would do the trick for Jenzite silver. And then again some of the Jenzite boats may have sailed south with the morning wind. They could rejoin the main party by sailing up a little river called Bird Creek."

The meeting took place at the high table in the hall. When Maxim saw that Jaygo was to be present, he knew Shona was in the hostel watching John Miller. The Rancher's order and the presence of the Third Consultant kept the hall empty. The four of them sat alone in the long sun-dappled room with the striped bulk of the lifeboat to remind them of the matter in hand.

Los Smitwode had taken the chair; he was admirably succinct; the question of a new search had arisen, based on the information given by John Miller and certain other reports. Jaygo held up the map that Maxim had prepared; Gurl Hign had not seen the map prepared and had not read Junik's report. Now the TC passed it to her and she read slowly, moving her lips a little. Maxim caught Smitwode's eye and asked silently for permission to speak.

"I believe that a vessel should be sent at once to the Sooree River," he said, "to search for the two survivors who came down with John Miller . . . the doctor and the crew member. If possible a land party could go through the jungle from the river to the site where Bulk One fell. But this is a long trek. It might be better to have a search mounted from Silver City for this capsule."

"Excuse me, Dator," said Gurl Hign, "but a search for

this Bulk One might be mounted from this Station. The way over the hills and across the bit of sand and the jungle on the other side is much shorter than the way from Silver City or the Sooree."

Los Smitwode was wearing a thin smile. Maxim knew that something was up; he saw Jaygo's look of apprehension.

"What is known about the Sooree River, Mam Hign?" asked the Third Consultant.

"It's a damned uncomfortable place," said the Rancher. "The river runs through the heart of the swamp forest or jungle; it's hard to make a landing or a beachhead. It has the blackpod swamp, a pesthole for fever, at its mouth. The last person to sail up it was Cap Destris; next year he set out west and was never seen again. This was the year 1063. I think the shadow of Destris lies over the Sooree; we give the place a wide berth. Sometimes traders take up fresh water from its outflow. Even the Delfin will not go there, maybe because of the fresh water."

"How far did Destris go up the river?" asked Smitwode.

"About forty kilometers. Then he came to backwaters and silted channels. He turned back."

Jaygo burst out in a low voice:

*"Tell them, Magister! Please tell them!"*

Los Smitwode drew a paper from his red folder.

"Here is a page of General Recall from John Miller. Perhaps we should hear it read, Dator."

Maxim began to read the neat cursive script of John Miller.

*"Landfall made six four twenty-two sixty-five twenty-two forty, ship time. Dawn on host planet. Capem Tree good splashdown in broad river flowing through virgin forest estimated two hundred ten kilometers southeast of entry corridor over northern landmass.*

*"All A-OK, lifeboat functional, Doctor Valente, Ensign Chan approved air quality. I rode door unit of Capem; river swift flowing; we came over two low falls at the second I was swept away. Doctor Valente, Ensign Chan had lifeboat. I rate both high for survival.*

*"My function slightly impaired by striking submerged rock at the falls; current carried me into large lake or inland sea.*

220

Maxim drew breath and saw what was coming. He stared at Gurl Hign and his excitement reached out to her.

"A lake?" she demanded. "An inland sea on the Sooree?"

He read on:

*"Visibility poor, low mist. Sonic disturbance of air and water in the lake. Indistinct sighting very large life form, giant aquatic animal swimming in lake. My systems reacted badly to query magnetic field of this creature; loss of consciousness. Functions further impaired in red sea, encounter with dense mass sharp weed."*

Gurl Hign did not speak; she nodded at Maxim and he read again:

"Very large life form . . . giant aquatic animal . . ."

"Of course," said Los Smitwode, "we must not lose sight of the objective. The purpose of the search is to find two human survivors, one a Doctor."

"It is a good sighting of the Vail, Eminence," said Gurl Hign, "the best since the Outwandering. The search will be made both for the survivors and for our lost friends."

"What do you propose, Mam Hign?" asked Smitwode.

"We must wait until LaMar returns with the *Comet*. He is the only trader to be trusted with this search."

"I agree with the Rancher," said Maxim. "I will sail with LaMar if possible."

"I wish I could go myself," said the Rancher, "but it will be harvest time before the journey is complete."

"Then that is the plan for your search, Dator." said the Third Consultant.

Maxim thought of the palace of gray stone, the peeling murals, the broken heliographs and that old man and woman who waited high above the Western Sea by an unlit fire.

"The Envoys have kept their faith for more than fifty years," he said. "What if one of the Vail does survive on the Sooree River? Who will address it in their name?"

"You are the Dator," said Gurl Hign, "you could do it."

"Be damned to that!" exclaimed Maxim. "Jaygo Manin, you are the heir of that Foundation! You must go with LaMar."

"Dator Bro!" said the Third Consultant in an icy tone, "must I remind you again of the purpose of the search . . ."

At last Jaygo looked up, red-faced, almost sullen, and said in a flat childish voice:

"I will not go."

The look he gave Los Smitwode was one of pure reassurance.

"I will not go," said Jaygo, regaining some composure. "I am needed here. I will brief you for a possible encounter with our friends the Vail."

"You are the heir of the Envoys, intern Jaygo?" asked Gurl Hign quietly.

"I rejected my birthright long ago," said Jaygo. "You have spoken my title, Mam Hign. I am an intern, a member of Doctors' College."

The Third Consultant gathered up his papers and handed them to the intern. He gave one long sigh, perhaps a sigh of relief, but Maxim could detect nothing of the love and dependence that he guessed might lie beneath the cool mask of his face.

"We must get back. I am doing doctor's rounds this day. John Miller is sleeping . . ."

"Sleeping?" asked Maxim in surprise.

Los Smitwode smiled broadly.

"His own word! Miller spoke briefly this morning. Good day to you, Mam Hign, Dator Bro . . ."

The two doctors left by the back door of the hall and Maxim and the Rancher trailed to the front verandah to watch them climb the grassy slope to the hostel.

"What do you think," Maxim asked, "will we find them . . . the Vail or the survivors?"

"I am a fool for not thinking of the Sooree River," said Gurl Hign. "The Delfin knew about this, but they fear the Vail. As for the humans, could you go well in a lifeboat like this one we have here?"

"It is a marvelous thing, Rancher. Food, medicine, everything is there. It would serve them well."

"Mind you," said Gurl Hign, "it might not be a bad idea if a doctor did go along with LaMar."

Maxim had been watching the hostel closely and now he saw Shona Dun Mor come out. She walked down the hill toward them.

"Of course," he said, "a competent nurse aide might go on the voyage."

Gurl Hign laughed aloud and thumped him on the shoulder.

"Cheeky devil!" she said. "Ask her, then!"

She stayed for a few moments or went away. He did not know; he had lost track. He watched Shona come on and on until she climbed the verandah steps and stood beside him. They looked at the river in silence; there was no one about except young Ben sitting on the ramp eating plums from the wooden bucket in the sunshine.

"Come on," he took her hand, "let's walk back over the bridge! Let's climb up to the waterfall!"

She smiled at him.

"I've got work to do!"

"So have I!" said Maxim.

As they came down the steps, Ben said:

"Can I come, too, up to the waterfall? And bring my kite?"

"No!" said Maxim firmly, remembering how small brothers were dealt with. "Better take those plums to the kitchen before you get sick."

He felt in his pockets for a suitable bribe and found two sweets wrapped in ment leaves. With a sudden qualm of conscience he wondered what kind of a reading Ben the vesp might get from those relics of his journey over the Western Sea, but the boy simply grinned and popped one in his mouth. Shona laughed and took up a handful of plums. They walked slowly the length of the rambling Station House, then they began running together down the paths and ramps toward the bridge.

## Chapter XI

### The Flight of the Hawk

Gurl Hign sat in the meadow and let the morning sun shine on her bare arms. She looked at the tall cairn they had built together for Frenck and laid her hand on the warm red stone that covered the grave of Coll Dun Mor. It was Freeday, the last before the harvest; over the river

Jame Denny, the schoolmaster, was trying his new harvester on a corner of the plantation by the Jenzite village. She sat on a mossed stone and drew out the brass telescope. She was taking it to the lookout on Ben's kite-flying expedition, to cast a look at the jungle, but it would do to see over the river. The village sprang up like a collection of toy houses, well-tended, with the flowerbeds glowing, smoke coming from the chimneys and other signs of life. It was tenanted by five, six young couples who had moved across the river and taken up residence in the sturdy Jenzite houses.

She got the grain field in focus and began to smile. Denny and his helpers were coaxing the new harvester. Its rotating drum rolled a ways and then stopped and needed adjustment, but it had cut a wide swath through the corner of the rye. Gurl Hign lowered her telescope to the wharf; she could see yesterday's garlands and scarlet kelp strands still curled on her boards. The *Comet* had sailed, her dear LaMar was gone again. And after one short month Shona had "signed up," had "declared her intention"; in the traditional words of Rhomary, she had married Maxim Bro and now sailed with him on a honeymoon voyage. Some days Gurl found herself thinking in the way a mother should think: a good match, Shona would go to the city and live in the New Town, never see the dusty alleys, the dark corners of the Warren as she had done. For all his bookish innocence she liked Maxim Bro, felt in him a dogged patience that she admired. Besides he was not quite the soft-handed city man, he understood fruit farming, rode his parmel better than anyone on the Station. . . .

The wharf was empty; the *Seahawk* was in dry dock, Cap Swift and her crew had taken themselves off to the shebeens of Derry and Rhomary. The *Colleen Cross*, the *Comet*, the *Faithful* had sailed the south coast; there was no sign of the *Dancer*. She caught a flash of sail and raised the glass again. Why it must be the *Dreamer*, the Kellys' pinnace chartered by summer visitors. Other years there had been three or four parties who sailed on the Gann or in the ocean. Perhaps the rush would be on when the news finally hit the world. There had been already one thunderous reaction from Rhomary: letters to the Doctor's Eminence from the Council and from Doctors' College. Any search would be subsidized. An expedition to a crash site in the far north was being undertaken. She could not tell whether the Doctor was pleased by this dry stuff. By now, or shortly,

224

the city would know about John Miller and the expedition to the Sooree.

She looked at the hostel, just below the meadow, and saw three persons seated at the breakfast table on the back verandah. John Miller drank a little water, she knew that, but he didn't require food. Gurl Hign was not quite prepared to stare at them through a telescope; she wished that John would stand up, walk about a bit; and at that moment he did. He came to the rail, as if to turn the hostel's larger telescope on *her,* but instead he gave a slow wave. She waved back, grinning. So tall, and the slightly halting movements made him somehow more human than ever. She remembered the way Frenck had moved after his sickness . . . what Junik, long afterward, had diagnosed as a slight stroke. It struck her suddenly that John Miller might be able to see as far as the meadow clearly without any telescope at all. She felt a prickle of discomfort until he turned slowly away and walked back into the hostel. Down at the wharf the pinnace had reefed its bright sail and come in. Picking up supplies?

She lifted the telescope and saw Trim fussing with a cargo net. Two of the summer visitors came down the gangplank and strolled about on the wharf: a young couple. Well, they were not dressed for the simple life. Gurl had one other young couple on her mind and she could not help making the comparison. The contrast between this pair and the two lovers who had sailed on the *Comet* was enough to make her smile. Shona and Maxim were high-colored, strongly built, altogether more solid and, to her eyes, more beautiful. These others were tall and pale, the young woman's face was fine but cold, even her smile was cold, her hair was red-gold, confined by a silver fillet; the sea wind softly lifted her cloak of spring-green jocca cloth. Her companion had the same coloring; perhaps they were brother and sister. He was a slender smiling young man in green leather, his own cloak ruched and pleated from head to heel. The silver fillet on the girl's hair caught the light and so did a brooch on the young man's cap; their faces were hidden now and then in a soft blaze of light, as if the sun had caught a dew-drop or the top of a wave. Gurl Hign held her breath.

She moved the glass, searching the deck of the pinnace and found the third member of the party. An older man leaned on the rail of the little ship; she could see a streak of white hair running back from his pale forehead, the rings on his strong hands. There were two young servants taking baggage below decks, besides Dan Kelly and his son Shawn sailing the pinnace. She was so far away, here in the sun-warmed meadow; when she lowered her glass the three travelers were no more than colored manikins. To put her suspicion into words, to relate it to Maxim Bro's report, unread, lying on the desk in her office, was to break a spell. Gurl Hign stood up, clumsily, and backed a little until she stood beside the red slab of stone. She sat down in the grass again and rested her body against Coll's grave, as if she would draw out those visions that he had shown her twenty years ago. Three persons, tall and pale, beside a well, walking in a garden, their faces transfigured by the love Coll Dun Mor had felt for his benefactors. Their coloring had been different, she remembered the fall of silver-blonde hair on the young woman . . . but color, shape, everything could be *changed*.

She raised the glass again and saw the young woman beckoning to someone above the wharf; she watched still and grew cold with fear. Her son Ben came running up to the travelers. She could see him smile; she could see them smile at him, hovering their hands above his shoulders, not quite touching him. They turned their backs, showing the boy off to the third man, leaning on the ship's rail. Ben Dun Mor, the image of his father, the same age as the boy those others had befriended. Gurl was drawn to her feet; the spell would not break, the dream had become a nightmare. The scene dissolved almost at once: Ben bowed politely, the travelers mounted the gangplank, the pinnace was ready to put to sea. She followed Ben, running back up the ramp to where his kite lay and when she looked again the *Dreamer* had taken the light wind and was sailing gently down the Gann. Gurl Hign sat down in a heap and almost smiled at the thought of herself running and hallooing down the long, steep slope . . . if Ben had gone aboard the ship.

She muttered to herself, trying to calm down. Ben came through the grass carrying his kite in his arms; it was a big black-winged kite that he had made himself from paper-bark and bent wood.

"Come on!" he said. "This is a great morning! The wind is just right!"

"Who were those trippers aboard the pinnace?" she asked steadily.

"Did you see them with the glass?" he grinned. "They

gave me half a credit. Vail knows why except that I said my name."

"From the city?"

"They didn't say. There was one thing, Ma . . ."

"What?"

"Perhaps all rich folk are like that, but they had a strange light."

It was a game he played only with her; Ben had insisted since he was about four years old that every person had a special light, an aura. It shone out about the head and shoulders for a few seconds when he first saw a person on any particular day. The usual colors were blue or dull-green; Little Diggy Dit was unusual, his aura was pink; a few people had an unusual bronze tone.

"What color were they?" she asked.

"A gold light," he said. "Pure gold. All three of them."

He turned toward the path leading to the lookout.

"Hey Ma, d'you think Earth folk have different lights?"

"Surely," she teased. "All the colors of the rainbow, all the colors the Vail can see . . ."

"I could have gone to the Jenzite village," he said, "to watch old Denny's cutter, but this is much better, Ma. Do you think any of the Jenzites will come back?"

"I doubt it," she said. "They have everything they need."

"Now they are lost, like the Vail," said Ben. "This world is full of lost things."

"Only because it is *a world*," said Gurl Hign, "a damned big place. We'll hear of the Jenzites again and if all goes well on the Sooree. . . ."

She could not put her hopes for the Vail so bluntly into words. Ben went on, taking the path to the lookout at a pace that was much too fast for her; she plodded after him. The sky above the lookout, a wide gap between two saddles of the Divide, was a pale, luminous blue. Ben, half-way up now, released the kite and it soared up in stiff, wavering flight.

"Slow down, for pity's sake!" she called. "Ben!"

But he ran on as if the kite were leading him to the top of the pass.

2

Chan planted seeds and cuttings of the earth plants from Bulk One on the banks of the stream; they grew but did not flourish and one by one they died. All she had left were a few plants in pots that climbed feebly leaf by discolored leaf up the sides of their wretched shelter. Even Alice the goat would not eat them.

"Doc," Chan would say, "we have to get back there one time. Get more plants, load of that loozy jungle dirt."

And he would reply.

"Sure . . . we'll go back . . ."

Would they go? Was it important? He could hardly think of the future; what happened in two long days' time was as remote as earth. It was difficult to keep a diary, it was impossible to develop a routine, he did things out of order because they were small, heavy, boring tasks. He was disgusted with his attempts to be a naturalist and the drawings of bract-insects, urchins, gray birds in his notebook. He longed for the immense patience and the innocent eye of a Darwin. At least Chan was getting her strength back after the fever but when had that been? Five, seven, nine long days ago?

They watched over Alice as much as she would let them. She rounded out very slowly.

"How long before she has them?" asked Chan.

"Gestation period five months," he said.

"Shee-it, we'll be dead."

"With twins," he said, "and her small size, it might be sooner."

"Look, she knows we're talking about her . . ."

Alice began to nod and beck and caper about, kicking up her heels, then she came and nuzzled for more food.

So the warm brown mornings, the stifling noontime, the dopey afternoons and blue evenings lengthened out and wrapped them up like embalmed corpses, lying in the shelter, feeling the gravity drive them into the ground. Evening was still a little better. They talked by the small, voracious camp fires. Chan had been thinking about the complement of the *Serendip Dana*.

"Fiver will mean trouble," she said.

"What way?"

"Divided command," she said "and the ranking officers of the real crew, the service, don't have pull over the assigned mensh."

"Tell me who they are again, the assigned mensh?"

"The Silver Cross Maintenance. Plainly bad muggers and shape-up skull crackers to the last strap and spanner. I don't know why a lot of space mechanics should get this faggidy, long-ago, crack-troop profile."

"But Ryder said the feeling aboard was so good."

"He didn't have much contact with the Silvos. Hell, Doc, I've had a snotty young sub-ensign *draw a weapon* on me because the stamp on my inspection disc was quote 'illegible.' "

"What did you do?"

"Damn near broke her arm."

"How?" he gulped.

"Like this . . ."

Chan rose up beside the camp fire, stood in a slouching position, a sloppy approximation of attention, then lashed out with a stiff, left-legged kick that looked as though it would have felled an ox.

"I was given right," she said, "but the Silvos blackmarked me. I had so much strife I got excused from inspection duty."

"Weren't there some other assigned persons?"

Chan began to laugh with a sob in her voice.

"The Konos. You saw them, Doc. The media, the entertainers. They were such sweet, funny heads I swear they could gag their way to mother heaven. What will they do? Most of them were in Fiver."

He remembered a group of singers, a tumble of clowns and pantomimists, a boy and girl who danced in strips of silver foil. He had seen them live and on video. He thought of the poor Konos sitting about in full makeup, falling into melancholy attitudes in the soft jungle, sequin tears clinging to their white cheeks.

A day or more after this particular talk something did happen. He went out one morning and Alice was gone. He felt an immediate fear but damped it down, searched casually, did not call very loudly. By the time Chan emerged from the shelter he was ready to panic; they behaved like parents whose child is lost, moving about half crippled with anxiety. The jungle. The desert. The base of the hills. They walked and called for hours. A portion of the sled that had been lying near the water's edge had disappeared. In the afternoon he took the lifeboat into the swamp; Chan remained in camp in case Alice should come back.

He poled warily through the maze of channels feeling the same frustration after a couple of hours as he had felt after days and nights. He rowed and called and poked fearfully among the sticky black branches of the swamp trees.

229

At last after deceiving himself twenty times he heard a faint answering bleat; he pushed through into another channel. There was Alice, balancing with delicate footwork on her raft of insulator board, floating in the reddish water. He rescued her tenderly and went back to the beach where Chan greeted them with a few tears. They never worked out how Alice got washed away but like a wise child she had learned enough to keep away from the water's edge.

Then the brown and blue longeurs of the new world rolled over them again; he watched the hawks wheeling over the hills but still said nothing. Was Chan strong enough? He walked several kilometers into the belt of deformed trees on the edge of the desert and saw nothing but more desert, nothing that could have made lights on the ground. That same night, or maybe the night after, he awoke in the tent, burning hot, from a dream of the waters of that inland sea.

"Min-mer," he croaked through dry lips. "Chan . . . I got the name . . . minmer."

"Fever!" said Chan, looming above him like the sea monster. "You have a burn like a bad re-entry."

"Incubation!" he grated. "Swamp. It is swamp fever!"

He went into a rigor, shivering with grisly chills as he thought of the alien organisms pullulating in his bloodstream. Then time lost its hold on him and he wandered in sweet alpine valleys, argued in lecture halls, dissected the dead, giggled over an English mnemonic for the facial nerves. He lived and died on the *Serendip Dana,* bound for the planet Arkady. He rowed through the swamp. He heard the voice again, deliberately directed himself, part of himself, deep in his fever dream, back into the inland sea to hear the voice again.

He began to come out of it, feeble as Chan had been, barely able to sip his boiled water.

"I remembered it all," he whispered.

Then he began to cry, tears were streaming down into his beard.

"It has gone again. . . ."

"Sssh . . . wheesht," soothed Chan, holding up the notebook. "You told me to take it down."

In a matter-of-fact voice she read off the text of the message . . . if that was what it was . . . and he found it exciting.

"The tailed star rides and there is a minmer fallen from the sky. Have you found your way to the stars again? I am

230

the last. Tell that to the minmers. Have they improved their spectrum? Go well, minmer. Go down to the red sea. Keep the sun at your back."

"What do you think it means?" he asked. "What is a minmer?"

"You are . . . I am . . ." said Chan.

*"They are . . ."*

Her face was clouded.

"Doc, what does that mean? There are no other humans on this planet. There can't be . . ."

"Why not? You had a whole list of lost spacecraft."

"I don't believe it, Doc. But I did think . . ."

"What. . . ?"

"Something humanoid."

"The monster spoke the message in English."

"Shee-it, Doc, you heard soothing communication and translated it in your poor head!"

He lay in the miserable shelter and Chan tried to feed him a balanced diet. They had plenty of food left but it was dreary as the plastic film in which it was wrapped. Who could distinguish between a wafer of protein additive and a gelatin capsule of essential mineral and trace elements (may be taken orally or used as a suppository)? Crusoe urchins were a delicacy; they had four tubes of lemon lift that they were keeping for special occasions. Alice, the omnivore, ate seaweed, plastic, cloth and the powdery bones that he had found in the sand.

He regained his strength fairly quickly. One day he woke in broad daylight with Chan shouting and yelling wildly in the distance. He rushed out of the shelter armed with a hunk of driftwood. She was standing in the sand quite a long way off, not far from the place where he had found the bones. Alice came rushing past him, bleating in panic, and burrowed into the shelter. As he toiled in Chan's direction she pointed to the desert and did not stop shouting. A large animal was moving away among the fantastic tree shapes.

"I see it, Chan, I see it!"

He saw it but he did not quite believe it. It was a lumpy creature that moved easily and swiftly with a waltzing motion over the desert sand. It had six legs. It looked rather larger than the skeleton he had found but so far as he could tell they were of the same species.

When he came up to Chan she was sitting in the sand and weeping.

"What did it look like to you?" she asked.

"Nothing on earth," he said. "No . . . that's wrong. It looked like a kind of a camel. Chan, please don't cry."

But she cried aloud and he sat down in the sand and held her close to comfort her. They clung together and he looked at their new world, the sand, the bare slopes of the hills, the pitiful campsite in the shadow of the swamp and he understood her despair.

"Look at the tops of the hills . . ." he whispered.

She wept still and would not raise her head. He stared until he found the place: a rock wall, then a long bed of loose stones and far overhead the place that he called the Pass. A hawk or two wheeled overhead, over the very summit of the hills. Was that a faint scurf of green on the Pass? Presently they got up and trudged back to the shelter, in time to rescue his notebook from Alice who had forgotten her panic.

All the long day he walked around the perimeter of the camp, jogging when he came to the strip of beach. At night he took medication and fell into a long dreamless sleep. When he woke with the sun just reddening the pale sky over the distant reaches of the swamp he knew what they must do. He began to fill one of the boat's kitbags to make a pack.

"What is it? What are you doing?" demanded Chan.

"We're going over the hills," he said. "We are going up to the Pass."

"You're not strong enough, Doc. I couldn't make it either."

"*We must!* This place will be our death. Look how we are."

"But that hill. . . . Why don't we take the boat, get out through the swamp?"

"No! There's fever in the swamp. Chan, we could get up to that pass in a few hours under normal earth conditions!"

"There's Alice! What about Alice?"

"Chan, she's a *goat*. She could climb up there in an hour! I'll carry her in the sling until we get up a little."

She argued all the time they packed and when she finally gave in and began putting on her boots he saw it was because he frightened her. She was afraid he would leave her alone.

Their bright, tough, colonists' gear was fine for climbing; Chan had the harness of her silversuit and he made

232

her take two oxygen bottles. They divided up the food, water, medical kits; when their packs were on he almost fell face downward in the sand. They caught Alice and gave her two protein wafers and put her in the sling, made from plastic sheeting. It still had a faint brimstone smell that recalled Bulk One. Alice thrashed about a little, then settled. He took a long piece of driftwood for his alpenstock; they each had a whole tube of lemon lift and went off, not looking back at the camp.

The rock wall, which he had thought would be the hardest part, was easy; he went last, heaving on Chan's hindquarters. She groaned and swore and found hand and foothold as easily as a kid climbing a tree. At the base of the long bed of loose stones he released Alice and she went skipping and dancing up the slide while they panted and cheered. She stood at the top and bleated for them to come on. They started up and it was hideously difficult; they toiled on the slipping, intractable stones for hours.

They came to a place between walls of stone that shut out the light of the rising sun. Nothing grew there, not the least flake of lichen. He made two attempts to reach a shelf with his rope, then a third. The shelf was about the size of two bootsoles; he moved on to another, smaller, for himself, then heaved on Chan's rope until he felt himself blacking out. They sat on their perches and snuffed oxygen. They could not see up or down very easily; he made a wrong move and his driftwood staff went clattering down below them. If they went forward at a dangerous angle they could just see the vast purple-black expanse of the swamp.

But the going was still possible; he went on, two more shelves, and came to a huge boulder. Alice came over its crest, saw that they were still following, flicked her stump of a tail and was gone again. He swarmed over the boulder as Chan negotiated the last shelves.

"Come on!" he called to Chan. "It gets better!"

Yes, better! The Pass really was a pass, not some trick of the light he had seen from below. Two saddles of the hills rose on either side of a flat plateau; a broad scour, the beginning of another rock bed, reached curving down toward them. There was a spongy covering on the rocks under his hand, green growth on the plateau. The hills inland so clustered and were so hazed with green that he could have sworn there was a spring rising there. He looked up blinded by the light and saw the hawk birds, closer now, wheeling over the saddles. He turned back to Chan, shouting, but she was nowhere to be seen. He ran back, showering stones.

"Chan, Chan . . . it is better! We've made it!"

She came over the far side of the big boulder with a smile between set teeth that made his heart ache.

"I see it," she said. "Doc . . . I'm sorry."

"What. . . ?"

"I broke my foot some way getting to this loozy rock. I can't . . ."

"There's no other place to go!" he said. "I'll set your foot or make it comfortable."

"No," she said. "I'll last. Where's Alice? You do it, Doc. Go take a look through the Pass."

She lay flat on the top of the boulder, her face a pasty gray, gray as the stone. He turned up the last broad scour and saw a flash of white at the top: Alice had reached the grass. And the hawks were wheeling overhead . . . large birds, maybe flesh-eating birds, birds of prey. He ran upward waving his arms at the hawks, fighting and gasping in the thin air, his heart doing more than any heart of earth, any human heart could do. But he was hardly human; he had become a new creature.

He tried to shout and it came out with every sharp breath as a feeble bird cry. A single huge bird zigzagged into his line of sight; surely it had seen him, seen Alice, peacefully cropping the green grass. He shouted again and looked back and saw that Chan had revived. She was crawling, dragging herself up the scour and pointing at the great bird. Then he looked up and it was coming down, a dark wing-shape blotting out the light. He stumbled toward Alice across the grass; he flung up his arms to fight off the hawk and there was a sharp impact and a tearing sound. He found he was clutching in his arms a large kite made of bent sticks and dried papery bark.

He let the kite fall and began to fall himself, to sink down in slow motion onto the grass. A slight shadowy figure came over the pass, then ran back, then came again. A young boy.

The boy, running and shouting, seemed to be reaching for both of them: he was the boy, the boy was himself, the boy was proving their common humanity. Then the boy stood still in an attitude of controlled fear and addressed him.

"What *is* it? What *is* it?" said the boy.

234

"It is a goat," he said. "Nothing to be afraid of."

A stocky figure came striding over the pass and he was able to crawl forward a little. He looked back at Chan who was crawling on and on up the scour, laughing and shouting and crying out to high heaven. He staggered to his feet again but could hardly stand; he was caught and held by a short, brown-skinnned woman in a white leather tunic.

"Minmers . . ." he said.

He gripped the woman tightly so as not to fall down.

"You are the minmers!"

Her black eyes were very bright.

"Yes!" she said. "Yes, we are the minmers!"

"Please," he said, "help her, help Chan."

He pointed and the woman set him down and went past him to help Chan. Alice went dancing over the Pass and the boy ran after her. He shrugged the pack from his back and steadied himself on his hands and knees and crawled through the thickening grassy covering of the pass. His breath was coming a little easier; he looked down into the valley. He saw things that could not be believed; the river, the wharf, the strange huts and houses. He saw the boy and a few men and women coming up toward him over grass and stone, running out of houses. A peal of bells began to ring.

# Epilogue

## *The Dawn of a New Day*

---

Two days out from the Gann Station. Maxim was suddenly awake and alone in the big bunk in the *Comet*'s forward cabin. He turned his head and saw Shona, wrapped in a blanket, peering sleepily through a port.

"What is it?" he whispered. "Come back to bed!"

"Don't you feel it?" she whispered back. "We're hove to . . ."

He sat up. The motion of the ship had stopped; he could hear a murmur of voices above their heads.

"Perhaps it is this sea mist," said Shona, "perhaps LaMar has found something floating."

"What, in mid-ocean?"

He stumbled out of the bunk, hit his shoulder blundering into the curtained "head" of the honeymoon cabin, splashed water on his face from the washcrock in its clamps. Then he came back wide awake and did what he wanted to do, namely take Shona in his arms again. There was a banging at the cabin door and Poll Grev stuck her head in, coughing loudly.

"Save your strength, Dator," she said. "Wanted on the bridge."

"Damn you, Poll," said Shona adjusting the blanket, "open your eyes, we're covered, more or less. What's the matter?"

"A message from the *Dreamer*, the Kellys' pinnace that was trailing us."

The mate went off and Maxim struggled into his clothes. "Stay here," he said. "I'll bring your breakfast."

She lay in the bunk again and watched him with a smile that turned his heart over. He wished for the hundredth time that they were on a desert island, kissed her and went away, crawling up and up the ladders to the bridge.

236

LaMar strode about in his billowing sea-cloak. The winds that drove them northwest had become cooler in the last half day; captain and crew had been watching the weather. There was a long yellow bank of cloud far away to the southwest that could stand for a big blow. Now a patchy local mist had sprung up on the sea's face. The *Comet* swung nervously on her sea anchor, eager to be on her way.

"Sorry," said LaMar, showing white teeth in his dark face. "You recall that hired pinnace?"

"Poll Grev mentioned a message?"

"They were trying to catch us up," said LaMar. "We saw their light signals last night and misread them at first. Now they're anchored in that patch of mist, a boat is just coming to us. Dan Kelly shouted some garbled thing about the doctor."

"Is that a strange way to handle in mid-ocean?" asked Maxim. "I hope there is no trouble at the Gann."

"I doubt that," said LaMar, "but what would the bluggy Eminence find so pressing?"

He went to the rail and looked down.

"I don't understand that mist," he said. "Perhaps it is Gline's ghost ship come to give warning."

He took up the speaking cone from the deck and roared over the side.

"Ahoy the cocker! Is that you, Dan Kelly?"

Maxim saw the tiny boat and an upturned face.

"Message for yourself and the Dator, Captain!" called the man faintly.

"Come aboard . . ."

Maxim was ready to run down into the waist of the *Comet* to see the man hauled aboard but LaMar kept his captain's dignity and the pair of them waited. Dan Kelly was a ruddy-faced sailor, middleaged, with a game left leg that explained why he had left the trading fleet with its longer voyages and turned to ship building and charter boats. He held out a sealed letter in the Third Consultant's neat minuscule script.

"Open it, Dator, it is addressed to us both," said LaMar. "How did you come by this, Dan?"

"We were going down the Gann to the ocean, Captain," replied Kelly in a singsong voice. "The morning after you left, it was, with a gentle wind, all sails set. Suddenly the bells rang out to the signal post at the river's mouth and all the semaphore towers were set to call us back . . . for the carrying of this message."

"What in dry hell . . ."

"I think some persons are found," said Dan Kelly. "I could not get much sense out of the boat coming with the letter. It was the Dit boys, Billy and Diggy, half mad with excitement and talking about a man and a big woman and a strange animal, all come over the pass in the Divide."

"An animal?" asked Maxim.

"A wee white thing the size of a dry-hog and the Rancher said it was called a go-at."

"A goat!" said Maxim. "Great Vail, a goat!"

He broke the seal on the letter and began to read aloud, so excited himself that he stumbled over the words.

> " 'I must inform you, Captain LaMar, Dator Bro, of the arrival of two human survivors from Capem Tree of the Serendip Dana. They are, as we expected,
> Valente K.H.J., Physician and Surgeon
> Chan T.N.R., Warrant Officer, Second Class
> the companions of John Miller, separated from him on the Sooree River. They have had adventurous journey through blackpod swamp—also report loss of Bulk One, only plants, birds surviving plus one female African Dwarf Goat, luckily pregnant with heterosexual twins . . .' "

"What in dry hell is he blabbing about?" exploded Lamar.

"One of each," said Maxim. "A race of goats for Rhomary!"

He read on:

> " 'Since these are the humans your expedition set out to recover you may decide to call off the search.
> " 'Signed and sealed
> Los Smitwode, Third Consultant.
> " 'P.S. Dr. Valente seems to confirm the sighting on the Sooree River.' "

"Thank you Dan," said LaMar. "You've done us a great service. Can we give you breakfast?"

"I must get back, Captain."

"What d'ye make of this damned mist?"

"Perhaps it will clear when the sun gets high," said Dan Kelly.

"Did you see that typhoon buildup in the southwest?" asked LaMar.

"Likely it will turn inland," said Kelly, blinking his watery blue eyes. "I must go back. Shawn is tending the *Dreamer*."

"Got a good charter? Some cotton rich?"

"Aye, from Derry. A married pair . . . the Stines."

LaMar watched Kelly all the way as he returned to his boat and was cast off.

"Another queer thing," he said. "What's with Dan Kelly? How did he strike you, Dator?"

"A bit shaky," said Maxim, "but I thought that was his usual manner."

"Not at all. He was wafty. I'd not expect him to have drink taken at this hour of the morning."

LaMar shook his head, wondering, and looked again at the doctor's letter.

"Well, we have our survivors. Would you rather go back to the Gann and talk to them?"

"Whose decision is that?" asked Maxim, hedging.

"I could consult with my officers or with the whole crew," said LaMar seriously, "but the word is mine alone."

"It is a strange thing . . ." said Maxim, and he realized, almost for the first time, what a very strange thing it was. "It is a strange errand to go hunting a vanished sea monster, but I do not think it is without worth, without meaning, to find the Vail again. Why now, think of it, we can ask the survivors what other life forms have been found in the universe, we can have the true names of the stars again. . . ."

"Our own names do very well," said LaMar. "I wonder what the Eminence means 'seems to confirm the sighting.' "

"He's twisting," said Maxim promptly. "Smitwode thinks nothing of the Vail but his conscience would not let him leave this out. And the Rancher would urge him to tell us."

"Aye, she would!" LaMar gave a great bellow of laughter and clapped Maxim on the shoulder.

"We go on! We go on!" he said. "Gurl will have her sea monster. . . ."

He shouted orders and the *Comet* sprang into life and rode on to the northwest through the patches of mist melting away before her prow.

239

"Curse it," said LaMar, using his glass. "There . . . there is the thing that worries me just a little."

He handed the glass to Maxim who saw, far away on the horizon, between the patches of mist, a thick, yellow-brown clump of cloud.

"A typhoon?" he asked. "Isn't it early in the year?"

"A little," said LaMar. "It would be pure bad luck if the buster itself came this far but even the fringe winds could be mighty fresh."

"What is the trader out there that is overdue?" asked Maxim. "Will it be caught?"

"The *Dancer*," said LaMar. "If she's afloat she will ride it out. Cap Varo is a moody devil but he knows his business."

"Have you sailed to the edge of the world, to Cape Gline, very often?"

"Often enough," said LaMar, "and it has the worst weather I've ever been in. Gline was right of course . . . what looks like another arm of this Red Ocean is the beginning of the largest sea of all. These busters are proof of this third ocean."

"How's that?"

"The typhoons rise up south, on the equator. I think they must rise up over water . . . a belt of calms where the pressures are queer."

When Maxim returned to his cabin with a laden tray he found Shona at the open port staring out to sea.

"Great news! Survivors at the Gann . . . What is it?"

The expression on her face had made him pause.

"Just for a moment I heard the bells of the pinnace," she said. "Sweeter than ours. Look there . . ."

He looked and the mist had lifted; the *Dreamer* was getting underway in a patch of sunlight, her rigging hazed with gold. Then the little boat was out of sight as the *Comet* held her course for the Sooree.

They sailed on for a day and a night through the same late summer weather. Then in the night a sailor fell from aloft into the sea; the *Comet* hove to again and the man was picked up. Maxim kept to his cabin, heard LaMar roar and curse on deck. Shona came back from nursing the man who had been rescued and sat on the edge of the bunk.

"LaMar is nervous and so are the crew," she said.

"But the man is all right?"

"Wet and shocked," she said. "The ship heeled over or he would have fallen on deck."

"What is it then?" demanded Maxim. "You are nervous too . . ."

He had decided that a honeymoon was a test of nerves rather than stamina. They were cooped up on the *Comet* with no regular duties, only the hope that everything would be perfect. He was longing for the trek up the Sooree River.

"You should have come up," said Shona in a low voice. "I wish you could have heard what young Davey said when they got him aboard."

"Tell me . . ."

"He talked of lights in the air."

"What, you mean meteors? Another starship?"

"No," said Shona, "something like Elmo-fire. Globes of light."

Maxim felt it like a blow; he crouched up in the bunk gaping at her.

"And I heard something . . ." Shona's voice rose hysterically. "Maxim, they have no idea, we must tell LaMar."

"Hush, sweetheart," he said. "We're getting too far ahead. What did you hear?"

"Bell sounds . . . very faint and sweet."

He shook his head.

"Are you sure of it?" he asked. "I told you all that long tale of the shape-changers because it was haunting me. Even now it is like a wire in my brain, a dream that will not fade. Is it haunting you too?"

"No," she said simply. "Remember how I heard the sweet bells . . . from the pinnace."

Maxim held her close and remembered. He began to curse as fluently as LaMar.

"They are out there," he said. "I feel as if I had been tripped and fooled all over again."

"The *Dreamer* is far astern," said Shona, "or so the crew thinks. But there is a bank of that strange unseasonable mist lying to the west."

"LaMar found Dan Kelly strange in manner," said Maxim. "The man was controlled, I guess, so that he could not say too much about his passengers, even if we asked awkward questions. He had a look of poor Milt Donal, the merchant."

"But the message was delivered," said Shona. "What is their plan? Could they hinder us?"

"Yes," said Maxim, considering. "Yes, they could numb the minds of a whole crew and leave their ship wallowing.

I'm not sure how far their powers reach in other directions —pushing, raising a wind—who knows?"

"Should we tell LaMar?"

The ship was underway again. Maxim went and looked out into the starry night from the port, craning his neck to see up to the bridge. Another day and a half would bring them to the mouth of the Sooree if the wind held.

"No," he said firmly. "We've no proof, only vague imaginings. We're *not* being held back; this thing with the sailor Davey was an accident."

He came back and kissed Shona Dun Mor.

"I'll write a report," he said.

She hid her face in a pillow and her whole body heaved; she laughed at him until he took measures to prevent it.

"Oh Vail," she said, gasping, "I have got me a Dator."

That same night they walked about on deck; there were two sailors on watch, besides the new lookout and the man at the wheel. The moon was down, the season's comet hung in the eastern sky; Maxim remembered the Western Sea and the yacht *Arrow* skimming over those still, shadowed waters not far from the hollowed shore. Now the *Comet* rode sturdily through the endless surges of the Red Ocean; land was a smear on the horizon to the north and a dark line to the east. That was the blackpod swamp. To the west the tropical storm that LaMar feared had settled over the Six Seven Isles. Even the sea-smell was different; there was a tang of spices here.

Shona leaned against him and they searched air and ocean carefully. There was nothing unusual to see, no lights in the air or on the water, no sounds but the rough music of the ship herself, creaking, straining, leaning in and out of the shallow trough of the waves.

"No sign . . ." said Maxim.

"What would they want out here?" whispered Shona.

"I think they have become curious at last about the fall of the starship."

"When I was little," she said, "I had an imaginary playmate, a kind of boy-girl, very clever and brave. I called her Luralee, after one of my father's teachers from the mysterious Ensor family."

"I will put that in the record, too," he said, smiling. "You must tell my Uncle Urbain."

"I am more afraid of him than of the shape-changers or the Vail," she said. "And even more afraid of your mother and father and all your kin in Edenvale."

"They will love you," he said. "They will eat you up and give you good advice. Old Urbain will think all his birthdays have come at once."

"We were alone on Rhomary but we were never alone," she said. "We changed our nature but we didn't change at all. We lose all manner of things and find them again."

"If I send out a prayer," said Maxim, "it is for any new folk fallen down in the rescue capsules. I've never been in the swamp forest but I hate the sound of it."

In a day and a half the swamp forest was all they could see, crowding down to the water's edge, blue-green and black. The mouth of the Sooree, dead ahead, was wider than the Billsee, its pure greenish waters churning under the *Comet*'s keel for more than half a day; the water butts were all replenished. Everyone was excited; the lookout and the boys and girls on watch sang chanties to each other and roared out, calling for the Vail.

"Dry hell!" cried LaMar, holding the wheel himself as the trader entered the broad stream. "They will yell more softly if one of those big beasts sees fit to reply."

They sailed slowly upstream, taking careful soundings, and anchored at sundown. They were sucked into the sticky blackness of the jungle night; thick mist seemed to well out of the tree-growths and vines on the shores. In the dawn there was a moment of excitement; the lookout spoke of a shape in the mist but when it cleared there was the river empty as before, and silent. The soundings were difficult and the wind so light they were almost becalmed. Ahead the river had narrowed suddenly, though the path of the main stream was still broad and clear.

"This is as far as I feel able to go," said LaMar to Maxim.

It was siesta; the crew slept; the pair of them were in the captain's cabin poring over charts.

"We've come a little further than Destris," said LaMar. "The river has changed since his time, for the better as far as getting a ship upstream, but I still don't trust the place. It is all shifting silt down there and I'm damned if I let my ship run aground on a sandbank that was not there the night before."

"Then we need a flat-bottomed boat . . . the lifeboat," said Maxim.

"Yes, that yellow-striped creature should do very well."

It had been brought along slotted into the ship's long-boat.

"I will go," said Maxim, "and so will Shona."

"I will send Poll Grev with you," said LaMar, "and Trant the bosun's mate."

"The one they call Tug?"

"Short for Tug of War," said LaMar. "He is the strongest man aboard and when he goes anchor man that team wins."

"Let us make a start today," said Maxim. "I think it will be hard work rowing upstream."

"Fine," said LaMar, "but please, Maxim Bro, go canny. Watch out for any freshening of the wind and come back to the ship."

"But the tropical storm has lifted from the Six Seven Islands . . ." said Maxim.

"Yes, it turned inland and it should not bother us," said Lamar, "but these busters are unpredictable. If it turns again we are in trouble."

"What would you do?"

"If it came from land," said LaMar, "I would have to lay out to sea. I could not wait or send boats to look for you."

"What should we do in such a case?"

"Put up the full cover of that lifeboat and burrow into some muddy inlet until the blow was over," said LaMar.

"Captain," said Maxim seriously, "do you believe this report: 'an inland sea on the Sooree River'?"

"It's possible," said LaMar, his dark face grave, "but how large a sea and how far away . . . ah, that's another question. The Sooree is a mighty river; compared to it the Gann is merely a stream. The Sooree reaches far, far inland to some mountain range we've never seen and can only guess at, like a distant planet in a sun system. If an expedition went up the river to its source we might stand on the tops of those unseen mountains and see the distant north, the polar regions, that no man has ever seen. But your lifeboat will take you safely a few kilometers and a few days away."

The lifeboat was laden with food, water and a few of the original pieces of equipment. Maxim had logged its provisions and for the most part left them behind at the Gann. The thick liquid in tubes, the bricks, sticks and pellets that passed for food were ingenious but horribly unpalatable . . . they were for a Rhomary museum. He had kept the clever beakers that could be heated with a flick of the wrist and the food was all good Gann produce.

The Sooree was wayward; all four members of the expedition rowed hard . . . with hoots of encouragement from the *Comet* . . . and the strong river currents twisted the lifeboat this way and that. Yet they moved, with the good help of Tug Trant and his muscles, slowly, slowly toward that narrowing of the stream up ahead.

"Well," said Poll Grev, wiping the sweat out of her eyes, "we are now in unexplored territory . . . beyond every other expedition."

Yet they still hung in the stream like a waterfly with only a short stretch of greenish water between the garish striped lifeboat and the *Comet*.

"Dator," said Tug Trant in his light, soft voice, "you think we'll find 'em?"

"I'm hopeful," said Maxim. "Right now I wish we could row into a shadow . . ."

"Your rowing is still pretty uncrafty," said Shona. "You need more practice."

They rowed again and kept on until they did find a shadow. A huge leather-winged umbrella tree stretched far over the water sending down a fine tangle of aerial roots. Poll cut them with her machete and they rowed up the tunnel and came to a new place.

The Sooree divided into sandbanks and cross channels stretching for kilometers up ahead to a wall of swamp forest growth that closed off all but the sluggish main-stream. There were yellow, blue, white bract growths glimmering on the sandbanks and above them hovered the bright-wings, mimicking them in the same colors. The light changed and changed again as they sat and watched; darkness was waiting in the swamp forest ready to pounce on them.

"This looks strange enough to me," said Shona. "How would it be for a poor star traveler?"

"Let's make camp," said Poll Grev, holding up her hand to test the wind.

There was a heavy stillness over the river that made talking above a whisper difficult, too loud, a sound that might wake sleeping monsters.

"Let us make a portage," said Tug Trant. "We'd do better in a channel nearer the main-stream."

Crossing the sandbanks was back-breaking labor; the sand was soft and dangerous and they were afraid to drag the boat for fear of hidden snags. In the last hours of daylight they waded, heaved, lifted the yellow boat, settled it in the channel Tug Trant had chosen and washed themselves in the green water. Maxim felt his muscles trembling with exhaustion. After some food all four explorers lay down in the boat without a single bawdy "honeymoon" joke from Poll Grev and fell asleep.

Shona was crying out. Maxim surfaced as quickly as he could through layers of thick sleep. Then he was awake in the boat as it rocked and bounced in the channel; a strong wind howled through the blackness and the air was full of tattered plant fragments from the swamp forest.

"The storm . . ." cried Shona.

"It is turning!" shouted Poll above the rising howl of the wind. "Tug, shall we . . . ?"

"Try for the *Comet!*" Tug Trant's soft voice did not carry and they all huddled down in the lifeboat with their heads together to hear his words. "We should get in the mainstream and try to return to the ship."

There was only a single narrow sandbank between them and the mainstream.

"Won't the *Comet* be out to sea in this typhoon?" asked Maxim.

"Bless you," shouted Poll Grev, "this is not the buster . . . only the fringe wind."

Even the narrow sandbank was almost too much for them. The wind, to Maxim, was of terrifying strength; it was a wall, it was a blow from a fist, it was a stinging whip of many tails. He held to Shona protectively as they worked, then his feet and fingers slipped, he was flung away against the far bank of the channel. Shona came after him, groping in the darkness and shrieking against the rising tumult. After instants of real panic they were able to cling to the boat again as it plopped into the churning water of the Sooree's mainstream. They rowed like demons and made swift progress downriver, then the lifeboat twirled in a maelstrom and the wind slackened just a little.

The blackness of the swamp forest was suddenly lightened; Maxim could see the water, the sandbanks, the black line of the jungle trees bent and flattened. Poll Grev uttered a shout of fear: above the forest on the western bank, linking earth and sky, was a great oozing, coiling wall of yellowish cloud. Sharp bursts of rain stung their faces and they heard an unearthly sound, an eerie whining note, the voice of the typhoon before it struck the river. Some hoarse voice cried "Hang on!" and Maxim realized it was his own.

He fastened himself to two handgrips on the side of the lifeboat and felt Shona beside him doing the same. He thrust his body against hers, laced his legs across her to anchor her more firmly. His direction had all gone; a wall of water that seemed to be racing upstream engulfed the boat, then another and another. They gulped air on the crests of huge waves. He knew nothing but the watery darkness full of leaf debris and the frail strength of the lifeboat and Shona's body close to his own. He never knew when the darkness and the buffeting went away: long before that time he became unconscious.

He felt sunlight on his face and then a gentle touch; his body ached, his face seemed to be thick with silt. He breathed deeply but did not open his eyes; his first thought was *"I am alive!,"* his next a wracking wave of pain and anxiety: *"Shona!"* He uttered a groan and the light touch that moved over his head and limbs was withdrawn. Maxim sat up and vomited water and scraps of vegetation. He wiped his face with his hand and peered into clear, bright sunlight, dancing on green water. The water stretched far and wide on every hand; he crawled toward the water, dipped his hands in, washed his face and drank.

He felt an overpowering weakness, a strong lassitude in his body and a lightness in his head. He thought *"Am I alive after all?"* and turned his head. Shona lay curled on sand, her long hair dabbled with the black and blue-green leaf fragments. He tried to stand but could not and crawled to her side. She was sleeping peacefully, her face cool and clean, her breathing regular. He kissed her forehead and for the first time began to see where they were.

The island was all of sand and silt, an extraordinary cone-shaped island; the yellow lifeboat rested on the top of the cone and its passengers lay on the sand, each about three body lengths from the others. Maxim crawled on and examined them all; Poll Grev's coloring and breathing bothered him a little. With awful slowness he patted her cheek, shook at her shoulders, tried to turn her over. She stirred, groaned, woke up just as he had done.

"Are they . . . ?" her voice was hoarse, ruined, just as his was replying.

"All safe."

"Where . . . ?" said Poll, sitting up.

She began to retch helplessly and got rid of water and leaf fragments just as he had done. Maxim held her forehead and tried to answer her question.

"Island," he said hoarsely.

But that was not enough; the green, fresh water stretched far and wide; the shores of the green sea were rimmed with swamp forest trees and with piled walls of silt and sand. The shoreline was uneven, hollowed into bays and inlets, some of them dark and overgrown as caverns. A formation of this kind, a huge dark cave, roofed with forest vegetation, was very close to the island. Maxim stared at this place for a long time with a glimmering of light beginning to penetrate his own darkness. The waters of the inland sea washed gently in and out of the cavern.

*"Maxim!"*

Shona's voice was filled with terror. Maxim and Poll both spoke at once, overlapping, to reassure her. He was able to stand and run, staggering and falling to her side. At the same moment Tug Trant woke noisily, still, in a half-drowned condition, the strongest of them all. He sat up at once and backed away from the water's edge, making gargling noises. He was frightened.

"What is it?" asked Shona, clinging to Maxim.

Maxim looked into the water and felt the hair prickle all over his head. An eye in the shallows, a single huge eye, then slowly, gently, the creature crawled onto the sand. It was covered all over with dark brown fur and was man-sized, a little larger, without limbs, a kind of giant sea caterpillar. It crawled onto the sand and soft whimpering sounds came from it.

"Ah-lo," whispered the sea beast. "Ah-lo . . ."

And at last Maxim, whirled and battered by wind and water and by the seas of time, knew what it was he saw. He went forward, full of wonder and delight.

"Hello," he said, hunting for scraps of ritual. "What may we call you?"

"Shamut," said the sea beast. "I will be called Shamut."

"What is the meaning of that name?"

"It is an invented name like the others. Perhaps it means the last."

"O Vail," said Maxim, "are you the last then?"

"Minmer," replied Shamut, rearing up on the island beach, "I am the last. I am one and I am all."

"We were washed into your sea during the storm. Did you form this island for us?"

248

"Yes, I did."

"You . . . one of your kind . . . did the same long ago for Sean Manin, by the Sea of Utner."

"Minmer thinking," said Shamut, waving to and fro so that Maxim glimpsed the long connecting fronds that led back into the sea from the furry body.

"How minmer thinking still grates. *Long ago.* Do not force me to remember . . ."

"Vail," cried Maxim, "do you not know it? The Envoys have kept the faith for years; I bring greeting from Ishbel O'Moore Manin, the Thirteenth Envoy, and from her heir Jaygo. There are many of us on Rhomary who have never given up hope of seeing your race again. Generations of mankind have carried your shape, your words in their minds . . ."

"Oh, the minds of the minmers," said Shamut.

The voice was a little altered, more resonant; Maxim thought he could recognize sadness and irony.

"It is the hardest concept to grasp," said Shamut. "You perish utterly and come again, from one bright day to the next, like shoals of small fish."

"Vail," said Maxim, "we find it difficult to grasp your vast size, your physical appearance. Show yourself to us . . . swim into your sea from your cave yonder so we can take in your greatness."

There was a strange breathing sound, almost a chuckle, from the furred sensor as it slid back into the water.

"Then see again . . ." said Shamut.

Maxim turned back to the others and found them frozen in strange attitudes. A wave washed out of the dark jungle cavern and its entrance was filled with a writhing blackness just below the surface of the water. A patch of broken water, larger by far than the island itself, moved out into the inland sea. Then four, six sensors rose up thick, mobile and glistening; the water heaved and parted and a huge mound of greenish-black appeared, growing, twisting and flowering into three protoheads. The Vail rode upon the waters of the inland sea; it filled the air with sound and vibration, notes of thrumming richness that conjoined into a mighty voice:

"Minmers . . ."

The minmers shouted in reply: they stood on the crest of their island waving their arms and hallooing wildly, waking echoes in the nearby cavern in a release of pure joy.

Then Shona turned aside, brushing away her tears, and began scrabbling at the compartments of the lifeboat.

"Quickly!" she said. "Oh heaven and earth . . . has it kept waterproof?"

She brought out the marvelous apparatus, quite undamaged in its pack. It was no more than a slim box of metal and plastic, still bearing a strong resemblance to its ancestors in the displays at Rhomary. She pressed two buttons, as John Miller had instructed her, and peered and pressed again so that the Vail was caught and held in a stream of jewel-bright holographic prints. Then they turned the camera on themselves and Maxim, holding the result, found every instant in time so captured, as poignant as every other. He saw three colonists, grinning in the mad light of a world that was still new. He made a mental note that he must be sure to write a caption on the back of the prints for the assistance of future archivists. "Poll Grev, Maxim Bro, Leo 'Tug' Trant, Landfall +243, 3rd Sept. 1102 New Style, Inland Sea on the Sooree, at the finding of the Vail. Photographer: Shona Dun Mor."

"Will it come talk to us again?" asked Tug Trant as they ate and drank, sitting in the lifeboat.

The Vail was feeding too; its seines spread out to the shore and sometimes a sensor reached out and plucked fodder from the swamp forest.

"I think so," said Maxim."

"Here it's calm," said Poll, "and the buster has spent itself . . . see that rag of cloud, it must be out to sea . . . but I badly want news of the *Comet.*"

"They want news of us, too," said Shona "We can't stay too long in this place."

"What of the *Dreamer?*" asked Maxim suddenly with a glance at Shona. "Could the Kellys' pinnace ride out that storm?"

"Surely," nodded Poll, "but the summer visitors would learn more about the pains of a shipboard life than they had expected."

They sat and watched the Vail, foraging, swimming, half-submerged or canted out of the water on the farther shore, its sensors busy repairing some damage the storm had done on the strange sand walls it had made. Maxim saw that his vision of the Vail given him by the shape-changers had been accurate but softened; from this perspective the creature was too big, it dominated them, it bewitched the eye. They lay and dozed in the scanty shadow of the lifeboat and Maxim, trying not to sleep, found that he had slept. The island was in shadow and the cave was tenanted again. He sprang up and went to the water's edge.

"Shamut. . . ?"

The adapted sensor was waiting; it came around the island in a long rippling wave and rose up in the shallows at his feet.

"Minmer?"

"We will go down the river in our boat and look for the ship that brought us here. May I ask a question?"

"Your aura tells me you will ask several."

"Do you recall the other ones, humans who passed by in a boat like ours? Who fell down in a spacecraft?"

"Fallen from heaven? Yes. Those *were* minmers? The thought of you creatures so contained, whirling among the stars, grates unbearably."

The sensor drew in a little and Maxim feared that contact might be withdrawn.

"Vail," he said quickly, "let us come again. Let an Envoy take up the dialogues."

"The tailed star rides," said Shamut, "you have come in the same season as before."

Maxim realized that he was on the brink of an even greater diplomatic error: the Vail could break contact, dismiss them for another seventeen years.

"Ah, no," he said. "Shamut, I pray . . . not so long. I do not mean to grate but I must talk of time."

"You know very little about it. How could you?"

"I know that the tailed star, your comet overhead, returns only three or four times in a human lifetime. Let us come in a few months, when Brother the binary partner of our Sun rises higher in the western sky."

"Minmer, you force me into chill waters. I am the last and I carry all our lives within me. This is the time of retreat and sorrow."

"Shamut," said Maxim, "the drought is long past. The Western Sea, your former home, is just as it was. You could return to it again, over sea and land."

"The Outwandering was painful . . ."

"We could help you," said Maxim, "we could help you cross the desert."

"Help me?"

Maxim laughed. "A thousand minmers would come to smooth your path," he said. "A canal could be built over

251

the Long Portage leading to the Western Sea. We could bring you home."

"Grandiose thoughts and limited senses," replied Shamut. "Minmer, you mean well . . ."

"Shamut, I have a name. I have a name like the Envoys Sean, Maria, Patrick, Rayn, Brian, Maire . . . I cannot pretend to be only a part of the minmer race, some kind of anonymous fairy creature. I am one person and these grandiose thoughts are mine alone. I am Maxim Bro, Dator of Rhomary, and I spend my life doing what you hate to do or cannot do. I remember, I collect data."

"Zimbro," said Shamut, after a pause, "Minmer Zimbro, what can you give me of all your store of knowledge? What hope? What grain of sand? What pearl?"

"How far do your senses reach?" demanded Maxim. "If you search about you may find some old friends. I would say some other old friends, but I do not believe you count the minmers as your friends even yet, for all the hope and feeling we have poured out toward you. But that other race, the race who told of U1, Thet and Essoon, the race of strange capacities who put on a shape to be beheld . . . I believe they are here, if you can make contact with them."

There was a heaving of the water in the dark mouth of the cavern and the Vail swam out and positioned itself behind the furry body of the sensor, some distance from the shore. Maxim quailed at the sight of the waving protoheads and the great lamps of the Vail's eye clusters. Shamut said no more; the adapted sensor slid away into the water. The Vail swam off into the very center of the inland sea and its sensors rose one after the other straight into the air and so remained, a grove of giant trees, moved by the wind, as the last light faded in the east.

Maxim flung himself down on the beach trembling with disappointment. He buried his face in his hands.

"Come on, Dator," said Tug Trant, laying a heavy hand on his shoulder. "Don't let the big beast upset you. You have the courage of ten men to talk to it so long."

Shona came to him and so did Poll Grev; they rocked him in their arms to comfort him.

"I'm a bad Envoy," said Maxim. "I've no talent for it."

"Should we go now?" asked Shona. "What was the talk all about? Have we been dismissed?"

"We must wait till morning," said Poll. "We can't try

the Sooree in darkness. Is the Vail angry or will it let us stay here?"

"Surely," said Maxim. "We'll go at first light, Poll."

"You're tired," whispered Shona, soothing his brow.

It was true. He could hardly keep his eyes open for weariness, a weariness of body and mind that made him scarcely able to lift his head. As they sat beside the boat in the warm twilight he curled up on the sand with his head in Shona's lap and slept like the dead.

It was Shona who woke him again; by the stars it was past midnight.

"Maxim . . . look there . . . at the end of the lake!"

The forest darkness was not so thick here on the water; the shape of the Vail was just visible, its sensors relaxed again. There was a sound, faint but unmistakable, that rode in the air like bell music. Globes of light danced around the lifted heads of the Vail and there was the muted vibration of its answering voice.

"They've come," whispered Shona. "Do you see?"

They were alone on the sand; Tug and Poll had settled down in the boat under the canopy.

"So they have come . . ." said Maxim.

"*How* have they come?" whispered Shona.

"Through the air in this shape."

"Will they show themselves this way in daylight?"

"I don't think so," he said. "If the pinnace is anywhere about they can come and go easily. In daylight they will be human: the Redrocks, the Stines. . . ."

"Our imaginary playmates."

The distant movement of light and sound went on and on; the Vail communed with the shape-changers and Maxim sighed, unable to take it in, limited in all his senses. Yet when he made out Shona's face in the summery darkness he felt joy again for being where he was and for being human. He sent out his prayer again for all humans on Rhomary, in the dry towns or at the Gann or on the seas or stumbling through the swamp forest on a world just discovered. So he slept again with Shona in his arms and when he woke at first light he was not sure that all he had seen in the night was not a dream.

The Vail was not about as they pushed off in the lifeboat. They paddled in a wide arc into the inland sea and headed for the main stream; there was suddenly a patch of broken water spreading in their narrow wake.

"Here it comes again," said Tug Trant. "It must have scooped out some depth down there to hide itself."

They still paddled and the Vail rose up, terrible and blue-black and of monstrous size, not forty meters away. The huge voice sighed above them, the fully diapason of the Vail that seemed to shake earth and sky.

The lifeboat was seized by a swift current, a furrow opened in the water and they were propelled along it faster than they could row. Their assisted passage carried them rapidly downstream past the wrecked sandbanks and flattened edges of the swamp forest where the typhoon had passed. They rowed out again into the broad lower reaches of the Sooree, calm as before, and they raised a cheer. The *Comet* rode safely at anchor and there beside it was the *Dreamer*, the Kellys' pinnace.

"There now," said Poll Grev. "The *Dreamer*. And I'll bet the visitors are below decks resting their poor heads."

An answer to their cheer was already ringing out from the deck of the *Comet*.

"What were the words?" asked Maxim. "What did you think the Vail said, at the last?"

"Go on," said Shona. "You heard as clear as any of us. You are not such a bad Envoy as you thought."

So Maxim repeated the words and heard it in the voice of Shamut, the last of the Vail:

"Go well, minmers. Go well and come again. Or send some others in your place."